I0831669

GALAXY OF THE DEAD

GALAXY OF THE DEAD

BOOK 3 OF

WRITTEN BY EFREN STAT

 Published in the United States by
Elemental Stone Publishing

Book and cover design by Guy Galzerano
ISBN (Hardcover): 979-8-9923088-6-0
ISBN (Autobook): 979-8-9923088-7-7

Printed in the United States of America
1 2 3 4 5 6 7 8 9 10

Second Edition

To the Wooden Giants.

Chapters

Prologue – Classy Roots

A Giant Mahogany tree stood in the middle of the rain forest. Its branches rustled in the strong winds from the North, though its branches weren't only moving from the wind; they moved with a majestic vitality because a great war had just begun.

The crackling in the sky to the North showed one humongous black cloud and three blissfully white tornadoes rotating around the dark mass in an effort to try and force it away from the forest. The puffy outline of the black cloud evolved into rugged edges, giving it a defined and detailed sharp contour. The smooth arches that usually symbolize a cloud's shape were no more.

The black cloud flexed into this toned form and black lightning streaks flew out of the top half of the cloud. Black bolt after black bolt tore into the upper atmosphere and sometimes haphazardly into the Tasmanian marauding tornadoes. The dark cloud progressively forced its way forward, closer and closer to the darkening summer green rain forest.

Zip! The sky was relentlessly being ripped apart by lightning bolts. Zip, ZIIIP! ZAAWAP! The extremely powerful electric discharges leaving crackling particles in its wake. Residue static edging for more than just a bolt of action.

Further up in the sky hundreds of storm threads fell upon the black cloud, only these bolts were zealous white and crystal blue.

The earth rumbled and shook as the sky made a loud scream, different from the crash of the thunderous lightning. A sound that grew louder and louder as it approached with the wind. Suddenly the black cloud's full mass splintered apart and was left with two great holes in the middle of itself. The screams in the sky ended and two more tornadoes rose in the high altitude, joining the other three to face off again with the slowly coalescing black cloud.

One of the white tornadoes quickly died out and formed into a woman's body with a long black leather coat. Throughout the forest the voice in the sky was heard.

"Your time has now passed. Dark days end now, Ruzo!" Her eyes shone with pain, anger, and remorse. She spun like a ballerina and formed wind circlets around herself and twisted the air back up again.

"You are no sister of ours!" Her voice was completely enraged. The fresh tornado complete with speed wobbles.

The tornadoes dashed about the black cloud and streaks of white and black bolts raced out of the battle-sphere in every direction.

* * * *

A leaf fell, bound for a weird journey downward. Such a loud world that surrounded that fallen leaf. Where was the peace it was so accustomed to? No more delicate breeze from atop the tallest tree, a caterpillar tiptoeing on its cuticles, or morning dew blissfully gathering together before their slippery lemming of drips and drops, It was only left with a slow drowsy float down the creaking hollows.

As the leaf flipped in the air it peered at its lost wooden attachment. The distortion of the slanted brow of bushy green, a fat swirly knot for an eye, and a squirrel hole for the other. The leaf settled upon a long, crooked branch that looked like a witch's nose, and then slowly slid off of its girth. It continued to fall, still floating past lower canopy branches and a trunk of vitality, now taking its majestic transformation.

An area of bark split four ways vertically. It cracked and created high-pitched creaks. A steady exhale poured from the vertical cracks that continued to grow longer and longer.

A roar blew the leaf past dozens of trees with similar height.

"AWAKEN!"

The leaf eventually fell and descended upon the massive roots of the Samauma and Giant Mahogany trees, breaking the earth. The horse size roots were then fully liberated from the earth and stretched over the rain forest floor and bush, causing the forest floor to become extinct in moments, banishing all the color from flowers and herbs, leaving its mean and green brethren to transcend.

As the massive bottom lumbering roots stretched out, so did the extending branches closer to the top. Branches for miles and miles praised the higher tears of the sky. Arisen, the trees radiated with power and energy. Their power licked the molecules in the air and charmed them for their own. The sky changed, and from all directions, as far as the edge of the world, dark clouds formed and migrated around the lightning blasts. The winds ripped and thunder roared, clouds broke apart and tornadoes heated up. It was a stormy scrap occurring out in the sky's metropolis.

****

With war in motion Mother Earth placed a wealth of spirit into the roots of the Battle Worn. These specific Battle Worn were called Landtos, known as the smaller trees that reside along the outer edge of the rain forest, loyal beyond measure to their Mother Gaia, our humble planet Earth.

The ground grew moist with the heavy rainfall. The day turned to night with the massive black cloud hanging very low, taking over the sky, almost fully blocking out the red sunset.

The sliver of the sunset's red tint ignited the angels' blood fury towards one another. The airborne battle had been chased deep into the heart of the forest where Ruzo, otherwise know as, Mareridt, whizzed through the gaps of her lumbering, tumbling trees which tried to block the trailing angels who wove in and out of the wooden gauntlet creations. These gigantic wizard trees moved defiantly to close gaps with their huge trunks, creating thunderclap booms.

As the red sun settled, more dread lingered within the darkness. A whistle sound broke through the wind and branches, racing through the rain forest, and an angel broke through the top of the trees and black clouds. She halted in the sky and gathered the last light of the sun into her right palm, and moments later the sunlight blasted through her other hand, jeweled with five emerald rings. Rain thundered down on her silhouette, a bald chick in a soaked ragged robe cradling two pure spheres of light where her hands should be.

Her sunbeam followed the ripple in the forest where the other angels were in chase, as a snowflake fell upon the hovering angel's luscious lips.

****

Prologue

An army of Battle Worn sped through the forest abyss, intuitively knowing where to move because of their leading roots feeling out the free soil that lay ahead. Some slapped the mud with their hasty roots and others dove into the wet soil and popped out four tree lengths ahead of the heavier ones.

The trees dripped with excitement to be Awakened once again for the great cause of protecting their Mother. They moved in on the cautious Giant Mahoganies in an assault. These Giant Mahoganies were usually on the good side, only their life link was summoned by Mareridt, the rebel angel of the six Sky Sisters.

The Battle Worn sunk halfway into the dirt to wrap around and tangle the barbaric Mahogany roots together. Pulling and twisting each root out and over the next. Taking teams of Battle Worn to carry through their timbering assault.

When thuggish wooden octopus roots revealed themselves for a fight, the Battle Worn climbed the Mahogany trunks with their branches, like ice picks climbing a cliff, leaving the cliff scarred, overwhelmed and in ruins, ready to lumber down.

Some of Mareridt's larger elemental summoning trees also had a craft in tackling, and were simply brutal with their size. They would grab Battle Worn with their conscious roots and in one motion slam them into the cold snowy dirt.

The snow, now a sappy mess with the smell of fresh-cut wood and bubbling wooden heated hearts snarling in the rapidly freezing climate.

* * * *

Flat night settled into the forest and the war plundered on. Nothing was seen but slow tussles in areas, trees annihilating each other in the blizzard white. There was not much fighting other than this, it was more stalking tranquility, watching and searching for the enemy.

Mareridt sat in the higher Giant Mahogany treetops wearing a smoldering black chest strap and green skirt. Her dark caramel skin blended in with the bruised tree trunk. She looked down through the snowy branches and noticed a walking angel with her Landtos guardians on the powdered rain forest floor. Mareridt whispered through the wood, readying her minions.

Twenty yards of canopy suddenly shook and dropped loads of

snow on the walking angel. Mareridt dropped with her black blade sizzling through the cold air, hungry for her sister's blood. In the instant of the death strike upon the snow-covered angel, the Battle Worn surrounding the sister formed a barrier to protect her, and the wooden shroud burst into flames when hit by Mareridt's black blade, Landtos trees splintering off, slowly burning to ash.

Suddenly a push of force knocked Mareridt back, yet the dark angel's strength only allowed her to be knocked back so far. It was two against one now, but variant numbers only alluded to variant tactics.

Mareridt plunged forth, this time with sonic speed. Yet again, a force hit her, and she flew to the side, putting her just out of range from slashing her sister with her dark blade. Encompassing the apprehension of force push retaliation, Mareridt used her sister's summoned wind, along with the cold elements around her, and blasted her two angelic sisters with shards of ice. She exhaled. Her dark angel form was pleased with the destruction.

Three angelic figures, however, were in the shadows behind her, with an army of Battle Worn silhouetted and up for a fight, their eyes smoldering green.

Moments later, the dark angel was thrown through the center of two huge Mahogany trunks, and after a long unconscious flight she crashed into the wet desert sand. Splintered and dead, she lay in wastelands.

Gentlemen of the State

Gentlemen of the State

Moving quickly, the three of us rushed around and over tall wooden fences, using windowsills and other building masses to animal through residential yards. For example, that tree Pads used to help himself combo jump over a guest house.

A chase like many others that usually ended up with us in some new area just large enough for our size, breathing hard and smiling at the happy glinting eyes shining after running out of the devil's grasp.

I am Kraeno, nicknamed Krae, the biggest of the three. My jump wasn't as agile as my brothers', but my heart was just the same. We ran alongside each other no matter what obstacles were in our way; we moved through.

Splinters flew and hit the sidewalk. My shoulder felt a flash of heat, but even pain at this moment felt great. My head was tense like a bull darting through a red flag. The sound of snapping and loud, quick creaking explosions finally reached my ears. Before that it was a couple milliseconds of *Korn, Reclaim My Place!* I hit the street with a sprint full of momentum. I knew my brothers were close behind, but then I got another feeling of contact. Slam! A red pickup truck hit me from the side.

Good timing, Dick.

Sprawled across the hood I could hear the door open, and this little fuck ran out and did a downward stroke to my chest with glistening Mr. McSharpington in his hand. Sprinkle me a fudge stick with caramel on top, this damn sequence of pain wasn't over yet. I was tossed on the street headfirst.

Then came the real pain. Under the truck, I could see the hole in the fence where I came out. The sidewalk was littered in a full brawl showdown. My two brothers A.D and Pads weren't hesitant in acknowledging when to turn on survival beast mode, turning them into shining madmen. These moments of rage were so focused and pinpointed. I could almost see the glow around them.

One punk flew that way, and another dropped to the ground like throwing a bag of peanuts from a ten-story roof. However, more of these fools dashed around the corner and through the fence. My two fierce brothers hit the lawn, overwhelmed by the puffy bodies of the territorial street gang getup.

If you haven't noticed, we don't like to be subjugated to staying in one area and not the other. That was what got us into this mess. Hopefully, the lawn owner will stop jerking off behind those blinds and call a medical truck. I'm just not sure we were meant to win this one.

I rolled on my back and looked up. Up there watching us was a canopy of branches, seemingly in wonder at what us young Creates were doing, scuffling around. I felt like that tree was keeping our souls from leaving this street and never coming back. *Thanks. I guess.*

****

It's snowing, no more California beaches, hot babes, and warm breezes for a while. Our landlord took us up North to his winter home in California to recover from our injuries.

There was an L-shaped couch that all three of us were lying on. My feet hung off one end, Pads legs off the other next to the fireplace, and A.D laid in the middle. I think he got it the worst out of all of us. After those two hit the ground during the fight, A.D hung his body over Pads. Pads was our little brother, and you know, got to protect your kin. A.D was the eldest, and I'm one year from him.

A.D's name stood for Adrenaline Devil. Even lying here all bloodied up by stab wounds and scrapes, he'll still think of a way to flip the couch and get his heart racing just for a second. Yet right now, every cough and laugh could very well pop a stitch.

The band *Sprung Monkey* was our entertainment for now, playing on the red, stickered-up boombox.

Pads, laid out on the end, swaying his foot to, *Get em outta here.* I lay there rereading Sandman Slim, and our older brother lay there watching the ceiling.

"Why not? Pads as the grower, me as the high climbing builder, and Krae as the manager of the operation."

"What you mumbling over there A? You go taking too many of Jeff's daughters Oxys again?" I said.

"Pass me Korea Krae. You wouldn't know how to charm a girl if you had a baby toe ring and a puka necklace." A.D said, a smile crinkling on his face. Two long cuts ran down his jaw, and his right eye was puffy and black, along with a neighborly crooked, smashed, and lacerated nose.

"I may not be as pretty as you princess, but at least I can bend my arms rather than having 'my fair lady' shovel food in my mouth," I condemned.

Passing the pipe meant putting the pipe in A.D's mouth and lighting it for him. There you go, big guy. Hope that green medicine makes you feel better because I am not getting up again. The pipe was from South Korea, where our grandfather fought in the Korean War. He gave us each an old relic before he passed away. One was Korea, a bamboo pipe as long as my forearm and plated with metal chakra carvings all around it. Just having the gifted artifact around makes the pain go away.

A.D's right index and middle finger were smashed while he was on the ground. His left hand, forearm, and bicep were stabbed. Three times in the same arm. You might as well cut it off with that kind of time to stab a guy. Those young street gangs are all the type that became twitchy and scared to death when in a fight. My guess was that their eyes got all blurry, and they just swung and took strikes at bodies and clothes they recognized as their prey.

Yep, I remember my first scrap too, but I slowed down my second one.

Then there were my injuries. I can tell you one thing, getting up to 'pass the pipe' hurt like hell, but I'll poke two balloons with one needle and take a piss while I'm up.

Peeing still stung from the catheter that was pulled out of my bobber the morning after the jam fest went down. It's been exactly one week since the day we pissed off Central Coast's worst. I guess those firecrackers A.D threw in their window weren't as celebratory as we thought it would make them feel. *Happy Fourth, bitches!*

We waited by the door for them to burst out with chins high and a million curse words on their tongues. As they poured out, tripping on a surfboard leash we strung up right outside their door jam, we stood at the end of the yard, closest to the street, yammering our little taunts to get us really fired up like true adrenaline junkies. As I said before, we don't like dodging trouble, especially if it's trouble with people that do stupid shit. So we bolted and had our fun running. Then boom! I get hit, and I'm down just like that: one broken eyebrow with a good scar from the pavement, a two-inch stab wound in my chest, and a bruised leg, back, and shoulder.

That left little Pads. What put him down to begin with were a couple of blades in the back. Any other droopy-eyed feeling of his was from the hatred that lashes out so violently in the world today, so thoughtless and mechanical.

We lay, we sat... We waited until we recovered.

* * * *

The time shifted like a planet of poems. Words flowed by, pushing through space with Shakespearean fluidity. They twisted and twirled, letters double-helixing like a dragon in flight. I saw a rigidly pointed piece of tree bark twirling in the open portions between worlds and stars, gracefully positioning itself with gregarious humor. A piece of bark tattooed or marked in some strange fashion. A piece of bark with a point of end, the point of no return, yet an apex of a beginning, point'torious of our new patriotic world.

My mustaches blew through the solar winds-

I woke up to a long bubbly fart blowing air right past my face, like a car with a faulty exhaust trying to get started, puffing out smoke every now and then. My right arm stretched out quickly to punch A.D in the ball sack.

Well he was feeling better.

Everyone was awake with smiles on their faces. A fart in this family was a good way to settle an argument with our dad. After a fart like that all seriousness would be set aside, and it's cheesecake on Friday mornings. With mom, as soon as you got to the middle of the fart, it would conclude in a binocular smack across your face, causing the fart to squeak out into a high pitched, burrrpuff, and rip your shorts.

"I was having a good dream, weirdo." I drained

Shaki, aka Shake, was leaning her elbows on the couch, palms cradling her chin. The landlord's daughter…

"What was it about?"

A.D and Pads were still giggling, probably thinking it would be funny to say my dream was abo-

"What was it about? A pretty piece of poo sitting on your lap and whispering sweet sweet... shit."

I sat up. My wound felt less like a grizzly bear holding me down with her clawed paw, and more like she just put one claw inside me to see what human tastes like. That's right you grizzly, stick that long index claw in your mouth like you just dipped it into a bee nest and scooped out a nice chunk of golden honey. Mmm.

And screw these guys, what are they all laughing at?

"I was swinging on a vine in the forest at the edge of this cliff looking over the ocean with hundreds of whales breaching and diving." Taking in a deep breath, I looked over to where there was the sound of a snowy branch scratching on the window. I'm not letting you in, Mr. Branch. I thought we went over this. It's too damn cold out there.

I turned to look at Pads and A.D, who were sitting tight, grinning, always entertained with my stories.

"I was with a short-haired blonde that swung on a vine next to mine. All of a sudden, she swooped by, and with one ravenous slash she cut my vine. All in good fun, I guess.

"I plunged into the deep ocean. It was a whole new world that clamped a serious chill to my bones. Thousands of whales, sharks, and dolphins streamlined around me through the clear sea. Then I closed my eyes and reopened them to see a piece of bark floating through the stars."

Shaki gave me eyes like she would be giving an old bard singing glorious stories of young knights. The boys abandoned their grins and looked anywhere but into the eyes in the room.

Before our Uncle Favin took us to California, we grew up and lived in Northern Ireland. When Pads was only ten, our parents died. After their death, we each had our own experience with the woods, and we each had similar dreams that ended with space bark.

Urn Journey

9 Years Before

Our parents' funeral was loud and filled with music: fiddles and violins, lutes and guitars, drums and bass, and one ballistic saxophone. People loved our parents, and they came from all different walks of the land. Most wore long coats with torn edges and hems. Their clothes were a plethora of colors with plaids and patchwork, blending amongst the forest of Spring. As they talked and waltzed around, clinging to their cups with every step, their beers and beverages would tilt and spill to the earth. In every conversation or dance, someone would be rejuvenating the dirt with their mug. Sometimes, whole drinks would fall, and then they'd prance back to the grand table to refill. As young boys of 13, 12, and 10, we knew this was how they grieved our parents' deaths by getting the dead drunk and the earth with it.

A man in a blue button-down shirt and a panda tie walked up to us while we sat at the base of an old oak. He knelt down, and his colorful girlfriend in a green and yellow splashed dress stood behind him, smiling at us. The panda man looked all three of us in the eye for a long time and then slowly poured his drink at our feet, still looking at our, I imagine, rock-hard faces.

"Ye brave lads keep your minds abit you and close to yees oots..." He said with a thick accent.

He looked back at his girlfriend, who was now smiling at him.

He let out a deep boast of a laugh and stood.

"We ill me' again when you've grown some bark on tha ol' chest o'f yours laddies. Grievances fo your folks." With a nod he was gone, walking toward a keg at the cooler station, only to lift it out of the ice bucket and throw it to the side.

The party went on and we sat there watching under the forest canopy in Lagan's Landing, our town and location of where our devious hearth resided.

A month after our parents were cremated, A.D, Pads, and I traveled to a new land with our Uncle Favin. Favin took us to the Netherlands where the forests were deep and the hills rolled below the high mountain tops.

The first night we left the cabin, Favin told us we were going to travel to a destination with no means of time or complication.

"The land breathes around us, boys." Favin said.

"This earth cares not of time, but of the limpid sense of life and death. Good and Evil. Our lives here have no ticking clock to them, and we are but ghosts of the forest."

A.D tilted his head in a benevolent way. "Limpid?"

"Yes, Boy. Limpid, no emotion for pain and suffering, only reserve and strength are recognized here in the valley of the wood." The sun settled into the canopy of trees as we shuffled to a stop and dropped our gear. The four of us ended up on top of a rise in the middle of a hill surrounded by a platoon of Atlantic White Cedars, slim and average height with single trunks running high up before the branches spread into large wings over the dirt-flowered floor. The sun set in the direction we came, with the sunlight fading into the great Cedar branches. The sunrise in the East will be our morning guide, but until then, we watched the hills of green treetops in the distance run for miles and miles.

That night, we ate our pots of beans around the deep hole we dug for the campfire, while Pads sang a lively song sitting across from us, flames licking at his chest.

I march along me pitiful road. I march poised with a bold toe.
The badger at me side has flies n hungers for cheese,
But I have a wager, he pees on Frachier.
Dippity do n slippidy dee, wet to his knees. Hehe.
Now run in the wind and fart in the dark, I swear I saw a lllawyer.
He might save Pads or She my parts,
But I guarantee she's jazzed for pleaaasure.

The song didn't quite make sense, but we loved him just the same. He took two big gulps of his drink and exhaled loudly, seeming relieved of a good song and drink. Pads could live his whole life with just the simple things. A lifetime of song and drink was a well spent lifetime indeed.

A.D threw twigs into the fire from afar. He was slouched at the base of an oak, its roots creating a comfortable barrier for him to sleep in.

I pulled out my nuts... and grapes, and grubbed down a little before sleep consumed me.

****

One of my eyes cracked open to witness a orange glow tickling the dark sky. While slowly opening that eye, my other eye followed and turned to look at our crew. My brothers were sleeping, however… there was no sign of... Slam!

Dirt and leaves flew up from the ground.

The sound and shock of the earth made my eyes shutter and forced to wince. Our guide, Uncle Favin, jumped from the lower branches of the White Cedar A.D was sleeping under. The jump must have been around 15 feet, impressive for an early bird.

A.D's eyes were open as well as his mouth, but he still lay at the base of the tree's roots.

"I thought a tree was timbering down on my dreaming body."

A.D opened his mouth to say more but instead leaned back and grunted with his arms across his chest, trying to get to a more comfortable position, eying our Favin like he was A.D's malicious Parrot that just woke him up by poking him in the balls with its beak.

Why poke me in the balls of all the damn places?

Just as A.D was bewildered, Pads was in awe. My guess was he was awake to see Favin's Kate Beckinsale's Underworld landing.

"Boys ye best be getting ups and fetching to your breads to feed yer core. We have all day to journey to our destination and set up camp where your parents will finally rest." His Scottish accent was sweet and motivating.

We complied and rose slowly. Unlike other children our age, we had no problem quickly obeying our elders. We had respect for Favin, and he had respect for us. When we were growing up the people around us never let up moving in a productive manner and - doing the do - in revolutionary sequences. It was always one chore, duty, or activity to the other. It really seemed like whatever our parents and their friends did became hobbies to them, which then morphed into a freaking joyous lifestyle. If you're to live your life, might as well be happy about whatever you may be doing. I remember watching Pops clean the toilet rocking out to *Korn, Beg for Me*. Funny part was he was cleaning it with Franky's face. He owed Pops a new truck. Pops looked back at me with a big smile as I stood in the doorway; it looked like an everyday chore of cleaning up the bathroom.

I watched Favin's back as I rolled up my multicolored blanket.

He looked to the sunrise, fiddling with a leaf between his fingers. His back was big and torn from all the factory work, but his green tattered coat, long with two coattails, showed that the factory was not where his heart anchored; it was the woods. His dark ruffled hair sat a couple inches from the coat's collar and his earlobes hung low with one plump golden hoop earring; the other, a green twisted vine formed in a loop. Based on how he looked, this was his stomping ground.

So, back to the three of us. We were never too keen on keeping still for long. We knew that while alive and in our human form we must work and play. An object in motion stays in motion. Thank Mr. Newton for turning our family's blood into boiled liquid metallic hydrogen. The more words you use, and the bigger they are, the more truthful they usually sound.

We finished packing up the cooking pots and got started on the walk down the hill through the dense forest of Cedars and Pitch Pines. The branches above us lingered and creaked, and sometimes, after a creak, a bird would squawk and fly away.

The walk was long, and I could feel the stretch of my shoes forming to my feet. Not until the next day, when we put them on again, will we realize how much sweat soaked into our soles.

Sometimes, Favin did short running spurts for ten or fifteen minutes at a time. It felt good dodging trees, quickly jumping from side to side, and striding forward toward open paths of the forest. It's different than running suicides for football or rugby. It felt right to move quickly through the wood. Almost as if the trees gave us that extra boost of power to propel us forward. It's a particular feel in the wind and air; the air seemed to be breathing with us, not just us breathing it in.

I watched Favin in front of my brother Pads; every step seemed like a progressive dance. And then, as the pace became more natural, we all broke off into our own different deer paths.

The sun had shown directly overhead as we glided through the trees, transitioning out of our run and stride, run and stride conservative pace. When I looked to my left, I saw Favin and Pads ghosting through tree trunks at a distance. A.D was ahead to my right. It seemed he became absorbed in the wood and took it upon himself to extend his already long strides.

I moved onward, quickening my pace, just about at a run. Keeping my distance from A.D, I waited until there was an open clearing ahead where there wasn't much side-to-side objectivity. When the time was right, I sped forward to pass A.D where he could see me in his peripherals. I knew he'd be sprinting in no time, so I started my sprint just a moment later.

Moving fast among these great Cedars was a thrill. I chose a path with limited side-stepping; however, every three paces, I completely had to turn my torso one way, a full ninety degrees, and then the other way, a full ninety, causing me to adapt the action of pushing off the trunks to get my legs around the base quickly.

Once I could feel the heaviness of my heart, we both reached a line of Spring colored trees in a glade of varied heights. On the East side, sitting across from us were trees lined up like Queens of the forest evaluating their guests. The two in the middle seemed like they had carvings in them, possibly natural yet intricate indentations. Their branches mantled the over-story of the glade, leaving openings into the sky in curious locations, carrying themselves as if growing in a pattern; a branch abruptly stopped and turned to circle around an opening while another branch cut through the middle.

I got a familiar feeling about these old unrecognizable symbols as I stood there looking up with A.D by my side, the sound of our panting now completely filling my ears.

"Guess I won," I said.

A.D glared at me and then looked past my left ear.

I turned around to see the rest of the pack gracefully journeying into the glade. Pad's chest barely moved; guess he wasn't huffing air like us. And Favin looked around the glade in a wide eyed joyful grin. It's how Pops looked when he saw an old friend.

"Ah, so you've found Macaton's Crossing. It is said in legend that the ol' Wiser trees separated themselves from the Battle Worn trees here. They made a line, whoever passed to Landtos would study from their roots and reside as warriors, and whoever stayed beyond Macaton's Crossing would study the sky and muse as sorcerers... We will march through the Crossing and set up camp at Many Streams River, in the heart of these Redwoods, Sycamores, and Ciders."

The Landtos, on the western side of the forest, had the smaller, more dexterous tree forms. Legends were told that the Battle Worn were warrior trees that could merge into the dirt, having their roots dig through the earth to reach their destination. The whole tree could move through dozens of yards in a matter of seconds. Depending on soil frequency, wet or dry, the Battle Worn could sometimes entirely disappear underground.

The Macatons were fully rooted to their grounds. Their height ran up to the sky hundreds of feet, like Sequoias and Redwoods, or Mahoganies and Samaumas. The wiser of the forest bunch, the Macatons studied the sky. They were said to have magnificent wizard and elemental powers.

These two groups were separated after the Great War of the Six, a time when Mother Nature lost one of her daughters to nefarious ideals. A time that the Kalmc brothers only thought of as myth and legend.

Many Streams River

We approached the river with little creeks and streams splitting off from the main channel and meandering through the woods. Some streams ran down rocky hills surrounded by red oaks and redwoods, trickling down into ponds and trailing into small waterfalls.

"This be the spot boys, let's gather some wood, make a fire and clean up." Favin said lightly while looking up into the trees surrounding us.

The night passed on and the moon rose high above us. Favin took out the urn and showed it to us for a moment. He delicately wrapped an orange-red, intricately sewn scarf around the urn and placed it in Pad's light brown satchel. Pads took the satchel and stood there waiting for orders, the brown strap crossing his chest.

At ten years old, he was easily the nimblest and most agile of us. He was also a very good climber and felt no different being fifty feet up than standing at ground zero.

He also loved our mother and father very much. Actually, all three of them were inseparable. Pads was a very good sidekick for our parents, yet now they were gone, and because of that he didn't talk much, only sung his bewildering little songs.

"Padrick, take your beloved parents' ashes to that fallen tree there." Favin nodded to the location behind Pads, where a fallen tree loomed high over the gentle river held up diagonally by another fallen wood.

"That branch is in a perfect spot." He exhaled while ruffling Pad's curly brown surf hair.

* * * *

The urn broke on the top of a jagged rock sitting in the middle of the river right below the long branch where Pads lay, tranquil arms hanging limp on either side. The orange, reddish scarf blew in the light wind in his right hand, his cheek resting on the tree bark. The moonlight glistened on the water flowing downstream, and the slim river with the blue light of the moon illuminated the greenish-gray particles of ash. Hundreds of little streams connected to the river and whispered to the new elements that flowed through. The ash spread, and the current took our parents in all directions throughout the forest waters.

The three of us stood on the ground, silently watching the majestic flow.

Favin stood with the tips of his boots touching the water line. A.D sat on the balls of his feet, elbows resting on his knees, watching tenderly. And I, feeling like a puddle of mud, gooey with the transcendent love of my surroundings, felt something move at my heel. I looked, and it was only a root.

After a while, the orange scarf trailed by, floating on the surface of the steam.

The Trees Move

When Pads was 7, I was 9, and A.D was 10, we lived in a small rural village in Northern Ireland, Lagan's Landing. The green hills were clean-cut and neat, accompanied by epic trees plotted around for miles and miles. The thick, deep forest was a bit further on the horizon and took a little longer to walk to. However, the light always beamed through the canopy as if the forest was being blessed with holy heat.

During these times living in Ireland, five miles away from town, the trees were like our babysitters. Our school was a house filled with books like our barn was filled with car parts. Both portals into deeper understanding of the mind and machine.

Reading, hanging out, sleeping, pondering, and climbing with, on, or around trees was what we always had our minds set on after the afternoon chores.

One day, Pads finished cleaning up the house while A.D and I were switching out the master cylinder in the night-blue Bronco. Pads ventured off to the Juniper, a twisted trunk that looked like five trunks bent in an arch bonded and twisted together. The cumbrous twisting of the branches was like heavy trunks themselves that tilted and brushed the grassy green earth.

The sky was blue, and the overhead sun still watched our lone Juniper tree and warehouse. The Juniperus Phoenicea was very close to the barn that we were working in, just about forty yards to the right of the barn doors. I stood up for a second to take a drink of water and looked out the window to see Pads finding a nice seat in what would be the top of the Juniper, with a bushy peak that only rested five to six feet from the ground. The cockpit made of branches supported him flawlessly, and Pads played like he was some star-fighter pilot.

"Hand me the crescent wrench, will ya."

I handed the crescent to A.D and knelt down next to him. He was putting the clutch back together and tightening bolts on the firewall.

"What do you think Ma and Pop are doing at old lady Parls' place? She hates to have any kind of visitors. Living in a house of old text, she is." I mused.

A.D finished on his bolt. "Krae... let's bleed this sucker."

We switched positions and I went under the Bronco and opened up the bleeder nipple.

"In," I said. Fluid leaked out and into a cut open water jug.

"Old Parls has a lot of history with our folks. Ma and Pop are all smiles whenever they talk about her." A.D said.

"Out," A.D let off of the clutch.

"In," I said, and A.D pressed the clutch in.

A.D started to drill his opinion again, "She was there when Pads was born, she did some kind of ma-"

"Out!" I said.

I could hear him release the clutch. "In."

"Parls is the reason for our parent's meeting, Krae. I bet you never knew that."

"Out... How does that feel?" I asked my dear older brother.

"Good. Good work lil bro."

I stood up, shrugged, and brushed dirt off my right arm looking at A.D through the driver's window.

"I knew about that. Parls brought them together so they could search out an ancient book. Pops as the navigator, cause he has been to the crazy land of U-Graves, and Mom because Parls trained her to search for those diabolical artifacts." I splurged.

"Hm, something like that," A.D relented.

I turned to look out the window and Pads was gone. But Pads wasn't just gone, the whole tree had vanished. My face felt contorted in weirded-out curiosity. My legs moved me to the warehouse's double doors looking outside. I felt A.D brush up against my shoulder and stop.

Pads was sitting in the exact same spot I saw him last. The Juniper was not completely upright but definitely more so. The branches still hovered inches from the ground as bigger roots waddled and stomped forward. The smaller roots dug into the earth, pulling the mass along every protruding inch. Pads and the tree were headed for the cliff looking over the Irish Sea.

We were in a crisscrossed mind fuck as we peered at the strange yet beautiful movement afar. What in the deep depths of the nineteenth Hell did Pads do to that Juniper? A.D started to run after Pads. I started after him, running towards the slow, yet consistent tree, gripping and ripping up the earth.

There was excited yelling. We were calling 'PADS!!!' While at full, blown-out sprints, and Pads was calling out 'Cool!' and 'Ya-ho! Whoa, guys look at me!'

We got to the Juniper and skipped at its side. Now that we were this close all we could do was watch this reality in awe. The tree approached the cliffside revealing the vast sea and the blue-lined horizon.

"Jump Pads, for Christ sake, the freaking tree is going to take you off the cliff!"

When Pads started to realize that maybe Juniper did want to go for a plunge, he moved his legs to get ready to hop out of the wooden cockpit.

I slowed down and just stood there, and right before Pads situated himself to jump, the Juniper sunk its veiny roots into the green grass. The three massively twisted roots under the trunk stomped along for its final halt. The branches fluttered and beat against the trunk. The rest of the roots radically jolted into the earth, kicking up dirt and flinging it aloft in all directions.

The Juniper really spruced up since seeing it in its last location. Standing joyously more linear and holding happy Pads with great pride while looking over the Irish Sea.

A.D and I both looked up at Pads, confounded.

"I said, 'Go Mr. Woodtwist,' and we went," Pads said with a big smile. He looked down and patted the trunk with merriment and gratification.

Interesting thing about the Juniperus Phoenicea is it's usually found in the Middle East or holy lands of Jordan. That tree could have just been ready for a grander view, or it could have been traveling to get to Pads for thousands of years. How it knew that Pads would eventually end up in the Ireland Isles is some real serious star gazing. What else could a tree do? Or what else would a tree do to fulfill its whimsical duties? Even if that's just enlightening a good lad's consciousness of earthly secrets.

* * * *

It was an evening of brisk shivers, a year after Padrick's encounter with the Juniper. The cold bit the barrier of our home, but excessive heat production bellowed onto the hearth. So, I set out of the soft harmony of our home and into the cold woods to make a campfire. I loved doing things I didn't want to do, because, in the end, I am usually glad I did...

I arrived at a good spot sheltered with surrounding Ash Oak—good wood to set fire to. Close by, there were bigger Ash trees that still had green leaves on their limbs. I started the fire with about ten pounds of kindling, making the fire burn easy.

I sat there listening to *Atreyu* on my Mp3 and opened my red worn book, *The Complete Adventures and Memoirs of Sherlock Holmes.* Sitting there enjoying the energetic and conclusive Mr. Holmes with our great narrator and an excellent sidekick for a doc, Mr. Watson. The flickering orange light danced over the pages, casting a dreamy, cloudy look on the paper.

In the depths of a juicy investigation, I felt a strange power at my back, warm however very overwhelming. I unplugged one earpiece and read on.

Doctor Watson must have been the coolest doctor I have ever listened to until the Love Line radio host, Doctor Drew, came on air - *California Living Bay Bay!*

A titanic gust of wind blew against my back and almost killed my fire. I turned around because this was all very curious. I've been out here before doing the same thing I am doing now, though, for reasons I was not sure of yet, I got a strange feeling of being hovered upon by an enemy.

Deranged as I was, I put both earpieces in and nodded my head to the music. If anyone or anything wants a piece of me there is a good stick of fire that I can use to shoo them away or burn the holy shit out of their eyes. It was Sherlock Holmes that pumped me up for a death match, not so much the Atreyu, though it was a nice background melody.

I read on.

The trees cast shadows that rollicked around the fire.

I read on.

My peripherals caught a dark tree's shadow drifting into my left. Thick midsection, thin at the bottom, and long pencil thick shadow branches that stretched out and out.

I read on.

Wait. In my quick observation there was a super thin bottom to that tree shadow, as if it was not even connected to anything. As if it was just a wisp stretching on...

What the! And then it began. My book faded to black, and I dropped it on the dirt in shock. I tried to blink away the blackness, but it didn't work. It was midnight, and a fog of darkened tint rolled in. Everything got more and more dark till I could hardly see the flicker of flames in front of me; however, the flames inside me were just igniting.

A great force grabbed hold of my throat. This was a grip not like a brother's punishment but a grip of relentless hate. I felt a tug, and my ass drug on the dirt an inch back. I hadn't moved at all except for that little tug, so I knew the fire was still right there in front of me. Blind, I roared and ripped out my earphones and reached behind me to try and grab my assailant, but it was just icy air. I slammed my hands in the dirt at my sides and tried to stand up. It didn't work, and I was losing air. I didn't know what the fuck was happening. My eyes were wide open in anger, but I couldn't see shit. My throat was being choked, but nothing was there to choke me.

I shifted to my right, desperately trying to get out of this voided stranglehold... I felt another tug, and I moved backward another two inches. I was so pissed I started to yell.

"Bloody!.. Take me if you can!"

After my outburst I relaxed and let the dark force seep into my bones. I breathed in. Deep. When I breathed out, I pushed all my energy and power out of every pore from head to toe, instinctively rolling off to the right in the same instant.

Free, I could see again, and the fire was hot with blazing flames next to me. I looked up to see what was after me. The waning crescent moon aided in revealing a dark shadow beast from the closest Great Ash. It sat in the air, reaching up to the stars.

While it hovered there in gluttony, I grabbed the largest stick with flames on the end and walked toward the darkness. I poked at the Ash Shadow and it vibrated and slicked away from the flame, and then became a solid dark shadow again. I grabbed Sherlock Holmes and looked at the towering shadow. The Mp3 lay on the ground, blasting *Slipknot, People equal Shit*. I spit at the Shadow.

"You two will get along just fine, you-"

Flustered and aggravated, I left it and walked the fuck back home with the fire stick in one hand and Holmes in the other.

When I got back to our cabin I told my brothers what happened. Only then did dear A.D tell us what happened to him not too long ago with a girl named Jesse.

Our brother A.D had a funny way with women, even at the time when he was a little fourteen-year-old hoodlum. His idea of having a good time with a girl was just like having a good time with his brothers. Really good ideas, at least in our experience, came with manic conflicts and exciting consequences.

It was three in the morning, and he began to elaborate on what had happened to Jesse and him about a month ago.

"We were having tea at Lilly Piddles Cafe, and we decided to go have a picnic in the Wych Elms forest. We got a ride into town with Pops before, so at the time Jesse and I didn't have any fast transportation."

A.D smiled, looking down in remembrance.

"These punky high school kids were hanging out front by their bikes. I started telling Jesse about how good those free chocolate muffins were as we were in earshot of the high schoolers. The boys pushed past me and ran straight inside Lilly's. By the time they got back outside with empty muffin hands, two of their bikes were gone, and Jesse and I were on our way to the copse of Elms."

A.D was referring to something similar to a woodland area, similar to a forest, but the trees were a lot more spread out and had fewer woodland species involved in the proximity. Wych Elms were tall with big droopy branches that would shoot up and outward to create a large shelter of shade, like a tree fountain. When their branches were bare they could look very eerie, especially in the right setting.

"We got there and I opened up the bag of muffins. I bought them all so the other brats wouldn't get any, even if they wanted to pay." A.D cheered, very happy with himself.

"Get on with it, what happened with the wood?" I asked, half jokingly, half serious.

"...We sat there under the largest Elm, eating our muffins and resting on the thick trunk. My hat was over my eyes, and Jesse idled a few feet away, looking into the copse of Elms... All of a sudden though, Boom! And I'm slapped. My hat dangled on one side of my head, and she just sat there looking over her shoulder with an ember in her eye. I bewilderingly asked why, and she just turned away. Girls were very inquisitive to me at the moment, but soon I found out what was happening."

He lifted his shorts enough to see the huge welts above his knee and a bloody scab from a slash on his thigh.

The Ancient Demon Doomali

The sky boiled orange and was broken apart with black clouds that moved quickly from one edge of the flat land skies to the other. The city in the center of this foreboding desert reeked of insanity. Buildings and roads were splattered and flooded with different colors of blood that ran along the littered contorted streets. The chaos was created by the dead that constantly fought for survival.

From all the realms in the universe, their departed came here, the Galaxy of the Dead, a grip of solar systems made for ghosts and war. The inner Galactic Bulge was the sole power of death itself. It streamed lambent blackness into the heat of surrounding suburb suns.

Circling through the Galaxy were worldly massive dragons that destroyed anything that roamed in space, feeding off the dead energy from other planets. They were called Moon Zealots, the oldest beasts in the universe.

There were good and bad planets in the Dyathsake Galaxy. The heavenly planets were further out in the outer rim, the Halo they called it, and the ghost planets and moons were scattered all around each solar system. This way, there was always a place to dump the double dead, the dead that died again in the semblance of Heaven and Hell. The planets of havoc, of pure manic chaos, were as close to the dark power of the bulge as possible - The Inner Galactic Fuck Fest.

There were five different kinds of life in the Dyathsake Galaxy. Even in death, there is life. The first were Demons that were born in the Galaxy. Second were the Ghosts, who were the dead that had died again. The third were created from the dark power of the bulge, Hellhounds and other beasts with a future in the nightmare business.

These beings are not demons, who are born through lineage and forebears; they are created by the elements of space, a section of space that is more mystical than scientific.

The fourth kind was our kind, the dead that died in other regular galaxies and were now eradicated in Dyathsake as their old material selves, only dead. The final beings were the Togmehoians, the Lords of the Galaxy. Unlike common demons, these were the Lucifers and Odins of these demented, angelic worlds. Both born in death and absorbed with the dark power of the bulge or the holy light of the halo. This one world in particular, Plaztex, had an orange boiling sky that looked as if it were rippling with heat, soothed only by rapid blue and black clouds that raced through its skies.

A protracted zoom focused in on a demon named Doomali, standing on the balcony of his spire loaded rooftop, a location attractive to any drunkard's eye.

****

Ghosts were being shipped away to their phantom moons in gigantic gray spaceships dotting the darkened orange sky, as a pack of three women walked into a bar. One of them was wolf-like with steel bracers, and the other two were human.

Doomali stood by a staircase at the end of the bar across the room with a muscled, dark, shadowy beast humanoid. Parts of the beast's skin faded in and out, becoming transparent and then full again. Doomali, in contrast, was a solid mass of demon flesh, with spikes on his forearms and a metallic beard that pointed down to his collarbone in three different directions. His face was tattooed with red war art, characterized by spirals and sharp finishes contrasting his pit black face. His beard itself was a metallic trident with red swirl rune marks, complementing his teeth of steel shards. An attractive fellow nonetheless.

In Dyathsake the demons had a lot more respect and power going for them, however, there were times when the demon guilds recruited humanoids. For this to happen, the humanoids would have had to survive these death planets long enough to gain a name for themselves. Whatever the name would be, they gained it by surviving through the fires of Hell.

Most humanoids were completely taken aback by the whole, being in Hell thing, and died again within the first day or two. Others accepted their fate and usually survived on their rage built up from their path towards a grunge destiny. One of those types would be Hantos, the shadowy beast that stood next to Doomali.

Face in half transformation transparency, Hantos heaved his heavy bottle that he was drinking out of. The bottle flew across the room at the doorway, and SMACK! It was a dead-on headshot to one of the human girls that just walked into the bar. The glass broke, and she fainted to the desert tile. While the bar slowly increased its deranged anarchy, Hantos walked over to the woman on the tile and sneered at the other two. Behind him, a three-eyed, three-armed beast was strangling another devilish character while pounding him with his two extra fists.

During the chaotic breakdown of the pub, Hantos dragged the knocked-out girl up the stairs behind the bar. Doomali santered over and spoke to the two women before he walked out.

"You gonna go after him?" He said in a slow drawl.

An unsure "No" sound came from the wolf-like humanoid, her knife half pulled.

"Then get out of my pub," Dommali said with a smile full of shardy teeth.

"I'll make sure to give your friend your condolences." He walked out of the bar with their shirt collars in each hand. Overhead there was a yellow, sand-textured sign that read, Burning Christ. The regulars called it the Big BC.

Three of Doomali's soldiers greeted him at the front street. "Back to the Citadel my Lord?"

Doomali tilted his head up in disgust and let go of the cowardly pair of women. "Aye."

He continued onto the desert streets, and his soldiers followed with long black scythes and spiraled blades attached to chains at their hips.

Up ahead, a gang of dead humanoids walked towards Doomali's crew from up the street. They looked tough and like they had survived Dyathsake for a while. The leader, a wide mouthed rock man, fanned the others out with a look and a nod. They commenced the attack as soon as they spread.

The dead loved to attack guarded demons, especially if there were only four to their dozen. The legend was, to drink the blood of a demon was to gain demonic powers and become a hybrid of blood and fire, making them harder to kill and a more desirable recruit.

The gang's attack was well planned. Four of the bigger troops had quick spring-out shields that spanned out in the blink of an eye. The rest of the gang carried heavy crossbows and scimitars.

Our dark hooded Doomali maneuvered himself around one of the shielded humanoids and patted away a scimitar blow from the assailant behind another shielded brute. Doomali grabbed both the troops in front of him and threw them fifty feet into the air. He slid to the next, crouching under a scimitar slash, and then grabbed hold to heave upward and send a third up to dangle in the darkened wind.

A human stood before their leader rock man. Doomali walked over casually, caught the human's bolt that he just shot at Doomali's face, spun the bolt around, and stuck it in the foolish creature's forehead. A second later, the rock man was high in the air and falling to yet another loud crumpling end.

Behind Doomali, the rest of the gang lay slain on the dusty ground. Two of his guards wiped their scythe blades on the double-dead's ripped and ragged clothes. The third was bent over, pulling out his spiral blade from the neck of a tall goblin. Its blood sprayed out onto the street.

As they continued their stroll up the street, they approached the great Citadel. The building ran four stories higher than any of the other buildings in the city, and a large balcony hung out of Godzilla's reach over the street.

Doomali was the son of the Togmehoian of Plaztex, the planet they were presently on. His mother was a demon, currently in the outer regions of Dyathsake fighting the noble dead.

The noble dead rested as heavenly creatures, powerful and ruthless, with good morals and judgment. The noble dead fortified the outer rim of the Dyathsake Galaxy. Only the wise, compassionate, and orderly life forms from all over the universe were allowed onto their Halo lit planets.

Doomali strode inside the Citadel, leaving his guards in the arched doorway. Tapestries of weird horned beasts seizing the walls of pandemonium were spread throughout the entry room. Doomali peered at one with Moon Zealots that twisted in between worlds and stars; the Galaxy's fringe was bright with goodness and dark with evil at its core.

The stairs were draped with a blue carpet that climbed the floors of this kingly Citadel. Yellow sand columns decorated with dark blue flags hailed a yellow diagonally ripped symbol through the center of them. These colored banners filled the huge room's walls, floors, and roof.

Doomali reached the top of the stairs and headed towards the balcony. Flapping in the wind, two blue and yellow flags stood tall in the corner's edge. A lord and four of his sorcerers awaited Doomali's arrival.

"Why hello there Doomali." The voice echoed multiple times in all surrounding minds.

"Father."

"Our most powerful demons are ready in the catacombs along with our best physicists, sorcerers, and warriors," said the Togmehoian, Saul, Doomali's father.

"We have devised a method of possession that is more..." He smiled, placing his hands behind his back and gazing out over the city.

"More rooted and to the point. Ha. With it you will bring true wreckage to the humans."

"Their space productivity, to my understanding, has more highlights than any other star system." Six inserted, one of Saul's high wizards, Lord of Ghost Moon Larus.

Larus was where they did massive possession testing with their berserkers. They'd find 'voluntarily' blase minds and possess them from the other side of the Dyathsake Galaxy, honing their skills so that when holding onto a living creature, it was like leashing a pet, only from universal lengths.

Six had sharp horns sticking out of his voided face, holding two shadowy red eyes. It was a wonder where his voice came from; it seemed to be projecting from his body of trapped souls. When his dark gray cloak went slightly ajar, there were white cloudy skulls that peeled out. With Six, his hobby for possession went far beyond most.

Doomali and his father's ideal plan was to rip a hole of fear into Earth within the Milky Way. Then, as there was chaos and loss of hope, Doomali would gather his core troops and infiltrate Earth's major space base, gaining the largest vantage point of all and creating Dyathesake Starships with Earth's resources.

Doomali, "Aye, take me's to Lagomos Catacombs, the dark bridge of vibration and phantasmal vipers."

When they left the balcony, the Togmehoian Father and Doomali took the lead, striding through the palace halls of the Citadel. Father Saul placed a warm hand on his son. His cloaked sleeve hung heavy with a battle orb, completely hidden, though the sleeve rippled majestically with flagish waves of concealed power.

As the rune-scarred demon Doomali walked by some catacomb cells, his eyes rolled to the side, staring at a beast trapped behind the bars.

"Hell-O!" Doomali then screamed, boasting his guts in his yell. Full blown out, mother fucking 'you're going to die' scream.

The beast screamed back immediately, almost keeping up with the noise of Doomali, but all it took was a minute of that death roar to put fear into the beast's eyes and settle it into the corner of the room. The beast didn't move much after; both of its shoulders almost touched either side of the cell walls. He was a hairy fella like a werewolf slash 'beauty and the beast' monster, leaning more on beast. He looked at Doomali, curious; however, fear gleamed in its eyes of eternal doom.

Doomali snarled and turned away to walk through the catacomb corridor. The entourage picked up again, and they walked down to the depths of the laboratory.

****

Blue spirit vapors rose from the cracks of the floor. The feet of the legendary demon warrior lay thick on the wavy stone.

"We made a portal of bones and lit the spirit vapor with the ancient dirt of Pantoon and roots of Brekinvale luster." A black shaman said with his robe of shadows wisping in the spirit vapor rising from the X cracks in the stone beneath him. His tough horns had a texture of a flowing lava haze, his face hard and momentarily certain of murdering hundreds of beings.

Pantoon is one of the first cities of the dead, and Brekinvales were the trees that blanketed its earth.

The black shaman's eyes rested in space. The smoke twirled across his cheeks as it met the retiring air coming from his jagged toothed mouth.

"Glasir. One golden leaf as well as one golden hope for Tienilla. The first Sky Sister holds the golden leaf Scepter as a last hope to protect her world..."

Other forms of shaman lab wizards hung around the catacombs, listening in on the conversation. 'The lords of the dead will come to living mend', a thought that rang in all their ears. The stone worked prophecy was written on all the surrounding walls.

BAS DOOM HAL PEAKNOLUM SHHHLEIP

"With the golden leaf, we will set our horns deep into the mortal's roots," said the chief lab wiz, like a wolf snarling in your face.

"Mareridt," Doomali breathed in a whisper, and the blue spirit vapor turned red.

'Doomali, the deadliest of dead. Bark of danger.
Breathe even stranger.
You seek a path that turns Mr. Suffering on end.
Laughing hysterically, craving psychos merrily.

The Ancient Demon Doomali

Strips your spine and blows blood in your mouth.
A site caved in, withholding anyone who could shout out.
Doomali, a broken demon that likes his grapes on a string.
Can throw you up and demand that you sing.
A fa la la la, plump, and there you are... ding a ling ling.
Dead again to succeed fate's ring."

Gently setting his lute down on his lap, a lab wizard deep in catacomb shadows finished his singing whispers and watched the possession party craft their plans.

Mareridt

White puffs pressed sluggishly South around high mountain peaks. Whirlwinds blew at the face of a voluptuous cliff.

A single gust blasted into the side of the mountain. The peak rumbled for a moment and then settled back to sleep, like a disturbed ogre woken up by a wild ram's headbutt, leaving a fat hole in the rubble. Out of the dirty smoke appeared a figure of a woman with reaper-like wings on her back that jetted out and then swooped down in an arch to her ankles. Her forearms also had dark, petite wings that looked thick and tough.

Her spine straightened to align with the ascending mountainside, crouched and dangerous. She rested in the concave that her body formed when blasting into the mountain. Her hand dripped blood that fell into the broken rocks of her present sanction. Her eyes drifted toward the broken sky of thirteen visible moons, then jolted down. After a moment of pondering in her elevated jolly madness, her dark-winged body followed just as fast, down towards the red city of Pantoon.

The mountain whispered, *Mareridt.*

Mareridt, an evil, now dead Sister of the Skies on Earth, was once beautiful and eloquent, but nonetheless rebellious. Her dark mind took her further into insanity because of her great power as a Sky Sister. Now after being dead for so long her talents in demonic possession were top-notch, bad to the bone, skin your soul, crazy, freaking, stuff. This is what she was, an intrusive dream matriarch bitch, the one and only Dyathsake has ever had.

She once was kin with the six Sky Sisters; however, infested with a dark conquest to rule over the humans and make them inferior to nature. In a conflict of ideals, she turned against her sisters and raised an army of disillusioned Wood. The Wood honoring any who had the ability to call them for aid. For men also cut them down ruthlessly, with no kind hand, so they, in turn, were upbeat for a rebellion.

There was a mass of very intelligent tree clans. The code to become Awakened was so intricate only Mother Earth or her descendants would know the prayer; thus, the connection and bond was very strong, a power which made the world grow.

When Awakened by a Sky Sister the Wood honored and followed without question. Mareridt's lies and skills of delusion deceived the Wood's loyalty to overthrow the other five Sky Sisters.

After the Great War most tree clans were split. Mareridt's forsaken trees grievously moved to one side of a forest while the other clans, who battled against Mareridt's rebellion, moved into locations that surrounded the exiled forsaken, keeping them in check for eternity. The Woods of Mastbos Brenda, in the Netherlands.

Invitation

Back at the landlord's house, Shaki sat on the porch stairs patching a hole in my plaid sweatshirt. Her hands gracefully wove in and out of the fabric, steady even with the cold air of mid-November.

The boys sat on the foldouts, eating their cereal. Pads with the brim of his bowl pressed to his mouth, taking more gulps than chews. A.D, his slashed arm thick with fat purple scars, held up his spoon, leaving his bowl to sit on his lap, soaking the cereal in the milk, kind of like mine, only mine was already empty.

I didn't think I would be able to eat this fast after the laceration on my chest and broken ribs, but everything on us seemed to be healing accordingly.

This weekend we will all go snowboarding. Test out our rejuvenated wounds and finally have some fun outside of the house. Being stuck inside was really starting to wear on us. All we did was read books, listen up on our tunes, and prank Shaki and her dad - our landlord, back in Central California.

Yesterday, before Mr. Patrick got home from work, we used two full bottles of ketchup to litter the snow in the front yard. Then we threw Pads in the mix. He laid face down right in the middle of the doorway with a glob of ketchup smack dab on the back of his curly light brown head. We couldn't have done it any better. I must say that it looked like a slaughter fest carnival massacre, prime and professional like, something that would scare the balls right out of the neighbors.

A.D and I rested in a couple of trees, both flanking the entrance to the house. As soon as we heard the engine of the black Suburban pull up, all smells went dull, and the noise of my excited heart rate filled my ears like a deep bass.

Shaki was with her dad, and as they got out of the Suburban, Shaki stepped in the red goo mixed with bacon fat. She gasped, and they both stared wide-eyed at the scene, seriously taken back for a moment. It looked as though Shaki was about to jump right back into the truck. Mr. Patrick, however, ran right where we wanted him, directly in front of the doorway where Pads lay limp.

A.D threw the first snowball.

All sounds were lost in the void of anticipation, and then. Smack. The snowball exploded right on the back side of Mr. Patrick's head. I threw from the other side, missing a few and nailing a couple of good ones. Our laughter made it really hard to aim.

Mr. Patrick stepped over Pads and ran into the house. A couple snowballs hit the front door and Pad's butt.

Pads rotated over and squeezed the mustard bottle so it sprayed straight up into the air.

"AHHHhH!"

Little Shaki did get back in the truck after witnessing her pops slowly becoming the abominable snowman. Her cute face peering through the front windshield. We had a short stock of snowballs left, but we made 'em count and lit that little glass barrier up. Good times recoverying indeed.

Shaki was now finished with the white patch on my plaid sweatshirt. I set my cereal bowl down and walked over to grab the sweatshirt. None of us had a shirt on, and it was getting just a little chilly. I wrapped the sweatshirt around and zipped up. The patch was on the shoulder and the stitching looked tight.

"I have a hole in my undies. Do you want to patch those?"

"You don't need those patched A.D. Just use it as your poop shoot," Shaki happily mocked.

"And Speaking of poop shoots, my pops picked up your mail when he was down south. It's mostly junk, but there was a letter from your uncle."

A monkey jumped out of the kitchen window with a letter in one hand and grapes in the other. First, he threw the letter on the porch. Slap! Then, he threw a clump of grapes at Pads and pounced back inside.

"What the shit." Pads grumbled.

Shaki picked up the letter. "Here it is."

Pads gulped the last of his milk and indifferently took the letter from Shaki. "Iceland… From Favin Tork."

A.D stood up and threw his bowl ten yards off the porch and into the snow. He snatched the letter from Pads. "Well, read it already."

A.D opened the letter.

"Elo Champs."

A.D looked up from the letter at his brothers with an open smile.

"Hope your recovery is going well. A good friend and myself have discovered an ancient relic that has been in your family for ages. Get your rest, heal up, and fly over mid-winter. Directions are on the back. This be very important lads, something that'll really twiddle your nips."

A.D looked disappointed. "Aww, no snow bunnies this season."

"We don't even have a place to live. We can't stay at Mr. Patrick's forever bro." I said, sympathizing with A.D's feelings. Those snow bunnies were cute, and what's even better about the winter season was hanging out with our northern crowd, which we never got to see, Alvero and the Alaskans.

"We could stay at Alvaro's Krae," A.D said vibrantly, like it was the most intelligent idea ever.

"A.D since you're in a 'take charge' mood, why don't you go pick up your bowl and then buy us tickets for Iceland. We're going." I said.

A.D looked over at Pads. Pad's arms were crossed, and he was nodding affirmation with me. A.D then set off to do his chores. Once he started moving early in the morning, he would find productive things to do till sundown.

Shaki, in her sweatshirt and sweats, raised her arms. "Maybe I can come. Can I come?"

The gears turned and the silence yearned. The pillow of friendship was ripped from under intricate metal heads. Passion lingered like a spoken prayer never heard. True compassion wasn't the duty of the tortured monsters we were. Our nerves ran with problems that could occur, spilling out lava from the uncontrollable heat of denial.

Why was trouble so welcoming? It invited you in and everybody else. If they jumped off a bridge, would you as well? Hm, ya I probably would, even after watching trouble disappear in the morning mists below the lemming bridge. I would begin to wonder where it would lead. Greater salvation? A great rush? Nowhere? Or is trouble the meaning of what is really great in life? A practitioner of death.

"No Shake, you got other stuff to do. Favin is probably just going to show us an old book or something. When are old relics that interesting?" I said with a hint of sarcasm.

"Yeah right, just going to the airport with you guys will be an adventure."

I looked at Pads. He was sitting there grinning and looking down at his feet. Then he looked up at me, shaking his head, shoulders bouncing from his giggles.

I watched Shaki's excitement dissipate, but her drive still burned deep.

"I'll even give you my crossbow." Shaki exemplified.

"How do three split one?" I asked.

"Trade off... I'm going to go buy my plane ticket now." She stalked toward the door.

Pads chimed in with a mischievous smile to turn any doubting heart.

"Who said we were flying?"

A Pirate's Life for Me

We have weapons too - our freaking freak like minds. Keep it sharp, keep it keen. Usually, during our few excursions with Favin, they've been littered with physical and mental trials, adventures to add to our collection of epic stories, and ingestion of everlasting wisdom. So, we decided to take a little more time and prepare ourselves for whatever Favin had in store for us.

We rocked back and forth on this ship rather than swiftly flying with meek humming jets and wispy looking clouds.

Just one day before this rocking freighter, we were sitting on a train going cross country for four days, until we reached Maine. Boring as it was, we still managed to be productive. The one hundred and fifty dollars we spent on dry food was finished within the first two days, and after that, it was munching constantly on train food; an accomplishment in itself eating that stuff. Orange peels, pear, apple, and nectarine cores were all over our little bunked-up berth.

Shaki tried to clean up every once in a while, but we really took our work seriously. Books scored the middle floor area between the four bunks, and everyone kept to their own little bed, reading or eating, or perhaps sometimes stretching in the middle area; regardless, we rarely left the berth. Shaki, once again, was our pretty little butler, Winston Smith Shaki.

Pads was under A.D's bunk, and I had the bunk above Shaki. We read and shared interesting information about Vikings, historical battles, the different trees or lack of trees, weather forecasts, social activities, patterns in their government, and all there was to find about Iceland.

When Shaki wasn't completely disturbed or out of her mind being locked up in such small quarters with us, she occasionally pulled out her Iphone and looked up a couple of additional interesting facts; however, with us, we really connected with books. Holding them and looking through them was our Zen.

One time in our bunk studyhall, Pads threw a book up to A.D, *Large Forest and Tree Species Lost in Iceland.* The book flipped ajar, and I caught a glimpse of a quarter of the page. It was a gray crosshatched picture with a rainy day feel to it and a great tree, widened with long curling branches, standing over a cliff, seemingly puffing its chest out toward the dark sky.

A.D caught it and flipped to the page Pads wanted him to look at. A.D's face crinkled and eyes narrowed, scrunching close together. I remember looking back down at Pads afterward. He tightly squinted at me as well, with a hard pondering frown.

I looked up at the top of the train's ceiling and fell asleep. I had one of those dreams again; this time, it was a tree whistling in the wind happily. I felt like the tree was trying to hint at something, always whistling and nodding to the side.

****

So now, unlike the train, we are scattered amongst the ship. I watched the great waves of the Atlantic Circle slam against our haul, again and again. I looked back a couple flights down the bridge stairs and A.D was on the stern's deck, taking a break from his pull-ups on the overhead railing. He looked out, watching the swells majestically chase after the sunset.

I turned from watching him and focused on the helmsman.

This guy was hard to talk to.

I acquired my quizzical face, "Could you and your crew possibly throw a fish net out while ferrying back and forth?" I watched his face, looking for any trigger that would unlock his madness.

"Ever think of a little gravy with your beans, helmsman?"

He stared into the sea bluntly. At first, he angrily mumbled about 'seeking the twins in the sea.' He then got a little louder. "The fish don't be jelly fed B Z, most be a little looney, water bandits, not the tings bove but below. It just not right to Tracher."

Puzzled as all hell, I picked up a scent that lifted my chin. "What he meant is…" The Lady Captain refreshingly greeted. Her fierce light blue eyes anchored at the ocean's edge.

Tracher, the helmsman, turned his old, rugged head around to acknowledge the Captain that just walked onto the bridge. He nodded and went back to looking toward the sea.

She continued, "The kind of fish we would catch would scare guests away. This be bad for business." Her hair was dark, long, and knotty, looking as if it was washed in salt water every day. She had a nose ring, eyebrow pierced, and golden earrings covered both her ears. Her presence bled authority. The unique and formal way she dressed alone showed that her pirate-ridden explicitness was all in the past.

Perfect, I thought to myself, again thinking of 'perfection'; the word throbbed seductively in my thinker. I looked into her eyes.

"What is your business on the bridge?" She asked, shifting into a more malevolent tone.

"I merely wanted to know how your ship ran. Such a large ship ferrying just people back and forth from the US to Iceland seemed interesting to me, especially on such an unconventional path."

"You idiot!" Her voice was harsh but extremely steady and controlled.

"You are lucky you found us on the docks when you did. Now leave us, boy." Her eyes and body never wavered an inch. Strong she was.

And after being shut down, it was hard to remember what I really wanted to ask.

"Happy to be aboard Captain." I followed my words right out the door and down the stairs.

A.D was working out vigorously, strengthening himself after all that food and laying around for months and months. He was still facing the end of the ship, so I slipped by him and went down into the haul. I heard shouting below, cheering even, and then a girl's voice, "Get 'em Pads!"

I turned right to venture down to the crew quarters instead of left, where the guest quarters were. Pads was sitting across from a crew member with an Indian feathered spear tattooed at full length on the inside of his right forearm and a feathered arrow on his left forearm.

The tatted guy was winning and was about to submit Pad's knuckles into the table's splintery wood.

Pads barked a grunt, getting the fellow's attention, and then spat in his face. Pads then swung the spear back the other way, like a quick beat in a metronome, thumping the big guy's fist on the far end of the table.

Outraged, the man got up and started to shove his way through the other crew members. This guy was really big actually.

I got in the way though. Pads was still sitting in the chair, proud of his win and ready for anything. That damn kid. I grabbed him with one hand without looking, pulled him out of his chair, and pushed him toward Shaki, who was already drifting toward our inviting guest quarters.

I looked at the guy and couldn't help but laugh a little.

"Listen mate, what's done is done, we are outta here."

Still outraged, the tatted guy yelled at Pads, saying he'll crush him and throw him into the sea. He probably could and could get through me pretty easily as well, but he didn't, and we went back to our room while Pads sang the West Ham United Green Street Hooligan club anthem chant.

I'm forever blowing bubbles,
Pretty bubbles in the air,
They fly so high,
Nearly reach the sky,
Then like my dreams
They fade and dieee!
Fortune's always hiding,
I've looked everywhere,
I'm forever blowing bubbles,
Pretty bubbles in the air!

When we reached our room Pads immediately started doing crunches. I looked at Shaki and she was all excitement. Her dark tan collarbone stretched out, golden eyes wide, and her puffy cheeks a little red around her broad nose. She opened her fat lips, exhibiting her white teeth.

"Those guys had it coming, just a bunch of seabirds waiting for their next meal. I was ready to knock seven shades of shit out of them if they touched Pads." Shaki gleamed with semi-gritted pearly whites.

"Well, I'm sure they would have liked that Shake." I indolently plopped down onto a cot and began my pensive slumber.

Before I slipped into the abyss of pitched starlight, I heard Pads.

"Krae get out of my cot, you drunk piece of..."

Then I remembered. I left my flask of rum with the old helmsman on the bridge.

Iceland

The deck's steel was dented and cold, like the blue wind swirling around our massive ship.

I rested my forearms on the railing, bumping my chest with the cold steel as the ship rocked. We layered ourselves with jackets on top of sweatshirts. I wore my sweatshirt of multicolored patches under a blue and white Mexican poncho. The rag always left me warm and humble.

Occasionally, a spray would wash onto the bow in front of us, the three brothers.

I could feel the Captain's eyes watching, but it didn't really bother me. We were just so very anxious to get off this ship. I've been having the worst nightmares on this boat. Crippled ghosts and mutated demons simply blistering out of the water. Whats more is the crew talked of the same dreams, making everyone a bit more skittish in the dark at night.

Out in the distance on the ship's port side were white peaks, slowly melting into lush green mountains. Then, on our starboard side, there were rocky broken-up hills guiding us into Reykjavik's bay.

Village of the Isle

I looked under my Converse and saw the light wooden dock under my feet. My gratitude to be ashore melted away as I felt the bigger crewman with the spear and arrow tattoo step between the others and bump my back.

"See you later, Twinkle Toes," he said as he walked by me, his face bright with insanity as well as joy. This guy's ideal belief was that fucking around was the purest of lifestyles. A face that said, I will bring my people together and do my best to stress their boundaries and push their buttons for outcomes of blissfulness. An ideology that ongoing pranks kept the mind thinking in the present; a mind that kept its gears turning was a mind that had no chance of ever dwelling in cruel realities.

Spear and Arrow's shoulders looked like they'd crack me up. No tickling business. Literally, crack me in two with an easy two-foot bull rush.

He arrogantly pranced along the dock toward the lit-up tavern.

"Hey. Lord of Basackll." Funny way to say-

"What'd you call me, little Twinkle fairy?" The big guy turned to face me with an intelligent grin on his face, slowly lifting an eyebrow.

I continued, "Ball sack." Letting the words slip out slowly, emphasizing the 'double L' and 'ck'. My finger pointed to the water while I stepped a little closer to the crewman, who seemed like he would enjoy throwing an anchor on a man's chest and laugh wittingly while watching him try and get up.

"Fuck you-" he was interrupted in the air while falling into North World water.

Splash!

However extravagantly outraged, his boys still maintained their heads. They didn't want to waste time throwing me in when they'd just have to wait for me to get out all wet and frostbitten, only to acquire a means of redemption for their fellow brother of the ferry. So they got right to swinging and throwing fists up, in a weird semblance of bringing me down. Bringing me to the docks, Ha! Docks and drops were nawskis for me, so I got right to it as well. I started by throwing a long, drawn-out punch to the middle of the riot.

Pop!

I threw both of my hands over my shoulders, surprised about the direct connection. Damn, that felt good, and now my adrenaline was jacked.

Twitching eyes intermediately going from focused to blurred, then back to a renewed focus. Nerves unraveling and unconnected. It was like a green parrott flying overhead in slow motion on the clearest of days.

The world became clear, and all sounds slowed. Focus picked up every hymn, while the spirit watched the body move. Rage and love were the only things that could grant the same level line of jacked adrenaline with some wildly erratic frequency.

My rage elevated when I remembered I didn't like people. I jiggled solidly through the mass. Some bodies flopped down in front of me, and others were pushed slightly to the side with my fists bowling through the line-up of crewmen, trying to hit as many of them as possible with each throw.

My love elevated when I caught a glimpse of Pads behind me as I was hit with a right hook that swiveled my head around.

Look at lil Pads. Isn't he the best? Let's beat their asses little bro. Wait, It looks like he's about to…

Smash! I fell into the bodies surrounding me, throwing their knuckles my way.

I 'pitched the bay' and blurp toddley burrr tea... Knocked out goes Krae.

****

Hm. I'm awake. My eyes opened to a ruined and rusty golden sign, 'The Village Isle'. Looking down, I could see that I was leaning on a wooden pallet and sitting in the dirt. Under the sign, Pads and A.D came out of the front door, chatting it up. The *Metallica* song *'The Day That Never Comes,'* played in my head while I waited.

"That's real nice leaving your boy in the dirt all alone."

"Wha you say, Kraeno?" Pads said in his soft yet aggressive tone.

I put my head back on the pallet. Damn, I was exhausted.

"You mumbling fool," A.D noted, then stared off to the west.

"I sacked you good Kraeno, you owe me one brother."

My eyes tilted at little Pads. My hand rose up and flipped the finger in between all the rest. Pads was hunched over, resting on his knee right in front of me, just staring.

What's with these guys today? Stareaholics. I heard Shakes walking up in her dark gray boots.

I had to gather some strength and not look so much like a retarded fish caught and thrown out of water. I leaned forward and rested my forearms on my knees, looking right into Pad's light green eyes.

"How you doing Krae?" Shaki asked with a wide pearly smile. Innocent little chick; if we all got our balls eaten off by wolves, she still wouldn't know the difference between a guy who's feeling good and a guy who wants to eat bullets.

I gave her two thumbs up without picking up my arms.

"What's the news, Shake?" A.D asked, still looking west down the main street, parallel with the harbor docks.

"No buses going to Favin's until tomorrow morning." She paused and looked us over.

"There's a motel right over there though," She aimed her pointer finger down the road to the west. "We could stay there for the night."

Shaki continued again, after a patient moment of waiting for a reply from us.

"Another thing! There is a lady who is having trouble with her house. She says the earthquakes ever-so-often, cracking her walls and jostling her things... I think she's crazy, speaking about some Kraken to all the locals."

Pads was still fucking looking at me. I laughed.

Pads helped me up merrily, and we all started walking toward the motel.

****

It was twilight and the water looked a deep blue gray. The docks depopulated and men bustled away in conversation.

Now at the motel, Shaki grabbed the keys at the front desk, and we walked down the hall to our room.

I headed right for the head. Wonder why they call it the head? It sounded like a shipping term, like the head was at the front of the boat, therefore being the head or the head of my pee-pee, which then equalizes back into a bathroom term.

I finished my leak and started washing my hands and face. Sometimes, the sink was a man's best friend. A great rejuvenating cure can be as simple as a splash of water.

I got a glimpse of my face as I dried off. I had big face line creases between my cheeks and jawbone, like little boomerangs dividing the cheeks from the jaw. My temple was a little swollen with a crescent scar crossing the brow, and above all that beauty was my colorful mustache, black, light brown, red, a small bit white, yellow, and a hair of blue.

Realization! I was starving. I opened the door.

"Fooood..." I moaned.

"We already ate when you were knocked out," A.D said indifferently, clicking at the TV.

"Try the tavern; they have some white pasta there that's suuuper dank." Pads added in.

I grabbed Pad's old black windbreaker and bounced out into the motel hall. After that, I shut the door and checked the jacket pockets. Cigarettes. Alllrighty, where the hell is the... Lighter! Pad's old busted eye shamrock zippo. I lit up and walked outside.

The house right next to this motel looked a little crooked. I started walking by the house and toward the inn, all the while looking at the cigarette smoke rising up into the air in front of me. Wait.

Simultaneously, I heard a creak and saw something move in the corner of my eye. I looked back at the house. Maybe that lady wasn't as crazy as everyone said.

As I was coming up to the tavern, I tossed the cigarette in front of me and gave it a good step twist as I walked by.

Pads, you joggled my brain pretty good, buddy.

Reaching the lit area right under the faded golden sign, I tugged Pad's black jacket tight around the shoulders, and all of a sudden, The Village Isle's red metal door swung open right in front of my nose. I caught a whiff of spilt beer and moved aside as a drunken stampede of crewmates bustled out.

One wagged his finger side to side at me, smiling like a hyena with his pack about to go laugh themselves to the bottom of a barrel.

Laugh away, you schmuck!

I opened the red metal door and pushed past the mass of crew and dock lads that littered the joint. I headed for the bartender. There was a good open spot right between two handsome-looking fishermen talking.

"Pasta, sir, and lots of it," I said to the bartender, who was cracking open a beer for another mate.

He looked at me with his black hair knotted to his shoulders and pointed down at the bar.

"Pasta is whatcha want, huh kid?"

I just looked at him.

"Four-Fifty." He said.

"And an anchor steam," and then I sat down between the fish mates.

"Nine-Fifty." He looked over my shoulder and back at me worried.

"I got the money man, it's alright." He took the cash and went to the next lad.

The tonality of a hundred low barks were bouncing off the back of my head, and hot air flushed down my shoulder blades.

I spun on the stool, noticing during the spin that the two fishermen were cracking their knuckles.

"You mimicking a chipmunk big guy?" I said to the crewman with the spear and arrow tattoos on his forearms. He had a wide face and a dark buzz cut.

"Do I look like a chipmunk, Killer?" The crewman said gregariously, quieting the bar.

I really wanted to slap both of his cheeks at once and say, 'now you do chip'. But then I probably wouldn't get my pasta, along with not having any teeth to eat it with. But who needs teeth for pasta?

Instead, I smiled and said, "I don't know, can you sing?"

I'm not sure why I keep calling this guy strange names, like Mr. Ballsack and Chipmunk, but they seemed to roll off the tongue.

I heard the bowl of pasta touch the bar top. I turned, grabbed my bowl and fork, and took a bite while looking at one of the fishermen boys sitting next to me, then swiveled back to Spear and Arrow.

"Listen... um, what the hell's your name crewman?" He didn't give it.

"Listen big guy, hope there's no hard feeling from earlier." I took another bite, then started talking again with a mouth full.

"It was hot earlier and thought you asked to go for a swim." I took another bite. "Now I just want to eat in peace."

"What was that? You want to eat in seas?" The crewman laughed, and the tavern laughed with him.

"How bout I buy you guys a drink?" I spun around to the bar and downed my pint.

"Five more barkeep! Quickly, Sir." I urged.

All of a sudden I was tugged off the stool. I never would have guessed.

"Drink your beers asshole, what the hell you want with me."

The mass of crewmen excitedly lifted me up and began walking me toward the door, with water ashore. I didn't struggle a bit. It was actually quite comfortable; I think my dark hair caught air, yet it would have been nice if they took a little more time with this.

The red metal door opened, and guess who? My brothers stood under the wedge.

"Oh, check it boys. We have ourselves a couple more midnight mermaids."

From my point of view, the tavern lads were getting pretty riled up from this, and my brothers weren't likely to surrender as easily as me. I looked over my right shoulder, and my pasta was sitting on the bar top. Come to me, baby.

"Bring it," said Pads, I love you little brother.

Then, right when a yellow haired fellow started lunging for Pads, a lady burst through the door and slid between them.

She screamed, "My house! Someone help! Please!" It seemed this was one of those times when a sane person went insane, and you had to listen to them because, well, everyone wanted a taste of fresh insanity. Old insanity we throw to the curb, but fresh... The present events must be monumental.

The lady proceeded to plead. "Please, please."

I shrugged my way out of the crewmen's grip. Not an easy thing to do I might add, even if they had already somewhat let go.

Spear and Arrow, jacked and wide with bulging muscle, was the first to respond, "Lead the way, Miss."

We all ran out onto the street. Pads and A.D were on the first string of household heroes, with Spear and Arrow and the lady. More than half the tavern ran outside.

Well that should be enough for the little lady's problems. So I went back inside, sat down on my stool, and finished the beer sitting next to my bowl of Alfredo pasta.

"How about the other four beers, Guido." I asked the barkeep.

"What was that?" He expressed passionately.

Man, I really can't get a break around here can I?

"Beers my friend, beers," I said, with him glaring at me. We looked at each other. I shrugged my shoulders and mouthed, beers bro.

He finally turned and started pouring pints. Good boy. Now for my honey-loving pasta.

Tree House

Dirt and dust hung in the air surrounding the lady's house. Looking at the two-story home from the outside, it had a horribly slanted roof and there were three to four windows for each wall, with half of them broken out, looking like something you would see in a haunted roller coaster ride.

The house shook every which way, rumbling, and flinging the lady's furniture all around the inside. It slammed on the ground again and again, from this corner to that. Pads and A.D stood there with quizzical expressions. A.D held a stern smirk, dominating the kid inside him that wanted to laugh hysterically and throw eggs at the windows.

The lady of the house sat on her heels facing her front door. She simply watched the dancing settlement go ape shit.

The blonde fellow that had lunged for Pads back at the inn, grabbed the shoulders of the two guys flanking him and pulled them down to knee level, peering into the dark gaps under the house.

"Wha the…" Blondie exasperated.

Pads and A.D did the same thing and took a look below. Pads planked, resting on his elbows, and A.D bent with one knee on the ground and the other tabling his arm. A.D stroked his half-inch beard and turned to look at Pads. Pads, entranced by the flailing house, waved A.D to follow him. They both got up and raced to the rear end. A couple of the crewmen trailed their lead.

In the backyard stood a remarkable great oak. It had a massive trunk, mothering huge branches that held up bushes of green. Possibly the only tree in the barren lands of Reykjavik. The men stood there watching the eerie tree and the shadowy house rustle around in one spot.

The backyard had no lights; it was like night and day compared to the street that separated the house from the docks. Their eyes dilated and focused, searching for the origin of the chaotic wreckage.

An old man waddled in between the group of men and flicked on his flashlight. It was the motel manager. He shined the light on the back door, then the broken grass, which pulsated in a wavy pattern, mirroring the fluctuating depths of underground movement. The old man then ran the light slowly up the trunk of the great oak, and the light vibrated for a second, close to the tree's center.

The chill itself now snaked around every man's spine and squeezed enough to shiver their souls.

The group decided to dig up the ground and find the root of the problem. The old man gave the flashlight to Spear and Arrow and stumbled off yammering about puns and crumbs of sorts.

The men were alive again, as they once were when they first carried Kraeno to his icy plunge. Boots skidded through the dirt, racing to find shovels and more lights. The group was scattered, but the adventure seemed fresh as Spring.

Pads looked at the back door and hiked up his shorts to his thighs, then leaped side to side, dodging the earth that was unbalanced and most mobile. He prepared himself for one final leap toward the back door of the house right as the broken rear foundation slammed into the ground. Pads slipped to a halt in the wet mud, but regained his positioning. He had enough time to quickly pounce on the door and grab the doorknob, pulling it open. The door now swung frantically in and out, knocking Pads to the mud. The house bowed forward, and the door slammed shut. Pads stood there wobbling from the shifting earth.

"Pads what the fuck are you doing?" A.D yelled, "Get the hell away from there."

The shaggy, dirty, light brown-haired kid took another leap toward the back door. This time the house was tilted east, on its side. Pads opened the door and was flung inside as the house tilted west, crashing on his back onto the laundry room floor.

A.D stood looking at the jiggle-beast house, listening to all the crap smash against other crap, watching the house leak in extravagant places because all the pipes were torn out. And then A.D saw a light go on inside and got a glimpse of Pads being tossed from a door wedge into a closet.

Spear and Arrow returned from the docks with a small anchor held with both hands, chain trailing behind him. Crew members and dock hands were quickly returning with shovels and lights. They began to sink the shovel edges into the soil with heavy grunts, throwing chunk after chunk up into the air. Spear and Arrow stood in the middle of everything digging like a dog with that small silver anchor. It was like a giant's pickax with a chain connected to it.

The back door swung open, and out came Pads, gripping two shovels and a broken lantern.

"What you going to do with that buddy?" A.D humoriously shouted at him, as Pads tossed one of the wooden handled shovels his way.

A.D caught it, and Pads threw the lantern in the mud. "That's one mad tree house, A. I picked up the lantern only to have it smashed into my chest by one of those roots blasting through the floorboards." Pads looked down at the dig zone.

"Let's get to the roots shall we." Pads shouted.

"Rude roots reckless rioting routing wrinkled wrenches right out to rounded reliable ring rules." A.D watched Pads shoveling away, waiting for a response which Pads was too busy to give. A.D decided on a much easier slogan to raise morale. "Ground and pound baby!"

After a few minutes, the load of digging was finished, and the veins of Lady Earth were revealed. The men stood amazed, breathing hard, leaning on their tools, peering at the wooden worms shifting around in the trench.

"Cut it off from the house." Someone shouted.

Spear and Arrow grabbed the chain and whirled the anchor around beside him. He exhaled a loud grunted roar and landed a solid finishing blow to the center of the largest root.

The house dropped flat on the ground, and within moments, the roots suddenly slipped out of the foundation. Like a Kraken elevating its tentacles over your ship's masts, the great oak's roots rose out of the dirt, suspended in the moonlight overhead, creating that drastic pre-collision suspense.

Then, Plow! Gravity dropped those heavy roots, and they popped them up like dolls on a trampoline. The roots then came back around to the slowly crumbling house, clawing through the backside and leaving their mark of destruction in the ruins.

Most of the digging crew was laid out in the dirt and mud. The others who didn't get completely knocked up and thrown across properties started helping their friends get to their feet. A.D lay looking up at the stars, taking deep breaths. Shaki held Pad's head, diagnosing if he could remember who he still was.

A puff of smoke lingered from the rear side of the house. Kraeno walked up gradually with Shaki's gift in one hand - the black, full spread, tactical crossbow; on the tip, a bar towel, and little vodka bottles duct taped around the bolt head. The bolt salivated, and the smell of gasoline filled the air. Kraeno stared at the heart of the shadowed bark. With the moonlight cast behind the monster, its silhouetted shape and contortion reeked of something evil.

The roots whipped around the sky, hovering above the broken bodies in the mud, slamming down on anyone who might try to get up. Blondie was one of the brave ones that tested the wooden hydra. He got up in a hunched-over run only to fall to a root slap across his face, resulting in a sound that echoed through the yard like a broken jaw or eye socket.

Kraeno stood in the mud still staring at the heart of the great oak. Taking a long drag from his cigarette, he blew out a line of smoke that cloaked the crossbow, and pressed the cigarette onto the soaked bar towel.

As suddenly as the bolt lit in a bulky flame, he had the crossbow up to his face and the trigger pulled. The crewmen and his brothers lay there watching the little fireball race toward the tree's trunk in seconds. The fiery bolt thunked into the bark, breaking the vodka bottles and splashing flames all over, revealing the twisted face in its cracked bark of ugly knots.

The hydra flailed about, slamming into the ground and the surrounding bodies, smashing anyone in its path of painful destruction. The men jumped up and gathered their broken neighbors, hobbling out of the tree's reach. Shaki tried to pull Pads away, but she didn't have the strength. Kraeno jogged up, twisted his hand in Pad's shirt, and dragged him to A.D. then twisted his other hand in A.D's shirt and drug both of them closer to the motel.

In all of its flaming glory, the roaring great oak was now fully uprooted and slowly chasing after those running toward the docks. However, the tree was too large to fit through the gap between the lady's ruined house and the small fish n' tackle building. The furious roots pounded on the house, and the trunk checked the still-standing foundation beams until the whole house collapsed. The tree was getting used to moving, and in its killing fury, its tenacity became increasingly more formidable. Orange mist seeped from the wooden slits of its eyes as black clouds rolled in front of the moon, and darkness consumed the night. Facing the demon oak, terror reaped the cloudy air.

The fight for survival now took place in the lamp-lit arena of Reykjavik's harborway. The street was in chaos. The big crewman, Spear and Arrow, was in the middle of it all. He jumped diagonally across a gap from the street to the edge of a dock. As it wagged under his weighted pounce, he jumped again into the nearest fishing boat.

Spear and Arrow's quick evasion turned the demon oak's attention to three other lads who were attempting to follow him, astonished by the plundering horror. In their stupor, one of them got caught by a thick root and was then punished into the cold sea.

The other crewmen and dock hands headed for the inn. The blazing tree roared from a deep crack in the bark and chased the mass towards the inn. Half a dozen guys got inside; another three got twisted in the tree's 360-degree root twirl.

The tree bashed against the front of the inn, destroying the Village Isle sign completely, leaving only lonely chains above a crumpled red metal door. Roots enveloped the doorway and the front interior. Aside from the roar of the tree bashing against the inn, and the yelling of the crewmen, zealous shotgun blasts were heard inside.

The great oak lunged at the doorway, widening it with each hit as it pulled the stone blocks apart with its roots. Glass broke at the base of the tree resulting in a pool of flames. Another glass broke, and another. Molotov cocktails were being flung one after the other.

The bartender ran out of the back alley wielding his shotgun and threw another Molotov cocktail at one of the last bushy branches on the demon oak. He then started pumping rounds into the tree's fiery face, four shots at a time, then a wide-eyed reload. Knotted black hair hung down to his shoulders, and his chin lifted high in the air, letting rounds fly. The grit of his teeth showed that he was pissed and wanted to tear this wooden devil apart.

The tree stumbled back but then quickly jolted forward, breaking most of its smaller branches on the inn. The brick crumbled and the fiery tree was inside, burning the building down to the ground.

The demon oak was enveloped in flames, but the fire only toasted its bark and boiled its sap. The tree's wood was heated and charred, making it more monstrous and deadly.

Screams were heard from inside. The bartender worked on getting the rest of the people out into the back alley while shooting shell after shell into the protruding roots.

Spear and Arrow was huddled with two crewmen organizing a massive net behind crates on the docks near the inn. Kraeno slid in beside them with the tactical crossbow, moving to the middle of Spear and Arrow and the other crewmen. He grabbed the front of the net, then tied the finer netting to the bolt and tugged the spring line back, locking it in.

"I'll shoot for the roof. If it sticks, we can run up and entangle the bastard!"

The men started to protest, but Kraeno was already on his way to the street.

He took the shot and the net trailed behind the dark bolt flinging across the sky. It thudded into a fiery thatched roof and only after a short hesitation did the net team run at the tree, two men for either side.

The tree's flames were dying down. The Molotov cocktails were high-proof alcohol, but nothing that kept malevolent flames continuously burning.

During the tree's tousling rage the men wrapped the net around the roots as the tree twisted and roared with vicious blood thirst. The cracked bark, where its mouth seemed to be, dripped droplets of tiny fireballs. Higher on its trunk a hole smoldered red and black from a past fiery blaze.

Kraeno dropped the net, backed up, aimed quickly, and fired another fat bolt at that smoldering eye. Embers flew and it sparked up into a busty flame. The tree finally moved away from the inn, bricks falling and tumbling behind it. The crossbow bolt holding the net was jerked out of the roof, but the net covered the tree's top branches and rear roots. Spear and Arrow still held the net tight from afar, tactically rolling and twisting it around more insurgent roots.

The bad part? It was coming at Kraeno with slow slapping strides. The tree with a fiery bolt for an eye stopped at the streetlamp post and pulled it down with one of its larger branches. With the bottom bolts of the streetlamp, the demon tore into its trunk, leaving sharp runes and symbols. The cuts began to glow orange with heat and mystical power. The great oak roared again, bending down to get a good look at the man with the crossbow.

The tree crept forward. Still powerful and mighty. Without stopping, it threw the lamp post to the side, casually killing a young boy who was watching the unbelievable event in close proximity.

Kraeno retreated one slow step at a time, while carefully reloading another bolt, unsure of the damage it would have.

Behind the tree a man sprinted over to the dead body of the young boy and then brutally cried out while raising a machete in his right hand. He got to the smoldering oak and climbed up the roots, making his way to a mid-level branch, chopping away at the trunk while screaming battle cries of mournful sorrows.

One of the other higher-level branches was cut off, but the madman's machete didn't just cut the wood, it cut the netting as well.

Within the next moment, a free branch grabbed the man and lifted him inches from its toony features in the trunk. Hot sap spit out onto the man, changing his battle cries to cries of horror. He was then thrown into the ocean as the tree continued towards Kraeno.

The net lifted off the ground and suddenly became real snug. The crewmen had tied the net to a truck hitch and tugged the tree off balance, leaving it frantically roaring as it fell. After a small quake as the tree hit the ground, the rugged bartender jumped up onto the trunk and worked his shotgun surgery.

A couple chainsaws came out of the woodwork and started zipping away, and within minutes the crewmen had chopped up one dead, fucked up looking log with orange heat steaming from its cracks that soon faded out.

Plateaued, Kraeno looked across the smoke of the dead oak and saw Spear and Arrow standing there looking right back at him. Kraeno gave him the finger, turned around, and walked back into the old motel. Spear and Arrow watched Kraeno walk away and then went to the bar for a drink.

****

I stayed out of the way while the living picked up their smashed friends. I laid out on the ground by the motel room's fan; that kind of performance kept you heated no matter how cold it was outside. A.D slept on one of the two beds with a bandage wrapped around his head. Shaki had to give him four stitches right above his right ear.

Four clinics arrived after the tree fell. They passed out medication, like morphine, hydrocodone, oxycontin, demerol, and all kinds of other names I have never cared to pronounce. A.D received some morphine, and we stashed the extra pills away for another time. If Mother Earth was really a tormented sprout ready to throw the gloves off and brawl down, then we were really going to need some medication in our front pockets.

Pads and Shaki were outside in the night air, making sure everything was steady. After extreme events like that, you never knew what exactly was going to happen next.

Unfortunately for all of us, Mother Earth could be an aggressive assailant. Sweet home on Earth was no longer as sweet. Nature wanted to rip us to shreds, and understandably so. We've ruined her, flattening out to almost zero respect for nature, creating dumber and more ignorant, industrialized babies of dumb dumb dumb butts. Stop wasting shit and start growing green, then maybe our Mother wouldn't have a bounty on any Sucker Two Legs.

I could only imagine what snowboarding would be like with monster trees everywhere.

I took a shower, a long hot shower. When I got out, there was a dark-haired woman with long legs in tight green breeches and a black Nirvana hoodie standing by the front door of our room. I dropped my towel and covered my tits. I've always wanted to do that.

"Cold shower little guy?" She asked unabashedly.

I picked up my towel and went around the bed to where my pack was. She stood by the door. I looked her over again. I remember her from our parents' funeral. She was the gal with that panda tie guy.

I did a deck change, "Came to pick us up?" I asked, smiling, thinking about the dead tree outside.

"Yes, and let's skedaddle before Icelandic Agents get here. Is he okay to move?" She nodded toward A.D.

"Ya, A.D is alright. I'm Kraeno. And yourself?"

"My name, is Cid..."

"Well Cid, I remember you hanging out with that Panda tie fella, is he with Favin?"

Her white skin pulsed red, and she smiled looking down.

"Yeah, they both at the ranch." She said fast, snippy, and obviously in love with the Panda Man.

"There was a lot of work to be done after this disturbance of soil."

I was puzzled, "You mean…" I hinted outside.

She nodded, "Now get your brother ready; I'll send the other one in to help. Chopa Chopa."

Cid walked out with her yellowish tassels tied with bells dangling from her dark green boots. Her tight green breeches forming her butt great.

I packed up most of our stuff in a couple minutes. I threw my backpack together and put it over one shoulder, then picked up the duffel bag with Shaki's crossbow and two more bolts and tossed it on the bed. I didn't bother waking up Brother A.D, so I put his backpack on my left shoulder, picked up the duffel, and headed outside.

It was still night out, but the police floodlights lit up the area like it was Friday night football. Pads put A.D in the bed of Cid's truck with fluffy padding from our packs.

The street was lively as a summer festival. The lady Captain, her henchmen, Tracher, and Spear and Arrow, hung close to the docks watching the clean-up. An investigation was happening around the split wood of the great oak. I could make out some of its rune blade-like designs the tree had carved into itself with the lamppost. They no longer glowed, but the carvings showed definite signs of unique intelligence and magic.

Pads hung around outside with Shaki. Shaki stood proud with wary eyes. She came on the right adventure, and she bloody well knew it. There wasn't anything getting at us without her being there to do something about it. Shaki belongs. She can run along with our wolf pack. She made the cut.

"I'll ride in the back with A.D," I started taking off Pad's black windbreaker and threw it into his arms. I unzipped my pack, pulled out my blue and white poncho, and hopped in the back. A.D moved around a little bit, but his eyes were still closed.

The little Toyota started up and music popped on. Through the back window, I read the green digital writing on the radio, *Soulfly, Umbabaraumba.* Cid put it into gear and Pads turned the volume knob up. Cid looked across at Pads and Shaki, and they smiled back at her.

The truck rolled by the three the salty dogs close to the dock. Pads and I watched them as we drove away, and they watched us. I had a feeling we would be seeing the Captain and her ship soon enough.

Soil Churned

Two hours later, we were driving through the woods in the middle of the night. This was usually a comfortable venture for me; however, after the recent shindig, it felt like we had no business in the middle of hundreds of potentially mean, green wooden giants.

A.D and I rested on our packs lying against the cabin wall. Our eyes traveled with the speed of the truck, making the overhang of the forest green, blur into a mossy sky. The cold breeze blanketed over the truck bed, keeping us out of the icy wind.

My eyes wandered forward and saw over the canopy's apex a chimney and white smoke running smoothly into the pale night sky.

"Home at last," A.D said while letting out a deep breath of relief.

I wanted to say, 'hey nay, Cali way,' but the funny thing was, this place did have a homey feel to it.

I could see them as we broke through the complaisant woods. Sitting on the roof were Favin and Mr. Panda Tie, their cigars competing with the chimney.

Cid slid the pick-up truck in front of the house, creating a dusty entrance and bouncing pebbles up that clattered against the exhaust.

"Don't burn the pad down, Uncle. I'm not sure the forest isn't too kind about fires," Pads yelled out his window.

"Pads are what you'll need as soon as I get down from here, Mr. Kalmc," Favin said while bouncing up and preparing down. In his younger years he would have jumped, like the morning leaps in the Netherlands' forest. However, Favin definitely grew some years on him. He reached the bottom by the time we all were out of the truck.

His long, tattered, patchworked coat, mostly greens and browns, snapped down and up as he walked. Every patch on that coat was from a rip or tear, and every inch of that coat was patchwork. We gave Favin a good forearm shake and a mammoth hug for all the missed years.

The panda tie guy fell down from the last branch of the tree that led to the roof. He looked the same as he did at our parent's funeral; clean-shaven, puffy, swollen arms, bright eyes, and a great big smile. He wore a long-sleeved, woolen shirt and worn Levi jeans. Sticks of celery were in his back pocket, along with a piece dangling from the side of his mouth.

"E Lo Lads, who be dis misses?"

"Shaki, and you are?" Shaki asked, as sweet as pie cooling down on a windowsill. She looked at the panda guy and Favin simultaneously. I can't wait till we find out the panda guy's name. Panda Guy seemed so objective.

Favin butted in before Panda Guy could speak. "Along for the journey, I see," Favin said, inspecting her subjectively.

The smile grew on his face. "Well, certainly a journey it has become, eh? I am Favin, a guardian of sorts for these three. And this is Panda, good company, and a loyal friend to our family." Favin looked at his friend and gripped his shoulder tight.

"Now come inside. I want to look at you in the light."

A.D farted with a completely blank face.

"You dog you, I say!" I said this while we jauntily started toward the house in the middle of the mischievous forest.

It was funny, usually when arriving at a family or friend's house after a long trek, we would arrive in the dim of morning, the night sky ceased in dawn light. Comfortable was a good description for this time before the sunrise. A new day. Here to witness it from the beginning, together.

We sat around the kitchen eating pie and fruits, filling in Cid, Panda, and Favin on what happened last night. They seemed excited about the story, worried, of course, but not amazed. Their faces were hard and pensive, thinking of what was to come.

"We haven't had much sleep either, lads." Favin said while taking a bite of apple pie with a wooden spoon.

"What happened in Reykjavik spooked the ranch considerably."

I looked at Favin, stared in fact. I was just a hint bit confused on how they knew about abominable tree demons before we told them.

"Go on," I said.

My Soul by The Cancel, played on the speakers hooked up to Panda's laptop computer. The instrumental version created even more angst in the room.

Panda stood by the window next to the climbing tree to the roof, looking out into the backyard. "Ye see Laddies, tha tril bee not the oly tril tha may bees coming to leaf…"

"How did you come by your name again, Panda? Express…" A.D snickered into the conversation. His head was freshly buzzed and buffed because of the stitching behind his left ear from the rooted debacle earlier. It seemed we always got bloated with pride after a new scratch from scraps.

Panda walked up, getting really close to A.D's face. Eskimo kisses like. "I be climbin trils tea meech weh I was a lil lad, tha why tey 'all mey Panda." Panda struggled to speak slowly so we all could understand him. He went back to his window, happy as a green pea.

I puzzled out tril meant tree.

"Alright alright, that can come later. I have something to show ye boys. It's about your ma and da." Favin waved us to follow him into the living room.

The room had a red cushioned desert feel to it, with couches sprawled all around, open to one wide window that showed the deep forest behind the yard. The sun was just beginning to rise, and the backyard had a tinge of gray lighting. There was a fat barn outside, and it looked like shiny metal circles and squares rested on its walls.

Favin slammed a massive book down. The Book of Tree, it read.

It was fat and old, and I thought I should start running again; I called everything fat now to gloomily contribute to my own newly found physical attributes.

"This is your family tree boys, the past and present of what your bloodline is capable of." All three of us were huddled around, attentive to Favin and this book of our legacy.

Favin continued, "Your ancestors trailed back to the times of old parchment, when trees were still semi-awakened and capable of doing much more than they are now. Very few people knew of their whimsical existence. The people who had, however, were honor-bound to serve Mother Earth and the prosperity of the world.

"These trees were the middlemen who found and trusted those who had proven worthy and honorable. This wasn't a hippy dance gone mad with pagan enlightenment. This was our Earth promoting families to guard the world while she slept, resting and conserving her energy.

"Our Mother loves life and the living, boys. This is why she and her overseers, and might I add, her rooted paladins, rest in this ambiguity of life and evolution. Their fate is in mending our planet with wholesome souls, nothing more. With this creation of an evolving natural clinic, they would rest blissfully.

"The honor-bound families were given increased human abilities and powers, like tough skin and regenerative features of the body, nothing too ludicrous, just enough to keep the families living through trials of confliction."

Favin turned through pages as he talked. We looked through the pictures and we took turns watching his lips move. I could smell that awesome pie from here. Smelt so good.

Favin talked like a plane in flight. It wasn't going to stop until it landed.

"Millions of years ago, when our Earth was born, she herself gave birth to the Sky Sisters. At different periods in time, she created a daughter. The first was sister Tienilla, raised by Mother Earth to guard Mother Earth; however, it was very difficult and too severe to enlighten a child with no one to speak to. Tienilla being raised correctly was crucial, so Mother Earth awakened the trees to guide the little one into her administered destiny. They showed her humanity with all its flaws and imperfections, as well as their strengths and ambitions.

"Then once Tienilla was a full angel of Mother Earth, Tienilla raised the next daughter, and so on until there were six; Tienilla, Freya, Shay, Kendra, Blitzen, and Ruza."

Favin turned the page to a stormy black sky and what looked like a disorganized lumberyard in the middle of a forest.

Metallica, Orion was turned up by Cid, looking over the forest out past the back porch. The bass rumbled through the large window pane.

"A thousand years ago, there was The War of the Six, a war when Ruza changed into Mareridt, a las who got bored of compassion and desired destruction. These written pages, and this," Favin zigzagged his two index fingers down the dark sketch, "illustration of the war, was drawn out by a Battleworn who defended Mother Earth from Mareridt's assault."

Favin looked into our eyes. "And passed the pages onto our ancestors, which are now in this very book, and now in this very room. Mareridt is the one who began the grievous awakening before, and she may be the cause for what happened in Reykjavik last night."

"What you're saying is that we... us..." A.D rotated his finger, directing it toward everyone. "Are the guardians of Mother Earth...?"

There was a silence for a moment or two. A.D leaned back on the couch and peered outside.

"That's freaking awesome!"

Through the window, smack dab in the middle of the dug-up yard was a tree tossing colorful balls and clubs in a circular motion up in the air. Other branches twirled clubs and passed them under limbs and bushes of leaves that still held on through winter. Another branch threw colorful balls straight up into the air and cycled them back up as they were coming down, looking like a clockwise rainbow waterfall.

"What a magnificent juggler!" A.D applauded, still awed and amazed. I could see behind the entertainment that individual trees were slowly unearthing and coming around to the barn. As they waddled forward, they pulled the steel off the side of the barn and picked up the metal pieces leaning in the dirt. Most of the trees looked extremely different than each other.

"What are they doing?" I growled. Curious if these were more of the killer trees we encountered in Reykjavik.

Favin happily swung his trance over to us. "Don't worry Kraeno. These woods are with us. They're a clan of Awakened that rotated their hibernation period to help guard our Mother, Gaia. They are merely warming up before their daily training."

I got up off the couch, dazzled by what's been happening in Iceland thus far. I walked into the kitchen and passed Shaki at the door jam. She seemed bewildered, in bliss and astounded. I could stick one of Panda's celery sticks up her nose and she wouldn't even notice. I reached the sink and spouted out some water in a cup. I finished it and poured another. There was a scratch on the window. I looked up, and it was the climbing tree used to get up onto the roof. Its eye and knotted nose took up the whole kitchen window.

A branch pushed the window open.

"Good morning Mr. Kalmc," the heavy, echoing voice behind the branch said through the window.

I nodded greetings, filled my glass, and walked back into the living room.

It seemed like the whole forest was bustling. A tall Redwood and Sequoia slowly wove through the rooted trees and made their way toward the yard. The Sequoia stopped a little behind the barn, and the Redwood followed. Then they both sunk their roots into the ground and remained static.

The climbing tree outside the kitchen window slowly wandered into the backyard, red berries falling to the ground with every rumbling step.

"That is Bear, a Rowan tree, native to the island of Iceland."

I remembered seeing a Rowan tree in the Icelandic books we were reading on the train cross country. Favin filled us in that a Rowan tree usually stood alone, yet this one was their forest's leader and used earth bond poltergeist shrouds that covered miles and miles as a spiritual haven.

"He is the clan chief and warden of the forest," Favin finished explaining while one of the thickest Oak trees I have ever seen passed over a large golden shield encrusted with a bear crest welded onto its steel. Rowan Bear grabbed the shield with one of his larger limbs and entangled the bear-crested shield so it could flex in and out of its timber, staying controlled and stabilized through the outer branches on his left flank. Bear's other branches spread, and his trunk's facial features closed and vanished.

A wind gusted and circulated around the Rowan tree, blowing off some more berries. Smaller than the rest, this tree stood summoning winds, possibly mixed with a poltergeist essence, like a sorcerer. I say poltergeist because it felt like the wind was alive, dancing with the clouds and swirling around, massaging the air around Bear.

The winds blew and the surrounding Oaks, Maples, Gums, and scattered about Birchwoods all slapped the soil and sunk their roots into the earth, suddenly losing all face-like features as the Rowan tree had.

"What are they doing now?" Shaki asked.

Cid was coming back inside, and she responded to Shaki's question. "Bear is communicating with his clan through roots and wind. Possibly discussing what happened in Reykjavik, and why you…" Cid paused, looking outside. She sighed and then continued, "Trees are not just beasts that lavish and claw, like the one you saw at Reykjavik. Some can be foreseers of the future or even sorcerers of the elements around us," Cid said in her slight Scottish accent.

I looked out in the yard with amazement and started diagnosing each tree. The juggling tree had inked up quills scattered about, blending in some places with his leaves, and popping out in other areas as if the quill had origins from a parrot, parakeet, or rosella. Ink stains were splattered on sections of his wide, thick branches, as well as on the juggling balls and clubs too. There were very intricate designs with these little ink spots in fact, exactly like tattoos. An artist, a writer…

Hints of broken arrows were hidden deeper in the core of his branches; a snapped shaft here, half a shaft and arrowhead there, feathers, quills, and artifacts. Everything seemed wrapped up and locked down with twigs and smaller limbs. Everything seemed old except for the tree's vitality.

The juggling tree's stump was short and stocky, with his branches forked, widely extending outward so they hung only eight feet from the ground. He was a joyous looking oak, and a real wooden renaissance pleasure.

The most energetic trees by far were the thin and delicate, comparatively, little Birchwoods. Their restlessness showed when they were rooted and swayed side to side like they had ants in their sap, always twitching and swaying. Their group couldn't disguise themselves as regular patient sprouts for the life of them. Even without the wrinkles in their pale bark to make out their faces. They had this vibe, like they were ready to jump out of the dirt and dash around, which reminded me of Frankie in fourth grade. He had A.D.D.

Bare branches covered the Birchwood trunks, and long blades hung from every other limb. Each blade was vastly different from the other, but most were shaped as Arabian daggers, curving to one angle like a crescent moon.

I looked behind the Birchwoods and there was a heavy Gum tree sitting up straight, towering over the house with many trunks jutting out and racing toward the sky. The other heavy branches protruded out in all angles. One wrinkled root was out of the dirt, tapping and shuffling the soil around. An identical Gum with red bark leaned against the backwoods.

The Willow standing next to the Juggler Oak looked like a great assassin. Its large crown hung low to the ground and shrouded its wood. From its shaggy appearance and many leaves, I got the feeling that the Willow was very old, meek, and content; a perfect tree for veiling an army of ninjas.

The last two trees were rooted close to the Rowan Bear. Nearest to the house was a bare-branched Maple tree with a bonsai contour, which exhibited an open space in the middle of the zigzag trunk. To the left of Rowan Bear was the thick Oak who had passed the golden bear shield over. His thick roots bubbled out of the ground. Its width was as wide as a truck, and its multiple trunks rose half as tall as a Sequoia. I looked up its height, and the higher I looked, the more my balls tingled and shriveled up into my stomach. If we went up against this guy at the docks, the whole village would have been destroyed. A true natural born bruiser.

Pads walked out during their earthly sermon and stood between the Bonsai Maple and Rowan Bear. Pads was analyzing the woods like me, only there was never the slightest fear in his eyes when around the wood, as if our parents were reassembled into the heart of Gaia. They now rested in the earth, water, and air, making trees an ancestral reminder of their true souls.

Without hesitation, Pads wandered close to the awakened trees. No one told him not to, because we were not a family that held each other back. So, we followed him, and our group headed outside onto the porch.

"The human families that guard Mother Earth are the Totem Clause Sentinels. We keep a grove of trees awakened and trained for precautionary defense," Favin whispered between A.D and me.

The wind died down, and the dreamy buzz went away. I heard the birds start chirping again, the sound of the creaks and moans of branch joints, smelled the fresh-turned soil, and felt the sting of cold air coating the tip of my nose. Even if Earth was being attacked by a dark angel, it was all sort of worth it to see this degree of natural animation.

Rowan Bear lifted his roots and stepped a bit closer to Pads, the rest gathered in as well, creating a semi-circle. The taller trees didn't really move too much, but the Birchwoods clanked and clattered forth, twisting, and battling with each other along the way, creating six tornadoes of swords, knives, and hatchets.

We lost sight of the six Birchwoods when they twisted into the shaggy Willow, with its dome crown of low-hung limbs. Suddenly the clanks of steel stopped. The next second dirt flew up with little bits raining down onto the porch. The Birchwoods swayed in front, anxious, restless, and spasmodic. Each twitch led a swing of a branch carrying glinting blades, which were easily blocked by the next spasmodic Birchwood.

Pads circled around, saying 'Hi' to each tree, and eventually Rowan Bear took voice.

"Our honorable companions, we tip our crowns to you as we brush our leaves against Mother's belly. May our roots be your shield against the unknowing."

The hollow eyes of the Rowan tree didn't have good nor evil qualities. We were amongst Battleworn and heavyhearted woods. Favin once told us, the wood was only able to recognize strength and intelligence. The wood had compassion for the beings of Gaia, but only with certain qualities. Their thoughts and intuitions were influenced by peace and prosperity for their Mother. Whatever the case, they will do what they must.

A chill ran down my spine.

A.D and I looked out into the crowd of semi-skeletal woods. Winter branches made these trees look even more beastly. We stood there stone-faced and watched their hollows.

After a moment the trees bowed their crowns and then spread out like they once were.

The day was still very gloomy, and the weather must have been regular for the ranch, which was only a couple of miles from the coast.

I peered out, and the bladed frenzies scurried around the yard, clinging and clanking, blocking and retaliating with their fast, branchy strikes. The juggling tree returned to juggling, only with a newfound cosmic concentration. The gum twins pulled gear and metal out of the barn, layering themselves with artifacts and materials which were hammered to fit their trunks. The Bonsai Maple had her back to the crowd and focused herself within the clouds.

Pads patted the huge Oak standing beside the Rowan tree. Its bark had deep grooves like mountain ridge after mountain ridge and valley after valley, rounding its worldly trunk. Pads wasn't young anymore; however, his desire to tree climb always made him seem like a child. He continued to pat the massive Oak, and the Oak didn't seem to care.

****

The feeling of warmth flushed over my face as sunshine broke through a dot in the clouds. The Redwood and Sequoia still rested in the same location. Their high branches turned up toward the sky, like arms raised in a prayer or victory.

The clouds started wisping apart over our abode, reaching a border circulating in a measured circumference. How these clouds reached this defined perimeter was even more astonishing than trees walking or talking; instead of clouds floating casually through the sky they were being pulled up higher and higher into the atmosphere, like a vacuum in space sucking up the fluffy gaggle of water molecules. The clouds rose in a rounded ring conglomerate, reaching the brink of our globe.

A red ball bounced off the porch, hitting Panda square in the nuts. A low monotone tree voice called for "music".

Panda benevolently threw the juggling tree's ball back, walked across the porch, and pouted while pressing the power switch for the speakers. *Working Woman Blues by Valerie June* bumped on.

I looked back toward the sky.

The sky looked like a sun arena, an open space with a golden eye peering down amongst the land. The clouds lay as a barrier, a fog bank, to outside eyes.

"Te la is no all the tril know, it bees te ski as well." Panda noted for us, while turning up the porch stereo. Cid got close to Shaki's ear and whispered what he said, in clearer context.

"Brilliant," Favin announced. Truly, it was pretty cool to watch. The massive Oak and Rowan Bear got into the mix of summoning elements and weather works. Pads perched on one of the massive Oak's extended arms, watching as we were; however, much, much higher up.

As the crowd settled, one little cloud came out into the sky arena. It darkened, and moments later, I could feel the massive Oak gripping the earth. Suddenly, a fat bolt of lightning ran down from that little dark cloud and blasted a steel shield lying on the roof of the barn. The shield slid off and landed at the Redwood's roots.

Another cloud majestically formed and expanded quickly, growing teeth and one large puffy arm. The sky clapped with thunder as the arm reached out and swallowed the little dark cloud. I looked at Rowan Bear as he rested. He was perhaps giggling, as a tree does, with hollow eyes squinted toward the sky and hollow engravings glowing green.

Harsh winds passed, lightning crackled for minutes at a time, clouds formed and battled, and the exterior cloud barrier still flowed toward the higher atmosphere, defining the stadium of the sky arena. Colossus elementals were formed as hasty Helios puppets were used as a tool to tune the tree's abilities and perfect the summoning of conscious natural disasters into our world.

Totem Clause Sentinels

"So burning wood at an evening campfire doesn't set them in a fiery rage?" Shaki asked Panda and his girlfriend, Cid.

Wearing black sweats and a tight dark green halter top, Cid replied, "Not all trees have been awakened, therefore never being born into consciousness. Many trees in Iceland are new or were recently planted because of the afforestation policy."

I looked over during Cid's lecture and saw her tits trying to poke through her top. I wanted to nudge lil Pads, but I decided not to. This tree business was getting pretty serious; it was best to be serious with it. It was best to get a drink.

Cid kept going, "When Iceland was raided by Vikings, they ruined the land with their primitive agriculture and excessive boat making. Then, as the Imperial Church finally settled in, they made Iceland their main location for lumber. This exploitation of the trees, along with the natural harsh conditions of the North, extremely penalized forest growth. However, Iceland has been trying to restore the forest environment for around a century."

I walked to the kitchen serenely so I didn't pull attention from Cid.

"This was when Panda started collecting tree elders and importing them here. See, trees were being shipped to Iceland from all directions, and massive amounts of trees were being grown here, and still are. So there were never really any second glances on a two-hundred-foot Sequoia traveling across waters from Europe. He found that juggling oak, Lingo, when he found me. Lingo was my only family at the time. He caught me as I fell from his tallest branch when I was nine. I guess Panda got a package deal, eh Pans?" Cid looked at Panda and squeezed his hand, obviously unconditionally in love with him. He peered into the fire with a tight, arrogant grin.

Cid continued, "Rowan Bear and the bladed Birchwoods were already here. It was Rowan who wanted a base for preeminent tree warriors to conduct their practices." Cid paused to sip on her tea.

"So, most of these trees in Iceland have never been awakened or have no insight on their natural duties. The animated tree warriors you saw before you today were ancient woods, either summoned by Mother herself or by the Sky Sisters during the War of Six.

Panda summoned consciousness in the massive oak, Afwat, the oak constantly by Rowan Bear's side, like a mob boss's right-hand man. He thought a massive tree like that had potential. A forest within a tree. A Macaton and Landtos hybrid. A retiring find for Panda indeed."

Shaki butted in quickly as to not interrupt completely. "Macaton and Landtos?"

"Macatons are the trees that study the elements. Landtos are the trees that study the land and their roots. For example, Redwoods study the sky because they are already very tall. And Birchwood trees study their roots because they're kooks," Cid laughed.

Everyone was smiling around the hearth, comfortable and toasty. Pads relaxed on the couch with his arms crossed and legs sprawled out on fluffy cushions while he listened to Cid and Shaki chat. A.D was doing sit-ups and talking with Favin, and I stood outside, far from the window, and drank wine found on the floor next to Favin's bookcase. It was a great delight to see my family safe through a window, as if the window was a shroud from evil, and I, the guardian, making sure evil never got a chance to peek in.

Favin got up, went to the fridge, and pulled out a jug of milk. He took a long chug from the carton and milk sloshed over his gray stubble. He then snuggled the jug under his armpit and packed his dark wooden pipe in the refrigerator light.

The pipe had engraved metal plates similar to those of our Bamboo Korea pipe. After his pipe was packed with fresh greens, he then walked outside. I became aware of myself stroking my stache and rubbing my sideburns.

It was butt cold outside. My shoulders wanted to turn in on my chest, so I pushed them back, pinching my shoulder blades together.

"What you up to bud?"

My only reply was a swig of wine to keep my teeth from clattering in front of him.

"Follow me, Kraeno."

I followed Favin to the side of the house. He stopped at the trunk of Rowan Bear. Favin looked back at me and lit his pipe, talking through his teeth and blowing smoke through his nostrils.

"To give aye rebirth," nodding toward Rowan Bear, but still focused his attention on his pipe.

"Taking a tree from comatose life to conscious demeanor is an intricate summoning."

Favin pulled in heavily and tipped the smoky pipe closer to Rowan, blowing the smoke all over the Rowan Bear's trunk. Green lit carvings flashed through the smoke. The sharp designs zigzagged and wove around in spirals and shapes, abstract to the regular eye. Beautiful. Reminded me of the art our mother used to do, and then again, it also reminded me of the great dead oak down by the docks.

"Every engraving gives unique and special powers, powers that are conjured directly from the summoner and the will of the land. Each symbol signifies abilities. Each mark engraved is life itself on the tree."

It seemed like the inner being of the tree was all green light. Green rays illuminated outward where the smoke was the densest. The engraved crevices shooting out the light slowly and sucking in the smoke.

Favin signaled me to come back inside. There were so many questions, questions about Ma and Pa, questions about Earth, questions about the freaking afterlife.

I stood there, freezing, as Favin went inside. I wasn't just cold from the brisk Icelandic air, but mainly from not knowing what was to come. I watched the green light fade back into the Rowan Tree's bark.

"My sister gave me the power of wind and thunder, Sir Kalmc. I would very much like to see her beauty again." The Rowan tree bubbled in nostalgia.

****

Bracelets clinked and rang as her arm went back and forth, easily digging through the bark with a light purple amethyst. Her eyes light green. Her light brown hair swirly and roughened past her shoulders. A dread knotted with crystals, stars, and twine hung between her feathered shoulder blades. She wore a dark earthy jacket, a long brown skirt, and high leather boots. Her smile brightened up the night sky, and the moon glistened on the hill's wet grass and the crystals in her hair.

She knelt in levitation amongst the air, carving happily into the stand-alone Rowan tree.

The wielded amethyst curved around in a spiral motion, finishing with a sharp thrust up and a sharp rounding curve down. She floated back a couple of feet, waved her fingers in a fashion that spun her golden bracelets in revolutions, and ignited the bottom bark of the tree with fire.

Smoke rose up and into the cryptic engravings all throughout the body of wood. A lime green light flashed forth, silhouetting the giggling girl with angel wings and her freshly awakened tree.

****

Back inside, I took back my couch groove and started tinkering with the gears of an old clock on the table. Favin plopped down in his chair, still smoking his pipe and drinking his milk.

"Your father was sort of the mobster for nature's wellbeing."

No googly eyes there. We all knew our Pops was involved in dark events occasionally. He had an art business when we were growing up. An artist who loved the color red. He could have told us he was a surgeon, and we would have been none the wiser. Right above his knees were two tattoos, one said Engi and the other said Vandr. This meant 'No Evil' in Norse.

Favin paused, reverted on what he was going to say, and went down another path. "Kraeno, what do you see in your brothers?"

I turned from watching inattentive Pads sit up and fart in A.D's direction, and looked into Favin's piercing eyes. "I see a couple of kids messing around-"

"That is exactly how your father and I were." Favin inched

forward. "But there comes a time in your life where duty becomes destiny and living is no more than a service. We are the Totem Clause Sentinels."

I snickered, a nervous trait when I become uncomfortable with chills.

"We! We are the last true guardians of Earth." Favin bounced back and sat deep into his chair, taking a long drag from his pipe.

"He searched for ancient trees like the rest of us, but his main agenda was keeping hardcore religious societies away from the marked trees of Mother Earth. The societies are still out there and still very curious about these wooden descendants. However, it is not, and will never be, their right to know. Death before discovery was your father's motto.

"Your mother was a whole other story. She traveled around the world looking for ancient relics and artifacts. When she met your father, they worked on distributing scrolls of summoner engravings for other Totem Clause Sentinel families, blueprints on what gives these trees life and power... Your parents were very important to the Sentinels."

Favin looked down at his pipe and sighed. He burped right after, and a puff of smoke came out. Everyone chuckled except for Pads. It was best to leave the fella be whenever Ma and Pa came up.

"After finding an emerald golden ring held down by thorny roots, your mother became very close to one of the Sky Sisters as well." He cheekishly remarked with a returning smile, possibly trying to lift Pads spirits.

"How did she find a golden ring under a tree?" A.D asked.

"She was on a quest to find Piper, an old tree that collected scribed pipes and musical war instruments. During the War of Six, Piper was a Landtos General in Northern Africa, when the five Sky Sisters battled against their dark other, Mareridt. Mareridt raised the ancient Macatons of the Mahogany trees and then tried to turn the sky into eternal darkness. After the war was done and Mareridt was killed, the Macatons grieved in their decision to join Mareridt and fight against their kin. There are as many fallen trees in that forest now as there are standing. We presume that during the war, Shay the

Sky Sister, was stuck in a jam and lost one of her rings.

"Coincidentally, while your mother was traveling through the forest, she was hassled by a hummingbird frantically trying to show her the path to a golden ring attached to a Mahogany root. Then, still in search of Piper, she followed the tweeting of this bizarre loitering bird, who eventually received her name, The Muse of the Forest.

"After The Muse of the Forest led your mother to the ring, she continued leading her directly to Piper on top of the highest hill. The bird pecked the golden ring out of your mother's hand and flew it to where Piper lumbered, heavy with ancient artifacts and things. There the ring lay, properly displayed in the dirt before the Landtos General.

"I heard your mother sang to Piper for an entire night before Piper acknowledged her presence.

"Eventually warming up to your mother's harmonic voice, Piper deemed the ring's discovery, and being the gregarious tree that Piper was, she asked for one favor from your mother. A celebration.

"So, an enormous festival was held in the forest a week later, celebrating the successful quest of an epic ring discovery and reestablishing a bond created between humans and angels. Many trinkets, spells, scrolls, manuscripts, weapons, shields, pipes, and other archaic collections Piper had were given away and traded to the Totem Clause Sentinels.

"In order for a Sentinel to trade with Piper, they had to tell a story or sing a song about how their ancestors came into the divine grasp of Mother Earth. While Piper was absorbing all the excitement, she demanded more and more musical entertainment. It was really the first occasion where the forest was able to unwind after the War of the Six.

"Men carried small kegs on their backs while women carried flowers to cover the forest floor, contrasting the leaves that hung drunkenly from the tree's branches. The innovative kegs swashed along, preparing to drench Piper and the fallen woods. The partiers spilled the ale all over the ground, soaking the colorful flowers into the earth.

"Having the awakened trees together again, as well as a fulfilled Sky Sister, the Mahoganies were asked to come forth and receive praise as The Forgiven. Another addition to a great celebration.

"During the ceremony, Shay and your mother became good friends. Little school girls huddled up chatting by their lockers, only these little school girls were the guardians of our planet huddled up chatting next to a keg.

"This being said, it would be helpful to have you three there when we venture out to speak with her during the waning moon."

Favin took a deep breath from his story and wiggled around in his chair before continuing.

"What happened in Reykjavik has led us to seek higher help and advice. The closest Sky Sister is your mother's friend Shay, who resides on the island Grimsey." Favin put up his index finger and hurried to the bathroom.

Panda picked up where Favin left off. "Weez' av sum jumbo boat tha weez' can fee three Macatons in ahh sum small Landtos."

Panda looked around, obviously conscious that he didn't make sense to us Californians.

"You four key stay ahhs long ahhs yous like. Le aboot ye's heritage ah-tea like. Jest make sure ye's foosh the tinker."

I huffed a laugh in the side of my fist, and Panda felt that was a good time to meander forward for a casual wrestle.

The gang wrestled around after that, and it seemed like a Christmas that we've missed out on over so many years.

****

I heard Panda's voice in the other room as I woke. His dialect was twice as fast as our spoken word. The slit of light from the sunrise put a warm, what I thought would look like, solar bandana on my face, worn as a superhero would wear a mask with two holes cut out for their eyes. The smell of syrup overwhelmed the room as if someone was dripping it down my nostrils. I sat up rubbing my sideburns and saw Panda chatting with Shaki in the kitchen and Pads eating pancakes on the couch with three red cushions. He was sitting so close I almost bumped into his plate as I sat up.

I lay back down, ready to take my second rest. I quickly remembered why I was tired in the first place, and again arose from between the couch and coffee table. I went over to Shaki and Panda in the kitchen.

"Morning," I grumbled while rotissering my shoulders to loosen up the stiff areas.

"Congratulations, it seems you got some rest," Shaki said in a mocking but also amazed tone.

"How do you sleep with so much excitement? We were up all night!" Shaki emphasized the 'we' by looking out into the living room where Pads and A.D were eating.

My head tingled, and an aching wave came rushing over my skull.

Those couple swigs of wine last night did me in kiddo, I thought.

"We haven't slept in a house for a long time. Train to Ferry to some demonic tree screaming at us. I believe I deserved some well-needed rest."

I grabbed a banana from on top of the refrigerator.

"What's on the agenda for today?" I felt my brows turn down and jaw stiffen in seriousness.

Shaki smiled, "We are headed to Grimsey."

Panda butted in, "Weez'," toggling his finger toward him and I. "er gunni go."

Shaki's hips wagged to one side when she slapped her hands on them. Blue ice flared in her eyes and just as quickly cooled to a melting glacier.

She giggled indifferently, "I guess the girls have a lot of work to do here, and you boys need some alone time." Her debilitating smile was forced as well as lonesome.

I pushed past her in order to get to the trash can on the other side of the kitchen. When I pressed the foot pedal, the lid opened up, and there lay two empty bottles of wine. The banana peel plopped on the glass, spread over one label and the other's corked end. I turned around and put my hand on Shaki's shoulder, squeezing just enough to let her know my words meant something.

"Listen here Shaki. After seeing a tree blast hot sap onto a man's face and throw em' aside like an apple core, it seems to me that things are most definitely changing on our here planet. If we are going to continue to see your pretty little smile, you're going to have to stay with the mightiest of the clan most of the time, not the guts of the clan. The guts will go into the belly of the beast," I prided, while looking at Panda, prepping the camaraderie bond we must have for whatever was to come next.

"Which one seems more your style?"

Shaki murmured, "The guts guys. I'll. be. fine."

Again, I walked through her and Panda to get to the living room.

"No. way."

Pads looked up at me, setting his pancake plate down, and Favin walked in from the back porch.

"Need you lads to pack food and water for a good three days. Meet outside when you're done." Favin went straight to his room, came right out with two empty duffel bags, and set them down on a couple of red cushions in front of us.

"Also, bring that crossbow; I'd like to try it out."

The Grim Grimsey

The air was chilly as I trailed Pads outside, a duffel bag slung over each of his shoulders. I heard music coming from the side yard and saw water jugs floating up to Lingo. As I walked further out, I could see A.D filling the jugs with a hose and one of Lingo's roots popping up the jugs to a secure area amidst his branches. There was a rhythm to their preparations, synced to a red stickered-up boombox playing on the fat middle branch next to Lingo's trunk. The song playing was, *Last Dance With Leon by Doctor Flake.*

Behind the barn there was a loud creaking noise, and while this Jurassic minute passed by with these majestic treefolk in a marvelous hustle and bustle, I realized that it was so unimaginable that my dreams couldn't even have illustrated the contour. Seeing so much movement from these regularly known vital statues was unbelievable.

Afwat came lumbering from behind the barn, dragging along a massive trailer with a large squid fishing boat.

****

I ducked down beneath the fog to retie my Converse. I wanted them super tight and ready for anything. The fog hovered right above my eyebrow with the leveled misty line split from clear air. The difference in transparency was incredible. It existed only till the bow of our fishing boat, then it continued on to be an eternal haze above the sea.

As I sat on my heels to the right of the Captain's conning tower, I looked closer at the cluttered deck: bundles of rope, tangled nets, huge roots sprawled out all over the long bow, and a fire extinguisher resting on its side at the base of the starboard railing. What a beautiful, extraordinary mess.

Boots and the bottom half of a multi-colored long coat turned the tower corner, halted, then crouched down.

Favin yelled, "I need the crossbow."

I gave him a thumbs up and turned to scout out the foggy path to the haul hatch. Haul hatch in sight, I stood up and headed for the entrance below. In my arrogant haste, I tripped and was suddenly thrown to the ground. A Birchwood's face rapidly popped out of the fog and sneered inches from my own. Its hollow words were comforting and frightening at the same time.

"Watch your step. Never know when you could fall on a knife." The Birchwood clinked its daggers together and gave out a hollow laugh that followed him as he disappeared back into the fog.

Seems the Birchwoods find death hilarious. There goes my deep philosophy of woods and serenity.

I stood up again, walked slowly to the hatch, opened it up, and called for the crossbow. Pads replied from below with an 'Aye Aye,' and I heard the clicking of the case. I looked in and saw Pads take out my fifth of rum and toss it to the floor, then pull out the crossbow and head towards me.

"Don't forget the bolts Ol'Paddy McHolloway."

He seemed hesitant, but eventually went back and grabbed them. Pads handed the cross and bolts up to me, and once again I stood up into the fog. This time I felt mean, powerful, and boisterous. Must have been the cross's doing.

I made it to Favin without a problem and held out the crossbow. He waved it away and asked for a bolt first, motioning for me to follow him as he moved through the fog while wrapping the bolt with a dampened cloth. The smell of gasoline reminded me of the night in Reykjavik.

Finally reaching the very front of our squid boat Favin took the crossbow from me and cocked the bolt.

"Light it," he growled.

Favin put the crossbow bolt head up close to my face. I lit the end of it with Pad's shamrock lighter. Favin fired, and I watched the flame travel through the dense mist. It flew for a solid ten seconds, then slowly drooped, vanishing with a splash and sizzle.

I felt Favin looking in my direction. I still couldn't see his face through the fog, only my right hand squeezing the railing.

"Give me another," Favin eloquently demanded, while shoving the crossbow into my chest. His hand still existed, separated from everything else, just floating there waiting. I cocked the bolt in the sling and put the crossbow into Favin's hand. I then waited and readied my lighter.

"Light it."

The flame flew a little higher arching way into the distance, and then suddenly, at the beginning of its descension, it came to a halt.

Thunk! We found Grimsey only a hundred yards out.

"Prepare for Anchor!" Favin yelled out behind us.

He pulled me in close and spoke in a loud whisper. "We won't know what to expect on Grimsey lad. Being as it is now," his chin nodded toward where the fire bolt landed. As I looked up at the flame, it swiftly let out. Favin's eyebrow raised, and he gave me a curious look.

"Shit." I wimpered, with a long and drawn out shh.

Favin handed me back the crossbow and went through the fog back towards the stern, I'm guessing to help drop anchor. I stood there looking out into the mist. What in the hell is out there?

****

My foot squished into the pitch black surface as Pads jumped out of the rowboat and ran over to stand close to the shore where our wooden allies were now ascending out of the water. This island didn't seem like an island in real life. It was shrouded by a void and darkened by some kind of haunting. The feel of it pulsated along my spine.

A.D hopped out from the back of the boat, slapping the shallow water, and pushed the boat out onto the muddy sand. We pulled the rowboat closer to the brush and watched Afwat, Lingo, and Rowan Bear come out of the water, their bark engravings spilled out radiant light as ocean water rained down from their branches, creating a stormy sound within their perimeter.

Favin pulled out a couple of torches from the rowboat and passed them around to Panda and A.D, keeping one for himself. We all met at the road's entrance to the inner Grimsey Island. Sentinels and Awakened scattered about.

Pads ran up Afwat and grabbed his billiard, which had no bullets, but crossed Afwat's trunk perfectly, snuggly interwoven between his branches. Pads used it as a ladder to climb up to the first heavy branch, hanging thirty feet from the ground. Rowan took the lead with Favin, Panda, and A.D, while I took the rear with bare-branched Lingo the Juggling Oak.

The forest we approached was horribly dark, and the waning moonlight only lit up the furthest hill like a rising halo. Our torches lit up the front row of the furious-looking Oaks surrounding us. The trees were covered with a wicked, light-green moss.

We walked on edge for about an hour until we reached a wall of wood in the middle of our path. Afwat stomped forward and wrapped his thickest root around the center of the wall. It creaked and cracked, as he ripped out one of the rooted moss oaks and hucked it toward the moonlit hill further up the path.

Suddenly, the forest tilted in, and a shadow rushed past us, blasting out our torch flames. Time felt lucid as waves of evil energy crippled my bravery. A.D and I stood, inoperative at a very inopportune time. The half-engraved symbols of the demonic oaks lit up with orange-red light as they approached slowly, like clowns would a toddler.

Pantoon

Three blind monks stood fifty yards out from a massive black gate of bones, metal, and gooey dark shadows. A cart was placed in front of them, covered by a horse blanket. Eighty guards stood posted at the gate.

The Gate General stood by the gate's opening gears, dressed in full black metal armor, resting his long sword on his plated shoulder. He told his Corporal to check the monks and see if they were legitimately 'the monks'.

"Check THOSE God Damn Blind mother-Fuckers CorporAL!"

The Corporal discreetly walked over to the front of the cart and whacked one of the wheels with the flat side of his short sword. He sheathed the blade and extended his spear out in front of him with his other hand, lifting the gray bandana that covered one of the blind monk's eyes.

Underneath, his eye sockets were massively scarred and tattooed, like a sunburst of rough skin ridges and ink slashed in every direction. The tattoos were of little crumpled up dwarf trees. Hard even to call them trees, really. They looked more like black blobs with spikes sticking out of the top and bottom.

The black armored guards resembled all the different factions of the Togmehoian families in the Galaxy of the Dead. The gate alone had eighty soldiers, but the outer region of the gate had thousands of barracks filled at all times. A military melting pot for every Togmehoian who wanted a piece of the Brekinvale Luster harvest.

It was said that the three blind monks were the only ones who could invoke more Brekinvale Luster. Ancient as they were, they knew this hellacious planet better than anyone else. They were known as the only native herbalists left in the Dyathsake Galaxy.

Pantoon

Pantoon, being the first world of the dead and closest to the dark galactic bulge, is the only world that can grow Brekinvale Luster, a black tree with vibrant red fall leaves, that grows plump, pale, purple balls of fruit.

Circular in form, the fruit does two things: First, it can nourish and sustain a body for weeks at a time by just eating one fruit, without having to eat or drink anything else to dissolve your hunger.

Second, it will give the mind an out-of-body experience, making Hell seem like the best place in the universe. This quality, mixed with other materials and solutions, also makes a prime substance for soul possession.

So, the monks stood there waiting to pass through the gate. Their scroll books at their sides, bordered and bound by Brekinvale root. Their dark brown, rugged robes hid their soft leather shoes. Deep hoods hung back behind two of them, and the third had his hood covering his bandana eyes with the bandana tails tied and resting on the top of his shoulders. The melted-faced Corporal, who usually did the regular monk inspections before they passed through the gates to harvest, did a slow, confident waddle over to the last hooded monk.

"Take off that hood monk…" the Corporal demanded.

The monk stood there with his nose in the shadow of his hood.

"Take the hood off monk!" The Corporal stepped in a little closer. The hood shook from side to side, leisurely.

The Corporal lifted his right hand to throw back the monk's hood, and just as quickly, his hand was met with a root-bound book. The monk spun to the other side of the Corporal and threw a book attack aimed for the Corporal's helmet. The Corporal blocked it with his spear hand. Yet, the monk was still spinning back around the other way, swinging the heavy root-bound book again, finally landing the hit and hurling the Corporal's helmet six feet into the air and knocking him to the ground.

The Gate General put up four fingers to the guards flanking him and flagged them toward the three monks.

The monk closest to the horse-blanketed cart grabbed its handles and raised the cart as if to go. The Gate General walked forward, planting himself in front, causing the cart to clash into his armored thigh when the monk took his first step forward. The General's face was distorted in displeasure. He stood static and watched beyond the covered cart.

The hooded monk tilted his head down. His face was directed a couple of feet from the Corporal's helmet. The Corporal's arm reached over his stomach to grab the hilt of his short sword, furious at the hooded monk standing over him.

"Corporal. Settle." The General ordered indifferently. A moment went by, and he lifted the horse blanket from the cart, uncovering half of the ostrich sized seeds fashionably placed inside. He looked at the hooded monk. His face hardened in the shadow of his I-shaped helm.

The hooded monk walked to the cart, put his root-bound spell book down, and turned back toward the four guards.

After an intense standoff, his head tilted to the sky above massive watch towers and giant barracks with twenty-foot tall doorways. His hood slipped back a bit, revealing his bandana and the border of his scarred starburst eyes. Another slash scar ran diagonally across his forehead and left eye socket.

Something was flying toward them. Another moment went by, and the Gate General raised his head to check the sky.

Zip!!!

A black blur raced across the cloudy, reddish sky framed by three of Pantoon's thirteen moons and a Moon Zealot slumbering in space beyond Pantoon's ozone. The purple clouds of Pantoon drooped low and trailed the blur hanging right over the Barrack city. Hell whores stood on top of one barracks and pointed at the action.

Guards unsheathed their swords and bowmen lifted their hunky unnecessarily accessorized bows and crossbows toward the sky. About two dozen bolts and arrows shot up toward the blur.

Mareridt back-flipped right above the popular black gate with a dense light purple cloud suspended above her. Blue pulses of power pulsated through the purple cloud overhead while Mareridt darkened, veiling her face with evil. Her black and red kimono looked as silky as her black and red braided hair. Floating in the air, she threw her fists at the dirt and the armored guards below.

Blocks of ice rained down from the purple cloud into the courtyard and on the ridge above the gate wall at each fist pump thrown. Above the gate's wall, on the ridge, was an invisible dome where surrounding wizards stood holding an impassable electric shroud.

Demons and humanoids both were smashed from the blocks of ice. Some moaned and screamed with their black armor crumpling in on them.

The wizards still stood on the surrounding wall, holding the invisible shroud protecting the town-sized enclosure of the Brekinvale Luster forest, looking over their shoulders, astonished by the icy destruction that lay in front of the gate. Their personal guards faced the chaos, not moving an inch.

Mareridt power kicked down from the sky onto the Gate General's chest, blocking his blade thrust with her black dagger poking out from her long kimono sleeve. The General descended onto the cart of oversized seeds, splintering wood across the dirt. The other four guardsmen charged but instantly became trapped in a massive piece of ice surrounding their greaves.

Patches where ice had fallen, bit the earth, eating it up, spreading where Mareridt's influence was most prominent, and freezing everything in its path.

Mareridt looked over at the three blind monks.

"Hold still." Her voice bubbled with danger and ferocity.

The hooded monk picked up his spell book. The other monk who lifted the cart before, dropped the broken handle to the dirt floor. They stood waiting patiently.

A sound of ice folding into armor and screwing into flesh osculated as the four frozen guardsmen twisted and splattered, forming a stocky golem coalescing from ice and black armor. It stood wide and disfigured. Its head, chest, and arms dripped demon blood. Mareridt nodded, directing the golem toward the incoming beastly looking guards, whose spears were already flung in the air, and short swords whipped out.

Mareridt looked up into the sky and raised her arms at the purple clouds. Her eyes were closed, and her kimono snapped with the hungering wind. As the first spear got closer, Mareridt madly opened her eyes and mechanically looked toward the spear approaching her face; the fray between her golem and city guards distorted behind the toss.

Simultaneously, she unleashed lightning bolts from the clouds into the mass of mobile metal heads, while stepping forward, letting the spear zip through her black hair, slicing some pieces away with the wind.

The golem made of ice and metal crouched in the death of the platoon of beastly guards. Mareridt rotated her hand clockwise to gather the scattered armor and lift the bodies just high enough to build on top of the golem. She then aimed her other hand toward the purple clouds and let her hand fall down again and again in a hacking motion, binding the golem with more ice and pure physical domination. A huge beast of destruction indeed.

A metal band skimmed around the sky on a half-built wooden platform. The singer leaned off the edge.

I DON'T KNOW WHY YOU HAVE WEAKENED ME!
NOTHING MAKES THE DAYS GO BY.
WHY HAVE YOU COME TO TREASON
YOU KNOW NOTHING OF MY HIGH....
Doom Doom Dap, Doom, Doom,
Doom Dap.. Da Doom, Da Doom,
Dap. DAP! Dap Doodley, Dap!
LET ME SING A SONG FOR YOU, LET IT BE SOMETHING NICE.
YOUR END COMES QUICKLY TO BE SURE,
OR IS THAT THE THREE BLIND MICE!

The Lieutenants surrounding the courtyard ordered more guards against Mareridt and her Elemental. Two demon guards rolled in front of the gate. Their heavy build made the roll seem lazy and slow. Their horns stuck out of their skulls and through their helms with competing spikes that covered their full set of black armor. Their arms spread to their sides like defensive linemen. The Gate General laughed while still lying on the dusty ground, wounded from Mareridt's kick.

As the golem walked past him, it stomped on his thick, armored legs, cutting the Gate General in half. He roared and giggled insanity, then stared, watching the golem walk toward the gate. His crazy grin turned serious as he simply lay there focused on the mayhem taking place.

A condensed circulation of icy wind formed under a larger purple cloud directly over Mareridt. She twisted and twiddled her fingers during her moment of peace to conjure up icy pillars of stalagmites in the packaged blizzard overhead.

When the guards closed in on Mareridt, she leaped into the air to grab and huck these giant ice sickles down at the ground where she previously resided, shattering them on impact and creating a sonic frost nova that blasted shards of edged ice at the constant rush of guards coming from all angles.

The guards were pushed back, sometimes lifted off their feet, and sometimes trapped with ice around their boots, faltering their balance. These nova blasts wore at the guards, creating slow and agonizing deaths for those around her.

A man with two swords crossed behind his back and steel bracers around his forearms hung under one of the gate's scouting towers double the height of the gate itself. His grip locked onto a horizontal tower beam, with only a small fall from the ground. His bracers were as thick as elephant legs, and one extra-large gauntlet allowed him to hang lackadaisically as he watched the two demon guards and golem face off.

The golem, now twice as tall and stocky as he was when first coalesced, jogged forward at a causal stride, eventually building momentum into a bull rush.

The demon guards crouched, digging their gauntlets into the icy dirt to use their grip to thrust them forward. As they charged forth toward the monstrous icy obstruction, one demon quickly rolled behind the other, grabbed the spinal spikes on his armor, and jolted on top of the other demon to match the golem's height.

They all clashed. Horns to ice. Spikes to dark metal. The demons were set on a rampage of plunderous pounds and checks from their spiked shoulders, forearms, and heads like bouncing gorillas. They went ape shit on the golem, slowly breaking the beast apart. The blood spilt from within the golem's flesh mass and black armor, causing the demon guards to slip in the puddle of blood and guts. The golem tried to push forward through the frenzied bashing from the demons, but with all their weight it slipped in the blood and melted ice, falling back and hitting the dirt with a boom.

Both demons jumped on top of the golem and proceeded to break the top layer of ice. Once the ice had crumbled, they ripped the dripping dark armor away.

Not far from her first ruined golem Mareridt stood surrounded by dead guards and ice. She slowly raised both arms, twisting her hands clockwise as the bodies on the ground slipped away from the rainbow pools of blood and elevated towards two invisible magnetic fields. The invisible area pulled what was left of the double dead guards together with blocky ice chucks and edged shards that came from the heavy drooping clouds. Her sprawled-out fingers slowly tightened into clenched fists, and two new golems were erected. She blasted them with a final blizzard to bind their limbs and joints and then flew up into the sky.

Below her, all the double dead souls started to rise from their bodies, appearing like a deep fog drifting towards outer space. Her ice golems were soul-reaving monsters.

Still on the other side of the bloodied outpost, the dual-bladed warrior watched Mareridt influence a brisk blue and white stream from a nearby cloud into the palm of her hand and proceed to shoot the winter beam at her twin abominations. After she was sufficiently happy with their mad and tormenting look, she blasted up further into the sky, leaving her pets in the courtyard.

He opened his large, gauntleted hand to drop to the dirt underneath the center of the scouting tower and then walked toward the battleground. As he passed the two accomplished demon guards, they were breathing hard from their last kill and had a set stare of rage at the two new golems that had formed to take the first one's place.

The warrior pulled both his blades out from his back sheath. SHLING! He pointed his blades at the stupid golems and began to spit out orders to his Lieutenant.

"Guard the monks, Lieutenant. It's time to FUCK, shit up!"

"Yes Lord Lancelot," shouted the Lieutenant.

Hell-bound Lancelot started at the two cube-armed golems. You could see blood pressing out of the mismatched pieces of armor and sliding down the chunks of ice. A blue, red mist lingered around them from the blood pressure squirting through the frost.

The golems rushed straight for the gate, pushing Lancelot out of the way. Lancelot blocked the massive arm with both blades pointed toward the sky and slid back six feet in the blood-soaked mud.

Looking down at his blades he realized he required instruments for bashing not slicing. Lancelot slid his swords into his back sheaths, picked up a double dead's tower shield and pounded it with his trunk thick gauntlet three times to reassure himself that it would protect him better than its previous owner. He clenched the gauntlet into a fist and imagined ripping those ice golems' frozen brains right out of their icy cubes. A charge was in order, but he walked up to the fight, watching the demon twins monkey around the roaring golem twins, waiting for his time to shine.

Above them, crossbow bolts flew towards Mareridt. Her eyes blazed with impatience, waiting for the golems to begin pounding at the gate. She took flight and started the long circle around the invisible dome shroud containing the legendary Dyathsake Brekinvale trees.

Mareridt zoomed past the wizards holding the shroud. Some raised a hand to shoot cylinders of fire at the wicked black blur. Guards stood on the ridge, watching her with steady eyes.

Mareridt stopped high up in Pantoon's red sky, concealing her position from the ground. She hurled a huge water ball through the dense purple clouds, then a fireball, then lightning; all having the flash effect of the elemental colors, blue, red, and yellow that illuminated the clouds below.

Quickly, she dropped through the clouds so she could see the courtyard. The dead bodies that weren't mashed together to create the massive golems, she now used to telepathically throw at the electric shroud that zapped anything and everything to vapor.

The pounding on the black gate was a heavy, blaring Thud thud,

thud thud. The sound of metal cracking skulls. The boom of metal ringing against metal. The twin golems mechanically reaped rhythmic terror on the black gate while Lancelot and the demons proceeded to smash and bash them.

Four long poisoned daggers appeared at Mareridt's side. Two in each hand. She aimed her plummet down towards four tall wizards standing ten yards from each other, hitting three of them like a halberd would hit a piece of fruit. The fourth wizard was blocked by a huge guard that was too big for his armor, leaving a lot of visible green skin. This beast caused Mareridt to have to twist out of his way.

After Mareridt's twist evasion, five flares went up high into the air about a mile away. She stopped her slaughter and darted straight for the three blind monks. A large purple cloud trailed after her, eventually covering her body and the entire unit guarding the monks. Nothing could be seen, only heard: The thud of soldiers dropping to the ground in the deep mist. A poisoned hulk guard on the dome ridge screaming in pain as his body slowly dissipated. One golem pounding on the gate while the other slammed the ground like a gorilla with ice columns for arms to threaten Lancelot. Lieutenants spitting orders, and musical tunes heard from the metal band's hovercraft floating off in the distance.

****

Mareridt stutter-stepped in her landing to slow herself down, and the monks were set down by her telekinetic air cell. They seemed as they were at the gate, calm and collected, only their hair was wind-blown and all over the place. Mareridt's kimono looked fresh with a few wrinkles, and her hair was still in a tight dark braid.

The land was an empty maroon desert with a small starship awaiting Mareridt, about half the size of Han Solo's. Mareridt poked the monks with the hilt of her knife up the starship ramp while swarms of warriors closed in on them. A moment later, the ship blasted off with the gate still down and headed up in the direction of the slumbering Moon Zealot...

The slumbering Moon Zealot took up the whole sky. It lay like a dragon floating with the stars, pillowed by another nearby planet, thirteen moons, and a dark orange sun almost black from the influence of its neighboring dark bulge, the center of the galaxy.

The Moon Zealot had craters instead of scales, mountain ridges and groves instead of joints and muscles, and its form rounded however intricately rigid, straightened but engrossed with curves.

Pantoon's sun was just beginning to descend under the Moon Zealot's perplexing chin. A zone of nearly a dozen crushed-up planets, thousands of ruined starships, and bits of dead forests. A broad beard that was good for collecting the dinner that fell out of its mouth.

****

Dark blue flags with yellow tears cut diagonally through the middle, blew at either side of Doomali. He looked down from the Citadel's balcony with a hard face. Red spiral tattoos twirling across from ear to ear, and his metallic three-pointed beard plated his wide chin.

A starship came into Plaztex's atmosphere in no hurry. It hovered a flag's length from Doomali's balcony, rotating, and finally landing in the street in front of the Citadel. Mareridt and three men with gray bandanas over their eyes stepped out.

So the plan commences.

"Take Mareridt's starship back to Pantoon in the fourth division. Our Plaztex barracks will have our Brekinvale and equipment for transfer," Doomali ordered in his slow drawl.

The flat sheet head with snake-like features nodded in acknowledgment and turned to go. A king cobra.

"Jezzzz," Doomali said at last earshot. "If you fuck this up again, I will destroy your whole species for all eternity."

Jezzzz half-smiled and nodded. He turned to go, but faded back towards Doomali. Complex to Doomali's eyes, Jezzzz was hypnotic in his advance, fluid as a dream, relaxing his prey to the point of immobilization. Jezzzz slithered from side to side and pulled out his long scimitar, slashing Doomali across the cheek and torso.

Doomali jumped back so as not to have his face cut in two. With no weapons, Doomali stood ready for the next attack.

After another slash, Jezzzz dove in for a stab and a poisonous bite. The scimitar sunk into Doomali's side and through his stomach. As the blade slid deeper into Doomali, he tilted his head back and slammed his beard down into Jezzzz. The bite was rebutted with three-pointed metal edges just above the cobra's fangs, only inches from Doomali's red spiral tattooed throat. Doomali picked Jezzzz's body off his beard and dropped him to the ground. He turned to look over the main street from the Citadel balcony, dabbing at the wound in his side. Mareridt causally approached from behind, taking her place in the anteroom.

"Max!" Doomali called out, cringing a little from his wound.

Max, a skeleton soldier, stepped in beside Doomali. Max and the guards were there during Jezzzz's assault; however, they weren't fast enough to place their blades into his wiggly snake torso. Jezzzz was also Doomali's main assassin, and one hard cookie to lay a hand on.

"Yes Sire?"

"Go along with the mission," Doomali ordered, anger forming after each word. "And make su-" He coughed.

"My men and I will make sure to successfully transfer the Brekinvale Luster, My Lord."

"Good. Now go."

The Skeleton Crew left, and Mareridt took Max's place, telling the monks to stay put.

"I see your... men." Mareridt analyzed in disgust, looking down at Jezzzz, "...are loyal beyond measure." Mareridt's voice was almost broken and faint, like she was conserving her energy for muscles other than her tongue.

Doomali turned toward Mareridt, holding his side. "Everyone wants a taste of doom in hell." He frowned back at the city. "Now tell me of your news."

Mareridt leaned her back on the balcony railing, looking at the three blind monks.

"Well, I have the monks. And judging by your men's flares they successfully drilled the hole under the Luster Dome and retrieved some of that damn plant." Mareridt's eyes glazed and stared through the monks, the Citadel walls, the galaxy.

"We can finally begin the possession."

Doomali reacted and walked back into the Citadel. "We have already begun, Mareridt."

Mareridt followed him through the corridors. "What..?"

"We are about to send our second test subject." Doomali responded, walking straight towards the catacomb's windy staircase.

Mareridt stepped in a spill of Doomali's blood, looking at it unpretentiously, and then jogged up to his side. "You idiot! You can ruin everything playing this like it's a game! You stupid demon! From now on you do as I say. And as I say ONLY!"

"As you wish, Lady of Nightmares."

They walked in silence down into the catacombs.

****

The Skeleton Crew marched off Mareridt's ship and into the middle of Plaztex's barracks on Pantoon. Soldiers scattered the square, dueling and training like old gladiators. Max stepped off into the dirt and looked around.

"Alrighty, boys, don't be distracted by the fleshies. Charlie and Whitey go find me some tenting. The rest follow me."

Twenty-six skeleton soldiers with blue and yellow sashes, some with robes or tied cloth, walked into the fourth division barracks. Standing there in the center of the room was a demanding demon with a red spaded tail flipping around like a pissed-off cat. The rest of the barracks was bustling with men carrying heavy machinery in and out. Crates were being filled and lifted, and the windows were covered with blue tapestries and designs. A massive cylinderic drill, the size of a twenty-foot Christmas Tree, sat behind the demon, with a hole just as big trenched in front of it.

"What's your business here you skeleton scum?" The demon asked Max, as Max approached the center of the room with two eight-foot skeleton ruffians flanking him. The other skeleton soldiers spread out wildly around the barracks, scimitars in hand.

Another flat-headed snake humanoid stood beside the demon.

Obviously, his right-hand man or slithering advisor.

Max bowed, "We come for the Luster. Doomali's demands." Max's jaw dropped and closed in funny ways while he talked with his old bones, jaw clicking and teeth clacking.

"Jezzzz is supposed to pick up the Luster. Now leave us immediately," The demon said, waving them out.

"Mate. You don't get it. Jezzzz is dead. We have Mareridt's starship outside and we are going to deliver those damn trees." Max tilted his bones to look around the demon. The snake man slid forward, enraged by the news. And the demon moved his body to block Max's view.

"You have a ship, eh? Well, that's a surprise for a mangy pir-" The thick-boned, eight-foot skeleton to Max's right ended the demon's yammer with a slick stab into his ribs. The skeleton to Max's left then nonchalantly stabbed the snake mate in the side.

Both the snake mate and demon were then shot in the head just as quickly with Max's crossed blunderbuss pistols. The demon and the snake fell to the ground, and the three skeletons walked over to the massive hole in front of the drill.

After the barracks' demon leader was killed, there was little rebellion. The skeletons cut down anyone who looked ready to scuffle.

Max peered at the hole with his deep black sockets. A dark tree lay on its side, taking up the entire diameter of the drilled hole. Branches bunched up and squeezed together. Thick ropes wrapped around its oily, dark, bubbly roots.

Max looked around the large barracks. "Under Doomali's order, these Luster must be delivered. Stop what you are doing and get them out of the hole and into the starship!" Max then proceeded to walk outside. The barracks' soldiers stopped working on taking apart the drill and started heaving the big rope, slowly pulling the Brekinvale out of the hole. The Skeleton Crew watched.

Max stepped outside, followed by his eight-foot skeleton thugs. The tents were already being made up to block any outside view of the tree transfer between the barracks and the starship. Charlie walked up to his Captain, Max.

"Sir the tents are under construction."

"Good. I want you three to move the dead into the ship. We need their bones… leave the snake." His boys went off to work. Max stood there; his grin was large. Things were looking up for him. The Skeleton Crew was back.

****

The catacomb was a large underground laboratory about the length of one city block. Most of the space was filled with dusty bottles and shelves, tables with tools and potions, cracks in the floor with blue vapor rising, and various creatures with lab coats and robes. The walls were all scribed with ancient demonology.

Mareridt walked to the end of a table where Doomali was being stitched up. A container of his blood sat on a smaller round table next to him. Mareridt picked it up and swirled it while looking around in the container.

"Demon blood." Mareridt said, as cold condensation puffed out like the words were trapped within her breath, leaving the chill of the word frozen in the cosmos. "So, your henchman... Hantos." She glanced over at Hantos and back again. "Can he be trusted?"

Doomali smiled at Hantos and then Mareridt. Hantos was a thick beast with skin-shifting abilities. Falling into Hell changed him into something even more than a camouflaged menace, something much more.

Doomali let his most trusted and honored minions of the other various galaxies' dead drink his blood, making them somewhat stronger and giving an edge to their niche of living and killing in Dyathsake Galaxy. A casual strength of will to move through death and hold onto a solid form. Hantos was now just as strong as any demon.

"Hantos is a perfect subject for our greater possession testing"- Doomali said.

Hantos nodded, tucking his brown thumbs under his brown belt with blue hands embossing his blue pants.

Six, the lead sorcerer of Doomali's house, came through the wide catacomb doors, his horns popped out from his voided face of red eyes, and his gray robe was mostly closed with a hint of smoky skulls poking out from where the fabric formed a V on his chest.

Saul, Doomali's father, walked beside him with an entourage of flagmen and three heavily armored guards. They all entered the massive room of the laboratory. The flagmen stood to either side of the door. The colors around the room were white, black, blue, and yellow. The only contrasting colors were those in the vials and potions that littered the room.

Six saw Doomali and glided over to them.

"My condolences on losing your General Jezzzz. It seemed we may have lost you as well if his fangs met," Six pinched at his opaque voided face where a neck would be.

Doomali waved off the conversation.

Six continued. "Max, the Captain in charge of the Skeleton Crew, has returned with thirteen Brekinvale Trees and eight bags of bones... I must admit the Skeleton Crew is very good at pulling bones from the double dead…" Six's voice sounded fascinated.

"And here, Lady Mareridt, you must have made just enough racket on the topsoil for the drill to drill under the Luster Dome undetected. A job well done.

"Now that we have extra bones to create a portal that can fit Hantos' body, let us gather together the dirt from Pantoon and the ancient Brekinvale root, as well as the monks, to keep the Brekinvale Lusters in good health. I believe we are well on our way to over-powering our first planet out of the Dyathsake Galaxy." As Six soothed out his last words, his red eyes searched the room, wondering where the blind monks had gone.

"Earth will be under my rule. You will merely use it for battlements." Mareridt advised furiously.

Saul strode into the humongous spell room where the portal was being created. He stepped ahead of Mareridt and spoke over his shoulder. "Mareridt, you remind me of my wedded maiden all too much... Once we break through the Glasir and open up a real gap in between our worlds, hopefully, she will stop battling against the outer rim and join us once again," Saul pondered happily, shoulders shaking with laughter. The Glasir was the Golden Shield of Gaia, blocking evil not born or created on Earth.

The heavenly planets that resided in the outer rim have been warring against the hellish galactic bulge planets for as long as stardust has been technically one massive blob in space. Demon lord babies were raised to hate the lords of the Halo. Glory, retribution, and respect, all had no more meaning than an ant drowning in piss. The lords of Halo Light and the demons were at war purely because of their traditional beliefs. One side desired destruction, while the other side desired peace.

Their war was usually balanced and always lingered in a continuous stalemate of black axe against white sword. Some old legends tell of demons transplanting over to Halo Lit planets and angels settling closer to the Bulge, all in the name of this mysterious Judge of Balance. If demons were put in angelic shoes, perhaps they'd see the light, and if angels put themselves in demonic boots, perhaps they'd see the excitement of the void. This switch of sides is literally an unexplainable reality in the Dyathsake Galaxy.

Sometimes warriors got their fill of death, resided their hate, and retired, while the other side found dead friends and family, igniting their embedded hate and driving them to passionately go to war until their blood thirst was quenched, only giving yet another the right of redemption. The cycle of giving death to one gives birth to the killing of another, a cycle that seemed never-ending, until now.

If the darkened Togmehoians could fortify a location in the Milky Way Galaxy for an influx of resources and a supply of soldiers, the Galactic Bulge of demons would have a solid chance of dominating the outer rim regions. Hell would conquer Heaven.

The portal was in the shape of a door frame, built with every kind of bone imaginable. It was only wide enough for four men and tall enough for a stack of three. The structure rested right over three X cracks in the stone floor streaming out continuous blue spirit vapor. Brekinvale roots lay neatly over one of the X cracks, making a tight little root bridge with Pantoon dirt scattered on top of it.

Hantos was naked with two dozen other demonic misfits that all faced Six, Doomali, Mareridt, and Saul. His body, although solid as steel, looked murky and vaporous blue, skin mimicking the spirit vapor coming up from the catacomb ground. All four leaders gave Hantos their own piece of advice before his spirit traveled hundreds of light-years through the universe.

"You will possess the spirit of an ancient tree warrior that resides on an island named Grimsey, Hantos. So, take your time getting used to its form and mobility. The tree's power will not be easy to subside right away. These demonic misfits will aid your possession as you will theirs," Six briefed.

Hantos itched his head and then started opening his mouth as if he was about to ask a question.

"The portal made mostly of dead Earthling bones will pilot your spirit straight to Earth. Once you are in Earth's atmosphere look for a ray of green light that shoots up from a Northern Island. This green light represents all of the legendary Awakened around Reykjavik and Grimsey.

We already sent Madman Pierce there as a scout, so there may be a red beam of light in that vicinity as well. However…" Six rotated his voided face around the room.

"We haven't heard from Madman Pierce in four days. The bastard probably went crazy as soon as he figured out the raw power of an Awakened. If this is so, his body in Plaztex will remain nothing but a vegetable, and it is believed that his spirit will roam the universe for eternity.

If you die there, you'll come back fine, just don't go 'insane' and forget to return. Use these lights to guide you and then choose the brightest light with the most scribe work. That will be the Awakened that you must possess. Possess the tree and kill the Sky Sister, which holds the Glasir. Mareridt will be there shortly to take over the assault on Earth."

Mareridt's eyes rolled as if she grew impatient waiting for her host body on Earth.

"Scare as many shit brain humans as you can. Terror will break their souls for us to take later. The Northern islands will be a creative start to our reign." Doomali advised, putting a hand on Hantos' shoulder.

Six rubbed at his belly of stolen souls as if he were hungry.

Mareridt took a step toward Hantos, "Make sure you carve in the symbols you should have memorized. These will enact the power and abilities of the Awakened tree as well as the new abilities you would like to have in tree form. I have fought with Earth Mother's wooden warriors before. They are both powerful and intelligent. Their spell cast can break the skies, and their roots can break the earth." She preached not just for Hantos but for all the demons around listening.

"These carvings will allow full control and possession over the tree's spirit. Over scribing their spirit is crucial to keeping them imprisoned. The carving will also let you tap back into Hell to give us information. This is our only source of distant communication, so get it right."

Saul wandered over to the bone portal and placed his palm on a large skull.

"We will follow you shortly Hantos, this is the day our Togmehoian house becomes legendary." Saul moved his other palm over the bluish spirit vapor and sprinkled the Brekinvale Luster roots and Pantoon dirt into the cracks. He then tightened his grip on the skull and crushed it, creating dust, which sprinkled into the vapor cracks as well. After a moment, the vapor hovered up, engulfing the inside of the portal of bones, creating a thin vaporous film.

Hantos walked through with heavy slouched shoulders and fell limp on the other side.

"Let your soul soar and find your wood," Saul whispered. "Who's next?"

The Grim Grimsey

I struggled to get a gasp of air, pulling oxygen into my lungs as hard as I was trying to pull my arms out from under me. Trapped under a fallen moss-covered oak, I quickly began to panic, imagining only life just inches from death. I reigned as a claustrophobic madman while a ruminating philosopher lay in the depths of my voided reality. Counterparts swiftly rustled in the sphere of existence. I felt the earth migrating, sailing in black sand. Power exerted into my spine. Power… My brothers…

A ray of air revived my spirit in my unconscious body. A stab, and then another, and I woke, peering up at a wizard who was in the shape of a tree. His branch retracted away from my chest and tightly wound itself around the golden bear-encrusted shield with a dozen other branches. Rowan Bear's wooden facial features steadied like a sea at dawn. His left eye was a fat dark hollow, and his spiral knotted nose was flattened like a late-night street brawler's.

I heard a large ripple through the air, and suddenly the golden shield thrust forward, exploding a boulder that had been thrown. The ground rumbled as if in rage, and my intuition told me something was at a full and ferocious charge. I closed my eyes and heard a loud noise, PunNn! Cracking wood hitting hollow metal. I held my breath to hear every skid and drop of debris.

In my anticipation of seeing a triumphant, shield-bearing Rowan, I opened my eyes only to see a charred piece of demon-marked wood drifting through the starry night above like a shared dream.

The fallen mossy lumber that had trapped me had been moved to the side, and I saw Rowan Bear's shield blasting back the frantic moss-covered oaks. Lingo beat at one by quickly rotating around it in the dirt and then flipping the moss-covered oak over him and slamming it back into the ground several times. Afwat simply bashed the trees like street weirdos, probably giving Pads, high up in his branches, quite a show.

Before I knew it, there was a pause, and the fight was over. Only then did the weird roars and crazy hollow blabbers make their way to our ears. A sound only a loony-toon in an insane asylum would make.

****

The night grew dark, and the demonic misfits from Plaztex circled around their boss on a cliff at the edge of Grimsey Island.

Now that they had possessed the trees, their moss-covered branches created eerie shadows on their sprawled-out roots and the hard-packed dirt. They were so close to one another that their boughs blocked out all starlight. Disturbed gazes stirred their party towards uncertainty and bewilderment. Some of the eighteen who were watching Hantos fight the spirit within this legendary tree also had occasional tantrums from their wooden frames' spirits as well.

A carved-out demon symbol was far more abstract than pagan sigils and pentagrams. So, Hantos began with two of his more mobile roots grasping a sharp stone to scrape the bark away, like a Japanese warrior committing to his Seppuku. However, whenever the engraving stone got close, there was a flash of rebellion.

Hantos danced in the heavy mist, roaring and tearing at his new body like he was trying to rip out his sappy guts. Relics and artifacts shook from his branches. A golden spyglass wobbled off a high limb, clinking on an old plated helm, and spun through the air, slapping onto an octopus-looking root.

In his berserk, Hantos picked up the spyglass and broke it in half, creating one very jagged steel edge. He held it to his trunk. The spyglass then chaotically cut into his bark, making a sign, a carving. Once it reached accurate depths, it majestically blasted dark red light out of Piper's bark.

Hantos now waddled to his own creaks and moans while carving out even more aggressive symbols to suppress the ancient tree's relentless spirit. He became more transparent and more hollow, eventually completely camouflaging in with his environment.

The rambunctious, ruinous body drifted closer to a line of rooted pines. His upper branches shifted as if the pine trees had swallowed them. On his other branched shoulder, the dark mist surrounding the cliff's edge started to become one with his tree form.

The roars settled.

From the Misfits' point of view, Hantos' existence was only established by his slow, daunting breath. The tree before them was now only a smuggled soul imprisoned by transcending darkness.

Piper had been a Chief Lantos General, Collector of Ancients, Sentinel Tradeswomen, Provoker of Tales, and was now grievously lost.

On this night, the Island of Grimsey was a very grim place indeed.

****

Rowan brushed bits of bark and sap off his bear-crested shield and then turned in the direction of the far-off roar. It seemed as if the sound came from a cartoon of King Kong on PCP. It must have only been a couple of miles from us. I decided now was the time to get back onto the boat. The path to the roaring lunatic was through hundreds of trees that looked exactly like the ones that just went Ya-Hoo on our asses. I simply couldn't believe this was real life. There were so many times I came inches from becoming a puddle of blood. I mean, what kind of tree chases you while spinning around in a tornado, stops, and tells you to, "watch my bladery wise guy," then goes underground, pops up next to a mean-looking moss-covered oak, and proceeds to tear every limb and branch from its trunk?

"Kraeno! Where the hell you think you're goin?" Favin barked.

I turned around, and my eyes had to slow down to process the scene. Afwat sat on two dying moss lumps, their red lights petering out the further he pushed them into the dark mud, with Pads hanging from his billiard like a sailor calling coordinates from topmast. The Birchwood checked his several blades and sporadically ran each of them by a sharpening stone perched on top of his trunk. Lingo held an evil oak upside-down while A.D wailed at it with two burnt-out torches. Lingo was happy bullying the oak, however, when he became bored of A.D's pounding, he took two sides of the moss-covered roots and tore them from root to trunk fork, right down the middle, leaving A.D in awe, a sound he will likely remember forever.

Panda crouched next to a wider moss-covered oak and dabbed his knife into the carved out grooves that bled the weird red light. He looked pensive.

Favin stood in front of Panda, "Whatcha doing Kraeno?"

I coughed. "-," and no words could escape, so I tried coughing out my words.

"It's time to go Uncle. If this-," I pointed below Favin's bent leg planted on a fallen oak.

"Is down here, then what the fuck is UP there?"

The roars continued, and my chills started chilling to the point where my skin felt like it had a layer of ice gradually freezing itself into my bones. My legs shook so much I knew the others could see them wobbling.

"What's up there, the Jester of Darkness?"

Favin walked over to me. "Something very bad is happening, Kraeno, and we need to do something - anything we can to make it right."

"Shit," I whined, looking over my shoulder at the waves washing up on shore.

I yelled up to Pads, still hanging high off Afwat's billiard. "What do you guys want to do?"

"Don't think we have much choice, Krae. Let's go see what this bastard's screaming about." A.D yelled back.

Rowan filled in, "The Sentinels will ride with us. Climb up, and we will cross Grimsey to find more of these damned spirits. Piper and Shay may be in trouble."

"Piper, the ancient tree that helped our mum?" Let's go bury an axe, I thought. "Can't I go get the crossbow first?"

Pads yelled down, "There's no time Krae, we need to go help... For Ma."

Rowan grumbled from above Favin and me. "Climb up. Try to stay behind my shield, and if anything gets close... Just stay behind the shield."

Favin and I climbed up Rowan's branches. I found a really comfortable spot behind the tip of his shield. Favin hugged a branch next to where Rowan's hollows were.

We turned around and set out for the darkened trail. The roars blared continuously, fragmenting my mind into areas that would fester with nightmares later. I just need one song. I closed my eyes and played a song in my head by, *The Sword.* The drums splintered into a hard beat as we thumped our way up the darkened path.

The one Birchwood who was with us popped out of the dirt a little way ahead.

"Let's dance baby!" And then dove back into the ground to tremor forth.

A little time passed, and we were on an incline with fewer trees. The soil in some spots looked dug out. More uprooted Hell-spawn.

The Birchwood tree named Mac, skinny and agile, slid down the slope to meet us. The sound of waves crashing on cliffs harmoniously replaced the daunting roars behind him.

"Rowan, there are two dozen crazed oaks right up that hill."

"What of the screamer?"

"That was a little harder to tell. There were grunts coming from a semi-circle that the smaller trees created, but I couldn't make out exactly who or what it was. Hiding in the pines it was." The Birchwood gurgled the juice from where his voice came, sounding similar to a growl.

Rowan took slow steps forward, one root after the other. I got a good bird's eye view of Rowan's bark face of serenity.

"Mac, take us to where you saw these things that took our brethren. If it's possible to show them pain, then they are about to feel a whole lot of it." Rowan's voice was slow and hollow, but filled your heart with courage in a way that only newly discovered legendary magical creatures could.

I got to look at Afwat's reaction while swaying side to side in Rowan as he climbed up the hill. Afwat's wide lateral hollow morphed vertically into several toothy shapes, as if he were smiling at the challenge.

****

The foggy night turned a hazy blue-orange. Halloween was coming early this year, and instead of spooking kids from the trees, the trees spooked us.

Favin and I sat on Rowan as he prayed to the skies. Afwat and Pads stood as Rowan's guard, and Lingo, Mac, Panda, and A.D circled around the hill close to the cliff side to get a nice flanking position.

I saw the mossy oaks from a reasonable distance, but they didn't consider us a threat, possibly thinking we were just part of the landscape.

Rowan continued to raise his branches higher towards the sky, and as he did, the heavy fog became more and more of a barrier with crackling light within. The blue light was from the main source of Rowan's creation. The more ferocious the blue crackling became, I knew the closer our little battle-royal approached us.

Half of the planted dumb demon oaks tried looking through their heavy moss-layered branches towards the crackling sky. The other half waited, scraping dirt and admiring their new wooden forms and glowing carvings.

Rain fell now, and the fog slowly began to rip away from the Island. A dark cloud was revealed with blue flashing light overhead. Before we knew it, the next color that seduced the gray Island of Grimsey was a daunting red and orange. The orange tint was heat exerted from Rowan's higher creation, making the barrier's misty dew look like a late foggy night, harnessing the orange light of hometown streetlamps.

Blue steaks blasted down onto the demon oaks, and the moss set a fire. Trees lit up in seconds and scrambled around in perplexity. One oak wiggled itself off the cliff, hoping for an icy plunge into the sea and an easy float on its back. The others threw dirt at each other and tried dodging the bolts that bombarded their wicked little gathering.

I watched, relieved that this fight hadn't been as close up as the other…and like a jinx, the persistent wind from the East stopped abruptly, and the next surface my bottom was acquainted with was the dirt of our ol' Grimsey Island.

Confused, Afwat waddled to timbered Rowan's side, looking at Favin and me for explanations. Pads slid down the billiard, jumped down onto Rowan's trunk, and rushed over to Favin several yards away.

During Rowan's befuddlement, Afwat latched his branches together with Rowan's and leaned back to pull him up, only to be interrupted mid-lift by an invisible force cutting their thickly tied branches in half, causing them both to fly backward. Afwat's 70-foot trunk fell down the slope, losing our massive security tree and bringing all the attention right to us.

So the big guy is out of the game. The wizard can't cast, and there was something camouflaged in the darkness...

I looked over my shoulder and saw Lingo pushing the flaming oaks off the cliff, one by one. The Birchwood, Mac, ran at another burning moss oak, striding towards us. It had a flat top and flailed its branches in a detached, emotionless manner.

Mac popped up in front of him, reaching eye level with the oak. He spun in a tornado frenzy McTwist that scalped the oaks upper branches, yet lighting his own self on fire, and continued towards the camouflaged beast of the night that was snapping Rowan's branches like a massive poltergeist.

I saw its roots when they changed from a mass of night to a brown cylinder with deep grooves spiraling around itself, crushing into Rowan's mid-section. Rowan swiped his shield to break free, yet more wooden tentacles raced at him, pinning his golden shield to one side.

The evil within Piper was a mass of obscure roars and monstrous grunts, making it easier for Mac to find beast. Mac Jumped on evil Piper, completely up in flames, gallivanting in the branches of shifty bark.

The charred Mac was tossed away, smoldering to ash; yet flames still attached themselves to the possessed Piper, making it look like it was actually a tree made of fire. Its bark shifted and transformed in the red-orange surges of heat. The chaotic helical of fire flowed at every wooden inch and the air grew demonically hot. In a rage filled with fire, it trapped Rowan, engulfing our leader in flames, and then turned its burning gaze on me.

I never knew evil until I looked into those eyes of Hellfire. Evil wasn't as erratic as rage or madness. Evil was deep within, the void of light, the creator of nightmares, a darkness old and ancient.

The hardest thing I think I ever did was look away from the hypnotic scene ahead of me. Looking away to see Favin and Pads hobbling up the hill, haloed with a blue star that rushed over their heads.

My dear brother Pads. A tear of happiness came, only to be dried up just as quickly as a flaming branch stabbed through my throat. Those pits of fire came close to my own, and in that moment, I tried to spit as much blood into the hollows of Hell as I possibly could.

****

A.D watched from afar as a tree engulfed in flame killed Kraeno with a branch through his throat. Kraeno floated there, suspended by the branch, spitting his boiling blood into the face of the demon.

A blue blur zipped through the red night.

It was Shay. She concentrated the moisture from Rowan's storm cloud to extinguish the flames burning Hantos, Kraeno, and Rowan. She hovered low while water slid down her bald black head and analyzed the situation.

"Piper… What has happened?"

Hantos stood there, bare-branched with red light glowing bright through his black charred bark, waiting for his next opportunity.

"I sense evil within you…" Her eyes glanced at Rowan's cloud, and seconds later thunder cracked.

"Goodbye Piper…" Her ringed hand maneuvered in three quick signs toward the sky, and then a blue lightning elemental with golden circlets around each limb came into existence.

It floated down with cadence and amplitude. Its electric energy shot out from all five ends. The elemental split Hantos in two with one bolt abruptly cutting off his final rebellious roar.

The elemental scanned the wounded, the dead, the field of war. It then made security revolutions around Shay as she dropped to the ground and walked over to Kraeno and Rowan.

Everyone tried to get close, but the royal starfish of bright electrical discharge flew down to keep a perimeter around Shay. Lingo went to Afwat to check on his situation, even though the dexterous juggling tree didn't have the size to help pick up A Forest Within A Tree.

Shay peered at the dead and then raised her attention to the living. "Panda man! What has happened here? I felt a disturbance with Piper and the Island." Shay took a deep breath to stabilize her frustration.

"I need to check on something, stay here… Are there any more of…" Shay pointed her jeweled hand at Piper's ruined trunk.

Panda responded, "I de know."

Shay flew up in her ragged robe, floating eye to eye with her lightning elemental. The dark cloud still stormed down on Grimsey. She spoke to the elemental in a beautiful, delicate tongue. The elemental flew to the cliff's edge and began blasting bolts of lightning at every tree in sight, floating through the moss oak forest, splitting all of them in half.

Shay flew to Afwat and raised her robed arms to telepathically lift broken Afwat out of his timber and to an appropriate rooted position.

"Afwat, I am sorry…" And Shay flew away to the North.

While Shay's elemental was wreaking devastation to all the trees on Grimsey, Afwat, Lingo, and the Totem Clause Sentinels gathered around their dead. Rowan, Kraeno, and Mac the Birchwood were burnt and ruined.

There was silence, and after an hour of blank stares, watching the dead lying in the dirt, the wind changed, and a rush of blue light came across the sky again. Shay gently settled in front of the grave Sentinel's faces.

"Well well well. I'm not sure where these abominations came from, but they are led by witchcraft that dreadfully threatens Mother Gaia and her kin. I never thought this could be possible… Afwat, please, explain what you know."

Afwat explained in as few words as possible with his low rumbling voice.

"This must have been what these… Demons were after." Shay held up a Golden Leaf Scepter. Everyone except for Afwat and Pads looked up at the majestic instrument forged by Gaia herself. Afwat's gaze was fixed on Rowan Bear and Pad's on Kraeno.

"Grimsey is a beacon of energy because of the Scepter. Piper was its guardian and my friend. Now you must take this burden in guarding Gaia and the Scepter from these dark forces… the other Sisters must know what is happening. I'm bringing the Scepter to Tienilla. She should hold onto it. You will need to join her to help protect it."

The silence lulled. A.D gritted his teeth as his hand brushed through Kraeno's wavy brown hair.

"So much destruction..." he said, in an almost inaudible voice. "Why did you destroy ALL the trees?" A.D's eyes filled with tears.

"Bury your dead and find out what's happening to Gaia!" Shay walked over to Piper and touched her charred bark with two fingers.

"I will miss you, Piper," Shay whispered, and then took off East, against the heavy wind.

Lingo walked near the cliff and sunk his roots deep into the muddy earth. He twisted, locking them in, wrapping around the hard substrate, and then ripping them all out to create a crater. He continued, making a large grave on the cliffs of Grimsey.

Flowers for the Dead

Afwat stomped into the cabin yard with Rowan Bear's golden shield attached to his back. His rear branches were bent inward from his fall at Grimsey, and the inner body of the forest within his branches finally allowed some sunshine to his previously shadowed core. Everything was bent out of shape, including the hearts of the crew.

Afwat placed himself in the backyard and faced the house as Lingo and the Sentinels entered the yard with slouched shoulders.

Shaki ran to Pads. "Padrick! What happened..? Where is Kraeno!"

Pads looked at her with eyes that glistened in the sunlight, holding onto a layer of moisture on the brink of breaking its watery spheres and building up into one fat drip.

The Redwood Gum stood behind Afwat and cracked a broken branch off his back in three swift sweeps.

The Awakened, or any tree conscious of knowing, were aware of each clan member embedded into Mother Earth, just as the Western Pacific Ocean swell rises to an Eastern Pacific tsunami. Urgency and alarm send sparks through Gaia's surface energy to transmit messages of death, birth, or subterfuge.

Again, there was a loud crack, and the Redwood tossed a wide branch behind the barn.

"We lost our leader. The Awakened who are able to travel need to protect Tienilla on the Island of Crete. She will need many to support her. I fear the worst has yet to begin." Afwat announced to the clan.

"What has happened Afwat? Where is Rowan?" Shaki asked. "None of your Awakened have said or done anything since you've been gone. Now none of you can explain where Kraeno is or what the hell happened out there!"

"Hell is imminent, yes. And it seems to me that Mareridt is looming over Gaia once again." Afwat answered.

"Where is Kraeno?!" Shaki yelled up at Afwat and turned to Favin, who was looking down, clutching his tattered multi-colored coat by his chest hems. His long ruffled dark hair covered his green eyes in strands.

He lurched forward.

"Answer me!" Shaki yelled again with a squeak, and was on the verge of tears. Her cheeks swelled and her bottom lip quivered. She walked up to Favin with her fist ready to pound repeatedly on his chest.

They were close enough now that Favin's defeated voice could be whispered to her, each syllable harder to say than the last.

"Kraeno... is gone, Shaki," Favin deflatted, still peering down at the ground.

Shaki shook, shivers running down her spine. Cid hugged her by the shoulders and guided her over to the porch couch. Pads walked over and helped Cid sandwich her in comfort.

Pad's hair looked like Favin's; it was droopy, long, and straggly, only his hair was dirty blonde. His shoulders stuck out of his gray tank top, and Shaki snuggled her head into his muscled grooves.

"A.D come over here." Pads said, looking at Favin, hoping that he'd snap out of it.

A.D's face looked identical to the hard wooden tree faces they were partnering up with. His two long scars ran down his right jaw and cheek. His bashed nose looked like a wooden knot, and his scraggly brown beard hung under the wreckage.

He ran his hand over his buzzed head and looked up into the blue sky. "We need ourselves a bigger crew..."

Kraeno where you at bub?

****

"I just love flowers. I wonder if they can talk too." Shaki's head tilted toward the sky. She had a bit of spunk, but her face was sullen and still in pain.

Pads looked out toward the Reykjavik docks with Favin's long spyglass. He spotted her ship.

"Come on let's go, Lady Captain is back."

Blue skies and sunshine reflected on the pick-up truck's black metal. There was a slight breeze on top of the lookout hill. They have been up on that hill for two weeks, every day, looking for Lady Captain's ship, The Saint.

Pads started the engine and closed his door. Shaki got in with a multitude of colorful flowers in her sun-bleached hair. Along with her tan skin and green eyes, she could pass for an islander.

Mazzy Star, Into Dust, played in the truck as they drove down the mountain.

The sun was setting by the time Pads and Shaki reached Reykjavik. They parked the pick-up in the Village Isle alley, and Pads walked in through the back. Shaki stayed in the truck listening to tunes.

The place was wrecked. The front of the bar was burnt, the walls were replaced with plywood to cover up the broken brick, and half the stools and tables were either gone or charred to little three-legged artistic works.

The place seemed quiet aside from the TV playing Samurai Champloo's intro song and the slamming of mugs on the wooden tabletops. The only thing that seemed similar to the last time Pads was there was the company. Pads scanned the room. No Lady Captain, only the long-haired barkeep. Pads walked across the room toward the bar, and the barkeep watched his every step.

"Ah, how's your brother doing lad? A great help he was during that damn tree tantrum. I'll tell you what, boy. I don't walk the same around trees anymore. I'll always be facing em. Some folks have even been burning the suckers down." The barkeep said, wide-eyed. His amazement at the situation was blatant.

Pads shook off the question about his brother. "We can't burn the only thing that is pulling carbon dioxide out of our atmosphere. There are already too many morons polluting our air."

Gosh it's Hell on Earth anyway we look at it. Either through real demons from Hell or the stupid fucking people that actually live here. Pads thought.

The barkeep was giving Pads a leery eye.

"We are looking for the Captain of the ship, The Saint. Have you seen her?" Pads asked.

"Seen her? Not yet." The barkeep glanced down at his bar top and circled his bar towel on the surface. "Why you lookin?"

"I have a nice proposition for her that she'd be interested in."

The barkeep's emotions were so obvious it was almost like he wanted everyone to know what he was thinking.

The barkeep swiped his bottom lip. "What'll you be have'n?"

Pads pointed at the tap with an anchor. The barkeep poured the beer and said, 'he would be right back with more ice.' Pads waited, drank his beer, and with only about a quarter of the pint left, he leaned forward to look over the bar. Ice was piled nicely in a medium-sized hill. Pads sat back down on his stool and finished his beer.

The barkeep came out and thumbed to the kitchen. "Through the kitchen and to the right. The room with the green door. Knock." He poked out two fingers like bunny rabbit ears.

Pads nodded and headed through the kitchen. He grabbed a short loaf of bread, took a bite, and walked up to the green door. Knocked twice. The door opened. Tracher, the helmsman of the Saint, like a wobbly Dionysus, looked Pads up and down. Pads tossed the short loaf to Tracher and walked in with a mouth full of bread. Several people were in the room, Lady Captain, Spear and Arrow, Tracher, and a group of other piratie looking chaps.

Tracher tossed the loaf and stepped in behind Pads. He whipped out a flask from his shirt pocket. Painted 'Irish I were Drunk'.

That's Kraeno's, Pads chewed.

Lady Captain stared at Pads with a smirk.

"So what's it going to be?" She asked while discreetly sniffing the air as if to try and smell Pad's bones quiver or flinch.

Spear and Arrow sat with one hand on his seat in between his legs, while his other hand was half-fisted on the table, just waiting for Pads to do something stupid.

"Don't waste my time, boy." Her deep anger dwelled. Spear and Arrow was losing his patience based on Lady Captain's current mood.

Pads went over to the table and picked up a pint of beer to wash down the rest of the bread, breaking it apart in his mouth. A fellow had a speaker box in his lap that raged harmoniously. The volume was turned down, however, the tune and yelling still set the stage. *The*

Bled, Meredith.

Pads choked and coughed. The bread was so dense and dry that he spewed beer and chunks of bread up in the air. Spear and Arrow mechanically got up and grabbed Pads by the collar and shirt tails.

"No more spitting tricks from you!" Spear and Arrow growled, obviously still sore about their arm wrestling match.

Tracher opened the green door, and Spear and Arrow threw Pads out. Pots and pans hit the ground, and Pads bounced off the aluminum dishwasher. The green door closed.

Pads got up, rolled his eyes at his ridiculousness, cleared his throat, walked back over to the green door, and knocked twice.

The door didn't open. Pads knocked twice again. Tracher finally opened it. His hand melodically rose up to take a hit from his flask, eyes glazed with a grin.

"We need your ship and your crew," Pads said confidently. This time it was the Lady Captain who spat out her beer.

"And do what? Practice your pencil dives in the Atlantic. Milk your brother's nips? Run from the deranged trees to some island with more trees? What is it you want boy, Speak!"

Pads took a moment, "A special transport over to Greece." Spear and Arrow straightened, and Lady Captain glared at him, setting him at ease.

"Aye... What's in it for us?"

"Viking treasure."

The Lady raised her eyebrow and then patiently glanced around the room at her boys.

"Proof, lad."

Pads texted Shaki to come in. A minute went by, and two knocks were heard at the green door. Tracher opened it.

"This here is Shaki. She always stays true to her deals. Hence her nickname, Shake. We shake on it, and you'll get the rest of your gold when we are done with your ship. We have our bargain. You in?"

Shaki stood there with three large pouches tied around her wrist and her hands on her hips.

"Let's see..." the Lady mused, curling her finger for the pouches.

Shaki walked over to the table and pulled her pouch string, letting them chunk heavily on the wood. She left her hand suspended there, like a magician revealing the climax of their trick.

Without looking up, the Captain eagerly shook Shaki's hand. The shake caused a perfect, lively little Plumaria flower petal to fall from Shaki's hair and land on Lady Captain's hand. She looked at it amused and then up at Shaki.

"So you're the one that keeps these Scallywags in line… Let's go over the plans, shall we?"

Going over all of the directions was slow and full of tension. Everyone flexed heavily in the middle of the room. Most of the shoulders in the room were turned in, except for Spear and Arrow lackadaisically leaning back in his chair.

In the upper corner of the room, Samurai Champloo's intro played again. The guy with a speaker box in his lap unmuted the TV. "I love this intro."

'Tomorrow night, meet at the small dock forty miles north,' The Captain instructed. Pads had told the captain to bring only her most trusted men.

Shaki and Pads bounced right out of the Inn, got in the pick-up, and left with the moon pinpointing Favin's cabin to the north.

"Pads. I..."

Pads turned down the music, speakers occasionally popping from the heavy metal bass.

"I am going with Cid to Africa when you guys sail off to Crete to find that Sky Sister…" Shaki stared at him, ready for an argument.

"Cid said the Awakened spoke about a girl in Chad. A girl who lives amongst the locals and who has a power felt through Gaia. It could be another Sister that needs help."

"You don't want to go back home? After everything that's happened?"

"That is exactly why I don't want to go home. I want to be a part of this. I want to fight with you, Pads." Her cheeks turned red as she looked down at the truck's shifter. "Not sit at home waiting for Hell to melt all my snow away."

Pads huffed, "So you're off with Cid to help a Sky Sister? I saw Shay in Grimsey Shake, they don't need much help." He waited, pondering the notion of Shaki diving headfirst into the middle of Africa, especially for a tan little blonde thing like herself.

"What use are you to the Awakened Shake?"

"They'll make use of me. You know, there's not very many of us guarding the planet from what could be a planet full of monsters. I'm a good addition, Cid even said so." Shaki put her chin up at Pads and then looked out the front window, watching the road surrounded by trees.

"To be honest, I have a feeling we aren't going back to the world we were used to for some time. I like having you around. We, Totem Clause Sentinels, need to stick together." A little monkey squeezed through the back sliding window. Propped up onto the center console and started eating grapes.

"Hey little fella, I guess swinging around villainous treetops isn't the most enjoyable hang time anymore, huh?" Pads chuckled with Shaki, and then the little Indiana Jones monkey threw a grape at Pad's face, making them laugh even harder.

****

The next night was wet and rainy. We peaked over the last hill in the valley and saw the ship coming in from the south. Hints of the bow poked through the southern hill's tree line. The dock was a small black pin stilted over the dark blue water glistening in the moonlight with an unreal crosshatch texture look because of the rain.

The trees rumbled behind us and six Birchwood silhouettes popped up close to the dock.

****

The ship threw out its anchors, and a crewman jumped from its deck to the dock. The song, *Sing About It, by The Wood Brothers,* played on board. Another crewman with short red hair threw his mate the tie-down ropes. The red haired crewman set a plank across the gap, timbering down between The Saint and the dock. He walked down the bridge and smiled at us.

"Come on, you scallywags, don't be scared." He let out a boastful laugh.

Lingo popped out from behind two unmarked trees. The metal and gear in his branches rattled and rang from the vibration! The red-headed sailor stumbled back and spilled his mug of wine.

The Gums meandered to either side of the large dock and tipped their crowns, dipping into the ocean water in a bow. The Birchwoods glinted in the moonlight, revealing their blades. Afwat, the massive oak, waited there watching the disorder with his green trunk marks and eyes gleaming through the branches of shallower woods.

The Kalmc's and Shaki approached the foot of the dock, watching the event fold out.

"Take care of yourselves… Sentinels." Shaki said, voice skipping when deciding what to call them. Brothers, Warriors, Buddies, Loves of Mine…

All of their eyes drifted towards the ship after their quick goodbye waves.

The Lady Captain stepped out onto the top deck with the gold and silver rings in her face glinting in the moonlight, her eyes focused on the humongous oak hovering over the kids from Reykjavik. The smell of broken sand and tossed salt came through the breeze every time the waves crashed under the dock.

"Johnny, pull the anchor, you bloody reefer!" The Lady Captain yelled while keeping the other half of her body from going over her helm railing. The mates ran to the dock ropes to untie. Flashlights raced around the ship as the Captain revved up her engine and put the boat into drive; simultaneously, Johnny, the totally jacked sailor, was heaving at the anchor with his hands wrapped around the chain. His forearms, marked by one spear and one arrow, swelled up with the struggle of pulling the anchor out of the ocean's sandy bottom.

The massive ship bumped forward and then jutted twenty yards out, creating a wake that brimmed the dock and sloshed on shore.

The illuminated great oak kindly came up behind Shaki, A.D, and Pads, and side-stepped to the water line, giving a great grunt, easily heard by the crew skittering on the deck of the Saint. His eyes peered at the shallow water before him, and he began to wade through, towards the Saint.

Near the end of the dock, Afwat made another grunt noise that only Pads understood. 'Jump Pads. Jump Mate'. And Pads sprinted on what was left of the dock, finally leaping to a long side branch.

Once Afwat became more submerged, Pads climbed with the water chasing his heels. He made it up to a curvy branch that stuck out above Afwat's half a dozen trunks. Pads gave it a slap and they came to a halt about halfway from the dock and halfway to The Saint.

"What is this!" Lady Captain's eyes looked stern, and relaxed now that her ship had enough distance from the crazy tree, unable to reach them. She could see its bright green symbols rippling under the water.

"We're out of here," Lady Captain announced without a doubt.

Pads looked down at Afwat, bubbles trailing Afwat's corky stare back.

"These are the trees that will help save us from those other bad trees." Pads yelled indefinitely. He also wondered if he could have said that in any other way.

The Captain of The Saint huffed her way to the wheel, while shouting back at Pads, "I saw what the last one did to the harbor of Reykjavik, there is no, FREAKING, way!"

The tide started to pull in, and the Saint drifted towards Pads and Afwat. The gums had their branches and crowns in the water and were manipulating the current.

"Johnny anchor down now!" The Captain screamed.

Johnny had just finished reeling it in. He shrugged off the indecisiveness of her orders and threw the anchor back into the water; only the ship was now right next to Afwat at the time the anchor hit the ocean floor.

Afwat turned and started back to shore. The Saint followed. He departed from the water with the anchor hooked around his larger central roots. After reaching the sandy beach, Afwat walked in a different manner, clumsy and shuffling through trying to regain his stance. A funny sight to see for such a massive tree. The Saint beached perfectly parallel with the little dock to its side. It was a medium sized ferry with three levels and plenty of space to roam about. The top deck did, however, resemble an old privateering vessel, just without the masts, and the middle deck was like the top, just with a ceiling.

Afwat walked up to the Saint and pressed its bow out to deeper waters and down. He hung over the ship like a menace, three stories taller than her.

"Don't worry, that's just Afwat, a forest within a tree. Lingo, massive and full of agility. The Gums, Red and B. And those devilish creatures are Apollo, Ares, Wobbly, Zeus, Nyx, and finally Athena." While Pads was introducing the crew of Gaia, the Birchwoods spread themselves out onto the ship.

By the time the crew had whipped out their harpoons, guns, and scimitars, the Saint was turned into a hostage situation. The red-haired lad seemed uncomfortable with all seven of Nyx's blades pressed against his back, and the rest of the crew ran away from the Tasmanian devils chasing them.

"We are taking your ship. The deal still stands, and you will still attain your gold. However, with the troop that you see before you…" Pads waved Afwat aboard, and he jolted forward, quickly dunking most of the bow underwater, wiggling onto the deck as gracefully as a large tree could.

"We thought it unlikely you would let us aboard, so let us explain what's happening on the way. It's a long ride to Greece." Pads said in a flat tone.

The wake from Afwat's entrance still pumped and pushed the ship forward and back. Athena cut the docking rope in five different places, all in one, various angled motion, while A.D and Panda walked on board as the ship inched away from the dock. Lingo was the last to board the ship, and after he swung up to the bow, like a kid putting one hand on a fence to jump over, the crowned Gums threw up a large net to Afwat and Lingo as Cid's going away gift to the Awakened. The gums then pushed the long-haired lady figurehead out to sea.

****

Out in open water, a large swell hit the bow's crumpled metal railing. The woods were packed onto the deck, and all of the ship's life forms were static, aside from the inevitable sea dance caused by the rock of the ocean.

It was pirates taking over pirates, and neither of them wanted to get friendly. The lads had no idea what to do against moving trees, and the moving trees - Birchwoods to be exact – still held a few of their mates hostage.

A.D began his walk over the deck to reach the glaring beauty standing amongst her men.

"Ello again," A.D said while strutting closer to the Saint's crew and her Captain.

Johnny, otherwise known as Spear and Arrow, halfway slid a large knife from his belt buckle and gritted his teeth.

A.D's eyes glimpsed at the knife and decided to try and put their crew at ease rather than piss them off.

"Okay… my brother Kraeno died two weeks ago from a scrap we had with demon trees… from Hell, like the one by Reykjavik Inn. If it weren't for the trees on this boat, we'd all be dead, and the world would be on its way to ruin."

The Lady Captain's chin rose for a second of compassion, then she turned on her stubborn pirate face again.

"Let go of my men then!" She shouted.

Three of her sailors were still trapped by the doodle of roots and blade-wielding Birchwoods.

"If you want us to transport you and your precious… cargo, then we'll need more, a lot more coin." She tugged at the front of her blouse as if it were hot in the middle of the Atlantic Ocean.

A.D grinned, "In good faith and hope for further agreements, we'll deliver your crewmen back." A.D backpeddled away from them a little, thinking he didn't want to get stabbed while he was yelling for Lingo.

"LinGO! Yo!"

Lingo responded with a devilish roar, "What!" Sounding uncomfortably too much like War.

"I need you over here bud," A.D said, reassuringly.

Favin cut in with a fatherly order, "Lingo."

Lingo squeezed by Afwat and slid behind A.D. He then twisted his trunk to reach for something behind him, and an old solid chest appeared with three big locks on the front. Lingo tossed it so the chest landed between A.D and the Captain, rattling with heavy coins inside.

For a second, everyone looked very confused. Their stares kind of wandered, and their legs jigged a bit more with the rock of the sea.

"Where the keys?" The Lady Captain said while looking at Lingo with inpatient yet intrigued eyes, taking full advantage of the chest filled with gold.

"Hold on. Lingo... Where are her crewmen?" A.D asked under his breath. However, everyone could still hear him loud and clear.

As Lingo shrugged, the Birchwoods fumbled around behind him, and two crewmen walked out of their grasp, cut up with blood-soaked tears in their torn-up clothes.

"Where is Red?" The Lady Captain asked. The crew looked around, curious about their Boatswain, a crew member ranked close to the ship's third mate. Lady Captain noticed the upper half of a Birchwood who held several bloody knives. She stomped across the tree roots that lay on her deck toward the whistling, nonchalant Birchwood.

The crew huddled around their Captain and peered both at Nyx's bloodied blades and the seven holes in the red-haired Boatswain's back. The silence panned out, exceeding the forbearance of the crew.

"Great! More Viking coin for the living!" The Lady Captain announced. Her crew members, half relieved not to have to fight killer trees in the middle of the Atlantic, yet half confused because they didn't; nonetheless, they cheered by their leader's side.

"Now, where's those keys?"

When Lingo's branches fanned out, they seemed to have many layers. He looked at Favin, and Favin was already looking back at him with stern approval. Large keys flew through the air from Lingo's top with a scorpion toss, smacking the chest's edge.

The Captain walked up with Johnny and had him try the three keys with the three locks for a few minutes, eventually unlocking them all and opening the chest, revealing a shining golden light that lit up the salty faces of the Saint.

"We're going to be rich!" A man in the back of the group yelled, and commotion filtered through the crowd.

Through the commotion, the Captain made the agreements.

"You got yourself a deal. My name is Captain Sharp, and this is the crew of the Saint." She smiled, "From here on, if any one of my men even gets nicked by one of those freaks, I'll pull the engine out myself and you guys will go nowhere. Best to sacrifice ourselves than have tree beasts ravage another poor town…

Tracher! Man the wheel and navigate us to the Strait of Gibraltar. Johnny, along with your duty as Quartermaster and Second Mate, you are now Boatswain too. Grab Colton and meet in the Captain's Quarters with the chest."

The Captain's Quarters was up the stairs, right below the Wheel room. Tracher, as old as he was, hopped to, and Johnny bossed Loid to take his spot moving the chest with Colton. Johnny walked by their side as they wobbled with their shoulders turned in from the weight of the golden coins. Everyone else stood still, looking bamboozled.

"Get to work, boys, and get ol' Red ready for a sea burial… Let's Go!" She yelled. 'Go' being the word that ignited the fire under their butts.

Captain Sharp turned to Favin and A.D. "I need to talk with you as well."

A.D blushed, cheek scars turned pinker, and he started his float towards the stairs.

"Not you Hun. You," Captain Sharp nodded at Favin and then turned to follow Johnny, Loid, and Colton.

****

The door into Captain Sharp's Quarters was very small and had a golden knob. The doorknob reminded Sharp to continue to open doors to her dreams. It also gave a homey flair, showing the true virtue of the vessel's being.

Inside lay a fat wooden table, bolted to the ground through a red and gold-trimmed carpet. The chest sat crooked in the left corner, embellishing a tapestry depicting a ship slanted on clean desert sand with a red sunset behind it. The fabrics, pens, and crossed sword hilts were all red and gold. Vintage and tattered worn maps sprawled out on the table.

Captain Sharp rounded the table to face Favin. Johnny and Colton, stood at the left side of the room, arms crossed, listening in and on guard. Sharp smiled, "So –."

The little Indiana Jones monkey swung itself from under the table to the top of it and made a monkey sound to Sharp, "eh oh eh eh." Sharp tilted her eyebrow at him and then the monkey hopped up onto her shoulder.

"Get off of me, you." She rasped, staring at him with her frozen lake eyes. He jumped down and propped himself up onto Spear and Arrow's tattooed arms, crossing his own in resemblance.

"Where did he come from?" Sharp asked Favin.

"I have no idea, Miss." Favin's tone was melancholy yet soft, like he breathed out the words, obviously still distorted from Kraeno's death.

Sharp gave one last sneer at the monkey and went back to the arrangements on the table.

"We are here." Sharp placed a yellow-haired figurine of a woman in a red robe just south of Iceland. She then dragged her index finger from the figurine to Ireland.

"We need to stop here to pick up a shipment, and I want your wooden friends to help us."

"Our route…" Favin ran his finger from Iceland, under Spain, and to Crete. "Stays the same." Favin looked at Sharp, impatient with bargaining. Her black coat had one button buttoned at her diaphragm. She wore a purple tank underneath that pressed against her breasts, pushing them up and revealing themselves in the crest of her coat. Her tanned skin darkened as it rose up to her chin. She had a sharp and petite nose with a nose ring. Her eyes were blue with a ring on her brow, and her ears also had piercings and rings, surrounded by dark hair.

"This shipment is important… for both of us." Captain Sharp said persuasively.

Favin shifted his patched-up, multi-colored coat behind his back, about to say something, however, Captain Sharp cut in. "I'll give you ten percent of the package, considering you have fewer men to provide for."

"What is it?" Finally piquing Favin's curiosity.

"It's guns, and this is how we are going to get them." Captain Sharp and Favin went over the plans all night, sustained by cherry pie and iced rum.

A Dream Come True

Tumbling, tumbling, and more tumbling, like a freaking whirlwind through cold space. I had the sensation that breath didn't come easily through hyperspace. I was a floating essence where air didn't matter. It's the weirdest claustrophobia in the universe. Tight but open. Restricted but free. Chilled, however, warm with excitement.

My vision rotated around and around. I went into a streamline position not to make myself puke. A needle-nose dive into the void. My path was a steady zigzag through the stars, on the fast track to nowhere.

Galaxies went by, and stars in the distance took every color and every size. I've been here before, in our family's collective dream with a piece of bark floating through space. A mark of our legacy, a dream I couldn't shake, only to be woken by a gigantic fart, baked. But this was real. I could think about wiggling my toes, and they actually did. This was no dream. I remember. I remember that damn demon that finished my ass.

I blasted by a sun, blue as the night's ocean, and felt nothing. The lighter blue solar flares arched and retracted onto my surrounding encapsulation, which acted as a protective high-speed tunnel.

The name solar flare made much more sense now. The solar flares look as if souls were streaming out of the burning orb, a nexus of power that gives life.

Past the grasping sun, a galaxy unlike any other lay ahead. Gooey darkness made up its galactic core while a halo of light began to spiral out to a pleasant outer rim. The core leaking darkness into the surrounding suns and planets.

My cylindrical space tunnel slowed when I approached the outer rim of stars carrying an aura of pure light and brightness. I felt at ease, I made it to Heaven, I did it guys. This was awesome. I could almost feel the warm breasts of sexy, angelic women. I should have died earlier. I wondered what came first, that dark bulge at its core or this holy halo surrounding the perimeter of an entire galaxy.

Suddenly, my tunnel shifted down, orbiting under this massive heavenly planet with white towers peeking out of its clouds. The clouds were so puffy. I nudged my body toward them, trying to break free from this encapsulating wormhole. Nothing worked; I drifted on my back, only to watch the world fade away.

Sluggishly disheartened, I turned around to streamline through space on my stomach, then boom, a jagged and lengthy asteroid was right in front of me. I looked along the span of the rock and saw one end that resembled a tail and the other a head with broken worlds as ears or horns. My tunnel drove straight into its midsection. What the hell was this cratered monstrosity!

At the last moment before impact, it shifted up, causing my tunnel to skim the ruined worlds of its skin. The tunnel shifted around one space dragon and into the mouth of another. I recognized the mythological beast because its bearded face opened wide to gobble me up… What happened to the angel boobies?

****

After a while, I stayed locked in the mouth of the dragon, immobile because of the shard-like tooth stuck through my thigh. There were hundreds of imprisoning black pointed edges and little shard-like teeth, barring my view to outer space. As my imagination caught up with reality the dragon's rock tongue lapped me up off the shard and sneezed me out to descend into a dust storm atmosphere, free falling into nothing but a brown hurricane.

Some of the dirty clouds slowly began to dissipate, revealing patches of an odd terrain ahead of me. Lava pits and black desert sand were what I puzzled together.

Pissed and regretful that I didn't become a priest back on Earth, I giggled.

My fresh hatred and anger from being killed and overcome by Hell on Earth birthed blind revenge as I fell closer to the scorching hot planet with lakes of bubbling magma. Dropping in the dusty wind,

I could see my target, an island surrounded by lava. I tried to swim through the air to at least drop onto the mainland of black desert sand, but eventually, I gave up. I'd probably die, or at least die again, from the fall.

Watching the world approach, I thought of Earth and all of its natural green and blue beauty. Lava exploded to my left, and the air quickened around my ears. The ground enveloped the sky, SMACK.

****

I woke up in more pain than I could have ever imagined. Pain you only thought of feeling when being chewed by a mountain lion or being cut up in one of those torture horror movies. I guess falling from space and landing on an island surrounded by lava would do some scary physiological damage as well. I thought it would be quick, but it was not. I couldn't die and felt that I never would. I was a puddle of pain. The heat melted my face while I laid there broken, thinking three words over and over again: What The Fuck?

****

The world darkened into twilight, and my agony lingered, turning my eyes into the back of my head. Blind and dumb, only able to hear my moans and the pop of boiling lava, I slid my broken fingers into the soft cracks of the hardened lava island, unable to grasp or clench, but it was enough to drag my body near the edge, inch by inch.

I slid up, pulling my body to hand, and then stretched it out again, repeat. Second by second, the heat singed my skin, causing me to believe that my hair and back were engulfed in flames. My twenty-third slide forward, and my eyes popped, and organs started to burst.

The next time I stretched my arm forward I dropped my hand into this gooey almost cooling exposure. I've reached the pool in 210-degree weather. I turned and rolled right in, cleansed, free of agonizing pain, just a burning chill that slipped the agony away. This was it…

Surprisingly, this wasn't it. Still conscious, I slipped into a dreamstate and then breaststroked forward, again and again, feeling faster, like the lava ran right through me. I was enjoying the submergence. I must have been in the after afterlife. A ghost floating through whatever I may please. Yeah, that was probably it, I'm a ghost. Yet, my body skidded along the shallower floor of the lava pit and eventually I rose out, feeling hollow, naked, and enchanted with a barrier of power. I looked down at my forearms and saw bleached white bones. My legs were a stark chill, my hips, my spine.

I felt great. Guess I got rid of my baggage. My bony toes wiggled through the black sand. No more fear, just a tingle of bliss. No more time, just a walk towards destiny. No more ambitions… however, glory rang in my hollows. I'm a boundless boned bruiser bewildered by what Hell had in store for me.

The Skeleton Crew

The black sand of the desert shifted to hard-packed dirt. In the barren flatlands, an outpost sat alone as Kraeno decided to walk through the abandoned gate and follow the music.

Electronic jazz music came from a wobbly dinosaur-looking thing rocking its head this way and that, jamming on the keyboard. Five other men sat around casually drinking out of their mugs and skull caps. The outpost was mostly just pieces of a large gate surrounding a bar which seemed to only have three kinds of liquor.

A man with a heavy metal gauntlet lying on the table in front of him sipped his cup leisurely. His eyes looked down and his head rotated to the side as if his ears were trying to pick up something interesting the others were saying while they sat at the bar.

One basic trucker looking fella rested his fat arm on his leather padded knee, snickering insanely at the other porky creature talking.

"I'd never try it again!" The pig face said with a snort.

"Dawsen, I'm not kidding, skeletons come from the pits, and you can't just shred a body of its flesh and hope its skeleton will dance to your tune. Trust me, it didn't work then, and it won't–."

Dawsen grabbed the guy's arm, pulled him close, and flicked out his knife. "Let's see how far we can get… hmmm? I'd love me sim bacon." Dawsen's hatchet face smiled and moved towards his first cut.

"WAIT! Dawsen! Try it on someone else. Wait!" The fella moved his arm back trying to break free, but Dawsen only squeezed tighter and pulled him in again.

Suddenly, another man, miniature in size and consciously looking away from the skinning, coughed to announce a new arrival, "Look," he said with his screechy voice.

Everyone looked out into the desert; there were no walls, just an overhang to block the suns. A mirage of a body with white stripes appeared to be walking into the outpost.

"It's a skeleton man! We pick him up and turn him in, and we'll get a good ration of luster fruits. I'll be rich for at leas-." The miniature man was squished on the bar top by a heavy metal gauntlet.

Dawsen pulled his knife back and received a slash through the belly and was kicked through the overhang beam into the dirt. The overhang creaked for a second and then crashed down in front of the bar. The guy pleading to be saved from a skinning ran away in the direction of the skeleton, leaving his motorcycle and beer mug behind.

The bartender stared at the man with one huge gauntlet and two curved blades slung out and dripping with blood. The man put his foot on skinner's chest and sawed off his head, watching the light in his eyes die out. After the head was separated, the man cleaned off his blades and put them into their sheathes. One hilt was made larger for a correct handle when using the metal gauntlet.

The skeleton walked up to the bar. "Ohhh, dead bodies... I'm not surprised to see those in Hell." He turned from looking at the decapitation and asked the bartender, "What'da you have that'll get an ol' bag a bones a good ol' buzz?"

The bartender stared with tilted eyes and stubby ears.

"What, you've never seen a skeleton before? What are you some kind of boniest? I'll have my buddy here chop you up, bro."

The skeleton looked at the gauntleted soldier who was now opening a flask and pouring greenish paste onto the hatchet faced man's head. The skin, brains, and blood incinerated. He picked the skull up with his gauntlet, turned it upside down, broke the jaw off, and cracked it onto the bar.

"Another." He said confidently and without menace.

"You know you remind me a lot of a legendary warrior named Lancelot. He was a fable, but still."

The skeleton looked back at the bartender. "Hey, while you're pouring, pour me one too, you dumb Frankenstein looking bastard."

"How long have you been dead?" He asked, running his gauntleted finger around the inside of his skull bowl while waiting for his liquor.

"Not sure. I was dropped on this planet and have been walking the black sand for twelve nights. You're the first Hell people I've seen… How long have you been cashed?"

"Nine hundred years... And I haven't met anyone who's known that name in a long time."

The skeleton's electric mind worked this over, tinkering with the possibility, age, name, appearance… Oh, and acknowledgment.

"You're freaking Lancelot, wow! The stories were true!"

Lancelot took a swig from his skull and slid it over to the skeleton. "Yes, that is me."

The skeleton drank out of what appeared to be a clone of himself. The liquor dribbled down his spine, down his bones, and into the mixed puddles of blood on the floor. He looked up, disheartened by the drink's non-existent effects on him.

Lancelot put his regular hand over the skeleton's shoulder. "Let's get you over to the Skeleton Crew; they'll take care of you."

The skeleton's hollow sockets shone with hope. He looked down and pulled a dirty blue sash and a torn brown vest from the headless double dead guy.

"I'm ready when you are Lancelot," smiling with all of his teeth.

He peered down again. "These guys must have pissed you off good." The souls began to escape their bodies and drift around aimlessly.

"What's your name kid?"

"Name's Kraeno, soon to be, Kraeno, Slayer of Demon Lords, Rude and Reckless Bud of Earth."

"HAHA! There's a demon lord in the next town over, maybe we'll stop by and see her."

Kraeno looked down again, searching for something. He picked up an axe from underneath the double dead body. Kraeno slammed the axe into the bar. Exhilarated, he took another swing, smashing the bar in half and toppling over the bartender. The skeleton of Kraeno stood on the ruined bar and swung his axe down onto the indifferent bartender's head.

The dino-pianist still played his tunes as Kraeno and Lancelot walked away.

"Why'd you do that?" Lancelot asked curiously.

"He heard us talking about killing a demon lord. This way no one will know we're coming."

Lancelot smiled and continued on walking, liking the company of his new companion.

A loud groan came from inside the bar, along with a couple of smashed bottles hitting the floor. Kraeno and Lancelot both looked back.

"Forgot to tell you, Kraeno. Bartenders are very hard to take out. Best to grab these bikes and ride out of here, or he'll catch up with us."

As they rode out of the outpost gate a growing giant rose up behind them.

Bartenders are monstrosities. Check.

****

Bottles crashed and splashed inside a tavern overlooking a large pond of bodies and weird short-beaked ducks. The clattering banter inside amplified anytime the front door swung open. The day was red, and the purple fog hung low, hiding the upper half of the tavern's top floor.

Kraeno ran his bony finger on the curve of his axe blade at his hip as they came to a pause before the entrance. His blue sash turned into a blue bandana. He lost the brown vest, wore tan raggedy shorts, and carried two golden hatchets that were strapped to his ribs ambiguously. Lancelot stood by his side, right arm gauntleted and swords strapped to his back.

"Shall we, Kraeno, Slayer of Demon Lords?"

Kraeno strutted toward the door as Lancelot watched, waiting shortly till he followed behind.

The door opened, and there stood a skeleton among skeletons. The clattering died down, the mugs ceased to clink, and all jokes came to a halt.

Lancelot squeezed by Kraeno into the entrance of the doorway, and a dozen daggers were pulled. They rushed him, thirsty for blood. Once the closest skeleton was right in front of Lancelot, Lancelot's gauntleted hand grabbed its dagger arm and snapped it in two.

Golden Axes unbuckled. Skulls cracked. Split bones rattled on the ground. White stripes flooded the entrance, and a flurry of daggers caught wind. Sparks came from steel to steel frenzy whirlwinds. Boots and bones skid in the hard-packed dirt. Skeletons pushed outside. Golden curves. Fractured spines. Snaps. Breaks. Gauntlets gone bowling.

A giant skeleton, fifteen feet tall, bossed his way through the crowd. He simply swept his arms to clear a path. There was no pause in the giant's step when he suddenly manifested in front of Kraeno. Kraeno looked up, and his gaze reached the giant skeleton's chest by the time he was choke-slammed into the dirt. The giant fell on Kraeno with his knee, locking him in place and shattering his ribs. The sight of them snapping gave the Skeleton Crew a reason to laugh and cheer again.

Lancelot lunged after the crouching giant only to be swiftly stopped by a quick dagger pointed beneath his chin.

The dagger stayed while the compilation of bones moved into view. This skeleton had a long kilt, holey brown boots, and thin red leather strips wrapped around his shoulders.

"Before we kill you, let's see why your guts told you to walk into the Skeleton Crew's Stoop."

Behind them the bar had bones nailed into letters on a long piece of plywood, *The Stoop*, trailed by a skull and crossbones.

The giant picked up both intruders and held them up like damp towels.

The kilt-wearing skeleton walked around them and started talking with a loud and commanding voice.

"Brother Skel, I know why you have come to Dinsee, the House of Bones, but why do you carry Demon Lord Melcruso's golden hatchets?" He asked with intrigue and curiosity.

"And why, my dear brother, have you brought a soldier of blood with you?"

A smirk came but vanished in a second.

"I recently came from the lava pits. The man by my side showed me to your… Stoop. We killed Lord Melcruso and her spawn to show our dedication." Kraeno reported in a strict monotone voice.

"Dedication eh? Did you bring their bones?" The skeleton leader asked.

Kraeno shook his head.

"Well, if you had, that would have shown... dedication... You, brother, I can see right through-" The leader and his crew of skeletons laughed.

"You have recently been killed by a demon on your home planet, and now you seek revenge. You and your friend here must be pretty good to finish off 'our' Lord Melcruso."

Kraeno's high cheeks drooped, surprised in their alliance, and instantly regretful of his assault.

"Whitey! Bring your lads and ride to Melcruso's castle. We need to find out if they know about our assailants. Hood up."

"Aye, Aye, Captain."

The leader turned his eyes on Kraeno and Lancelot. "You may have created problems for us youngling, but we do have use for you. Your fleshy on the other hand, will have to die."

Laughter and cheer came again from his crew. Lancelot clenched his jaw and looked down at his feet, still dangling in the air.

"Sir... Skel, this fleshy can wreak havoc. I believe keeping him will be more beneficial to you." Kraeno exasperated, which shocked himself.

Why the hell should I care... Freaking Lancelot that's why!

The leader motioned his giant to lower Kraeno so as to be eye to eye with him. He stared violently into Kraeno's hollows. Then turned, slid out his dagger, and stuck Lancelot right in the side. The Skeleton Crew behind him cheered again! Yee-Haws and clattering roared through the crowd.

"If his double dead soul doesn't leak out of him, I want him cloaked and hooded at all times. You are in charge of him brother." The leader said, while gritting his teeth. He motioned the giant to set both of them down.

"I am your leader, Max, and this is the Skeleton Crew."

Five cloaked riders raced north on their motorcycles covered in bones and skulls. Kraeno and Lancelot looked at each other, and

Lancelot giggled, blood trickling out of side of his mouth.

****

As soon as the crew went back into the Stoop, Kraeno went looking for clothing to drape over Lancelot, lying wounded where Max had left him. Under the orange sky, the desert ground was barren, vast, and empty. A tumbleweed rolled into Kraeno's bare bones. There wasn't one broken or unconscious skeleton to strip their cloth. After all that fighting, not one lay defeated.

Kraeno wondered if any children were sent to Hell. Tough place to grow up. Stacked on everything else, the place was a furnace. Kraeno instantly remembered the pond behind the Stoop. A great place to cool off, especially if it wasn't filled with double dead bodies. Or maybe that's how people cooled off here. Feign death, jump in, and get away from it all.

He hobbled over to the pond. His cracked ribs made the rest of him hunch. Kraeno grabbed the tallest humanoid and flipped her around. Her breasts were the only thing spared from decomposing. He cringed at her wide face; half bone half flesh, and began removing her cloak. He kicked her body, and it flopped back over to drown in the pond. *Faker.*

He hobbled back over to Lancelot.

Swamp grime covered the cloak sleeves, and the hood still had a bundle of blond hairs. Leftover skin residue from rot lined the inside. Kraeno held it out to Lancelot.

"You shouldn't have…" Lancelot paused to rearrange his stabbed body to produce a groaning voice. "Rinsed it off, did ya?"

Kraeno dropped the cloak by his skeleton feet and started to drag it through the dirt with his heel. He then knelt down and rubbed dirt on every part that seemed like the dead still resided.

"May it be as good to you as it was to her," Kraeno smiled and nodded towards the Stoop. It always looked like he had shades on because of his narrow hollows and the skeletal cracks around his temples.

Kraeno grabbed Lancelot's gauntleted hand to lift him to his feet. Skeleton fingers wrapping around steel tendons. Once he was up, Kraeno slung the cloak over Lancelot's shoulders and ensured the hood came forward enough that his face was veiled in darkness.

During the fight at Melcruso's castle, Kraeno and Lancelot fought back-to-back, slinging blades over each other's shoulders. After cutting down her flying, spiked-winged warriors, the two of them picked up the fallen enemies' spears and flung them at the next flying assailants, all while blocking, parrying, and dodging the poison that was shot out from Melcruso's pistols, tubed up to her veins. She was a fat demon bitch who was infatuated with skinny bridges leading up to her main fortress hall. With no escape, she died by a spinning axe to her face.

When Kraeno and Lancelot fled, shimmering shields lay on her stone floor, still melting away from her acidic poison. They littered the rocky hall like her double dead warriors, wings sprawled and piled in heaps. The siege was an unexpected rush led by a conjuring of a happy new companionship. The fact that Kraeno and Lancelot survived through it together bonded the two like brothers.

Kraeno remembered reading about the heroic Lancelot when he was younger. It was like a dream come true, fighting by his side.

Kraeno watched Lancelot tug on his gauntlet. I know why I want him around, but why would he go through so much trouble just for a mercenary reward for finding me… and turns out the reward was nothing but a dagger in the gut.

"Lancelot, why are you here, in the belly of the beast? It makes no sense."

"In this hell, an adventure only lies where death is rampant. I am an Adventurer."

"There has to be another reason." Kraeno started walking to the Stoop, his words trailing behind him.

Lancelot whispered, "There is, but that is for another time." They both hobbled up to the bone layered door of the Stoop.

Heavy guitar riffs and a groovy bass flexed the wooden panels of their decrepit hangout. Lancelot adjusted his cloak so that the hood still hung low over his face, but the rest of the cloak lined his spine for access to his swords crossing his back. Kraeno looked at his bare shoulders and arms. "Your skin…"

Lancelot continued to look at the door.

"Here, fear is the only thing that will kill you. I wouldn't last a second if I walked in fully cloaked, but I may last a minute like this." He opened the door and walked in, B lining straight to the bar.

The barkeep looked at them, the left side of his skull was crushed in and ruined. He handed Kraeno a red bundle of bandages, thunked two mugs on the tabletop, and proceeded to fill them with purple sludge. Every now and then a skeleton mate would come by, 'Welcome Skel' and 'glad to have yous matey.'

The two newcomers looked at ease and drank their mugs in a watchful silence.

****

The Five riders busted through the doorway. The music died down, and Max stalked through the crowd to meet them. He was a shorter skeleton compared to the rest of the crew, but even so, his presence exemplified an entirely beloved leader, shoulders wrapped in spiraled red leather strips, and his finely woven kilt still around his waist.

Max looked at his five fully clothed riders, "What's it looking like?"

"Well boss, it looks like Melcruso's castle is in chaos. Half her soldiers are dead, and the other half deserted the place, fearful that the Skeleton Crew will come back and finish them off." Whitey responded, turning his head toward Kraeno and Lancelot as he finished his sentence.

"Looks like we lost our winged allies, but times are changing and there's nothing we can do about it now… Doomali needs the Skeleton Crew again boys, so we will ride off to Plaztex at dusk. Doom wants us to recruit for his little possession scheme."

Max finished up his speech, grabbed Kraeno and Lancelot, and walked with them out back to the pond alongside the lengthy and low bone bikes.

"How do you feel, lad?"

"Great. Actually, all healed up. Well, except for the smashed ribs, but they are feeling a lot better. What was in that drink?"

"That's what all Dyathsakians are fighting for, the Brekinvale Luster. We water it down a little, of course, because it's so scarce, but it's really the only thing that soaks into our bones and feels like we're taking something in. It has this magical bond of healing…"

Max curled his bone index finger twice for us to come closer.

"And it also has the ability to release your soul into the universe, which in fact lets demons bond to other entities in different galaxies. Angels and Demons both do this. It's the ultimate drug and the ultimate weapon to shake the balance between Heaven and Hell."

Kraeno thought more intensely about himself and his skeleton form. All he had were these bones and some kind of essence that made him, him. His mind and soul ran throughout his bone marrow and his sight flexed outward, up and up and up, until-.

Max clacked Kraeno on the side of the head with his fist, and Kraeno's hollow stare turned into a heated gaze for a split second, his mouth tilted up to the corner, lifting his cheekbone.

"Don't go off to Lala land, Fella. There are many ways to use the Brekinvale, and just drinking my diluted version isn't going to get you home, Bub."

Kraeno shook with chills running down his spine; he felt good, really good, almost like he had his body again. Home…

Max looked Lancelot up and down and then reverted his attention to Kraeno.

"I'll call you Nopey, and you know why you're Nopey? It's because you didn't listen to me when I said cover this flesh bag up, you damned scallywag. Plus, you look dopey with that blue bandana. Why don't you fold it up so we can see that fresh skull cap of yours?"

Max's giant walked outside, to which Max paid no mind; busy signaling Kraeno on how to fold and tie a bandana.

"And you." Max looked at Lancelot. "The only reason you're not skinned is because you remind me of an old warrior my father always blabbed about; a man that would punch first and slash later. So, I'll call you Lance. Stay mostly covered until the crew gets used to you. You guys get a little leeway because you took down Melcruso's castle."

Lancelot looked at Kraeno mischievously, but Kraeno was too focused on making his little folds, so Lance looked back at Max with a stagnant serious gaze.

"Now, we have all night to build you guys a couple bone bikes. But first we needs the bone baby bone." Max smiled at one of his skel mates next to him.

"By the way, how'd you get past Melcruso's bridge guards?"

Kraeno looked up after he made the final tie on his blue bandana. "Lancelot took two shields and bashed his way up the bridge. It was easy."

Max clicked his teeth together in a laugh of sorts. "Ahh, it is Lancelot, I'd be damned. Pick one of these bikes. We're off to the Hellhound Den. Nopey, you ride with me."

****

Max, Soap the Giant, Patches, Lancelot, and Kraeno, all raced North in the red desert, cloaks flapping with their speed. Lancelot rode hunched over, like he was tired or wounded, but the look fit him. The others had their skeletal palms on their knees or just slumped forward, arms hung in front of them like apes. The one named Patches had a lengthy chain wrapped around his body, heavy as it looked, it still seemed he was enjoying his ride.

Kraeno kept looking down at Max's bike, wondering what kind of beast they got the bones from. The rib cage must have been gigantic, teeth lining the frame were as long as his shins, horns crossed in front of the handlebars, and a spiky spine twisted into a spiral bordering his exhaust, expelling clean white smoke.

Kraeno imagined that nostalgic wonderful smell of exhaust, yet the only senses he had now were shaded vision and stark hearing.

Max finally drifted to a stop and got off the bike. He turned around to Kraeno.

"Listen up," the others arrived and began dismounting.

"We," Max insinuated the lot of them except for Kraeno, moving his hand in a semi-circle while his finger pointed towards the sky.

"Our pulling the pack away and taking them on a good 'ol chase." The skeletons giggled with excitement at that.

"And you, Nopey, are going to be left at the Den." Everyone looked at Kraeno, searching for fear, wondering if he had what it took.

"There are usually only one or two left at the Den. Kill 'em and be ready for Patches and Soap to come by for the pick-up. You ready?"

Everyone agreed in their own way. Soap grunted, Patches said,

"Aye Aye Cap," Lancelot just looked out in front of himself, and Kraeno made sure his golden hatchets were buckled, then unbuckled his battle axe from his back and wacked the long hilt into his palm.

"Okay, let the hunt begin," Max roused while jumping back on his bike.

The crew roared towards the entrance of a large canyon. The other Dyathsake worlds twinkled in the black sky, lighting up the desert floor and turning the red dirt into a deep purple. Approaching the canyon, the cliffs were steep and curved like a wave curling over.

Just before the entrance, Max started fishtailing the backside of his bike, creating copious amounts of purple dust.

"Get off here! And remember don't let them crush your skull! Or you'll be a goner!" Max slid to the side, not stopping exactly but slowing down, and Kraeno popped right off and landed on the purple dirt in a roll.

The others were kicking up a lot of dirt as well, so Kraeno simply stood there in a cloud of purple dust, holding his axe with both hands, and listened to the bikes rev off into the canyon.

A moment later, he heard a multitude of mountainous bellows. He always thought he could imagine what a Hellhound looked like, but at this moment if he had an ass he would have shit all over himself. The sound of their roars eliminated the rumble of the Skeleton Crew's motors completely. Kraeno backpeddled, trying to stay hidden in the cloud for as long as possible, and heard the skittering of sharp claws on rocks chasing after a small buzz in the wind.

The cloud finally dissipated.

There, two football fields away from him, were two snarling Hellhounds slowly stalking forward with a comfortable perception of an easy kill and a pile of bones to gnaw on. They looked wet and covered in fleshy ooze. Their eyes were slits, teeth half as long as their legs, pointy ears, and spikes that popped out of their spine and casually rolling shoulders.

Kraeno lifted his axe, testing its weight, and placed the blade to his side, ready to slash. The Hellhounds began to gallop towards him, and then the gallop turned to a sprint. Before he knew it, they were thirty yards away.

Swing now. Fast.

Kraeno swung, his skeleton body was so slender compared to his battle axe it lifted him into the air; however, he nailed the curved blade right across the first Hellhound's mouth and ear. As the Hound fell it tackled Kraeno, tumbling them down into the dirt like a cartoon cat fight.

The other Hound pranced around, strafing the scuffle. As soon as Kraeno came to a crouch, the second Hound lunged at his shoulder, almost enveloping him completely in its jaws.

Kraeno was now stuck in the mouth of a Hellhound with his battle axe preventing its ultimate crunch. He desperately unbuckled his hatchets and chopped at the Hound's muzzle. The Hound grew angry and pressed down further on his battle axe. Then, he started to try to rearrange it like you would a vertical toothpick. Seeing his chance he pushed away of the Hellhound's mouth, ripped the battle axe out, spun, and slammed the blade right in between the thing's eyes.

Kraeno looked down at his diaphragm and saw teeth marks and scratches all the way down to his toes. A rib or two was turned inward and a couple more were broken in half.

"I need some more of that dri-" Smack! It was like a demolition boulder swinging through to obliterate him.

Kraeno's bones acted as a skimboard for the third unexpected Hellhound, while it clenched down onto his arm until it clipped off.

He felt good about it. He felt good about being alive even after death. What a time, he thought, as the Hound tugged at his spine.

A slight buzz was heard beyond the Hound's gurgling teeth while it thumped Kraeno into the dirt. He was lifted up again, but this time, instead of another bash into the dirt, he and the Hound flew, gliding in the gentle breeze. Then crash, they slammed into the ground, and he was released, given a short break to barely rise to his knees.

Without his bandana or any other rugged clothes, Kraeno's bare bones were picked up by Soap and dumped onto his lap. While shifting into higher gears, Kraeno looked out into the desert and saw Patches riding like a gorilla with a chain wrapped around the Hound's neck, which was attached to his seat and made of humanoid skulls.

The chain drug through the dirt with a Hellhound howling and clawing its links.

Patches and Soap rode side-by-side, bouncing the two Hellhounds behind them. Soap's was completely dead, with the desert floor tearing apart its skin. Patches' Hound on the other hand, snapped its teeth when it bounced on the speedy ground, eyes staring flatly, still alive, waiting.

****

Max and Lancelot rumbled into the lot behind the Stoop and parked their bikes by the pond. A heavy pole stuck out of the ground with a chain tied to it, and the other end around the Hound's neck, giving it a perimeter to stalk and hate everything near it. The Hound eagerly roamed the open circle it was imprisoned in.

"This one almost finished Nopey. Would have if I hadn't hooked him and took him for a ride. Yee-Haw BABY! I'm surprised the Hound hasn't ghosted yet. He's really starting to look like one of us." Patches chuckled, still watching the Hound snarl. Its shoulder was skinned to the bone and looked completely torn apart. Bone to raw flesh, to bared teeth, diagnosing it as a Skelborg, or simply a Hell-hound way ahead of his pack.

"I've never seen anything like it. Stubborn bugger, in't he?" Max hypnotically stated.

Lancelot walked over to Kraeno, who was sitting in the dirt. Kraeno lifted up his only arm so Lancelot could hoist him up.

"There you are. You look broken."

"The Doc said it's nothing that can't be fixed," Kraeno responded with a smirk. He later pointed over to the Hellhound, which had become a large attraction for the Skeleton Crew. Lancelot put a shoulder under Kraeno's unbelievably heavy bones, taking him over to the Hound. Kraeno nodded at Lancelot once they got closer, letting him know it was okay to let him go.

Kraeno and the Hellhound stood there looking at each other. The serenity of the moment drew Kraeno closer to the beast. The Hound's body showed calm and rejuvenated; its eyes, however, flicked fire.

"I'd stay back mate. He hasn't forgiven just yet." Patches joshed.

The other skeletons cheered and boasted, yet this was all muffled to Kraeno. He extended his arm and broke his cautionary stance to seem more like a pack leader.

The flick of fire ignited in the Hellhound's eyes, and he lunged forward, biting Kraeno's hand and sweeping his paw to rip the arm from his shoulder. The Hound pounced on Kraeno and howled the howl they'd all been wanting to hear, a ferocious acquaintance of one's madness.

Even without arms, Kraeno did a quick skull-butt and somersaulted away from the Hound.

The laughter roared, but was still muffled by Kraeno's adrenaline. His attention was all on the beast.

Soap charged into the Hound's ring and checked him back enough to grab Kraeno's arm and retreat.

"Here's your arm Nopey." Soap said, in a dumb and dopey way.

"Hold on to your bones Brother, they're your only ones. We can't reattach another's bones to you. Remember that." Max reverberated this and turned his back on him.

"The Skeleton Crew is off to Plaztex, gear up!"

"Nopey, the Doc will look after you. Don'chu worry." Max paused to look at Lancelot and then back at Kraeno.

"Enjoy building your bikes."

"Alright let's ride!" The skeleton bike rev'd up and Max wheeled out into the red desert going East.

Lancelot watched Max and his crew cruise out while kneeling down next to Kraeno.

"I'm going to set out as well. The A team needs their lance at the head of the fight, plus I'm also not as injured as you are. You are a no-armed scallywag." Lancelot thumped Kraeno on the shoulder with his massive gauntlet and left.

"Hopefully they thrust that lance of theirs where the sun don't shine!" Kraeno shook his skull to the silliness of his remark and the silliness of wanting to throw his arms up in hysteria.

"Bartender!"

Pirates

While the Saints, a name the crew members liked to call themselves, began their ceremony for Red - an ironic name after being stabbed in several places by the Birchwood Nyx - Lingo and Afwat untangled the netting that carried their rugged pieces of metal Cid and the Gums had fitted for them.

A.D crouched and watched the Saints prepare a dinghy with kindling and wood; the scars that ran down the left side of his face looked pinker than usual and stuck out more in the cold. Pads jumped around on Afwat, swinging on his empty billiard and climbing up to higher branches than he ever had before.

The sway of the sea had Panda puking overboard at the stern side while Favin patted his back and watched the Saints and the Lady Captain prep their dinghy and clean up their mate. The monkey was pressing down on Johnny Spear and Arrow's right ear while Spear and Arrow fiercely watched Nyx the Birchwood, who cared not a tinge and glared back while sliding his blades back and forth together.

The body of Red was placed delicately on the wood-filled dinghy. Captain Sharp pulled two golden coins out of her bosom and placed one on each of Red's eyes. The coins glistened in the sunrise, making his red bushy brows look like the fire had already started.

The crewmen hooked the dinghy to the pulley and lowered it down towards the calm morning sea.

Pads thudded down onto the deck, stomped to the nearest Saint, and softly spoke, "Doesn't he have family? A wife and kids? Shouldn't they decide what happens to him?"

A Saint with a blue hoodie marked with a diver's red circle and a white diagonal line going through it responded to Pads.

"We were his family laddie. We were his kin… until you TOOK

HIM AWAY FROM US WITH THESE ABOMINATIONS!"

Tensions dissipated, like cutting the rope to a trebuchet. All the hate exploded right then and there. The Saints charged at Pads, a few with their daggers out, and Pads stood there, still astonished at how quickly things turned around on him.

Right before a blade almost poked through Pad's bubble, Lingo slammed a piece of scrap metal in between them, knocking the dagger down and seizing the rest with a rattle of clinks.

"Stop at once!" Captain Sharp shouted, relaxing her hand from her sword hilt.

"Don't let redemption cloud your judgment; these things can kill us in a second. As far as I'm concerned, which most definitely matters, we are stuck with these trees for a reason, a greater purpose. So don't go triggering your blunder busters and get more of your family killed... Aye Aye?"

The Saints backed away from Lingo's metal shield and muttered, "Aye Cap."

The rope was retied to the trebuchet and the tension once again was nice and tight.

The monkey looked down from eating his grapes and pointed at Red's dinghy slowly floating off to sea towards the sunrise.

"Light the torch!" Captain Sharp screamed.

Her men scattered around for a second, looking for the matches and the torch. Once found they gave it to Johnny. Johnny heaved it as far as the dinghy, twenty yards out, but it missed by an inch and splashed into the water.

"You idiot! All of you!" Captain Sharp was obviously angry about the ruin of Red's ceremony.

"Tracher, turn The Saint Northeast!"

Through the helm window you could see Tracher take a drink out of Kraeno's flask and start wheeling the helm left.

Meanwhile, Lingo was handing Pads the crossbow with a gasoline wrapped bolt already locked in. Pads took it and then quickly offered it to the Captain.

After witnessing the entire fluidic teamwork between Pads and Lingo, Sharp took the crossbow, amazed at the offer, and jingled her earrings as she twisted around, aimed, "Light it," and fired the flaming bolt. The bolt flew through the salty air and lost velocity right after Red's dinghy. The crewmen looked at each other with curiosity on how the Captain would react.

The Captain tilted her chin up and squinted her eyes.

"Line her up East!" She turned around and looked up to Tracher in the helm, sounding with a tinge of saddening discouragement.

Lingo and Afwat glimmered in the sun, reflecting light in all directions because of long plates of metal strapped to their trunks and larger branches. Cid created specialized armor for both of them; Lingo being more dexterous, 'The Juggling Tree', had a lightweight, blue metal armor around his trunk which covered most of his face. His eyes showed like green emeralds in the hollow depths of his wood, and the perimeter of the rip in the armor for his mouth was decorated with a sharp curve going up; on the other corner, another sharp curve going down, like the armor gave him two long yin-yang teeth. This armor allowed his semi-bare branches complete freedom to juggle his tools, weapons, and shields around.

What blocked the Saint's daggers from Pads turned out to be a night blue Bronco hood strapped onto his long outer branch, reminding Pads of back home in Ireland when their parents were still alive.

Afwat being, 'A Forest Within A Tree' stood at the very end of the stern. Cid, there for most of the Awakened's training, knew exactly how Afwat executed his tactical guard, so she sculpted dozens of metal kite shields attached to his more flexible outer branches. The engravings on each shield told the story of his life.

After Spear and Arrow lit the dinghy with a spiraling flame bolt, the Saints dispersed and went back to their duties. Afwat pushed out Rowan's shield in the middle of all the rest, flexing his smaller leafy branches and twigs around the golden bear to hold it tight as if reminiscing his old friend's life with his own, honoring the death of his own with the death of another.

The sound of his branches and leaves rustled to the side, like a large boar dashing through brush during heavy rainfall. He pulled the shield back in and gradually started undoing his engraved story of shields. Lingo watched Afwat with pleasure, never knowing Afwat's story until then.

****

Later that night a troop of the Saints were circled around a wooden barrel playing dice. Four players rolled. Out of six dice they needed a four and one to qualify, after that the highest number won, which would be 24, four dice landing on six. The four rolling were Johnny, Pat, Stevie, and Lingo. A lantern hung outside on the wall next to them, illuminating the circle of gambling pirates, many of them lounging around amongst the roots and branches of Lingo the Juggling Oak.

Lingo knocked on the barrel with a thinner branch and threw down his wooden dice.

Five, Six, Six, One, Two, and Five. Johnny looked up at Lingo, curious if he had adaptability in the game.

Lingo kept the One and both Sixes and rolled again. Two, Six, and Six. Lingo grunted, enjoying the challenges of the game, and picked up the Two and one Six and rolled again. One and a Six. After each roll they needed to keep at least one die on the table.

Johnny and the others laughed. "You need a Four to qualify. Does luck run through your… veins Tree?" Johnny looked lost for words, still perplexed about living, talking trees.

Lingo's trunk carvings lit up with green light, and then he bent in closer, almost hovering over the barrel with creaking wood. He knocked on the barrel twice and then rolled his last die. It spun and spun, then fell on a Six.

The Saints roared; some laughed at him, and others gave more encouraging remarks for next time.

"My turn." Johnny's massive arm jostled the dice in one hand and let them fly. He rolled and rolled, eventually spilling four Sixes, a Four, and a One. Completely annihilating the other two Saints in points.

"A perfect 24!" The Monkey jumped down from Johnny's shoulder, collected the pit money, and jumped back up. Johnny took the money from the Monkey and fanned it out.

"Ahhh, yet another win. LET'S PLAY AGAIN!"

The Saints rabbled and shoved for who would take whose seat.

Johnny sat back in bliss, and Lingo withdrew, grunting all the way back to the stern, letting the rabble fade to a mellow clamor.

At the stern Afwat, Panda, Pads, Favin, and the Birchwoods hung out eating beans and rice while chatting about Sky Sisters, the Majestic Kendra in particular.

"I remember she had unique beauty that made woods choke on their life force." Afwat peered down, and his branch gradually pointed at where his heart might be. His voice boomed, for he was a long ways up.

"Rowan Bear, her guardian oak, her go-to bruiser when times got rough. He and Sister Kendra did well with weather enchantments together."

Favin set down his bean pan and spoke, even while still finishing up chewing the rest of his dinner.

"The first time we went on a journey together to the cliffs of Iceland, Rowan settled in by the cliff's edge and wisped up the cool wind from the Atlantic. His summoning skills turned into art, and his art reflected his passion. The wind curled together making a toy tornado, twisting slowly into hair, a proud bosom, and thick thighs. She was a pure queen of the sky. She hovered there, naked, as the wind tore at every crevice, finally making her complete. The wind elemental of Sister Kendra simply stared into Rowan's hollows, and then," Favin's voice broke. "Rowan sung to his Kendra night after night. In later years I would be asleep in bed and wake. When I did, I heard outside Rowan's soft but very low voice sing to his air elemental, always varying in size."

"Shaki would have loved to hear that Favin." Pads said with a smile on his face and eyes adrift.

Captain Sharp stood up at the helm tower, watching the group of wooden raiders and their allies chat and tell stories at the back of her ship. She was baffled at how much her world had changed, but she always took what was given to her with a firm hand and an open mind. This group could be the life or death of The Saints. She peered down below the spiral staircase at her men rolling dice.

And just like them, gambling runs in my blood. She thought.

The third night on the ship, Panda was mute pretty much the

entire time. His sea legs were even worse than the Awakened's. A couple of familiar Saints walked up to Panda and his crew and told them their presence was summoned by Captain Sharp. The way both of the Saint lads talked over each other and tried to finish each other's sentences could have been their dopey bone-headedness, or it seemed it could have been a trap.

"You are -," and then the other Saint would jump in, "All." Back to the other one, "expected at -"

"Cap Sharp's quarters." One crew mate looked at the other, questioning him if he said it correctly.

After the messengers left, A.D and Pads made a plan with the Birchwoods to escort them over to her quarters. When they were just about to head out, and the Birchwoods were jostling with eagerness, Favin abruptly stopped their charge.

"That's not how we walk the plank boys. This is." And Favin pointed to Panda, Pads, A.D, and went.

"Let's go, you hooligans. And don't stir up any trouble, this be a gentle course."

They followed Favin through the working crowd of Saints. Pads thought these ferry employees reminded him exactly of a movie he had seen with pirates before.

Johnny was at the base of Captain Sharp's stairs waiting for them.

"You remind me of a hostess at Princess Tea Time," Favin noted to Johnny, easily two heads taller than himself.

"You remind me of an old man." Johnny tried to keep a straight face, but it broke into a smirk.

"Come on up, the Captain is waiting."

They walked up and went through the small door into a large room with the theme of red and gold. The chest Favin gave them was still in the corner, and the map they were looking at last hadn't moved an inch.

"Hello Gentlemen." Captain Sharp said while finishing up tying her hair back into a dark bun.

"Tonight is the night that we hit the shore of Ireland… Favin, have your boys been briefed?"

"Aye."

Sharp eyed him, taking her time to ponder. Perhaps her thoughts shifted from Favin, the Saint, and her schedule to the far larger development of very bad events unraveling into much greater problems. Her eyes blinked back into the now and went on to what she was saying.

"Good, we hit the docks in three hours. Let's go over this again, load up our equipment, and we ghost in, and out of there."

Panda took a seat on the chest with the ancient Viking gold and put his head in his hands. Everyone looked at him, Johnny and the Cap, with fierce unrelenting eyes. The Sentinels, Favin, Pads, and A.D looked at him too, humorously surprised at his choice of seating.

The head honchos spent an hour in the Captain Quarters, and the rest of their time setting up tools and equipment before they reached the Ireland coastline. This was the first time both groups intermingled as one team, a stealth team to be exact, with all its irony.

Afwat and the Birchwoods were to stay on the Saint with the other crew members, while the stealth team consisting of three dinghies, one with some explosives and two demolition experts, Pat and Donny, and the other two holding Pads, A.D, Favin, Panda, Captain Sharp and Johnny Spear and Arrow.

****

The Irish coastal cliffs silhouetted by the moonlight showed up dead ahead. Captain Sharp climbed up to the helm and whispered to Tracher, "If those smaller trees get out-of-hand, tie the anchor to the urchin net, net them, and send them to the bottom of the sea."

Tracher winked his one good eye. "Aye Aye Captain."

Captain Sharp wrinkled her pierced bull ring nose to Tracher's hard rum stench.

"Backens and Safa get up here yeah!" Tracher grumbled down to the deck.

Lingo stood by Afwat and passed over all of his juggling boxes, scarves, machetes and balls, his ancient books, tomes, artifacts, arrowheads, quills, and finally, one horribly dented keg with stickers covering almost every single steel blemish. He shook aggressively to make sure there was nothing else, and one feather fluttered to the ground. He loosened up, picked up the feather from the deck, and gently placed it with Afwat on top of the dented keg.

While Afwat collected Lingo's possessions, he also set up a ropes course within his long columned trunks surrounded by heavy branches. From the top of the billiard, he tied a knotted rope to an upper branch so Pads could start exploring even higher tiers when he got back.

The dinghies were loaded and ready, just waiting for Lingo to splash into the water.

It was like a very heavy octopus with very little grace slipping into the water. The dinghies rocked vigorously for a moment, and Lingo grabbed hold of the three little boats and propelled forward with his roots, squid style.

A lighthouse in solitude placed on the most rigid cape stood tall, scanning the vast bay and edge of a seemingly infinite Ocean. In its beam of light, you could see the force of the rain coming down.

Lingo continued pushing the three dinghies towards the docks. The lighthouse flashed over the log and clutter. If anyone were to actually see them, they could respectfully be seen as driftwood.

Tracher loomed out in the distance, keeping the Saint on the fringe of the lighthouse's illuminating reach. He zigzagged the Saint when needed, leaving the anchor up just in case the Birchwoods were to become frisky. They'd shoot their urchin net at them and drop anchor so the little bastards would slide off the deck and sink into the sea.

Lingo approached a large dock with different colored shipping containers inside a barbed-wire fence. Once they hit the dock, Panda eyed out a spot to catch up on some sleep while the others sneakily tied up the dinghies and waited for the Captain. Lingo swam closer to the stone wall and the barbed-wire fence. He was the ladder, crane, and any extra muscle they needed to finish the job.

Once grouped, they all ran out of the lamp light and crouched in a shadow by the fence. Captain Sharp leveled her hand, signaling Lingo to stay put until they were ready. With her other hand, she scissored her index and middle finger, signaling Johnny to start snipping the fence with his bolt cutters. Her black coat looking very captainy this evening.

Everyone was calm, and there was no bad friction in the air. Panda even laid back on the fence and put his hands behind his head, obviously feeling much better on land.

After Johnny cut the first four feet, A.D and Pads squeezed through, then ran in different directions on the outskirts of the shipping containers. They ran with lifted knees and tippy toes, each of them holding stun guns, of which A.D zapped the air accidentally while in his covert prowess.

They needed to find the main warehouse in the middle of all the containers. The warehouse had just received a new shipment of guns, according to Captain Sharp's inside man. The Irish mob was guarding the area, but Captain Sharp needed to find out how many were there in order to know the necessary escalation of subterfuge.

Johnny was finishing up with the barbed wire while standing on Donny's back. A.D returned from around the left corner of the containers and gave a thumbs up. Pads drug a body around the right corner, his brown hair hung in wisps in front of his face. He turned around and gave a thumbs up too. Right then, Johnny cut the last of the barbed wire, and the fence rolled off in two. Favin waved Lingo to climb up.

Lingo put his larger branches over the wall and slowly rose out of the water, having the spillage attached to his branches match the noise of the rain.

Captain Sharp looked over everyone. She threw off her coat and was left with worn tight black jeans and a black long sleeve shirt. Her eyes said, remember the split. She eyed one set of them; Lingo and Johnny then nodded. She looked over at Favin and her two mates carrying the explosives, then nodded.

Lingo grabbed both ends of the split fence and crumpled them to the sides. The others pushed through and scurried past the lamp light overhead and split into two groups, left and right flank. On the right flank, Captain Sharp signaled Lingo to get low; his branches stood double the height of the shipping containers.

Suddenly Irish voices were heard, and they moved their way.

Sure something would go wrong; Captain Sharp waved Favin's team ahead. Time to switch to plan B.

"LISTEN. Lingo get ready to launch Pads and Johnny at the

guards. Can you do that?" The voices could now be heard from ten containers away. The atmosphere turned hot and urgent. Panic was on the brink. Lingo looked at Pads with his worried emerald eyes, but Pads paid no mind to the risk of the night and climbed up Lingo's trunk to his thick throwing branch. For Johnny, Lingo tilted down, allowing Johnny to adjust to being held by a living tree.

"Johnny go! We don't have time for this!" Captain Sharp ordered in a fierce whisper. Johnny huffed and lifted himself onto the branch, letting Lingo get a light grip around his torso.

The voices quieted; however, their flashlights started flooding the floor near the last container before the bend. Lingo stood five containers down, ready with human fodder. The Captain noticed the flashlight circle thicken on a container across from them.

Suddenly, an explosion thundered, echoing through the container's inner maze. Instead of the guards turning back towards the explosion they ran away from it and rounded the bend. They were in complete shock when they laid eyes on the wound-up tree, not only harnessing his most dangerous face, but also carved out with intimidating spell engravings and two wicked-looking humans ready for launch, which indeed they were. Launched.

Johnny flew through the air, trying to balance his muscular body while placing his knees ahead of him to take one guard down with a knee crash. Pads flew into the other guard like superman holding a stun gun in his power fist, the other elbow bent, hand resting on his hip, not intending to do so, but did so in his intuitive efficiency of flight.

The guards were down and the right flank group advanced forward. They could now see the warehouse. There were no more guards left, only a fat hole in the aluminum service door. The door started to rise up and Favin popped out, waving for Lingo to come quickly.

"There are two dozen crates. Way too many for our little dinghies, and we don't even have enough time to do two runs. Let alone one…" Favin looked behind him, and there were two more guards lying on the floor.

"They got a call out before we took em."

Captain Sharp was impressed with how fast Favin got the job done.

"We'll be fine, we have Lingo. Plus, the Irish Mob is efficient... but not that efficient. We'll be on board by the time they get to the docks." Captain Sharp reassured the group.

Lingo came out of the warehouse with six crates that read, RPG, RPG Rockets, M60, M60 LMG Ammo, M134, M134 Minigun Ammo.

"That's all? Grab two more crates, Lingo!" Captain Sharp demanded.

He looked weighed down already, but he turned around and came back out with eight crates. The sound of his creaking wood had Favin worried.

"Okay let's get a move on already!" A.D announced, and they left, jogging back to the docks where Panda awaited with the dinghies untied and ready for loading.

After they loaded up the first and second crates, the third crate weight put the dinghy deep into the water.

"We are going to have to swim with Lingo as he pushes the dinghies," Favin said.

When they finished loading the gun crates, they all jumped in the water. Everyone grabbed a hold of Lingo. Lingo grabbed a hold of the dinghies and started the float onward. With all the odd weight and angled resistance, they still made good time. Who would have known trees were so good at swimming?

Halfway across the bay, a black 2010 Land Rover and black 1960 Lincoln Continental pulled up to the docks. Johnny laughed at them with his other mates, Pat and Donny. Panda then sullenly pointed out the fast-approaching gunboat during their gloating.

A.D maneuvered himself to the closest dinghy and climbed inside. He picked up Johnny's bolt cutters and used their tip to pry the top off of the M60 crate. A.D looked it over, quickly trying to figure out how to put the weapon together before it was too late. He set the three parts of the weapon down in his lap and started to pry off the top of the ammo crate, and at that time, the gunship slowed down in front of them. Five armed Irish Mobsters stood on their Starboard side. At first, they were confused at what the dock thieves were riding on; a moment later, after not really giving a shit, they raised their guns in the rain.

This is the end. A.D looked back at his brother; Pad's chin dipped and bobbed into the cold Atlantic swell. Their eyes stared back at each other, conveying that it was time to be with their brother Kraeno.

A.D looked over Pad's right ear and saw Donny's mouth drop in an instant. Pads looked back up towards where the riflemen were taking aim and saw the Birchwoods soaring through the air, preparing to crash down onto the Mob's gunboat.

All that was heard after that moment were blades slashing through air and flesh as the waves crashed against the lighthouse cliff. The lighthouse flashed across the gunboat, illuminating the display of the Birchwood slaughter. Blood spilled off the side of the boat, and the night became immensely darker.

Lingo eventually swam up a little closer.

Nyx took to the railing and started a casual chat, "Can we hitch a ride back? Afwat tossed us over here." The Birchwood Nyx turned his thin trunk to glance one way and then the other. "And I forgot why."

Lingo continued on swimming. The Birchwoods dove in behind him and grabbed hold of his repetitively thrusting roots. No one said anything until they reached the Saint. Still in their near-death daze, they tried to stay as far away from the Birchwoods as possible.

****

The first weapons crate clunked on the deck of the Saint, and everyone previously on board rushed to help with the other crates. Afwat still stood at the back of the boat silhouetted from the moon behind him, a dark shadow of the Saint. His quick action of tossing the Birchwoods over to the Irish Mobster gunboat saved Captain Sharp and the Sentinels, and everyone knew it. Everyone also knew how the Birchwoods finished the job; yet the thought of thanking wood so efficient at killing humans was too much for them at the moment.

Captain Sharp jumped up on the crate that said RPGs and yelled over to Tracher at the helm.

"Tracher, head east for one hundred clicks and then turn her south." Tracher nodded through the window and then the Saint bump started to a speedy escape.

Captain Sharp looked around at her crewmen, wondering what to say next. That close to death took even her out of her regular forte.

"I want these crates in my quarters right away… Some may call what just happened 'close shaven,' well I call it a dance with the devil, and the devil never wins against Saints! We came ahead tonight, but that doesn't mean slack off. Now get to work!"

Captain Sharp stepped down off the RPG crate and turned to whisper to Favin. "We split the guns and get you to Crete within two nights, then we are history… those… things," Captain Sharp looked over Favin's shoulder at the Birchwoods looming over her crew, unpredictable and heartless. "They are too devastating. I can't take the risk any longer."

Favin nodded and watched her stomp off to her quarters located closer to the front of the Saint.

What a magnificent woman. He averted his analyzing eyes and headed towards Afwat. She needed time alone, and he needed to start planning for Crete.

A Flawless Prosecution

A Flawless Possession

Mareridt thrust her voluptuous tan breasts onto Doomali, making her cleavage become more like a dark crevice with two perfectly rounded spheres ballooning out to manifest a valley. Her tits nimbly nudged his chest as her fingers gently caressed his pointed metallic beard, the black wing on her wrist tickling Doomali's neck. She pushed away and looked into his eyes, an entrance into his black face covered with red swirly sharp curves.

"Is your demon army ready to awaken the spirits of Gaia?" Mareridt asked with a wicked scratchy voice and a cute chin down smile.

Doomali looked into her icy blue eyes, thinking only of what his name attributed to: DOOM.

"Yes, my army and I are prepared to teleport our souls to these 'treefolk' you so much admire," Doomali said with arrogance and a hint of annoyance.

Mareridt got on her tippy toes and peered over Doomali's three spiked shoulder guard. The three blind Breckinvale Luster Monks had just arrived at the gold-trimmed doorway of Doomali's barracks. Each monk stood with their head stuck on one of Doomali's shoulder spikes, or at least that's how Mareridt saw it.

Mareridt lifted her arm and clenched the air. The monks lifted off the dark stone with red indentations around their necks. They didn't struggle an inch, only hovered there indifferently.

"Look. It's the three blind mice who found my shell. I am so pleased. Now I will be able to wreak havoc on my angelic sisters as well as have a flawless image as the Queen of the World… Monks tell me of my shell. Tell me about my new self."

Mareridt babbled hysterically. The only thing keeping her spittle from flying out her mouth was her previous demeanor, imprisoned by the angelic grace of her natural being.

The monks were dropped back to the floor and sucking in wind.

"It is a warrior woman from Congo, Africa my Lady." The lead monk took deeper, recovering breaths. His hood hung over his eyes, and he calmly proceeded to tell her the news.

"We found through long meditation that this warrior woman has a ninety-nine percent success rate. Until she meets you, of course, my Lady. You'll have full possession and capability to transfer your spirit and abilities." The monk said in a sarcastic manner, tired of Mareridt's eyes filled with twinkling glory.

Doomali has never seen a larger smile on Mareridt's face.

"What do you mean success rate? You are saying-" Doomali was cut off by the hooded monk.

"Yes, her entire life she has always been right, always won, and has never been infected by a virus or sicknes-"

Doomali approached him quickly after he interrupted and lifted the monk by his throat. He gave him a tight squeeze and threw him to the far wall. He looked back at Mareridt's madness and youthful excitement.

Forgetting about the monks, Doomali congratulated her. "Well then, congratulations M."

"I'm going to need a General to settle scores for me down on land while I am in flight taking care of old rivalries."

Doomali moved to the bar and poured himself a glass of dark purple liquid. "I'll unroot my enemies wherever you aim me."

"Then, we take the brunt of the army to the Evergreen Forest in Congo. The rest of our possessors will scourge the world and create chaos for all to whimper in fear.

"At the heart of obliterating terror, that… Is where the Sky Sisters will come with the Scepter Glasir, hoping its worldly power will guard them from our plague." She laughed hysterically, eventually causing the Lord of Plaztex to shove his way through the reserved monks and exit his barracks entirely.

Crazy witch.

The Boys are Back in Town

Max and his Skeleton Crew casually rode in two columns through Plaztex's main street. Max pointed his index finger and thumb like a pistol at this raggedy, babbling lunatic shifting its way across the street, making Max swerve to the left. Whitey and Soap the giant were side by side behind Max, and as they passed Soap spun his ball and chain once and slugged the lunatic in the side of the head, leaving half his skull scattered on the red dirt and the other half stuck on the flail spikes.

Soap was drained by blood-sucking demons on his home planet, and it was a slow death they put him through. He said he would never feel clean in his skin after that, so becoming a skeleton was a blessing, lounging on his bone bike like clouds were rolling him through the desert grounds.

They rode past Doomali's bar, The Burning Christ, all peering at the door with a side glance under their deep hoods.

There was a hidden lot a couple blocks down behind a haunted shack four stories high. The Skeleton Crew dismounted from their bone bikes and waited in front of the Shack for Max's orders.

"To the Citadel. Soap, Whitey, Charlie, Boardx, Boardi, Slayadex, Stew, and Marty. Doomali wants an extra escort with his private guard to the Catacombs. The rest of you hold up here at the ghost shack or enjoy yourselves at the bar until we may need you."

The Skeleton Crew Hoo-raw'ed, and split up. Five skeletons knocked on the front door of the Shack.

"Hunnies we're hooome," and busted through the door. Screams of excitement shot out to the street. Ghost women from all over the universe swirled around the Skeletons entering the Shack like they were long-lost lovers.

As a Dyathsake ghost, you either died and floated up to the ghost transport ships, which took them to the ghost moons, or you died and stayed floating on Hell's surface, slowly becoming invisible to everyone except those who had loved them before. In this case, all the Skeleton Crew women either hung at the Stoop or stayed in this Shack, a place where they all idled and looked after each other, waiting for attention from their skeleton boys.

A majority of the Skel group went towards the bar, chattering with one another and jostling around like hot shots. One skeleton broke off from that main group, and B lined it to the closest fleshy standing beside the entrance, pulling out his saber, parrying a large broadsword, and stabbing the ripple-faced humanoid right through the side of his neck.

Lancelot watched this while waiting for Max's team to start walking down the street to the Citadel. He followed to see what was happening that required an extra guard for Doomali. Always an overseer Lancelot was.

As Max's team walked down the street, the other hell-bound humanoids, warriors, and ruffians eyeballed the skeletons meekly. Their reputation had skyrocketed from their previous mission with Doomali, as well as their supposed siege and takeover of Melcruso's Castle. The rumors going around said the Skeleton Crew rips your bones out of your body while you're still breathing and then makes your skeleton dance for you while your ghost drifts away to the ghost transport.

Everyone had uncontrollable quick glances, wanting to get a glimpse of the legendary guard but not wanting to meet their end. The walk through town seemed like an old western movie when the bad guys slowly rode through in the middle of the street.

Lancelot kept trailing the crew with his hood down low and all parts of his skin covered. No one messed with him; however, being so close to Doomali's father's Citadel, everyone still wanted to gain a reputation as a badass. They cherished the belief that they could move up ranks in Doomali's army or, at the very least, be accepted. Lancelot thought over this ambitious nature while watching an Ogre strafe, circling around a goblin with a bow and three quivers full of arrows.

Being a block away, the contest between the massive Ogre hammering away tiny little arrows, had a certain comical elegance, and behind the very small and very large gladiators, the Skeleton Crew proceeded towards the Citadel, chuckling their tail bones off at the match-up.

At the bend of the street, a house's length away from the Ogre, who repetitively charged the dodging archer, the Citadel came into view. The beauty of something so dark and evil kept Lancelot's inflexible focus. He found a thick wooden column holding up a porch's roof so he could oversee while hidden in the shadows.

An arrow blazed by his head, and he swiftly moved to the other side of the column, seemingly unworried about double death.

The Skeleton Crew made it to the front of the Citadel. Doomali's Citadel guards were equipped with their usual scythes and spiraled blades attached to their belts. The blue and yellow flags partnered with long war tapestries hung from the Citadel, darkened by the heavy Plaztex winds cast during hellacious night storms.

The wind simultaneously picked up right then, inhabited with mad migrating double-dead ghosts taking one last spin around Plaztex before catching a ride to a Ghost Moon.

The blue capes of Doomali's Citadel guard blew to the side in the haunting breeze. They stood there, taking a long moment of silence to test the Crew's patience and exert dominance.

Four of them eventually led Max's team inside, while outside the remaining two guards looked up at a massive dark cloud forming over the Citadel.

A Noble Determinant

Amongst heavy winds from the East, Kraeno carried around a machete with a disciplined face carved out of the middle of its black metal. He chopped at weird desert trees that had bark in abstract definitions and tones which seemed like bubbly muscles. He chopped along and only chunks of wood dropped to the ground, so he felt dubiously alright about it.

Kraeno collected the wood in a blanket, tied it up, and slung it over his shoulder with his left arm. His right arm was forever lost near the Hellhound den.

Things have been getting progressively better between him and the Hellhound they captured and drug back to the Stoop. Every couple of hours, Kraeno would walk into the ring with the hound chained up to the center pole. Tenth hour, bashed. Twelfth hour, bashed and thrown. Twentieth hour, thrown, bitten, and drug around the dirt like a rag doll, but every hour, Kraeno tried a new technique, a new posture. It was a tango between a beast and a chew toy.

During Kraeno's most recent attempt, the Hellhound charged at Kraeno, knocking him down once again, but this time it just lay on top of him and pretended to fall asleep. If Kraeno tried to nudge his way out from under him the 2-ton hound would half-open its eye to make sure Kraeno knew he wasn't getting away, then adjust his weight and close those devilish hollows again to sleep.

On this day, the hound seemed fully recovered. Some parts of its body now snuggled up to his bare bones but didn't heal completely over, and half flesh and half bone didn't seem to bother him. Kraeno kept thinking he would name him Fab, like Flesh and Bone, but the beast needed something more than just a name; he needed a pack, and that, Kraeno thought, could be him. A dangerous team in this new world he could now call home.

Fab was a stupid name, Kraeno thought while making a fire pit on the outside of the Hellhound's circular barrier. Guess I don't have the same flare for nicknames as our fearless leader Maxwell.

"Mr. Nopey, would you like treatment this evening?" A skeleton with a long white beard said in a regular voice but meant it to be patronizing.

"Yeah Doc, I'll need some luster for my ribs."

The hound bounced up and took three leaps to reach the fringe of its prison. It was right behind Kraeno at this point, snarling so furiously that spittle splattered over Kraeno's shoulder blades as he spoke with the Doc.

"Looks like he doesn't like your chatter, Mr. Nopey. Maybe you should try putting an end to him." Doc puffed his ribcage out at the hound, and the hound snapped his teeth back at him.

Kraeno crouched to try and block the winds that screeched with dying souls. He felt no push or residence, only a steady wind going right through him. Sometimes, he forgot that he looked like something from a Bruce Campbell movie.

Doc kicked dirt up on the fire and flicked his fingers, and blue-green flames instantly arose, pushing west with the winds.

Kraeno stood up, his blue bandana was tight around his white skull, and he wore black Arabian trousers that were puffy and ragged at the bottoms where his shins were.

"Doc, I have a bloody idea!"

"So you're going to kill the beast after all, well very good follow m-"

"No, Doc I mean the movie Army of Darkness with Bruce Campbell. He attached a weapon to his arm after he cut it off…" Kraeno smiled in nostalgia. "A Boomstick!"

"Ha, well we have plenty of broom sticks Mr. Nopey. Did you want to take up the janitorial position at the Stoop? I'm sur..."

Still in his own head, thinking about his arm's fate, Kraeno cut Doc off again.

"Listen Doc, I need a weapon that I could um, attach to my arm." Kraeno made the motion of sticking something onto the bone right below his shoulder.

"Come to the weapons closet then; I think we still have a couple of swords and things lying around."

Kraeno waited a second and watched the Doc waddle back to the Stoop. He then backed up so his heels were on the edge of the Hellhound's perimeter. The hound lunged again and again, testing the strength of the two fat chains wrapped around the pole. He settled back for a moment, quietly growling, wet muzzle centimeters away from Kraeno's spine. Kraeno turned around slowly, bent down, and looked into the hound's scarred eyes, running a color of stormy gray. The hound paused, licked his sharp teeth, and lunged again at Kraeno, who didn't budge an inch, only tilted his head forward a smidge so as to skull-tap teeth that were as long as his face. Kraeno turned back around and walked into the Stoop. The hound puffed out a bark and jaunted back to the center pole.

Inside the Stoop, skeletons still drank, laughed, and bustled around like salty sailors. Some sharpened blades, some were comedians preaching on top of tables, and others simply played casual tunes on weird instruments.

The door to the closet was open, and a lantern light was on inside. Kraeno had never been inside the weapons closet and never thought much of it, considering most of the Skeleton Crew carried around daggers and scimitars.

He walked in and saw Doc holding a giant spear with an obsidian arrowhead tip. Everything around, hanging on the walls, piled on the floor, strapped to the ceiling, was beautiful, sharp, and surprisingly much different than he imagined. Swords, axes, morning stars, katanas, hammers, guns, and more guns. It blew his mind.

"Why doesn't anybody in Hell use guns?"

"We like to do things the old way. Get close and personal. Did you know some of us have spent over a thousand years in Hell? Enchanting and cursing weapons is very popular in the Galaxy of the Dead. Most of these guns have old witchcraft attached to them. You'll pull the trigger, and it'll shoot right back at you. Funny Demon Trickery is what it is. Easier to trust a blade than handle a crazy contraption that spits fire out, who knows where."

Kraeno walked around looking at the guns and blades. Lancelot had the right idea with his heavy gauntlet. I would rather smash too, than sit at a distance.

He came across an ancient ship's cannon small enough to fit the stoop of his arm. There was also a duffel bag of cannon balls on the highest shelf; he could see the wicks and the rounded black tops peeking out of the bag. Kraeno grabbed the ladder and went up about five selves. He moved the bag of cannon balls, and a skeleton popped up from behind it.

"Hello there mate, you taking these fine cannon balls with ya?" Kraeno was still in culture shock from hanging ten in North America to falling into this bizarre Galaxy of the Dead, so he looked at the weird looking skeleton and said, "Aye."

"Well then, have you found the cannon?" The skel said in a thick Australian accent.

Kraeno looked around the room to see if there were any other slumbering skellys sleeping amongst the weaponry. "Aye."

"Ah, well you have yourself a time, ya? By the way what's your name mate?"

"Kraeno."

"Ahhh yea, Nopey, The new recruit from Sagara Lava Pits. It's a wonder how you pulled off killing Lady Melcruso. You must have been mad as hell. Hehe. But of course you were. What she do to you back in your home world?"

"I just want to kill whatever possesses my land, brother. I don't think it was her, but it doesn't matter; all big-shot demons must die in my eyes."

"Beautifully said Nopey. Let me ask you this. Do you know why you are a skelly rather than your regular fleshy, blood-bagged self?"

"Well, I landed on an island surrounded by lava. I feel like that had something to do with it."

"Yea! It does… Let me tell you a little something about the Skeleton Crew. We were all killed by a demon from 'Hell' on our home planets. They're always possessing shit they are." The Aussie closet skeleton gritted his teeth for an instant and then went back to being cheery.

Kraeno's hollows stared. If he had eyebrows, one would rise with furious curiosity.

"Yea, yea, I know. Nopey you are now with a crew of hooligans that want the same damn thing as you do. To find the source of these demonic possessions and put an end to them..." The weapon closet skeleton leaned over the bag of cannon bags and got really close to Kraeno's skull face.

"We found the bitch in charge… and we are now this close, this fucking close to killing her and every other demon scum involved."

Kraeno leaned closer too.

"Tell me who and I'll blow them to smithereens."

"It's the Togmehoian Doomali, Leader of House Plaztex, and his little witch bitch Mare-right, or however you bloody say it, from a planet in the Milky Way Galaxy."

Kraeno began to pick up the bag of cannon balls.

"Oh, Nopey, by the way, that cannon there is bewitched. It'll blow *you* to smithereens if you fire it."

Kraeno paused in thought and took the bag of cannon balls anyway.

After jumping off the ladder he picked up a Tommy gun and tilted it up to show the skeleton sitting up on the fifth shelf. He gave a thumbs up, and Kraeno loaded its ammo drums in the cannonball bag, slung it around his shoulder, and headed out.

"Doc, I got what I need. You think you have anything in your little torture chamber that could dial me in with this gun?"

"Let's go see." And Doc proceeded out with the obsidian-tipped spear he was holding earlier.

The skeleton on the fifth shelf yelled down at Kraeno. "Hey Nopey. When you're done killing all the demons on Plaztex come back to the Stoop and we'll go for a ride to the lava pits. We like to go over there with our choppers and throw the new recruits in ourselves. It's fun coming up with their nicknames that way!"

"What's your name Skel?"

"Names Max."

Kraeno nodded and started to walk out of the weapons closet with Doc.

"Another thing… don't lose any more limbs; it's a boner getting them back." Bone cackling faded behind him as the door closed.

****

Doc finished wrapping Kraeno's ribs in tape soaked in Brekinvale Luster. The tape was blue and matched his dirty blue bandana.

Kraeno lay on Doc's Mahogany-looking table and peered around the basement. There were tons of vases and jars filled with various bones. There were bone piles in each corner of the room, along with piles and piles of books. It was messy and packed with stuff that actually meant something important, which, to Kraeno, made him feel comfortable and at ease.

"I can't attach a Tommy gun to your arm," Doc said while he prepared his ratchet straps and welding gear on the table next to Kraeno. Doc created a metal helix cylinder-shaped arm that fit to Kraeno's bone stub and strapped around his shoulder. At the mechanical elbow joint, there was another set of straps for Kraeno's new blade.

Doc finished welding the tip of the obsidian spear to the tip of the black machete. He strapped three leather straps around Kraeno's new metal helix joint and three around the machete hilt.

"Now you can stab and slash bud."

He watched Kraeno flail around his sharp new arm.

Doc picked up the Tommy gun, "Why did you want this one?"
BanG bANg BANG!

The gun started firing all over the basement.

"Guess it's a hair-trigger. Sorry, Mr. Nopey, I could make a holster for your gun, but it would get in the way of pulling your battle axe from your back… I just don't see how."

"I'll just hold the gun in my left hand and drop it when I run out of ammo."

"Ahh, very methodical, Mr. Nopey, very haphazard as well, but that's just how we like it." Doc would have winked if his hollows had lids.

"Thanks Doc… I'm going to check on the beast!" Kraeno opened his mouth and gave a flat stare that seemed to darken his hollows, mimicking something terrifying. He opened the door and went upstairs to the bar. After he took a couple of steps, a wave of an out-of-body intoxication lifted him up and put time through space in a pillowed basket. He felt great, but he felt something was coming, something that burned with dread, a bundle of dread, something he had not felt in this world or his own.

A bottle flew across the room and smashed against a giant skeleton's breastplate. The skel laughed at the antics; nothing could hurt him, nothing could hurt us, but something came that could easily change this loving perception of an immortal brotherhood…

Kraeno shot outside and looked past his Hellhound to the howling winds to the East. There on the horizon was a black line silhouetted in different heights almost as if there were black flames flickering up from an earthy fire. Kraeno continued his gaze, and the black line became more defined.

He rushed back into the Stoop and glanced over his fellow skeletons, who also started to develop the sense that the atmosphere was changing; some even knew something bad was coming but still smiled at Kraeno's new machete arm.

A skeleton with curved blades attached to his shoulder pads ran past Kraeno outside. He came back within seconds.

"Turn up, *Empires Falling by Black Angels*! We have a bloody war party at our mists."

The music turned up, and the crew switched to their chaotic hustle, gathering their battle gear. Kraeno paused for a second, happy again about discovering a whole new afterlife, and continued down the stairs to where Doc was, giggling in his boyish excitement.

"Load me up Doc, we have incoming."

Doc handed him the Tommy Gun. "Go get 'em, tiger!"

Kraeno picked up his bag of cannon balls with his machete spear arm and sliced the handle right in half. He was impatiently pleased and picked up the bag of cannon balls with his Tommy gun hand instead.

He made it outside and stood to the side of the doorway. T*ruckfighters* played full blast on the outside speakers, and each skeleton stood somehow differently than the next, preparing themselves for a hellacious battle, laughing and joking with each other even more than they were when they were chilling inside the Stoop.

Five riders raced off and created a bone motorcycle circle in between the Stoop and the approaching army. The faces of the army were now visible, bodies of all shapes and sizes came at them with idiot fury soaked in rage, earlier marinated in hate.

The Hellhound watched the onward army war cry its way into Stoop territory.

Kraeno walked up to the center pole and behind the Hellhound, set down his Tommy gun, pulled out his battle axe, and started slashing at the chain tightly wrapped around the pole. The hound did a 180-degree hop into a fighting stance and glared at Kraeno while the chain rattled with every swing. Kraeno kept slugging away at the thick chain in the dense wind of dead souls. The music playing put him in focus, a celebratory tune for being in such a badass situation.

The Hellhound turned around and barked savagely at the charging army, spilling spears at the bikers to disable their circle.

The first chain on the pole snapped, and the hound's neck lurched forward. Thinking he was set free, he tugged against the chain some more, yet it wasn't enough. He needed Kraeno's help.

Kraeno watched the barbaric demon army form its crescent moon charge around the Stoop. He turned his concentration back on the chain and listened to the clash of steel on steel sting the windy air.

Four Horsemen with scythes pointed up at a perfect vertical angle were the first to clash with the skeletons. They galloped through the scattered barrier of bones with giant reaper swings and advanced, edging closer to the Hellhound circle. Behind the Horsemen, the tossed skeletons finally fell to the dirt from the quivering reaper upswings, while in front of them, there was a leaping hound restricted and ready to unleash.

Kraeno sunk his Battle Axe in the dirt, picked up his Tommy gun, and approached the hound's left flank. The two center Horsemen were only a gallop away. The gun clicked, releasing nothing but anxiety at a raging stampede of howling monsters pursuing a full-fledged genocide.

Kraeno shook off the insinuated explosion of the possibility of a cursed weapon.

At this point, the Horsemen were seconds away from driving

their scythe reapers into Kraeno and the Hellhound. Kraeno focused himself, slammed the ammo drum hard into his bony leg, put his machete arm under the barrel of the Tommy gun, and pulled the trigger. The two center Horsemen were filled with lead and thrown off their mounts.

The fire eyes of the two center horses extinguished in a blink. One of the surviving flanking Horsemen put a deep slash in the flesh side of the Hellhound's face, while the other Horsemen was lassoed with chains from a skeleton with a golden grill, shown in a crazed smile.

Kraeno looked around the circle and saw that the demon army had entirely overwhelmed the Stoop grounds. It reminded him of some kind of weird team sport in the shirts versus skins aspect, only now it was demon skins versus boner boys.

The demons and dirty heads ravaging around in a thuggish manner slowed their charge and kept their distance from the hound's circle.

Subsequent to Kraeno's spillage of Tommy gun bullets, a hatchet-faced gill lady swung a great sword at Kraeno's skull, and Kraeno had to block the massive blow with the Tommy gun, splitting it in two and expanding the crack above Kraeno's hollow. The Hellhound pounced on Lady Hatchet's face, knocking Kraeno down also, with the chain still attached to the center pole. After ripping off her arms, it pounced on another unsuspecting barbarian standing just inside the rim.

Kraeno kept swinging with one golden hatchet of Melcruso's and one machete morphed obsidian spear arm, to keep blades, teeth, and any weird sort of tentacle things from snagging him.

Close by, as a tumbleweed rolls through desert plains, a keg-bellied, narrow-eyed dude came from the East, obviously in the war party line furthest away from all the action. Lacking knowledge of the battleground and the carnage that came within the circle, he bounced right inside as the Hellhound gnawed on another dirty soldier, chain mail giving him absolutely no protection from those hell-born teeth. The keg-bellied universal specimen came at Kraeno with a large scimitar and shield. Its short snout snorted during his whole hopeful prance to fulfill a siege kill and collect the double dead's bones as a trophy.

During the keg belly's graceful climatic ambitious saunter, the Hellhound clawed him in the side and met Kraeno's stare.

"Noble!" Kraeno bellowed. It simply rolled off his tongue subconsciously, giving him and the hound more power as he yelled the name. *Noble.*

Kraeno snapped back into battle mode, buttoned his golden hatchet into the straps that crossed his chest, picked up the battle axe, and swung it at the center pole.

Dropping the battle axe at the cling sound which broke the chain and charged Kraeno's adrenaline, drenching the maniac deep within his bones, like a broken bottle at a bar turning a frat boy into a brawling terrorist. Kraeno stood there with a full pump, filling his ribs with power and incorporating a quick meditation from inhaling the hot air around him. His hollow stare moved purposefully around the battlefield, looking for a place to exert domination. He looked at the cannonball bag and reminded himself he had no fire, plus the long dead winds would put it out before touching the wicks. He then looked into Noble's gray eyes, grabbed the chain harnessing his tiger-like body, and leapt onto Noble's back.

On the back of Noble's neck was an area completely bare to the bone from the joy ride they gave him after the ol' Rookie Hunt. The bone was arched with no flesh attached, which made it a suitable saddle grab. He wrapped the chain around the arched bone for riding straps, and they took off into the thickest patch of demon barbarians who were swinging their weapons around like berserkers teaming up on his little skel buddies.

The cluster fuck was easy to tear a hole into with Noble's size, but mostly it was Noble's rage from being locked up. When he wasn't snapping his long teeth at the fleshy troop in front of him, he would turn his head and snap up, trying to whip around to bite at Kraeno. Kraeno loved the beast's murderous hate for all things that moved, and harnessed his mount's hate for his own. Kraeno chopped away with his machete arm, mostly spearing monsters in the face if he approached at a suitable angle.

The mounted team whirled around close to two other skeletons, slashing away at foes with their scimitars.

In between the pond of the double dead and the Stoop was a loud buff monster with one eye clamped shut and the other just barely visible because of his gang-affiliated bandana hanging low on his brow. He had just crushed Kraeno's neighboring skeletons with two silver hammers.

"I'm so fucking pissed right now, I'm soo fucking pissed!! You motherfuckerS!" The Minotaur-looking monster yelled and started to stomp its way toward the Stoop. Max put his first bullet in the middle of the monster's stupid bandana.

Kraeno went from watching the one-eyed monster drop to the ground to a skeleton on top of the Stoop's roof, sitting behind a turret with an extra-long barrel and a billiard of shells wrapped around him. Max, the mother fucking weapon closet hermit, was out to play.

Max shot at the bag of cannonballs. Ka-Boom!

Everything in and around the Hellhound circle obliterated or went flying.

Kraeno stabbed at a demon with wings, but it blocked his obsidian-tipped spear with its shield. *I'll call him Aussie Max. What a mate.*

Aussie Max let the turret rip through the encroaching troops of Doomali's militia army. The turret muffled the sound of the band, *TruckFighters* still blasting on the outside speakers.

The tip of the turret turned red and waved around from cluster to cluster, winged beast to winged beast. Max had his teeth crooked and at an angle, easily identifiable with a maddened rampage sprinkled with the joy of redemption.

The battle seemingly favored Doomali's troop. Skeletons were more rapidly becoming crushed or trampled on. Kraeno looked up to Aussie Max as some kind of last hope. He absorbed every particle of pain that screeched out from his bullets, which cast a sphere of influence on the Stoop morale.

Tables shift as time turns, and nothing is certain.

Kraeno cringed at his impending foresight when a large monster with a lion's snout and mane threw a boomerang at Max, chipping him so hard in the skull that he fell off balance and tumbled off the roof.

The winged demon that Kraeno was spearing at gave him a final shield bash and flew over to the turret. After two naive monkey pounds, it picked up the gun with its tripod still attached and hundreds of tight muscles rippled out of its skin while its wings heavily pressed down on the air to float higher into the sky with so much heavy weight.

The demon reached its most accurate latitudinal firing angle and then sprayed bullets through the roof, eventually causing the roof to collapse into the Stoop.

Kraeno tugged on Noble's chain in the direction of an open space. Noble followed, anxious to get away from his bare geometrical prison. They rode, zigzagging through the barbarians, monsters, and demons lunging at them for that one last thrill of a kill - a story to tell their buddies later at the pubs.

The winged demon with the turret reverted back to Kraeno's escape and started to make chase, even though Kraeno finally made it out of the arena. He was walled off from his past but revealed an open horizon to his future. The all-encompassing, never enclosing ring of being.

He chopped the arm off a dumb imp cheering at Doomali's victory, and Noble started to run extremely hard towards the eastern horizon. Bullets whizzing by as Kraeno looked back to see the winged demon unable to catch up.

Vapor Vipers and Stalactites

"Hello my dear Max. How is your realm of influence? Ever expanding?" Max looked at Doomali with a curious stare. He and his Skeleton Crew were here to fight; he didn't like to converse with Demon Lords. To him, they talked like idiots, always telling riddles that never made sense to him. Max stood there and continued to stare at Doomali's black face with red spiral tattoos.

Doomali, the obvious stud of Plaztex, had a nonchalant attitude today; he had too many plans to get bogged down with the small things.

"Well then, how was ending Melcruso's thousand-year reign over the Western Sagara Islands?"

Max smiled, finally knowing what Doomali was insinuating at.

"Those Lava Islands were always more ours than hers. She sat comfortably in her castle, never ruling, just soaking in her own poison, locked down by her skinny bridges... And just so you know, Lord Doomali, my crew never went there."

"Oh, now that is very interesting Max because rumors around the planet of Plaztex say that skeletons snuck inside, bounced her guards off the bridge, and finished Melcruso with her own golden hatchets."

Max half wanted it to have been him that ruined Melcruso, but the other half knew that a move like that would put the Skeleton Crew on the map as a disloyal alliance.

"We had a new recruit recently. He came to us broken and slippery boned. He and his partner took Melcruso's castle alone..." As Max ended his sentence, he felt foolish. He knew of Melcruso's castle and how difficult it would be to even get an army over her bridges and into her massive hall. Maybe the strength of the Skeleton Crew is developing into a feared and exalted race.

"Two freshies eh, two freshies ready to tear Hell apart. I would like to meet them. Did they come with you into the city?" Doomali quickly glanced around, looking for triumphant postures.

Max and his crew hated the word freshies, so instead of proud, they all looked pissed off and ready to rumble. The word was just too close to the word Fleshies.

"They are recovering at the Stoop. I'll be sure to bring them to our next job here."

Doomali laughed as if he had remembered something. "Yes, the job, let's get to it. Follow me down to the Catacombs."

Doomali guided the way ahead of the group; two of his guards were behind him, keeping a slow pace, and the other two drifted behind the seven ironically different looking skeletons in the middle. Mareridt strolled up to Doomali's side from a large room with one fat desk surrounded by hundreds of books.

A dark room in a random spot, Max shuddered.

"Hello My Lord." She glinted a smile of mischievousness, and Doomali gave her an easy nod.

The group began to descend into the catacombs, and Max felt more at ease. Being further underground soothed the warring bones of the crew. It was as if the earth had added a layer of skin over their rigid, spacey bodies.

Ahead of the group was a dark blue amethyst bridge with blue steam rising from the surrounding pool of heavy vapor. Looking down into the misty pool were swirly movements in the vapor - an interesting place for pets. The top of the catacomb was pitch black and sprinkled with sharp rocksickle shapes.

The atmosphere grew heavy, and Max kept feeling the muscles of the demon Doomali twitch. He knew something was out of place, so he abruptly stopped. With his long strides, Soap was already a couple of feet ahead of him.

As Soap looked back at Max for affirmation that something was wrong, he was just as suddenly picked up and impaled on the rocksickle directly above him. Smirking, Doomali walked under the impaled skeleton, bending his neck a little to the side so Soap's feet didn't brush his pulled-back hair with his toes.

Mareridt stood behind Doomali and raised her arms, thickening the vapor and raising the resident vipers above the bridge. One lunged at Max's shoulder, but he moved to the side and cleanly cut its head off. The other skeletons, Charlie and Whitey were wrapped up and pulled off the bridge into the blue vapor.

Slayadex head-butted a guard and was received with another guard's scythe colliding into his chest. Slayadex grabbed the arms of the guard and pulled him in close, rapidly sliding his daggers repeatedly inside him. The brothers Boardx and Boardi rushed for the witch, angered by her classic, stand-back sorcery.

Doomali pulled Soap's giant body off the rocksickle and used it as a hammer, slugging Boardx and Boardi away from Mareridt; enough of a hit to make Boardi bamboozled and receive a scythe into his blue-painted skull. Doomali then ripped his brother Boardx's skull right off his spine.

That left Max with Morty and Stew. Stew wrestled with a guard furthest back from the party, teetering back and forth at a standstill, using the bridge walls as their rope-a-dope. Max turned to Morty and watched while his rhythmic spiked knuckles punched into the guard's gut.

A guard from Doomali's side, who still had the upper part of Boardi's skull stuck around his reaper scythe blade, rushed at Max with his scythe high above his head. Max slung his one-shooter pistol out of his cloak and popped him in his rosy mouth. Max kept his gaze on Doomali's eyes and casually walked over to the guard Stew was wrestling with, took his spiraled blade from his belt, and chopped at the guard's spine until his arms were limp around Stew's bones, never blinking away from Doomali's stare.

Stew and Morty dropped in at Max's side, casual and indifferent from the fight. Not having lungs gave them eternal stamina. Their hollows deepened and the darkness of the unknown made the Skeleton Crew seem all the wiser and all the more terrifying.

Slayadex shook his dagger blades from the torso of his holey guard opponent and stuck his blades behind him into the head of a vapor viper that was wrapped around his neck. He tossed the dead viper back into its lair of fog.

"What the fuck is this, you filthy Togmehoian!" Slayadex roared.

Calmly and collectively, Doomali took a few steps forward, placing himself at the apex of the bridge.

"Skellys. What magnificent adaptations of Hell. If a demon kills another galactic life-form, that life-form drops to Hell with a gift of pity. This pity floods their bones with steel full of demonic strength, cursed with immortality and suffering. What a funny game the dark bulge has played on the Skeleton Crew..." Doomali's speech was uppity and high class, full of even more superiority than before.

A blue light approached behind Mareridt and Doomali; the light was twisted with shadows of tormented souls captured in the cloak of the one called Six.

"My High Wizard Six advised me to end your MC here on Plaztex. The closer you came to becoming my most trusted crusaders, the more comfortable you felt about finishing me. Well, now I'll give you the chance to take me out, Max. In the Lagomos Catacombs, the sole laboratory of demon possession on more vital planets."

A monstrous roar was heard deeper within the Catacombs, and claws scraped on thick metal bars. The roar persisted like a dog trying to get to its endangered owner.

The vipers still wiggled in the vapor surrounding the bridge, their heads peeking out occasionally, checking if they were allowed to attack. Mareridt stood back with her vipers at the ready in case Doomali failed.

Max pulled his mates back an inch by their ragged coats.

"Sounds too good to be true." He said with a smile and a quick wink at Slayadex.

Slayadex opened himself up to Doomali; his arms spread, creating somewhat of a bone wall, two daggers pointed forward.

"I have no problem finishing you myself, Doomali. You are but a freak born into high power. I'll make sure your little vapor slut will drop dead with her mouth around your tiny weenie. That is the only favor I grant you. Now, I shall slay you. Prepare yourself for ruin." Slayadex laughed hysterically while parrying Doomali's forward thrusts and needy, bone-thirsty hands. He did whatever he could to stay away from Doomali's grasp, counting every second of his survival as a better chance for Max's escape.

Doomali grew tired of Slayadex dodging his charges.

"Six! Release the Beast!" The sound of bars sliding open came to a crash. A noise of monstrous feet smacking against the cold catacomb tile echoed through the halls.

Slayadex gripped his daggers and wrapped the long red cloth hanging from their hilts around his wrists. Slayadex was his name. Slaying fools was his game.

****

Max, Morty, and Stew skidded around the slippery square corners and up the last flight of stairs. Once they reached the top, he started thinking less about their current situation and more about the majority of skeletons out and about in Plaztex City. A roar came from below, and the sound of bones splintering against catacomb walls put a chill to his own.

"Let's go!" Max began his sprint towards the long and wide flight of stairs running down to the entrance of the Citadel. They weirdly stumbled down the stairs, distracted by the demonic hunts and Heaven versus Hell planetary battle tapestries. Max wondered if Doomali would illustrate a painting of skeletons running away from giant blue vipers creeping out of smoky vapor.

They finally reached the bottom, and Morty tapped Max on the shoulder bone while looking tranquil at the top of the stairs. Max turned to see a massive beast hunched over on his fists like a gorilla. It was about the size of an elephant and probably as tall as Soap, but with meat. Max nodded to the entrance where two of Doomali's guards stood outside, scythes in hand and ready to put a halt to Max's escape.

Suddenly, two blades thrust through their bellies and slowly kept sliding to the hilt. The blades whipped back, and the guards dropped, revealing Lancelot in their place.

Max and the others ran up to Lancelot, looking for more of their crew to be there waiting with him. Only given a second of rest, Lancelot's eyebrows shot up, and his eyes widened.

A humongous crash rumbled the grounds outside the Citadel. The beast made its way down the stairs and probably made a mess of the entrance wall. Morty and Stew glanced at each other and ran back into the Citadel entrance, hoping to slow down the beast long enough for Max's escape. Lancelot's eyebrows flicked up with surprise again at the skeleton's loyalty to their Captain.

"Follow me. I know of a place down the main drag." Lancelot urged while back peddling and watching bones spray from the Citadel doorway.

They ran past a dead ogre littered with wooden arrows and turned into an alley where Lancelot had taken his spying post before. As soon as they turned the corner, a zip blasted through the alley and went right through Max's ribs. Untouched, Max sprinted at the archer, unthreatened by the arrows that followed the last. Max reached him and drove the guard's spiraled dagger into the archer's ribs. The archer goblin fell to the ground and bled.

"Come on, we need to make it to the ghost shack. What happened in the Citadel wasn't good."

"You think?" Lancelot said playfully.

Max took up the archer's attire along with his quiver and bow. The building adjacent to them blazed regularly with fire. Max stood silhouetted by the shadow of the flames, his small skull looking very disproportionate to his double-coated and cloaked body. Max threw up his hood and jogged through the alleys in the direction of the shack, tense to find more dead skeletons lying in the Plaztex City dirt.

Blitzen

Cid walked on wooden planks in a lit-up town built on top of a lagoon. Her gaze shifted like a metronome, up to the high windows of three-story houses, then down to the planks ahead of her, and then up to the tall, stilted houses on the other side. The clunk, clunk, clunk of the wood planks and creaks of the pylons holding up the town had made Cid enormously comfortable in this enormously dangerous place.

Before Cid was found by the youthful Panda Bear tie-wearing Santy Clark, she was a poet's daughter in a Scandinavian town called Aarhus. This town was structured very much like Pa Uris Da, Congo; other than being built of stone in the 16th century, Pa Uris Da's foundation was made of wooden planks and bamboo, which she hypnotically adored.

Cid's body rocked as if it was born on a boat amongst high seas. Her green breeches swayed side to side, with the bottom arch of her butt perfectly curved. She wore the top half of her blouse, half unbuttoned, and her dark hair in a ponytail.

The alley cats were shocked as she passed by, physically put into a spell that only allowed them to watch the woman of their future dreams slap the planks of the boardwalk. They were all put in this blissful trance that lured no harm.

Cid came up to a house with Christmas lights surrounding the patio, stairs, and upper balcony. The lights had the channel lit up in a slew of reflecting colors. Cid walked up to a door, which was really only a blue tapestry of three women swimming in a Celtic circle of braided hair, and noticed every window slot showed lantern light inside.

She whistled a bird chirp and waited, looking out onto the water.

Four little chirp whistles were heard from inside and Cid grooved in with some swagger. Shaki was there sitting on a stool behind a couch, only showing Nirvana written on her gray t-shirt and a coach shotgun pointed up to the sky with a smiling, puffy tan and freckled cheeked face.

"Point it back at the entrance. I'm not sure if I've been followed or not.

"There's cold beer in the cooler," Shaki cheered.

Shaki and Cid had been in Pa Uris Da for three days now. Their second night in, two intruders came through the front door, which was really the only entrance into the house. Shaki was sitting there, right behind the couch where she resided now, and she rose to meet the burglars. The burglars saw Shaki's shotgun and turned to run out of the house, barely shutting the door behind them before the shotgun blasts tore their backs to shreds. Instead, it splintered the door apart. Hence, the Celtic tapestry hanging in the door frame.

Cid popped off the bottle cap, and it flew up, bouncing off the logged ceiling. She walked over to the main room where Shaki was and sat on the stairs leading up to the bedroom.

Shaki slouched her arm over the barrel of her shotgun aimed at the doorway and looked at Cid. "Any luck finding us a door?"

"Nope." Cid took a gulp of the beer and started packing her long wooden pipe with weed.

"But, I did find something else." Cid smiled, flicked her lighter, and smoked her pipe.

As she blew out, she sighed in relief and relaxation. "Ahhh. What a night…" She looked up into Shaki's awaiting gaze.

"There's a tavern at the heart of the lagoon on a small little island. That tavern, you've seen it, has two large 'logs' bridging across on either side. Each side, however, is full of hooligans and mercenaries. Inside is filled with the toughest guys in the state, and tonight I found out why they all flock to this Tavern, which now seems like a fortress in disguise." She took another puff of her pipe, gulped her beer, and blew out the smoke.

"Please go on," Shaki said, happily impressed with Cid's story and tricks of intoxication.

"I made it inside to find this band playing instrumental polka up in the corner balcony. It was a jam of funky bass mixed with jazzy drums." Cid's eyes watched the ceiling, happily reminiscing the sound.

"Below them was a long bar and crowded tables duct-taped together from previous tavern brawls." She paused again, adjusting herself into a more comfortable position.

"The whole architecture seemed like a church, then converted to a mansion, then transformed into a tavern. The ceiling was five stories high, making it seem a lot larger than its already massive size. The walls and railings for the staircases were covered in slash marks and indentations in most places where no one could have ever reached, let alone swing a blade to hit that mark.

"This was my second curiosity, other than all the mean-looking men hanging around with their gear bags and weapons with them. They seemed like they could almost be a militia or some kind of force of mercenaries, yet they all were very separated and against one another. The men established higher up in the tavern tiers seemed a tad more gentlemanly, but I also saw one of them hanging another over the third-story railing being choked into submission.

"Now you might ask where a Sky Sister's influence would be in a place like this?"

Shaki responded almost instantaneously, "What'd you find?"

"As the music tempo increased, a majority of the men upstairs began walking downstairs like a meeting had just concluded or something. There followed a girl dressed in black shorts and a red and black flannel, sneering down the steps as she walked, shoving and bumping into any man in her way. Two thin swords were attached to her hips, and more were hung on the wall.

"This wee chick exuded so much rage, so much dominance, and so much power that at first I was taken back by intimidation, but then everything clicked. Those 'logs' placed at either side of the tavern actually had engravings all over them, engravings I missed at first because there were so many idiots on the bridge I never looked down. When I left, the engravings weren't like the Awakened, they were something else, something dark..." Cid sat there, taking a couple of quiet breaths while looking at Shaki, and then continued.

"That girl was a Sky Sister, Shaki. That army of mercenaries were her troops, and those trees were obviously demonic and turned on her, revealing why she chose men to stand in the place as guardians of Gaia instead.

"She seems horribly pissed off, so we are going to need to think this one through a wee bit. However, there is still one thing we have going for us. This Sky Sister was so furious with rage and hate that every single male around her was scared shitless. Because of her reputation, we white girls are presently the most feared in this area. It's no wonder no one whistles or dares speak a word to me without me speaking to them first. It's very nice. Fear. Control. Power." Cid finished jokingly.

Shaki passed her tongue across her upper lip, "She's mad because the trees have turned against her. Or so she thinks. We need to get Reykjavik's information to her asap!" Shaki straightened up and spoke with urgency.

"We are going to have to wait for tomorrow, Shaki."

"Why? Didn't you say she was just hanging out at the Tavern all pissed off?"

"Yes, but there was another reason why I had to leave so quickly."

****

Cid stood in the middle of the tavern watching Sky Sister Blitzen step down the long set of stairs, shoving men to the side rhythmically to the sound of the tavern beats. A tiny little girl with olive skin and two silver fully engraved short swords at her hips. One hilt's cuff was the head of a lion with the sword blade coming out of its mouth, and the other sword had two dragon wings guarding the hilt with an emerald in the middle decorated as its awakened eye.

Blitzen came to a meander and then stopped to watch over the main room of the tavern. Standing with both hands on the railing, her wrist wings, which every Sky Sister possessed, flared out and then folded back in. She stared straight ahead, eyes narrow and forehead scrunched up over her brow line. The man standing a couple steps above her reacted in bewilderment when she grabbed his mug and blindly tossed it down to the tavern 'arena'.

"Where'd my brew go?" Then crash. Blitzen proceeded down the steps, looking no one in the eye and simply taking their mugs and flinging them amongst the drunkards, which to her were only bombs waiting to explode from the sound of glass smashing.

To her, men had no chance against evil trees. To her, the human world was ruptured and close to its end. She antagonized the group to fight each night. The strong got stronger, and the weak faded away. Reasonable tryouts for what was coming.

The Wondrous Shell

A small village by the Congo River was surrounded by trees and protected by the good fortune of one woman, a woman who became the spokesperson and leader of their little village just last year. Her name was Beth, and everyone loved her. Her dark flawless skin, her bright green eyes, her strong-headedness to never give up, and the most impressive characteristic of all, she never failed.

Beth had four children who were all strong and obedient. When her kids failed in anything, even something as easy as reeling in a fish, she would punish them. Beth had no compassion or patience for failure because, in her experience, failure didn't exist.

When she stood up as a toddler, she never fell back down. When she got into fights, she always won. When she went hunting, she was always the first one back with the largest game. Arguments always turned in her favor. Her children were never a burden to her, only another supplement on her chain of success.

Her house was the largest in the village, fortified with columns covered with hop vines in a double helix twirl. A temple she created for herself after developing a business that focused on exporting foods and goods to other helpless villages in different states. Her jungle sanctuary has never been in any danger.

Beth's perfect success stuck to every operation she was involved in. Luck and timing were flawlessly on her side, and even though she didn't care to help others, she did so because it famously benefited her. Beth stood in the forest listening to the river flow nearby while she picked cherries from a cherry tree. She danced around the thick shrubbery of blackberry thorns and filled her basket with perfectly ripe and delicious cherries.

Overhead, the clouds ran together and darkened. Without a

change in face or hesitation in her step, she grabbed her cherry baskets and started walking back to the village, head bobbing to the bird chirps and rushing river behind her.

From a bird's eye view, the Congo River ran East to West; her village was on the Northern border of the Congo Forest, closest to the Atlantic Ocean. She was happy with her life and location. Everything was perfect how it was, but for once in her life, something was about to change, something she would not be able to shift with her luck.

Now in sight, barely visible through the dense forest and fat trees, her mansion lay twenty yards from her. The trees before her seemed to crouch and curl their branches, narrowing her path. Beth thought this very interesting. She approached the tree in front of her and curiously passed her hand over the carved out engravings in the bark.

After pondering over the deep indentations in the bark, she became convinced that her sons must have gone into the forest to hang on cherry branches and carve into the trees. So she continued back to her mansion with disciplining in mind.

At the dinner table that night, Beth became very frustrated with her sons lying about carving into the trees. Before she went to bed, she looked through their rooms in search of their carving tools and found nothing. In her discomfort, she proceeded to brush her teeth, wash up and fall asleep. She looked over at the clock on her wall, and it read 10:11. Her eyelashes fluttered, fluttered, 10:12, fluttered, to sleep.

****

Beth woke up with a mouth so dry she couldn't speak or hardly breathe. As she got up out of bed to get a glass of water, she fell right through her floorboards, catching a last-second glimpse of her clock that read 11:34 before she fell deeper and deeper, until finally she took her place in a very claustrophobic mine shaft.

Suddenly, no-faced mine workers from all over the shaft started walking in one direction. Beth followed in an attempt to find the way out of this nightmare. She walked with the workers, but space kept becoming tighter and tighter until finally they all came to a halt; this halt, however, didn't completely stop the compaction, and everyone still squeezed together closer and closer.

The air in the shaft seemed to be running out, and Beth began losing her mind. Everyone screamed in agony, everyone gasped for breath, and she stood there, mind boiling and melting away, creating plenty of room for what was filling her mind back up. Fear.

A voice thundered through the rocks. Beth thought it was her subconscious, there to save her from this nightmare. She slowly drifted out of the crowd, helpless and still ludicrous from being crammed into a mine. She heard the voice again, "Wakey, wakey."

Beth rose from the ground, reading the clock backward this time, 43:11, and then slipped back into her body. Her convulsions lasted only a moment, and when Beth opened her eyes, Mareridt's blue eyes were there, staring inches away. Slowly, incredibly slow, those icy blue eyes ghosted through Beth's irises. Beth's spirit rested, paralyzed by the fear of being paralyzed. Her body finally sat up and stretched out, but she was not the operator.

This must be another nightmare!

"Yes, I am a nightmare!" Mareridt said in her most wicked voice. Beth shuddered in the horrific reality of being taken over. Her chills pulled at her spirit, trying to lift off, trying to escape the maniac within her. She cried and whimpered. Almost dying and rising up towards the heavens, purely in fright, only to be pulled back down into her body by Mareridt.

"I'm keeping you around as a lucky charm little babe. Enjoy your cage." And then Beth's moans sunk away to a weak sniffle, and Mareridt relaxed. She opened and closed her new hands to exercise the nerves in her muscles.

"Perrfect." She said as she floated over to the mirror to see her healthy body. She watched herself for hours in front of the mirror, imagining herself hovering in front of millions, exerting her power over them, and residing as the Queen of Earth.

"What a wondrous shell." She clapped her hands to her cute little cheeks, elvish ears, and dark breasts.

Later, Mareridt walked downstairs with only her underwear and a red silk robe. She went outside into the darkness and crouched by the nearest tree. She mumbled witchery over and over, using her index finger to shape a design in the bark. She then started telekinetically pulling perfectly formed wooden spear after wooden spear out of the tree, eventually causing it to crack and slowly timber down onto another.

Deeper into the woods, there were moans and more cracking sounds of bark, giving some unusual vitality to the night sky.

Mareridt stood up and skipped into the forest to find her wooden minions. Trailing her were her wooden spears, haphazardly hovering in the air and ready to take flight in any direction she chose.

Panic

Shaki shoved the coach shotgun into a backpack and zipped it up. Cid took down the tapestry covering their cabin entrance, loaded it into her bag, and waited outside on the porch. The morning commotion from the outside villagers flowed through town like the chirping of different birds in one tree. They all had different stories to tell in many different dialects. Cid picked up one phrase repeatedly however, *The Forest is alive!*

Either the forest was the Awakened, or the forest was something like what the boys found on Grimsey Island. Regardless, it was time to reach the Sky Sister in the tavern.

Shaki came up behind Cid.

"I'm ready. Shall we venture forth into the belly of the beast? Tiptoe around the dragon's cave? Charge into the lion's mouth?" Shaki hurried after Cid, still impromptu compared to Cid.

Cid started her speedy walk on the wet planks above the lagoon. The sun shone through the strip of forest canopy overhead, and rain fell in irregular plops, accumuating above on the tall canopy of leaves then falling like a bloated elemental bomb. Some houses were even built on top of the sturdy branches above, looking more like tree forts.

The colorful birds chilling at the top looked down at the humans like they were crazy, all bunched up outside their homes, ranting and raving, pointing up at them like they were fearful of their flock.

Cid led the way, squeezing through the groups of people but also trying not to bump them into the lagoon. The people were waiting for something to happen, waiting for the forest to awaken and overwhelm their little town.

The ones with wide eyes and big mouths usually asked Cid and

Shaki for either help, a blessing, or a white girl dance of sorts to chase away the evil spirits. Cid continued forward, unaffected by their pleas and breaking their grasps as if they were inanimate cuffs looking for an arrest.

Cid turned her head to talk over her shoulder. "Look at that, looks like the whole town wants to meet with her now. Perfect timing!" Cid grumbled with angry sarcasm.

On the other side of the fallen Sequoias, closest to the tavern doors, were Blitzen's men blocking the mass of townspeople pushing and pulling to get across. A lot of them fell off the bridges, splashing in the water, still arguing with the guards, or yelling at the hopelessness of the day. It became so chaotic that Shaki started absorbing some of the panic. She looked left to right again and again, tipping off her focus and becoming more and more frightened.

Cid watched this anxiety attack only for a second before calming her friend.

"Shaki, look at me kiddo." Shaki looked right into her gray and stormy eyes.

"Breathe… we'll get to that Sky Sister. We just need to be patient and find a nice place to hang–" A large man, trailed by three women, plowed between Cid and Shaki's attempt at peace. Cid reached for Shaki in a hurry, trying to prevent her from slipping into the mindless panic. Shaki, on the other hand, changed, and was cool as kitchen tile in the morning.

"Shaki! Are you okay?" Cid gasped once she got a hold of her again.

"Yep, I'm better, I stole that guy's wallet." Shaki threw it behind her into the lagoon.

"And I have an idea on how to get into the tavern. Follow me!"

Shaki ran up to the nearest house, where a dog was snapping and barking at everyone passing by. She reached the snarling, bare-toothed punk dog and pulled the shotgun out of her backpack to point it in his face. Although the dog was just a dog and completely perplexed for a moment, it later turned its ferociousness to full, bite off your face mode.

Shaki reacted quickly by kicking the bull terrier in the face, grabbing the back of his collar, and picking him up to use him as an insanely aggressive shield. She handed Cid the shotgun and held up the dog by its butt to get a good hold of him.

"Watch my back Cid! We're going in."

Shaki ran into the crowd towards the back tavern bridge where there were more men than women. Shaki's idea was to push through the crowd with her snapping shield, and if someone was to get bitten, it was better a man than a woman.

All these people must have witnessed or at least heard about the tavern lady defeating the two monstrous Sequoias, so when an apocalypse did arise with more demonic trees, who would be the best person to go to? The demon tree slayer of course.

Shaki really didn't want to hurt the townspeople, but she was, in her heart and soul, willing. She charged over the dead engraved Sequoia, knocking people to the side while some fell in the water. Cid covered Shaki's rear while pointing the shotty at anyone who wanted to retaliate against them. Shaki made it to Blitzen's guards and threw the savage dog in the water.

"Tell your boss her sisters are here, and we need to update her on the Lantos!"

The Lantos were the old warrior trees that usually fought with their wood, not their spells and summons. The guards in front just looked at her with blank faces while the guard in the back told a smaller guard with a beret to relay the message inside.

Shaki turned around and saw the ignited red ears of the protesting Africans. Cid swiftly leveled the shotgun inches away from one's head. He lunged forward, and she checked his brow line with the butt of the shotgun. Another came at her, and the guard by Shaki moved up and punched him in the nose. Then there was a tight pull on their shirt tails, and they were on the tavern planks, headed inside, trying to keep their footing while scraping their heels at their backward stumble.

Cid turned around and gasped at the sight of their savior. She was very short, 5'2, tan, thin little waste with defining hip bones creasing below her red and black flannel. Her hair was dark with corn rolls wound tight on one side of her head. A skull and crossbones was tattooed in the corner of her hairline, marked as a permanent shadow mimicking her angry stare. She looked a bit like a teeny-bopper goth lumberjack, definitely dressed for the occasion.

Both Cid and Shaki felt weirdly at ease and in hysterical ecstasy, even though the Sky Sister in front of them seemed to be in hysterical rage. The prototype of comics with pissed-off Police Commissioners expelling white streams of steam from their ears was what they saw coming out of Blitzen. The image of her didn't quite synergize with a regular person's reaction to witnessing a radical angelic character, but her zest was completely enveloped with calm and collective energy. That was what made the moment so funny to Cid and Shaki, along with the Sky Sister's developing features of pouting – in the most dangerous way imaginable.

"Who are you?" She asked like a possible mentor would say to a stranger. Eager to know who they really were, as well as testing the tone of their response.

Shaki looked around; the place was very dark. It was hectic with preparations and running around, making the tavern look more like an armory rather than a drinking joint. She decided the eeriness came from the darkened corners of the tavern. For example, the plant sitting in the closest corner to them was being eaten by this pitch-black void, which also dimmed the lanterns surrounding that area. This made the plant look more like a hurricane weed, half lost in the deep shadow of the planet.

Shaki believed it came from the Sky Sister. Some sorcerers would prefer using light infused with their magic and quirky traits, while some prefer using darkness. Could this Sky Sister have gone off the deep end, just now becoming the maddened destroyer of the human race! Our odds were crumbling at every turn.

Cid's voice loomed in Shaki's ears, reminding her to focus back on the present and on what they were up against.

"-Sentinels from the North. We come with incredibly important news about the Awakened and the infernal demons that have left them restless."

The Sky Sister looked at them, turned around, and headed for the long bar top, assuming they would follow.

"My name is Blitzen. This tavern is a gathering place for humans that are willing to fight and follow me." Her tone broke into sharp pronunciation during her description of a soldier's duty. They reached the bar, and she turned around to face Shaki and Cid again. A dimple creased, revealing a quick smile from Blitzen.

"Now, tell me more about these demons."

Crete

Afwat grunted at the monkey sitting on the branch next to his cavernous eye and pointed with one of his longer branches at the ship's dark deck, insinuating it was time to go. Afwat scratched his trunk and waited for the monkey to reluctantly run down, skitter across the deck, and pounce up onto Johnny's sturdy, muscular back.

Johnny greeted the monkey and turned around to watch Afwat, the last of the plank divers, abandoning ship. He flicked his left nostril with his thumb and turned away from the massive splash Afwat produced, moonlit water arching over the railing.

"Anchors up, let's head to Crete's bay!"

The Saint drifted off while the team of Sentinels and Awakened swam to shore. Pads backstroked, watching A.D freestyle over the swells with the Saint floating away amongst the stars. The water was dark and reflected the sky, putting the Kalmcs at ease and in a trance. Pads rotated forward, slicing into the pitched sea, and watched Lingo and Afwat carry Panda, Favin, two weapons crates, a net of metal armor, and the Birchwoods to shore. They were far ahead of them, which allowed Pads and A.D some alone time.

Pads turned around, smoothly transitioning into a backstroke again. He kicked water up in front of A.D's solemn face. A.D fluttered the water drops from his eyelashes and continued swimming without missing a beat. A stream of water ran at different angles across his face, using the scars along his jaw as canals or mountain range blockades. The salt was thick here, and it looked like it already started crusting over A.D's forehead. Pads just watched him as they swam face to face.

"What is it, brother? You thinking about Kraeno?" A.D asked, through his huffs and puffs during freestyle strokes.

"I was enjoying the brother I still have while looking forward to joining the brother I lost."

"Brother." A.D said like he used to when they were little kids, subconsciously trying to squeeze in one last phrase of sensitivity before going to sleep.

"Ya?"

"I feel the exact same way."

They swam in silence and finally reached the others on shore. The two large oaks dripped a storm because of their zigzagged branches layered throughout the upper portions of their trunks. Their trunks opened up to the stars while their roots sunk deep into the sand, seeming to get their power back from being offshore so long.

A plastic bag of clothes fell from Lingo's upper branch right at Pad's feet. Pads and A.D took off their shorts, put on the dry clothes from the bag, and walked over to the weapons crates next to Favin and Panda. Trees were scattered about this side of Crete's island and condensed closer to an inlet and the gorge. They all looked alive and champion'ous. The power of the Preveli River flowing into the Mediterranean was noticeable even in the black of night as the waves pounded the sand.

Afwat stood facing the inlet, concerned with what may lie ahead.

Favin opened one crate with two miniguns fitted into the straw cushioning, like a minigun Yin-Yang.

"Panda, A.D, come take one of these."

Panda lifted out the black minigun, and as A.D lifted out the silver minigun, Afwat rumbled.

"No! We no disgrace Sky Sister with unworldly weapons. Only Me, Lingo, and Panda go into the inlet. She knows Panda from his Landtos venture through the Indo Tombs."

Favin opened his mouth to protest, but Afwat already started dragging his roots through the sand toward the inlet.

"I guess we'll wait here lads. Campfire and a song?" Favin looked at Pads alluringly, and A.D's ears perked up at the idea.

The three of them went to look for kindling and wood while the Birchwoods made a semi-circle as a camp perimeter.

Lingo, Afwat, and Panda were beginning to turn into the inlet.

****

Panda stood in between the two massive oaks, one twice as wide and twice as tall as the other, but both walked with as much grace as a lumbering oak could. They meandered the bank for a while until the leaves of the surrounding wooden guardians became brighter green and full of intricate vitality throughout their vines.

Panda tilted his head at the sound of a waterfall and suddenly became juiced with a feeling of ecstasy buzzing through his mind, body, and soul. He quivered at the feeling.

"Ohh, ye fell dat?"

Lingo bowed at Panda, enacting a nod of affirmation.

They continued around the bend, and Panda's legs trembled as if they were on the brink of buckling. He shook his head to try and wake up his nerves in an attempt to contain the hulking power of love and security that rested heavily in the atmosphere.

At the end of the inlet, a waterfall dropped 40 feet into a pool, where a willow tree sat in the middle of the cliff on a rocky ledge. The water reflected around the blue-green barrier of its leaves, pouring off the ends of its canopy.

Afwat lowered one of his longer branches to stop Lingo from proceeding. Afwat continued alone, slipping into the pool of water with decorum, and waited in its center.

The domed willow leaned forward, waterfall ricocheting off her sides. Her curtain-like leaves opened to reveal a woman with a very youthful face and soft brown eyes. Her hair was naturally green, tied back, and pinned with silver stripes as if Mother Earth made her out of vines and silver silk. She wore no blouse and had a slanted green skirt on, revealing one leg more than the other as she came out onto the rock ledge. Her rounded breasts were perky, and her face had no wrinkles. Her petite chin and nose created a too-cute figure that held a demanding strength from her luring beauty.

The scene was a perfect illustration of the fountain of youth with its mother of truth.

She looked out onto Afwat and behind him at his journeymen.

"Landtos, what news do you have?"

Afwat responded in his low booming voice, which bounced off

the water and echoed around the surrounding tree line.

"Sky Sister Tienilla, our ancient warriors have been fighting a dark and possessive evil. Our life force is being pressed back into the earth, our bark tainted with demonic scripture, our sap hot with fire. Evil, Sister Tienilla, which has already taken the life of the sorcerer Macaton Rowan Bear, General Piper, and Sentinel Kraeno Kalmc. It scourges our woods and plagues our Earth, seeming to be hidden everywhere we travel." Afwat rotated his massive trunk side to side, eyeing the woods around him, cautious of darkened eavesdroppers.

"My sister Shay told me of these new devils from Grimsey." Tienilla half whispered to herself. She pulled the Golden Scepter of Glasir from behind her dark green sash; her white-winged wrist made it seem like an angel's holy mace.

"I am Sky Sister Tienilla, the first Daughter born from Mother Gaia. I hold the Scepter of Glasir, the holy shield that protects our Earth." Tienilla raised the Scepter above her head, and her voice gradually became louder and more lovely.

"If you want it, come and get it." She concluded with a playful tone.

As soon as the last words left her mouth, her eyes darted over to the surrounding woods to her right. Like an actress spotting an assailant in the stands of her theater, she zoomed towards the tree that inched itself forward after she spoke the words, *Come get it.*

The tree stopped dead, realizing its mistake at her trickery, and tried to disguise itself in the other woods. Unfortunately for him, the other warrior woods tangled him up in preparation for the inevitable interrogation.

Sky Sister Tienilla's brown skin turned platinum white. She raised the Scepter up to the goony features of the mysterious tree, and the Scepter's leaf hilt bloomed, ejecting long thorns around her hand to protect its wielder. When Tienilla pulled the Scepter back, the thorns receded, and she stuck it into her sash. A snug fit because of her plump butt.

Tienilla flew up above the pool, the mist cooling her feet at the base of the fall, and she shouted her orders.

"All Lantos and Macatons, wooden guardians of our Mother, hear me now. I ORDER YOU TO BECOME FULLY AWAKENED!"

Panda felt a tinge out of his element and positioned himself on Lingo's lowest branch, sitting with his legs dangling below.

Similar to window lights coming on during a midnight street bustle, the trees circling the waterfall lit up with glowing green and blue light, filling the misty air with soft rainbow hues. The dawn sunrise turned the inland gray sky orange and red, harmoniously overlapping into a color flux with the green and blue power from the Awakened.

Afwat's engravings lit up as well, starting from his roots underwater. The dark blue pool exhibited the spiraled artwork of his life force and abilities, filling the water with transparent rippling symbols and patterns. His green light slowly crept above the surface of the water and made its way through his trunks. A vertical line crossed his hollow eye and ended a couple feet up from his face, fully engraved with rugged, lined symbols. In comparison to a human, he was fully tatted.

Panda looked down, happy to see the light reflecting onto his leg from Lingo's transformation.

The sky twisted in a multitude of different spots, turning it into an early morning birthplace of dawning storms. Clouds came from all directions to bind together and be shoved around by the hurricane winds, 360-degree gusts slapping the branches and leaves around. This surge of power manipulated the variance of colors, allowing visible detection of the stream of influence attached to its conjurers.

In addition to the power flux, Tienilla's aura and beauty caused Panda to suddenly faint. As he fell back, Lingo caught him with his branch that carried the net with all of his and Afwat's armor. Panda woke up, shook his head, and started spectating again.

The animation of other trees was soon unmasked. The energy of the Awakened was inescapably causing a connection of communal power. The imminent truth of demons in their ranks was revealed and abruptly solved with brute force.

Sky Sister Shay blazed into the event circle wearing her ragged robe. She scanned the hillside then uprooted a troublesome heavyset tree with her summoned spirit hand with five emerald golden rings, and threw him in the pool next to Afwat. Her bald head and dark skin seemed merciless in this rainbow-colored environment. She glared into Afwat's hollows, transferring her rage and revealing what she wanted done.

Afwat waded through the pool to the troublesome demon oak, kicked him up into the air with a thick root, and grabbed either end of his trunk. The demon oak's leafy top creaked and crumpled together while his roots mashed in an entangled fiasco as Afwat gripped both ends, wrapping his main branches tight around them.

The roar from Afwat's barky core echoed throughout the enclosure, just as the creaking and final snap echoed after he ripped the demon oak in half. Afwat looked inside both halves to investigate the villain and watched red luminescent light fade away.

Afwat dropped his enemy and then searched the perimeter. For a moment, the waterfall and the creaking woods were the only sounds heard after the Awakened tossed the demon woods onto the coarse and rocky sand.

Shay dropped down to the beach, banking the pool, and looked up her sister Tienilla.

"I tried telling you that there was a greater force we haven't yet quarreled with. Now that you've seen their disguise and deception, will you consider a gathering of all our sisters?"

Tienilla nodded indifferently, seeming unaffected by it all. She gracefully floated down in front of Lingo and Panda.

Panda hopped down from Lingo's branch and awaited Tienilla. He wore his green Hawaiian shirt unbuttoned, designed with white leafed patterns.

"Panda, Yes?"

"Yeh meh Laddie"

"I remember when you and a young girl saved the Indonesian forest from a lumber yard. Questionable tactics were used; however, you saved many ancient friends of ours. We thank you. You belong in our ranks during this dire time."

Panda nodded, "Ehm ehm," trying not to seem disrespectful because of his mutilated dialect.

Tienilla gave him lustful eyes and turned around to look upon the carnage. Panda stumbled back, letting Lingo catch his stupefied body once again. He could take a lot of unusual threats and skirmishes, but when it came to the most beautiful goddesses, he became mush.

In the pile of dead demon woods ripped apart by the Awakened, Shay had her foot on a goony-featured tree that grunted in his disfigurement. She interrogated him with her ringed fist.

"Who are you, and where do you come from, you little twig?"

The demon tree bubbled with faint, dying laughter.

"We come from the depths of Hell, lady. Where else?"

Shay looked taken aback. Tienilla approached her side to look down at the last of the demon trees.

Shay, still bewildered, whispered, "Why?"

"Mareridt rises again! And she plans to imprison you al-" Shay penetrated one of the demon tree's wounds with her summoned spirit hand, turning its hollows into flames, and as slow as molasses, she burned the tree into a charred crisp.

The two sisters looked at each other, puzzled and extremely worried.

"Panda man! Are you still with other Sentinels and Awakened?" Shay shouted.

"Yeh Laddie."

"Get them and bring them to us; it's time to teach you the ancient art of exorcisms. We have much to prepare for, and if Mareridt is already here, very little time to do so.

"Shay, go. Find our sisters."

Shay blasted off, and Panda hesitantly went running down the riverbank. *Lady coulda gien meh a lift.*

****

Panda came running up to the camp; everyone was sitting around the fire, and the Birchwoods were on guard.

"Wack op wack op! Teh Sissess ne us."

"We're awake, Panda. What's going on?"

"I'll tel ye n teh roe. Come n?"

Favin nodded and looked around the camp, the Kalmc brothers were quickly packing up the few things they had, and the Birchwoods were already bunched up and ready to head out.

"Where's Zeus?" Favin asked, puzzled. The other Birchwoods shrugged their bladed limbs. Favin had no time to look for a missing tree, and they were off onto the banks of the inlet.

****

Tienilla's camp was on the move. Under the waterfall and surrounding the pool were long inclined hills that created a bowl. Outside this natural depression, the Awakened trees were scouting the area for any spies, assailants, or other moving trees in general.

As the Kalmc party came walking in from the riverbank, Sky Sister Tienilla was showing a troop of Awakened how to block outside forces from possessing their woods. She used the dead demon wood as an example.

She carved three short diagonal lines at different angles and one hoop on the bottom line, then two long vertical curved lines down the middle of the whole face. It looked like a semi-colon with two semis and the letter P for the mouth, then two bow lines going through the silly symbol's face.

She turned around to her students and they were all carving into each other's bark, speedy although delicately so as to not mess up the demonic shield.

Another beautiful body with an angel's grace walked down the bowl from a group of Macatons silhouetted at its peak. She had a long black leather coat and blonde hair with a ring of yellow flowers resting on her head. She was barefoot and walked with attitude. Behind her the super tall trees were manipulating their environment and summoning elementals out of the natural substances around them.

She strutted up and peered over the Birchwoods.

"Aye, Birchwoods, nasty mother fuckers hmm. So you're Pam Kalmc's sons? It's an honor, though I am very sorry about your brother's death. He will be remembered." She spoke lackadaisically and bluntly, blue eyes caring but, at the same time, realistically knowing there was more to worry about than death and humble greetings. A half dozen little tree-sapling elementals danced and played around her ankles.

The Kalmc boys kicked around the dirt and avoided too much eye contact. Favin and Panda watched her with their jaws unhinged. She wrinkled her button nose and then pounded her knuckles together.

"Well, I need to show you guys something that might help with these demon bastards. I had Afwat open up the crates he was carrying and found your precious cargo."

The boys looked around at each other blindly as if ignorant of their weapons.

She giggled. "Don't worry it was smart to apprehend them, however that may have been. What I would do…" She turned her back and started floating in the air. Two of the little sapling elementals quickly jumped up and formed cute flowery anklets on her as she spun back around and begun conjuring up something out of the air, building it onto her right forearm.

"I'd put Tienilla's mark in the bastards. They'll probably be goners by the time you're even finished with the anti-devil shield."

She dialed in on the pile of dead demon trees, turning her head to the side to be heard over the waterfall and commotion going on inside the bowl.

"Watch this." She angled her left palm down at the pebbles on the beach and aimed her minigun made of air at the pile of dead wood.

"LET EM RIP!" And the pebbles steadily loaded into the air gun and shot out at a high velocity, ripping the woods apart. Everyone turned to her, shaking their trunks in admiration of her innovative bloodline.

She turned around with the air minigun at her hip. Pads took a few steps closer.

"Sister, we didn't catch your name?" He asked with idolizing eyes reflecting the smoking dead wood behind her shoulder. Tienilla, Shay, now her, Pads marveled at how different each sister was.

She shook away the minigun, and the wisps of air dissipated. "I, young laddie, am Freya, the second Sister. And I know what it's going to take to stop our sister Mareridt… Fire." She snapped her fingers, and a flame sparked up in the tall grass next to the Macatons. She started walking back up the hill, turning her spark into a fire elemental, yelling her lecture all the way up.

****

Pads and Lingo sat up on the rim of the natural grassy bowl overlooking the war preparations. Lingo whirled a skinnier branch around like a wand, trying to conjure up a gun like Freya. What was actually created would scare anyone under 10 years old. The black minigun sat in front of them on top of the weapon crate as his model.

Pads was sitting on top of Lingo's higher branches, watching attempt after attempt, absorbed in what tranquility he had left before the big rush of possible death and destruction.

"Lingo, buddy, maybe you should give that minigun a break and try something a little more your style."

Lingo stopped for a second, tilted his cordial hollows up at Pads, and then went back to waving his wand. A blob of air was formed with a cylinder and a hole at the end. Lingo gave a twitch and a puff of air blurped out. He lurched forward in his failed attempt and shook off his frustration.

Sometimes, to feel better, permanently engraving another thing into your body can be a self-reflective, progressive, and therapeutic experience. With Lingo's little wand branch, he ripped off a plank of wood from the weapon crate and used it to carve into his trunk shoulder farthest from Pads. Pads danced around the long branches to get to the other side and see what Lingo was engraving into himself.

"What's that?" Pads asked.

"It's a teleportation spell Freya told me about. It bonds me to her. If a raid goes bad and she needs my help, I can switch spots with her through a teleport. Instantly facing the threat and putting her, hopefully, in a better place away from harm. When the time comes and she's visible to me, I'll mark this symbol with a slash in her direction, and there you have it." Lingo answered in a deep woodsy voice.

On the other side of the valley, a group of scouts were returning. Next to them was a hovering angel sitting cross-legged like a genie. It was hard to see at their distance, but it looked as if she had a long blade resting on her lap. Another Sister found.

Shay was on the other side of the scouting party; her ringed hand glistened from the sunlight. In the middle of the Awakened scouts was a Birchwood completely entangled and spread out.

Panda fainted again next to the waterfall and fell into the pool as the hovering Sky Sisters rounded the hill. Favin dove in after him.

The scouting party brought Zeus next to the pile of dead demon wood, where two wide oaks spread him out like the lady on King Kong's island.

Freya waved Shay and the genie sister over to her location under the waterfall. Tienilla slowly walked up from behind Freya and stood next to her.

The power felt from four Sky Sisters together settled any anxiety the Sentinels may have had. Lingo, however, was off, skittering and sliding down the slope to get to Zeus the Birchwood, an old friend of his. Pads raced after him, full of energy, reminding himself not to run down too fast or he'll eat it.

Zeus, now heavily entangled, was surrounded by all the Birchwoods, Afwat, Lingo, and the Sentinels, listening to his demonic babbling. The Birchwoods chattered heatedly while the Sky Sisters talked under the waterfall.

"He's going to get out of that," Wobbly said, filled with ADHD energy, moving side to side, and back and forth.

"You think you could get out of that Stretch?" Apollo asked while twirling two knives up in the air repeatedly.

"Are you kidding? I'd spin right out and slip into the dirt." Wobbly laughed.

"He'll escape when the time is right. That thing inside of him is planning on something. Poor Zeus." Athena remarked, picking at her bark with her knife.

"Yeah, well what the hell is that thing in him planning then?" Nyx asked, pulling two blades back on his right side like he was about to start pitching at Zeus' trunk face, bluffing at the last second because the sisters were on their way down from the fall.

"Let's test this anti-demon shield out, shall we? Is everyone here?" Freya asked.

"I'll carve it into him," Nyx said, quickly approaching his old friend.

Zeus suddenly did a quick 900 and spun right out of the wide oaks' grasp. He plunged into the soil, becoming concealed. The beach started to tremor in front of Freya.

Lingo felt him underground with his roots and snagged him before Zeus could do anything to the Sky Sister. Lingo wrapped as many branches around him as he could, encapsulating him. He then shook him in a way that seemed like he was trying to shake the demon right out of him.

"Damn it, Zeus, COME BACK!"

Possessed Zeus froze his babbling squabble for a second, pondering his name. Then his hollows flared up, and a slow red light shone through Lingo's branches. All at once, a white puffy cloud turned black overhead, and a fat lightning bolt shot down towards the Sky Sisters. A lumpy, knotted oak glowed suddenly, making the Sentinels wince from its brightness, and blinked to replace the sisters with himself. Zeus' bolt zigzagged down and completely obliterated the intertwined branches and roots of the lumpy oak with a loud crack!

Nyx spun up behind Zeus like a Tasmanian devil.

"Quickly, create some room." He ordered calmly to Lingo, pointing at Zeus' trunk with the tip of his knife.

He finished the carving in a matter of seconds, and Zeus flopped around like a fish in Lingo's entanglement.

"Let's see if he's back," Wobbly said, standing with his antler-like branches touching Zeus' wooden cocoon.

Lingo pulled Zeus back to rest at his side.

"How about I hold onto him until he turns green."

Wobbly started like he was going to protest, but Sister Tienilla cut in. She now stood where the lumpy knotted oak had cast its protection transfer shroud.

"That's a good idea, Lingo." She then extended her voice to be heard around the bowl.

"Treious died protecting us, and now his soul is with our Mother Gaia. We are facing our greatest threat yet; we must remember that this is Mareridt's army of malicious demons from Hell. One hesitation could turn the tides of peace."

Freya flew up in four cylindrical revolutions and started giving a pump-up speech. Something about possessing the demons with fear and rampage, raping them with fire, chopping them in half, screaming terror in their faces, and ultimately dominating. Later, she began yelling about their ancient, magnificent history and all the old fallen warriors that will always be remembered.

As Freya preached, Tienilla gave her orders to the Sentinels, who stood there with constant chills running down their spines. Favin wrapped his fist behind Panda's shirt in order to support him up. The power in the sister's beauty alone was overwhelming and purely superior to their being.

"We need a ship to pull us through the ocean currents and navigate us to West Africa. Shay mentioned you came from Iceland on such a vessel. Most likely, they are still at the Cretan port. If not, find one. Persuade them to come to the mouth of our gorge. Also… bring lots of rope."

"How will we persuade them my lady? We've already killed one of their mates." Favin asked, reminiscing Lady Captain's stubbornness.

Tienilla put her hand out to introduce her sister, hovering in the air with her legs Indian crossed, dressed in loose breeches and covered in elegant piercings. Her dual-sided blade was twice as long as she was and rested casually on her lap, black tape wrapped around the middle.

"Kendra will take two of you into town. She will help with the persuasion." Tienilla said, her perfect boobies ironically bouncing up and down.

Kendra broke out of her float and swiftly made her way over to Pads and A.D. Her eyes flared up like green volcanic ash and her hair jingled with bells, shells, crystals, wrapped-up stones, and trinkets. While she held her blade with one hand, she glided her index finger under Pad's chin line with the other, his light green eyes surging into hers. A multitude of large bracelets on her wrist clinked together as one, and then she moved to squeeze A.D's fat, broken nose, giggling back to her sister's side.

Shay rolled her eyes and walked over to Lingo to check on Zeus.

"Now we must find Blitzen and Mareridt.." Tienilla took a deep breath and then looked up to watch Freya fly down and land from her speech. Panda covered his eyes, turned around, and took a deep breath.

Shay gently unraveled Lingo's branches, and Zeus' blue light flushed over her face.

Favin turned to Tienilla and Freya. "How did you find the demon shield?"

"There's an ancient clan that broke away from the church hundreds of years ago and dedicated themselves to demonology. Their practices are far from what we believe in, but some things were necessary to vault just in case. Now look at us." Tienilla stopped to look around, exemplifying her annotation with a stern and hard-breasted demeanor.

Freya stepped ahead of her older sister. "While you're searching for the ship Captain that brought you here, go speak with this clan. They are on the Cretan docks. You may get something useful out of them."

The Ram Horned Exorcist

A good-looking man in a suit and tie walked through the *thump thump* bass in a crowded club. His feet followed one after the other with a slow bob to his knees. A hand swayed to the middle of his waist with each of his confident, thuggish steps forward.

Strutting around like he owned the place came from being best mates with the real owner of the pub-e club, Luke, an entrepreneur slash grunge metal guitarist. The boss who loves rocking the whole building to ruins on Hippy Go Sucky Fridays.

A glass broke next to the strutting fellow, and he maneuvered a sharp turn towards the group of smug lads drinking their piss out of a glass.

"Might want to be a little more careful with your drinks boys." Before the strutting fellow even talked, the smuggers were ripping him apart with their eyes, and as soon as he opened his mouth the anger seethed into the air.

In Strutter's eyes, it looked like the group dropped a glass on purpose, testing Strutter's courage. In Strutter's eyes that meant words will never lead to peace. Nothing could be said to forgive these punks if that was the case. It was time to put a stop to them talking smack and blabbering out the same stupid shit over and over like every stupid group of punks goes on saying, even though technically, they really haven't said anything.

Crete was a tourist trap. It had beautiful clear water, hippy-yippy hotels and clubs, and historic museums to honor the Greeks. Mogly's, however, was the local rock n roll spot still standing; a good place to have fun, but a hard place to be a douche, like these guys.

The leader of the group got real close to Strutter's face and opened his mouth like threats were about to spill out.

Headbutt! Broken nose, elbow to the face to the guy to his right, while simultaneously quick push kicking the guy to the left into the bar. Strutter grabbed the guy by the shirt still bleeding from the headbutt and threw him to the bouncers, who instantly pulled the entire group outside.

The bartender and the couple bouncers around the corner were the only ones to see this. Mogly's was a labyrinth of hallways and rooms. Strutter winked at the bartender, walked through a long hallway, and zigzagged his way to the front of the stage, unabashed by the tiny bit of red splatter on his forehead. It's Friday and Luke's band was walking onto the stage with a full house.

As soon as the drummer took his seat, a double drum beat thumped hard from the speakers. The tempo was quick, and the drums overwhelmed every heart in the club. Strutter got a tap on his shoulder and turned around to Larik, head of security. They whispered a few words, and Strutter casually followed Larik through the mass of teenyboppers and hungry tune-heads.

There was a booth overlooking the club. A guy with beach-blown hair, tie, and surf shorts was with a group of girls in slashed and colorful dresses, laughing and throwing beer everywhere. The beer splashes made it halfway to the ceiling when the mugs slammed on the table. They all had big open mouths from yelling and singing over the stage music.

Classy Strutter slid in next to the boss at the booth. He grabbed a mug, drank, and shoved it into the boss's chest, who was still looking at the pretty girls across the table and yelling something that may have had some charm to it. He took the mug from his chest, drank three gulps, and ruffled Strutter's hair.

"Hiya Luke."

****

The instrumental electronics and drumbeats had heads flinging hair up and down. The double base dual drum rhythms tore up the airwaves and flowed in sync with the dub drops and electronic piano mastery.

Strutter was busy talking expressively to a girl who wore a green halter top with bells hanging on the bottom trim. Luke stole her attention by standing on the tabletop to take off his shorts. The girls went wild. One of them cupped a piece of his upper thigh. Luke stood there for a second smiling at them mischievously, then finally threw his black Dicky pants on and headed for the stage.

As he grabbed the mic, the crowd roared, and the music pumped even faster in the metronome. Luke's voice was rough but melodic, and passionate with death metalodies at the tip of his tongue. His throat was fat with veins, yelling his soul out to the world, desperately wanting the world to hear him, every single life source to listen to those forsaken bloody words of dangerous vitality.

Two brothers and a disappointed girl walked in the front door while finishing a fist pound with the doorman. As they walked through the twisting hallways and by the stage, they picked up on what was being laid down.

Time runs forth never tasting my bones of loreeee!
Our turn to rip the angels out of the gates of what they HORDE!
Blowing down righteousness to create new religion.
The time that knows us will regret its bloody pigeons!
Mother Earth is a hive!!
I can survive! Breath until the darkness subsides.
Mother Earth is a hive!
I can survive! Breath until the darkness subsides.

They continued through another hallway to the outside bar. The singer's voice thankfully faded out, and the atmosphere resonated down a couple of levels.

Kendra tiptoed to the middle of Pads and A.D to try and reach their ears. "The singer is one of the clan member's sons, that rebellious little prick. We'll get to him after we talk with this Captain Sharp of yours." Kendra said while landing back on her heels with an amused smile.

They took a moment to look around, and then Kendra pointed at a monkey sitting on top of some fake plant, slapping it to see if it would slap back.

Pads hustled in that direction where there was another corridor leading into another room. The monkey saw them coming and ran in before them. There sat Lady Captain Sharp and her team of Saints, all glued to the news on the telly. The text sliding on the bottom of the screen read, *Alert : Trees alive and terrorizing people all over the country!*

A clip popped up of a large fig tree with red engravings chasing a group of people down train tracks. Seeing this on the news was already crazy enough, but to add to the craziness, an oak broke through a fence bordering the tracks and 'coat hangered' the fig with a branch scrolled with green engravings.

The helmsman Tracher saw the Kalmcs come in while he was sucking on a bottle. He pointed and went 'um um' like a baby sucking on milk, trying to get his mother's attention.

A.D put his finger on his mouth to shush him, and Johnny 'Forearms' grabbed the Kalmcs' shoulders from behind.

"Hi lads, looks like you guys were right, eh? Let's go say hi to the Captain." And as he said her title, she turned around on her stool, eased Tracher's consistent finger poking, and gave them a cool gaze of tranquility.

"Aye, just the lads I've been meaning to speak to." Throwing her thumb over her shoulder to indicate the news.

"So what's keeping us from turning you into authorities so they can start cleaning up this big mess?"

Kendra stepped forward to create space, rose her arms up above her head, and briskly threw them down to her hips. Her bracelet circlets came together in a deafening clang and stopped at her little balled up fists and white wrist wings. The sound wave or whatever spell that came from her bracelets created a sphere of silence, blocking all frequencies coming in and going out.

"I am Kendra, the fourth born Sky Sister to guard our great Mother Gaia. Our sixth sister Ruza, now known as Mareridt," Kendra crinkled her little nose and looked to spit.

"Has risen from the Galaxy of the Dead, possessing what they can on Earth to eventually try and defeat us and open a demonic portal into our world, which would extend their battlements just enough to gain superiority over Heaven."

The Saints looked at her astonished, dumbfounded, and tranquil.

Lady Captain Sharp slipped out of her hypnosis and responded compassionately. "How can we help?"

Kendra glanced back at the Kalmcs with a haughty grin.

"We need your ship to help guide and transport our woodland soldiers to Congo, Africa. From there, we will take care of our little sister Ruza."

"Okay, we're in Fourth Born Sky Sister." Captain Sharp declared, still stupefied by the situation.

"Great, we will go with you to the Gorge mouth on the Southern side of Crete; I believe that is where you dropped off the Kalmcs and some of our Awakened before."

Captain Sharp rose in understanding and in preparation to leave.

Kendra turned to lead the way out and then remembered.

"We will need your assistance with something else, Captain Sharp."

Captain Sharp almost had her full demeanor back; however, she was still a little slow due to being in the presence of a goddess.

"And what would that be miss?"

"We need to grab that metal singer and have him tell us where his father is hiding out."

Captain Sharp clicked, and her character was fully back and definitely ready to smash some skulls. She nodded to Kendra and pushed Johnny out of the corridor.

"Go get 'em big guy. We'll take care of security."

Johnny aggressively made his way through the drunkards surrounding the outside bar and the crowded hallways. When security rushed to seize him, the other Saint mates kicked the back of their knees and rounded them up, completely taking them out of the picture. Tracher took a bottle of Jack from behind the minibar and continued to follow the riot, giggling all the while.

In the stage room Pads and A.D brawled with the two security guys in front of the band, while Johnny let his spear hurtle through the drum set, knocking the drummer five feet back; his arrow duffing the bassist straight into the floor. Johnny repositioned himself to grab Luke, already blinded by Johnny's monkey covering his eyes. Nevertheless blinded, he still swung his guitar at his face, and Johnny instantly ducked only to find a charging Strutter uppercut him off stage.

Johnny landed right in front of Pads as Pads knocked out a bouncer. Pads looked up and saw that mean-looking Strutter approaching them with a slow, confident gait. Johnny was still working on his recovery, so he was going to have to take this guy out alone. He taunted Strutter by waving him in with his sweaty palms. As soon as Strutter came to the edge of the stage, A.D made it behind him and wrapped him up by slamming a drum set over his head. A.D kicked his legs out from under him, and he fell rolling around, unable to escape the rawhide.

The owner of the club Luke again tried to crumple at least one of these troublesome patrons with a downward swing of his axe, but A.D grabbed the guitar neck, headbutted Luke, and threw him over his shoulder.

"We have him. Let's head out."

The bartender fumbled for her phone and tried to dial while her security team was getting demolished by Captain Sharp and her mates. Kendra briskly threw her arms down again like an elegant bird that only needed one flap to soar. The lights blinked off, P.A clinked, and all that shone through the darkness were Kendra's sunshine bracelets and silhouetted wrist wings.

"Follow me."

They followed Kendra and finally ran past her into the moonlit alley. Tracher was the last to clink his way through the doorway.

"Run to the Saint." Captain Sharp advised, and they ran through the docks and finally, after a jog through town, jumped on board.

A.D thunked Luke onto the planks of the ship. Kendra summoned a serpent of water that rose above the Saint's railing and began to splash Luke unrelentingly in his face until he woke up.

"Where's the Priest hideout?" Kendra growled and pressed her bracelet bracers into his neck, also tickling his nose with her wing. Whatever she had the bracelets doing, it resonated in Luke's face with excruciating pain.

"Pa was banished from the church for being caught passed out at the foot of the Cross with an empty bottle of Tullamore Dew and a quarter bottle of HayLiqs Whiskey. 'Wear a Crutch like a Crown' is what I always say. And that's the last I've heard from him."

"Where. Is. He? Demon lover!" Kendra rode upon the vexation she had for her sister Mareridt. She pressed her bracelets harder into his neck.

Luke shuddered with pain but stayed silent and stubborn.

Kendra got up from her knee and cantered over to the bow of the Saint. She turned around and looked like a seductive angel. Her tight tank top and loose Arabian breaches were worn perfectly. Cute, lively flower vines clasped around her ankles like her sister Freya. Her eyes could transform a rock into a moon. Eyes that held a far-off yellow glint from a lantern, accompanying green irises with gray mist coming into midnight streets. She walked back, causing the deckhands, not accustomed to her, to grab their chests and submit their devotion in their painful heartthrobs. Captain Sharp rolled her eyes at her crew but also couldn't help being drawn in by Kendra's beauty.

Kendra kneeled again in front of Luke.

"Where is your father Luke?" This time she asked with soft serenity.

Luke fluttered his eyes and breathed, "The Yacht Club." He then fell over onto his side and drifted into a dream with a smile on his face.

Kendra flicked away her trance spell, and everyone suddenly snapped out of it. She walked down the plank to the harbor dock, "A.D come with me; the rest of you prepare the ship. We need to be ready to leave as soon as we return."

Pads thumped his knuckles on A.D's knuckles, smiling at his triumphant brother. Funny how the idea of an apocalypse could be so easily brushed aside by a beautiful woman.

Kendra and A.D quickly walked across the harbor docks searching for the Yacht Club.

A.D stopped, "This is it," and tossed a penny at the wooden doorway of a large boathouse. A.D knocked.

"Hmm, how do you know?" Kendra asked, curious and amused.

"We lived in California for ten years, and there were many harbors with many Yacht Clubs. We knocked on all their doors..."

A plump Japanese girl opened the door. "Hello?"

"Yes, hello there, we are looking for Nathaniel Kragg?" Kendra asked politely.

"Of course, right this way." They walked to the main office to a desk surrounded by aquariums. The attendant picked up the phone and dialed.

"Mr. Kragg, there are two people here to see you." She looked up at Kendra and A.D, inquiring their names.

"Sister Kendra and her Guard."

A.D smiled and absorbed himself in the honor. He quickly reminisced about his journey and the fact that everything they did was in order to stop Hell from taking over their planet. His shoulders shook covertly from a Sentinels honor mixed with chills of what the future held.

Kendra stepped on his toes, "You ready, Adam?" She asked with a smile, probably conscious of what he was thinking. A.D nodded back with a smile, and they followed the attendant's hand that directed them down a spiral staircase. No one ever called him by his birth name, and A.D accepted the gesture with a greater hope for a better tomorrow. *My name is my destiny.* The thought quickly filled up his Adrenaline Devil veins with the suicidal energy he needed to save the world.

As they descended, A.D grew wondrous. "Whoa, we are probably underwater."

"Yes." Kendra smiled.

When they reached the bottom of the spiral staircase, there was a door with a window slit. It reminded A.D of the metal doors through deep dark alleys and down foreboding stairs, to be greeted by a massive grump with a low voice sliding a narrow slit open that only showed his chest, who eventually asks, 'Who goes there?'

Kendra knocked, and the slit opened up to a massive dude with a huge jaw and scar on his cheek, kinda like A.D, but A.D had two.

He eyed the two of them up and down. Some things will never change.

The door opened, and the house light flooded over them. A tan, lean guy with a spiraled ram horn tatted on one side of his bald head greeted them.

"Welcome Sister, follow me." He said with a calm and overly pleasant grin on his face, A.D had a good feeling about these people.

The den was holyesque and not by what was seen exactly but by the feeling from the deeds and conviction in the tenant's progressive techniques. The hallways were empty and regular. The rooms to either side of the hall were large and filled with books stacked almost to the ceiling. More of the ram horn tattooed folk occupied the desks in their cubbied rooms.

A girl with earbuds in and long bright orange hair sat on a pile of two dozen books and used twice that many for her desk. She smiled as she scribed and nodded her head, most likely to the music from her mp3.

"Follow the Topaz." The lean guy said smoothly. Pointing to the orange stones along the ceiling's edge, his forearm rippled with muscles that twisted around to his elbow. Everyone so far in this underground house of books had fit dark green robes with black sashes and black accessories.

They walked past the nodding girl and her brigade of affiliates down to the end of the hall and into the next room of fat rust-colored books and the old smell of crumpled dusty scrolls. *Bad Vibrations by Black Angels*, played on a speaker in the corner of the room.

A man sat on a stool at a desk, facing away from the doorway and looked down pensively at paperwork. One young woman and one young man stood at either side of him facing the entrance of which Kendra and A.D had just arrived. Their body language was meek and disillusioned. They showed no guard. They merely waited and glanced past the new arrivals and down the hall with the topaz lighting. Both of their eyes were yellow with blue starbursts.

"Ah, if it isn't the inner light of the Over-verse," Nathanial said like a wise guy, still looking at the pages in front of him.

"Sister, answer me this. Why did the Gardener plant a light bulb?" Kendra glanced over at A.D, and he shrugged his shoulders.

Kendra then straightened her sprine and gave her answer gingerly. "She wanted to create a power plant."

"Ah, yes indeed. A power plant should then, in turn, give more life to its environment, yes? However, now there is a deep darkness living within the Gardener's soil. What will she do?"

"She will do what is in her nature. Why question us?"

Nathaniel turned around to look at Kendra. His head had more hair than the other scribes; however, beneath his white wise hair were both his hidden ram horns wrapping down the back of his neck and behind his ears. His eyes now had a calm blue glow to them, like his guards.

"My apologies Sister, the recent events have made me apprehensive of Mother Nature's abilities against this ancient evil. I grow curious about your judgments, especially during these perilous occasions." Nathaniel huffed out an exhale.

He was an older man with a syndicate mind, yet he became ponderous within his wisdom of the deep, ancient underground history of the legendary Sky Sisters. The way he spoke was annoying, not so much the sound of his voice but the confident arrogance he exuded.

"Nathaniel, we as Sky Sisters have a duty to protect the Glasir Scepter in order to shield the robust nature of our Mother. With half or more of her woods already tainted by this distant evil, it would certainly seem like haste would lift our wings; however, being alive in such a small world for so long, speed is something we have done without for centuries. We will continue to take our time and plan our strategy against our Sister Mareridt with ease and foresight. She will hit hard and fast with the brunt of her force, and we will be there to respond to her so vigorously and so disastrously that *we* will seem like the hostile antagonists. Mareridt's belligerents will crumble and squish under our heels...

"Truthfully Nathaniel, we are confident that this wicked time will pass, and Earth will reside once again in its own teeter-tottering tranquility. Mareridt is against all five Sisters, who are much more mischievous and severe with the laws of combat than we were thousands of years ago. We will send her back to Hell." Kendra said with a mischievous smile of her own. "Crying, most likely."

"Also, I'd like to inform you that your clan's anti-demon symbol worked."

"We know it does Sister; even though your tactic seems self-sufficient, I'm glad it will pronounce itself as a major asset. The anti-demon symbol was founded by two of our Priests who did their own possessing. One would kill the other and revive him into a coma. While in the comatose trance, he would travel through the Galaxy of the Dead as a spirit and conduct experiments on the demons by possessing them and torturing them. When one of these demon bodies would finally give up and die, the priest would return back to our world, and they would switch, to rejuvenate the mind and document their findings.

"Unfortunately, the only thing they found useful was that symbol and the existence of an afterlife. So, our clan has always been ready for demonic return. We are humble exorcists. We use their weaknesses magnificently against them. The gated symbol of many punishments." Nathaniel made a sign with both of his hands and bowed his head.

"I give to you four of my best exorcists, each with a ship to help transport your war party. May you and your Sentinels rid the world of Mareridt's destruction."

"May I, Nathaniel?" The yellow-eyed girl guardian asked with courageous politeness.

Nathaniel nodded for her to proceed.

"Strike from the shadows when dealing with unfamiliar foes," she said with a hoarse voice yet relaxed patience.

The twin exorcist to her side spoke up quickly after her, "We should organize our own strategy against Hell. We have the experience we need to lead our own assassins. If our first tactic is to bluntly bash into our enemy, I believe that would be playing into the game of an army born into brutality." He finished, distressed with his leader's quick decision making. His reserved voice made A.D nod his head in agreement even though he had no idea what they were talking about.

"Franky, my boy, this is an Angel of our world. Their mere being increases success against these demons. You and Kale will bring Xer and Brac to watch and help where you can. Mareridt is our enemy, and Mareridt wants to see her sisters again, therefore Kendra and her Sentinels here will be in the fat of it all. No time to wait. One of them may already be in trouble…" Nathaniel said while looking into Kendra's eyes.

"Yes Kale, strike with keen eyes, but also hollow out yourself to become a definite guardian of our Mother. They need our help, so we will follow. Now go!" Nathaniel closed his eyes, turned around, and went back to work.

"It was great to hear you, Sister. May the wind always be on your side."

Girls Night Out

Blitzen had all fifty of her swords piled in the front seat of an old school bus. Shaki stuck her head out and watched the dust trail kick up behind a dozen buses and a dozen jeep escorts. Cid put her hand on Shaki's leg, and Shaki swung her head back inside only to see Cid's worrisome glare at Gaia's second-youngest daughter.

Through the short time they've known Blitzen, she seemed enraged and close-minded. 'Let's charge into Mareridt's army of woodland terrors and trample them into the Earth!' She'd say.

Cid and Shaki tried to advise her to find her other Sisters first, but none of their words ever settled upon Blitzen. She was mad, but probably more angry she was alone.

Up ahead, there was a massive storm forming and a dense dust cloud rolling in.

"Make camp here," Blitzen ordered the driver. She hung outside the revolving doors of the bus and waved an orange scarf around, signaling the convoy to circle up for camp.

They created their convoy barrier and rested at the edge of the storm. As they waited, the men's eyes showed a great deal. The frowning stares showed that they were openly uneasy while watching Blitzen and her backdrop of deep blue clouds and lightning steaks crackling down into a hazy wall of sand rolling and twisting up in the unnatural windstorms. Holding tension in their shoulders while watching the sun inch closer to the horizon and darkness creeping ever nearer.

Yet, a continuous nod and stare showed they had embraced a strong sense of awe and gratitude for having the opportunity to support such a badass angel of their world.

****

Mareridt used her lightning to split and burn any tree not under demonic control. Her storm was a thick circle around her army, which rested in its eye, untouched and unseen.

Doomali was dead center in the eye of the storm. He had thorns lining the entirety of his African Honeylocust bark. He marched his spiky roots forth and stood watching the inner storm between two of his awkwardly rotating bannermen covered in the blue and yellow cloth of Doomali's crest.

****

Truly an angel in disguise, Blitzen rolled her right shoulder and looked out into the thick winds gusting over the desert sand. Five magnificently crafted swords rotated around her body as she stood on top of the southernmost school bus closest to where the forest would be. Each blade seemed to spin in a different way with a different attitude.

Her white eyes squinted over the dirt-worn shawl covering her nose and mouth. She felt Mareridt's gloom, but that wasn't all. There was an intense power moving through the earth, a power she had never felt before in her lifetime.

Blitzen jumped down and outside of the circular encampment of buses to lay her palm on the soft dirt, her blades rotating around her with ease. After her quick diagnosis, she jumped back up to the bus roof and signaled her main soldiers to ready the rest of her men and prepare for battle.

She peered into the forthcoming desert sandstorm again and gritted her teeth under her shawl, brain sizzling in her mirth. She was glad her Sister sent such a heavy assault after her instead of hanging back in her fortified forest, but... she looked back at her men in the hazy yellow sandblast. Her men have never fought against brute demonic strength like this or anything close. *Best of luck to them.*

Using telepathy, Blitzen unraveled a rolled-up rug lying next to her on the bus roof. Forty-five epic swords flew into the air with ballroom grace in front of her. The sword hilts came together in seven tiers. All blade tips pointed up in the same direction.

It took a moment to collect and remodel them into one gigantic specter blade with forty-five different edges. All swords so unique and marvelously sharp, edged steel glistening in the last of the sun's light behind her. The horizon miraged the sun into a fiery sword, matching the surrealness of the bladed abomination. The last sword was etched with three interlocking triangles on the base of its steel before the hilt. It flew up to position itself on the apex of the sword's pyramid construction.

"Mazzbrick," she sighed, and Mazzbrick bowed and took its place, hovering far off to her right. It twirled in the air, glinting ever so often from the bus lights, however, still half concealed by the sand-blasts whipping through the wind.

Blitzen leaped towards the sky with her five brilliant blades still turning around her as her mystical steel guardians. Mazzbrick gliding in the air by her side.

Shaki took a deep breath. She noticed she forgot to breathe while watching the remarkable force head straight for where Hell's minions were thought to be. She looked over at Cid, reviewing orders and strike plans with Blitzen's Captains.

Shaki couldn't feel her body as she peered around the hustling camp. There was so much she was a part of now that her being wasn't even at the edge of her consciousness. She was there, using this body as a tool to fix the future, but she also had transcended even beyond death in order to safeguard other lives.

Her fear flew by her like the sandstorm that vigorously flew over her head. What happens when hope dies? Fear resides?

They waited for Blitzen's signal.

****

On this night, the full moon was exceptionally bright. Blitzen surged through thick winds and suddenly came to the eye of the storm. Mareridt hovered there smiling. Her face eerily dark even with the great light of the moon. Her aura was a cold twirl wisping around her red-robed body. Her platform was at least a hundred wooden spears, pointed at Blitzen and looking ready for launch.

An army of woods moved below, glowing red with intricate demonic squiggles and lines, tiny specks from the distance above.

Blitzen's surprised brow at Mareridt's new body turned into a vicious glare, and her five gyrating swords raced toward Mareridt.

Mareridt's spears mimicked the flying blades' actions in her defense and she vanished, zipping around the inner-storm at incredible speed.

Trailing her speed were dark blue icy clouds that froze the hazy yellow sandblasts as she flew through. Once content with her rings of ice, she hovered, smiling again, resting her arms into dense mini-clouds on either side of her. Blitzen charged again with her five blades interchanging spaces, ready to balloon out if Mareridt attempted another dodge.

Mareridt pushed her cloudy hands toward the attack, which was the motion to form an ice wall. Blitzen's golden sword sped ahead and stuck itself in the middle of the wall as she came up behind it, grabbing the hilt and shoving her way through. Mareridt was simply waiting with another mobile ice wall that blocked Blitzen's next downward swing that had so much force it put Mareridt beneath her.

Mareridt launched dozens of wooden spears at Blitzen to distance herself between them. During her onslaught of spear chucking, Mazzbrick, the great specter sword of forty-five legendary blades, came vigorously through the concealing winds, pointing its tip ambitiously at Mareridt's spine. Mareridt back flipped over Mazzbrick, slicing the bottom of her barefoot from one of its perimeter blades.

She transformed both of her dark blue clouds into two daggers of lightning, flashing in and out of miniature cloud hilts. Mareridt now chased Blitzen as Mazzbrick chased her.

Blitzen still casually blocked her evil sister's assault yet had no time for retaliation. It was a defensive fight now against her demonic murderous sister, so she waited while gritting her teeth, hoping that Mazzbrick would stick Mareridt on a blind turn.

As chaos swindled the air more and more inside the eye of the storm, Blitzen sent out her sword, with a pointy hilt, back to her bus camp. Within a fraction of a second, after another guardian blade quickly blocked a lightning dagger blow, Blitzen found the chance to punch Mareridt in the mouth. Blood trickled down her dark chin and slid across her jawline from her high-speed flying.

Mareridt screamed like a wailing wench and swung her daggers in a frenzy, seemingly giving Blitzen the upper hand in her sister's blind fury. This gave Mazzbrick another chance at a great swing, but was slowed by her icy trail and missed.

Dodging the frenzy without haste, Blitzen started to spin up in a whirlwind, leaving her swords to spin just as fast around her. Now, Mareridt was on the defensive, wavering in a clumsy disposition without her winged wrists.

Blitzen's blades now gained a static charge on them, just like Mareridt's, which created a lightning war, putting Mareridt constantly on the retreat from the dancing blades of Blitzen's Blitzkrieg. Sisters were always stealing from each other, even spells and abilities.

A tornado formed behind Mareridt as she was being repelled back. It zipped close to Mazzbrick, putting each one of the massive swords' swings a tinge off-kilter.

Blitzen eyed her sword elemental like a master commander would her best soldier, ordering off her elemental with a twitch of her tear-filled eye. Mazzbrick dropped down into the demon trees like a drill, causing the elemental tornado to follow as well, surely about to spin those uprooted deadheads for a good one. Blitzen hated how trees, being Mother's best creations, had to endure so much bullshit.

****

Shaki heard a sizzling sound coming from where Blitzen took off. Through the sandy, heavy winds, a sword with a pointy hilt came right in front of Cid's face, inches from her nose. It jolted down to etch a thick arrow in the dirt. The sword tilted up abruptly and raced back from where it came. In Cid's bus, the band *The Sword* played ironically.

"Alright lads, it's battle time. Let's head out," Cid yelled while jumping into her bus. She turned over the ignition and nodded Shaki over to hang out the window behind her. Shaki put her right hand on the 'Oh Shit Bar', while her left arm grasped a chainsaw.

"I wish everyone was here with us..." Shaki said.

"Don't worry, we'll finish the war before they even get here. IT'LL BE GREAT!" Cid said as she took off.

Shaki looked towards the back of the bus and brushed her dirty blonde hair out of her face. Cid leaned to the right to stop her hair from smacking her in the eyes as well. There were four men on either side of the school bus, each accompanied by two large oil canisters.

Three men sat in front with chainsaws and guns propped on their shoulders. Each of their twelve buses had similar formations, and each person believed wholeheartedly that Blitzen's plan would probably end up killing them.

****

Blitzen spun and kicked Mareridt in the nose with her heel, followed by a great slash across her torso with two spectral blades; the second only barely catching her chest. Mareridt retreated back and let enough ice out between her and Blitzen to completely deplete the heavy cloud above her into a white wisp.

Blitzen hovered there watching Mareridt flee and then looked down at the army from Hell. She now pitied the trees that couldn't withstand the demon's possession, and more anger grew inside her.

A steady line of blood dripped from her foot, gliding down in the air below her. As she lost track of its fall, she noticed it was coming from a stab wound in her thigh. She also noticed in the full moon's bright light, a tree that stood looking up at her. It was the only tree not moving and locked eyes with her in a very bizarre and eerie way, causing Blitzen to shudder. The tree moved slightly and then suddenly, after a moment, another tree came flying into focus, becoming clearer and larger with each second that went by. The demon tree had thrown another demon tree up into the air with some kind of flight engraving in its trunk to allow such contending elevation.

Blitzen waited and watched all in a comfortable illusion that what was happening simply couldn't be. The flying tree came to its peak and hovered there below Blitzen for a moment before it started to fall. One of its red engravings became considerably more vibrant than the others, and then another carving lit up around its bark. It unleashed a long branch that extended further and further, grabbing Blitzen, and pulling her down.

Blitzen's swords chopped at its thick branch but had trouble keeping up with the hacking while in her fast descent. Right before the final plummet to the desert sand, in the middle of the demon wood army, her scout blade with the pointy hilt came back and sliced the branch in one smooth and speedy stroke, releasing its Sky Sister from its grasp.

She fell through the cumbersome canopies, grasping to envelope her, and, PUFF, hit the desert sand.

Under the long swirly branches of these demon infiltrators, Blitzen heard an encompassing sound of wood snaps and timber creaks. Watching the hungry waddles of contorted monstrous faces caused the skin around her knuckles to pull tight white. Mazzbrick zipped away after a crushing swing overhead, trimming the upper levels of the encroaching branches surrounding her.

Blitzen ruggedly stood up and jetted out toward the sky to wait for her guardian. She flew all the way up to where the clouds were puffy and idle; the calmness relaxed her eyelids down. Everything looked at peace in the eye of the storm, however, Mazzbrick hadn't returned.

****

Mazzbrick swung at Doomali as the demon scooped up a nearby tree to block the forty-five swords. The goofy wood completely splintered under the flexible spectral of blades. Doomali quickly slid his newfound roots over to Mazzbrick and grabbed its hilted side in an agile rotation, then bashed the brigade of swords into the desert sand again and again, causing blades to be tossed in every direction.

With an eclipsing shadow slowly looming over Mazzbrick's collapse, Blitzen rushed to the cluster of fallen swords. Her five spectral bladed protectors followed in her assault, a tunnel vision of ferocity leading straight into the ground.

As she flew down, two short swords from shattered Mazzbrick flew straight into her hands, and she spread her arms wide in a Christ Air fashion, like a hawk swooping down on its prey.

Mareridt popped out of the storm right behind Blitzen and kicked her to the side, quickly pulling out a sleek lightning bolt dagger from her back, leaving Blitzen's limp body to fall to the ground.

Mareridt trailed her sister's descent and plummeted down onto Blitzen's stomach. As Blitzen opened her eyes to face the sister she so long ago sent to Hell, Mareridt stabbed through Blitzen's red and black flannel, piercing her heart, and lightning shot through Blitzen's beautiful white eyes. Her face remained stoic, yet disappointed. She would not give her sister that satisfaction of watching her grumble before death.

The earth rumbled and cracked, and sand spilled into the eternal chasms of time. Demon trees stumbled around to gather themselves, trying to lock into the more stable land masses while some slipped off the sandy cliffs and fell into Mother's valleys where her child would lay in rest, and her enemies would perish and burn in her merciless molten core.

****

Cid skidded the bus to a stop once she saw a branch swing through the sandstorm. *This is it.* Shaki pulled her chainsaw cable and started its motor. The saw rumbled and the chain zipped around. She jumped out of the bus and ran around to the driver's side.

A darkened, hunched-over demon Baobab tree, as tall as a lighthouse, appeared through the storm. The tree opened its mouth until the sandblasts filled its wooden yap to the point of spilling back out like drool. It lurched toward Shaki, moving along in a joyously slow manner.

Three more men ran out to join Shaki, all of them buzzing with chainsaws. The demon tree lifted his branches and plopped them down as if his day couldn't get any more fun. New planet, new form, new destiny.

The leading root advanced under the sand and swirled its tip to grab hold of the earth. Pulling itself forward like an octopus on the sea floor, now only five yards ahead of the bus.

Cid watched the lurching, hunched-over, Baobab tree with darkened bark move by her driver's side window. His engravings were little to none; however, the lit ones she could see looked as if Hell was embedded into its core. Molten fire and bubbling boils popped as the ridges of the old tree's bark singed. The demon tree passed by the driver's seat, and Cid saw the other school buses in the same lateral line as herself. More trees came out of the sand-buried air, and more chainsaws buzzed in the distance.

The Baobab demon tree hollows were set on Shaki. It slid its root forward into the sand again and dug itself right under her. She yelled out while sawing through the sand and root, "Acid burst this bitch!"

Then, out from the bus, windows with the cross beams and window frames taken out, came the green spillage of acid pouring into a pool at the tree's base.

The demon tree slowed, sinking into the earth just as fast as it moved forward. The bus backed up and turned in between Shaki and the other distractions right as the tree whirled around tossing acid all over the bus and flinging it into the windows.

"Run! Shaki, get away from the bus!" Cid yelled as she kicked the door open and ran out with two others.

Men from other buses used their AK-47s and pistols against the acid burnt demons. Some were met with a whirl of acid as back-fire, and some men saw the real demons of Hell come out of that storm. Most were quick and monstrous, enjoying a brief adventure into another galaxy to kill the living. They jumped on the buses and tore everyone and everything apart, no matter how hot the acid and bullets were.

One demon tree came thundering out of the sandstorm and threw a previously worthy combatant bus with three men inside high into the air. To Cid and Shaki, it appeared only as a thorny Honeylocust tree, but to fellow demons, it was the Togmehoian Lord Doomali.

When the bus smashed back into the sand a few flips away from the acid pour area, Doomali pulled out two of the men, easily sticking their bodies onto his wickedly sharp thorns, leaving them to hang there, dead. The driver had escaped for a moment but was caught crawling off in retreat by a quick and lengthy Acacia.

The Acacia swirled a long root around the driver's head and threw him over to Doomali. The squish sound of long thorns impaling flesh was heard even over Shaki's chainsaw. It wasn't death that filled the men's bones with mindless terror; it was living and moving inside a real nightmare. The ones that could still retreat did, while the others stood trembling alongside Cid and Shaki.

The lurching Baobab tree fell off to the side like an old stump. A large Wawona Tree with a humongous hollow hole for its mouth stomped on what was left of it, sinking it down into the acid, like how a gorilla would nonchalantly rest on their submissive opponent.

Then, as Cid and Shaki were just about to run for their lives, the earth began to rumble, and the sand slid into the crevasses created by the quick and humongous quake. The Wawona Tree waved a knobby branch goodbye and turned around to meet the others who were howling and parading around. The distortion in their warped, ghoulish features was stagnant and concerning. The demon trees used what human blood was left to cover their trunks with crimson war paint. Blood rituals weren't too far-fetched for gruesome demons such as these.

Fall, Fall, come on! Fall mother fuckers.

The earth cracked and quaked as the girls lay on the edge of the newborn cliff watching. A couple demon trees scrambled and fell along the freshly opening fissures, but most escaped Blitzen's dying manifestation.

They walked back into the storm, causally taunting Shaki and Cid to follow, even though they were now stuck on a desert island trapped by Mother's rift.

Tienilla's Fleet

"Clouds… they group up, they disperse, they settle. It's hard to manipulate land in resemblance to lighter elemental uniformity… Actually darn close to impossible. That's Mother's thing." Freya said, keeping her pondering gaze up at the diversified sunset sky and cradling the back of her head with her fingers interlocked together. Favin lay next to her on the stern's deck.

"The sky is ours. We could bring darkness…"

The marine layer behind them to the East hovered at the base of a mountain range and migrated towards the pillowy, ribbed clouds to the West. The Western clouds were a massive valley of scattered, wind-blown, sunset-colored puffs headed right over the fleet. The Southern clouds were stretched out, as still as if someone drew them on a canvas.

From all around the Saint, these clouds unified and slowly changed into a darker indigo hue, heavy with water vapor. It cast a deep shadow over the water and brought a chill over the crew, a chill much more than just having blocked the warmth of the sun.

"Or we could bring light," Freya tilted her ponderous gaze.

The conglomerant cloud split, parting around the sunset glow. A gust of wind blew in from the East, swirling the light red and orange clouds into a magnificent frame of the Western Mediterranean horizon.

"Whatever the case may be, in two days the sky will crack, clouds will form, and light will become hard to find... Darkness will bury bright spirits, and evil energy will conquer the melodic ambiance of our world." A swell smacked the front of the Saint and splashed water on the deck, gushing across the ship's planks.

Freya got up and rocked to the railing to peer over the rough, thirty-five foot swells coming out of the Gibraltar strait. Northern Morocco and the foothills of the South of Spain could both be seen as the Saint reached the peak of a swell. As they dropped back down into the waves' trough, they grew curious as to whether their ships would make it out of this flash tidal change.

Kendra walked over to Freya - steady as if she was walking to stand over an open grave.

"I feel a loss… Tienilla and Shay are out looking for Blitzen… Something happened Freya." Kendra held her black lightning bolt double-edged blade like she could conquer the world, but worry unmasked itself through her voice.

The Saint rocked inconsistently with the motion of the ocean, overly fluttering stomachs just enough for them to notice there had been an earthquake. A puff of black smoke rose into the open blue sky above Morocco, and then another puff only a few miles from that.

"I'm going to see what that's all about and get off of this sickening Monk," Freya grunted and took off South.

"Her name is the Saint…" Captain Sharp had been eavesdropping.

"This is highly irregular sea swell we have here. Does it have anything to do with the current… situation? Any ocean demons I need to know about?"

While Favin shrugged off the question, the swells raged and ate at the hull while occasionally slamming up onto the deck. Kendra walked toward the Birchwoods to watch the smoky puffs on land.

"Zeus was the nickname they gave me two thousand years ago," he rumbled as Kendra approached. He still pouted about the demon taking over his spirit, but Zeus simply couldn't pass up a chance to chat with a Sky Sister.

"I received the name Zeus in the year 439 when you were sending down your fat bolts into the forest from Mt. Olympus."

"I had a bad breakup with a Spartan Commander," Kendra giggled. Her lightning bolt blade thudded into the deck, and she looked over Zeus's permanently charred branches with the symmetrical side of her sword splitting her face into jagged halves. She then looked above the bow railing with Morocco in the distance.

Far across that sea, with great watery grace, the ocean shot up and created a cobalt blue elemental swashbuckling along the coastline.

****

Freya watched her shadow along the rolling swells for a while, thinking about what this could mean, who she was, and how she was going to be tested in the near future. She skidded her palm in the water before she reached the city. The spray behind her formed into a large water elemental, actually colossus in a way, stuck in its own element and prepared to hose down the city.

The crackle of gunfire echoed in the depths of the city, surrounded by tall hotels and buildings on every block.

Freya slowed her flight and signaled the water elemental to extinguish the large flame close to shore. She landed and looked into the eerie, desolate entrance to the main city, buildings blocking out most of the twilight sky. Vines grew along large wooden door frames and crept up boring windowpanes with shattered windows, filling office cubicles and hotel balconies with greenery. Moss partnered with thick interwoven vines sprawling across the street's asphalt and lamp posts in a fresh spread of foliage. Alas, this would have been a dream come true for a radical environmentalist; woefully, the greenery here was tainted and oozed danger at every stem.

Freya tugged on her black leather jacket to open up her shoulders for quickness and mobility, then tied her strawberry blonde hair into a ponytail. A tear slowly rolled down her cheek. Blitzen was her favorite sister.

The darkish vines slowly inched their way toward Freya's bare feet, and she floated a little above the second story and finally flew into the concrete jungle.

After the first bend around a city corner, there were three grocery mart fronts at street level completely engulfed in flames. The flames flickered horribly, ready to damage the entirety of the building's upper levels. The creepy sensation came from not knowing the depth of the weirder things that dwelled in hollow holes of the jungle. Deeper, darker, depths of meaner, stranger contortions. In this city's heart there was a disastrous beast spreading this meandering plague.

If demons weren't the probable cause of this, Freya would be all for Mother's vines taking over these overpopulated concrete cities. To Freya, people were annoying and dumb as shit. She withdrew a dial of her frustration. *They were lost. Lost and dumb, ya.*

The feeling in her chest twisted and creeked in on itself again... *Lost.*

More gunshots joined with men's battle cries, becoming louder and more pinpointed. Freya floated over to an abandoned car and put it into neutral, then flew to the burning buildings. Within a moment she extracted the building's flames, dragging them across the asphalt and into the steadily rolling car. She then flew up above the building's flat rooftops and played the game with a bird's eye perspective.

The engulfed car turned a corner with a broken militia firing at any vine or chunk of moss that moved. The militia was scared and nowhere close to the heart of the beast, who casually sat in a large intersection. Its branches infiltrating the top building levels, and the roots ate up the parking garages below. Freya rolled the car past the dumb and scared militia around another corner, and down the last street towards the demon tree's base, meanwhile splitting her fire up into the surrounding vines, using them as little ninja wicks. The fire raced through the vines heading straight to the demon core.

As the car bumped to a stop into the monstrous Cross Guard Tree, Freya used her embered vines to ignite and jump over to the car's gas tank. The resulting explosion left the wooden Cross Guard engulfed in fire.

As Freya flew out of the evacuated city, her water elemental dissipated behind her, splashing back into the rough white-capped sea. Revived in its place was an elemental gush of wind, aiding its creator with cognitive propulsion. Elementals always abide by their natural procedures, flowing, burning, staying perfectly still. However, with a bit of soul essence, these common elements become awakened stewards of their creator.

The fleet looked awesome to Freya as she flew back in, a bunch of toy ships in a hyper kids' bathtub. In the lead, the Saint, curved and colored like a shadow of the sea, with a sharp bow, an open deck, and three levels for cargo. It was a smaller ferry, and she was a little weighed down, but the trees made her seem like an entangled leviathan on the sea's surface. The four ram-horned exorcist ships looked more like pirates. Their horns engraved on their bows and sails smoothed and billowed from the consistent westward winds.

Water drops ran down Freya's cheek after she ran a wet hand through her reddish blonde hair. She giggled to herself as she watched the nineteen other tree bond 'ships' that tried to replicate their guides. The larger, less branchy Awakened floated under the rest as a hull of sorts; however, still relying on regular unawakened trees to float under them, fully submerged.

The rest intertwined together, forming a ship's curve, and some even had Awakened standing as the mast, holding up old torn sails from the ram-horned reserves. Their bond was tight and created funny little replicas of the ram-horn's schooners. Ropes were tied to all five guide ships to help tow the Awakened along. It was Tienilla's fleet, but really Mother Gaia's children off for another adventure.

Mad Max

Max and Lancelot rode to a stop overlooking Dinsee, the House of Bones. Past the blazing fire where the Stoop used to be, a dark pile of ash darkened the purplish dirt, and scattered bones caught the light from a dozen nearby planets with tiny proportional moons.

There was something so magical about this extremely crowded Galaxy of the Dead. A home of brutality, reality, and peace, if that made any sense... A place where peace is inevitable, ultimate, and eternal. Eternity is made up of peace, and inevitability in death is reality. The ones who live in an ignorant reality of terror and strife may lie in a world of damnation forever. Still, if you're open to exceptions, such as the belief that your reality of brutality is peaceful, then paradise awaits.

"There are fucks at the Stoop," Growled Max. He was infuriated by losing a major part of his Skeleton Crew in the city of Plaztex. He boiled with rage all day while traveling back. He even boiled at the fact that Saul, Doomali's father, couldn't name his damn city anything else other than Plaztex, the name of their freaking planet… Plaztex on Plaztex.

Max had changed entirely, and it made Lancelot nervous at every decisive moment.

"We are riding in. Hand me the dynamite and the detonator." Max ordered.

After the hand-over, Max took off on his bone bike toward the Stoop, straight towards the highest part of the flames. Lancelot unbuckled his two swords behind his back and followed Max into another bloody and broken battle.

They pulled up to a line of five hungry looking warriors, posing as kings of the hill, able to take the spoils of war and hang onto the territory. A dozen others like them were sitting around a smaller fire of skeleton bones and wood.

Max drifted up to them, threw the dynamite, wire twirling through the air, and pressed down on the detonator as soon as it dropped to their feet.

BOOM!

The heat wave felt good pushing through Max's bones, turning them orange for a second.

Lancelot kicked his bike peg down and revealed his two blades to the incoming dozen soldiers. Each blade slid along the first approaching monsters' stomachs before Lancelot did a downward slash onto the next couple of troop's chins. In front of him, Max rode in at an angle and rammed one of the heavily armored monster soldiers, sticking him with the bone horns welded to the front of his bike. Using the momentum, Max catapulted over the monster and gave it a solid knee to the face, pushing its chest off of the bike horns.

They battled for hours in the ruins of the Stoop. Doomali's troops were incredibly resistant to dying. Even when they were knocked out with a skull cracking blow from Lancelot's graphite gauntlet, they woke up later to jump back into the fight.

As the fight dwindled down, Lancelot ended up inside the back of the porous Stoop, looking through the tremendously broken and imploded ruins, flames still burning up its brick walls.

Max stood a little inside as well, a skeleton under a burning doorway. He pushed the head of the first smoldering monster he impaled with the horns on his bike off his super curved scimitar. Another monster hung, double dead, on the burning door with a bone sticking through its chest. Lancelot kicked a severed head with long black hair out of his sight, joining the fun of rolling heads.

The neighboring planets gently spectated the entire length of their fight, peering through the fallen smokey ceiling at Lancelot and Max, as Gods would do to any other victorious being that fought out of their skin.

Max looked out of the exceptionally large hole in the back of the bar. The pond was stagnant with more bodies. The bone bikes that were usually parked by the rear wall were all thrashed in a heap. He walked through the fire to see if anything was salvageable. He found a mostly intact skeleton brother.

"Other Max," Max whispered under his breath.

"Max…" Aussie Max said like he was gurgling blood or on the brink of death.

"What's up, Max? It looks like you guys had some party." Max laughed sarcastically, probably smiling for the first time since the ambush at Doomali's Citadel.

"You called me Max, Max… Thank you." Aussie Max said in a raspy voice.

"Don't mention it, you scallywag."

Max the Second rose from the bikes and shook off the dust accumulated by lying there for two days.

"I thought you were dying!" Max said in disbelief.

"Ah, I was just messing."

Max walked off and sat by his pond of dead bodies. Lancelot, who still watched and meditated in his post-battle rotations, was first thankful to have survived such a suicidal mission and, second, curious if Max had gone insane yet. He walked around the Stoop and over to the pond where Max sat. His kilt scrunched up at his thighs.

"What's the next move boss?"

Max directed his attention to Lancelot, only for a second, and then looked back at the planets and moons hovering in outer space.

"Who's that?" Lancelot nodded toward the skeleton pulling a motorcycle frame out of the pile of bikes.

"That's Max."

Now Lancelot was sure Max went coo-coo. "Max huh?"

"I took his name from him because my name was Max in the before life. His leader Duncan called me another stupid nickname, Skittles, or some pansy-ass name, so I killed him and became the new leader of the Skeleton Crew."

When Max had killed Duncan, he beat him up at a neutral bar while they were looking for recruits. Soap, Max's skeleton brother at the time, stuffed Duncan full of dynamite and blew him up. Once Max arrived at the Stoop, he had the remaining troop that watched their leader Duncan explode, blown up as well because they did nothing to protect him. After Max had reclaimed his real name back, Aussie Max went into a weird sort of depression, usually hiding away in closets.

Lancelot investigated the Stoop for a while, searching for what had happened to Kraeno. He took off after that. Lone Wolfing it once again on his eternal quest in Hell.

White Striped Recruits

Max went over to Aussie Max and told him it was time to go. Before they took off, Aussie Max put together a large trailer filled with all the bikes he could salvage, a stack of blades, and a bundle of clothes. Max told him to ditch the blades and clothes and replace them with digging tools.

They rode for two days' time, Max always ahead of Max the Second, otherwise known as Aussie Max.

When their bones started to tingle, they tipped over the nearby hills and saw a lake of lava spread across the mountainous terrain. Specks of white striped characters dotted the exterior of the lake of lava, dazed and confused, looking over each other in amazed horror.

Max dug his heel into gear and raced off down the hill leaving Aussie Max in the dust.

At fishtailing speeds, Max arrived at the patches of fresh skeletons. He noticed that the smaller islands were still packed with not just humanoids but humans from the planet Earth, similar to Kraeno's form. The islands probably became overpopulated, so the skeletons in front of him, now on the mainland, probably fell in first.

Max walked up to the lava's shoreline and yelled out to the remaining islanders, ignoring the skeletons around him.

"Hear me, you damned scallywags!" Eventually their fearful murmuring came to a stop, witnessing a clothed skeleton for the first time.

"This is Hell, all around you, the planets, the moons; the whole damn galaxy is the Galaxy of the Dead!" Max let that settle in for a moment and continued with even more luster than before.

"Join me, as the new Skeleton Crew, built upon redemption… The reason you stand on an island surrounded by lava is because demons put you there. Your destiny now is a bony one –" Aussie Max chuckled a little behind him, and Max glanced back, proud of his maddened humor.

"You were meant to melt and live as dead immortals." Max stepped knee deep into the lava.

"You were meant for the Skeleton Crew. You were meant to march on the demons that took your life. You are Hell's Reapers." Max rotated a full 360 degrees to make sure all of them knew he was mentioning them.

"Okay, skellys, let's go pull your brothers and sisters into the pool of enlightenment, the holy liquid of which is your destiny!" Max started swimming out to one of the islands and a few followed him right away. The people on the islands screeched and yelled, unaccustomed to life in Hell. Some of them dove in headfirst and accepted their fate.

More and more newly risen recruits started swimming in from the islands, and soon, Aussie Max saw an army of stark white stripes hanging onto Max's every word.

He treated them like friends, all of them like officers in his army, and ordered them to dig all the way to Plaztex. To conquer the city with a River of Fire!

****

Aussie Max led a scouting crew beyond the bone ship headquarters. They rode around to nearby outposts and stripped their buildings of bones and metals.

The new arrivals were learning quickly. Their morale was high because of the awesome redemption in the air and the feeling of having a family in the afterlife. Ruin, destroy, and take the bare-boned essentials they needed. No breaks in the mission leading toward a morale of destruction.

When Aussie Max got back to the digging crew from Melcruso's ruined castle, he saw how realistic Captain Max's idea had become. The crew dug wide and deep, not to mention far.

In order to ride this river of fire in style they created a skeleton ship. The bottom half of their ship was made from leftover bones from the previous Skeleton Crew, or whole skeletons that had created too much drama or grief for Max. The ignorant ones are unable to accept their fate and will never encounter peace because of their fearful spirit. So Max used the damned in another way.

Stonolf's Crew slash band mates, were killed by tree demons during their concert in Europe. Based on their present situation, these guys were taking their bony damnation pretty well. Aussie Max was able to loot some epic instruments at Melcruso's church and handed out the gear to the ragtag skeleton band, who motivated the operation and pushed the skellys to dig faster.

Stonolf called out, "Every sepulchral carving is closer to the tombage for those bloody demon cunts."

When Aussie Max had handed out the equipment, the band members leaned back, laughing with joy. The suave skeletons grabbed their new demonic instrumental pieces and started right away, nice and easy, with everyone usually joining in during their chorus: A band within the bone ship floating on a river of fire.

You can't push us around. (You can't push us around!)
You can't push us around. (You can't push us around!)
If you try, gonna lie 6 feet underground.
Papa' Ace loading up his mace. Little sister hiding behind the grandfather clock.
Got a couple rounds in the Chevy ashtray.
I don't know why I was made this way.
If we can't get in, then fuck what you say!
We the Skelly Crew running straight your way.
You keep looking at me like you want to jump.
If we let loose homie, you won't get up.
Little brother raised on the front yard gym.
Stands 5'2, nickname Sandman Slim.
Motherfucker thinks he's 6 foot 10.
Never seen a young man act so rough.
Never see a frown till you've seen that crown.
We just living our deaths like it's the four, five, Ten!
You know it's a fucking party when we get to town.
Yeah, I know a little something about getting high.
Yeah, I know a little something about getting drunk.

White Striped Recruits

You fuck with the Skeleton Crew and everybody rise.
So go jump in the lava if you feeling lucky punk!

The ship's frame was complete, and the white polished bones looked great engulfed in the red flames and lava goo that surrounded it. The bow and figurehead were a collection of skulls, their own as well as others gathered along the way, crossed with intersecting rib bones to make a wavy design. Bones woven so intricately together that it made for a well structured ship.

Max was submerged under the lava and dug ahead, making sure it was deep enough to pass through. He popped out every so often and threw three in his place, taking a break to check on the ship's construction and scouting crews.

"It is three weeks' time to Doomali's Citadel. Are there rumors of our approach?" Max asked, bored with all the digging but a little revitalized with the tunes from Stonolf's band.

"Hard to know for sure, boss. Skellys are a bit…" The heavy leg boned scout itched in his breeches, a tad worried about the bounty over their heads.

"Aye, we are outlawed, but we bring our natural habitat with us. Fire trumps all lad! I guess it won't matter if those damn demons see us coming, but we need to know when they come. Let's make two more scouting parties, okay? And I need recon eyes on the Citadel at all times."

The organization of a war party was so new to this little scout in front of Max. Everything seemed new to these newly risen recruits. It was a scary new world; however, like most things, it had its perks and occasional quirks.

The young scout's spirits shot up over his ever stretching understanding. "I have good news on Melcruso's castle. It had a drill. Shit, she had a dozen freaking drills, and now we have them, boss! We just need a team to go get the rest; we already have two on their way."

"Well, suck me fine Sally O'Feely, that's fucking great!"

In Kraeno's Berserk

Noble slowed and came to a halt right next to a starship in this new city called Transcendence. The superiority of architecture, roads, and monsters was bizarre considering everything Kraeno's seen thus far. The city was packed with creatures, so many that direct contact with one of them was inevitable with almost every step.

After escaping the Skelly Stoop, Kraeno went through a couple of late-night campfires and gathered information regarding demon armies joining for a raid against the angels of the Halo. Transcendence was like a giant Airspace headquarters for the demonic crusade. Kraeno thought it would be an excellent place to get some redemption. Gathering armies held collaborating demon lords.

He led Noble, or perhaps, with an examination of his slumped shoulders he exhibited, Noble led Kraeno. Noble sniffed the air and happily lapped up a warm breeze drafting by the open gate to a grim starship. It looked as if it dripped into the dirt, belonging to the world only as a disease. It had large collapsible wings and a green sewer glow to its trim, with green paint splattered on the side or green blood; it was hard to decipher anymore.

Noble benevolently cantered to the slanted gate with a playful black tongue sticking out the side of his half skel mouth. His muscles ripped around his open wounds still showing husky white bones, clean and sleek as if he had a metallic infrastructure.

The dusty companions boarded the starship without even glancing around to see if they would be detected, marching right up to the dining quarters. Kraeno pushed back his hood to peer around. His outer sweatshirt was dark green with red dust sprayed across it like old jet streams during sunset in a twilight sky.

How they came to pass unnoticed by the neatly uniformed guards required a great deal of luck. It may have possibly been a touch of their casual psychotic approach. It must have been difficult for the guards to decide what needed attention when everyone and everything was psychotic. It's as if being just the right amount of insane was the ultimate cover.

The other four sweatshirts Kraeno wore were the same but without hoods. If he was to be in disguise, he had to puff up his slim skeleton body.

He opened a clean cabinet and filled his satchel with all the canned foods. He threw one of the cans up for Noble, and the Hellhound stuck it with one of its snaggle teeth and ripped it in half with his paw, lapping up the orange slime on the ground in an instant.

Kraeno kicked the can to the side. His dirty skull tilted down in hypnotized depression and slump. His hollow sockets were vacant and displeased.

Good days and bad days, even in Hell.

Kraeno walked out of the starship, scuffed the dirt, and headed for the bar down the street; Noble followed him, giving Kraeno his space of despair.

In the Dyathsake Galaxy, a Hellhound was a beast that roamed and hunted, guarding and killing with its pack. Most of these prestigious slow-walking demons or hell-bound characters had never seen a Hellhound so ravaged and monstrous trotting city streets without preying on everything that moved. They were nightmarish creatures, roamers that scourge the land to keep damned spirits in a cell of panic and fear.

Along their walk, Kraeno felt the trepidation of the Transcendence citizens as they peeked out of the shadows, watching with an eye uncovered in the corner of their door frames. The Plaztex warriors and creatures less afraid eyed the two curiously. Kraeno desperately needed a dark hole to bury himself in.

He walked into the Lazy Jax Bar, followed by disquieted stares that clung to the Hellhound. The way Noble pranced foretold of dancing on their graves while ending their ghostly eyesight with sharp hemorrhaging teeth.

Noble walked around the side of the bar and took an easy leap onto the roof of Lazy Jax. He lay waiting above the black and white checkered sign for Kraeno. His paws crossed under his hairy chin.

The mood was muggy, meek, and slow, and Kraeno shook out his dusty pants in the same fashion. He really didn't care if his dusty pants were dusty; he just needed that moment to strengthen his mood. The last few days traveling to Transcendence on planet Plaxtex had gone well enough, however the week within the city had started to wear him down. He was tired of the nightmare.

Ghouls, bugs, monsters, ghosts, shadows, mini-villains, giant globs of rolling death, gore mounds, cannibalism, wraths, pure monstrosities doing gross and horrifying things. At least at the Skeleton Stoop, they were clean, they never ate each other, and they were a friendly enough lot. Now Kraeno was walking the streets of all the horror films combined. A universal collection of scary nightmares involved with every planetary culture. It was becoming too much. Kraeno was starting to realize he disliked Hell for being… Hell.

The Saloon Doors opened sadly, pushed with Kraeno's spearpoint hand. He slumped in with his hood slung low. In the back of the saloon there was a small flight of stairs next to the bar. Kraeno had two choices to get there: lurk through the shadows past dozens of ganker humanoid types or walk straight through the middle where everyone would notice him meandering around the tables and chairs. Kraeno, of course, had a different path in mind.

To his right, close to the door, there was a table with lycanthropes at every edge, drinking with heavy hairy muscles rubbing against one another. Their garb was all uniformed with yellow and blue colored tabards marked with a white slash symbol crossing their chests. The only thing that set their uniforms apart was the blood and gunk staining them.

There they sat, chatting about a Dyathsake planet with ten moons. Kraeno came up in his remorse and picked up one of their mugs, guzzling it down. The liquid spilled over his bones and started to mark the crotch of his trousers.

A blood-curdling growl rose from the closest Lycan to Kraeno, in sync with the beast's body leaving its chair. Then, all of a sudden, a soldier came through the saloon doors calling for his squad.

"Doomali and Queen Lextana are back; leave your drinks and get outside now! On the hop!"

Another blaze of luck, Kraeno thought in his muddled and wavering mind. The demon lord that threatened his world was coming right to him, and he wasn't getting ripped to shreds by these wolfmen.

Maybe it wasn't that bad of a day after all.

The Lycan who lost his drink turned back to Kraeno and swung with an open clawed uppercut. Kraeno, already looking downward in his depressed slump, moved off to the side and walked away, mostly dodging the Lycan's attack.

The Lycan jigged side to side, wanting to tear Kraeno apart, but his soldier buddies pulled him away and out of the saloon. Kraeno finished walking to the bar with a small burst of adrenaline and a limp. He sat down and ordered a drink. As soon as he peered into the clean dark reflection of whatever juice they gave him, he was poked from behind.

Kraeno looked away from his ghastly skeleton reflection and up at the oven head sitting next to him.

"Pretty thin, I do say myself. Pretty bone thin I do say… myself." Oven head said in a slobbishly dumb noise.

Kraeno tilted his head, looking over the square with an oven-barred helmet on.

"You have a cig?" Kraeno asked.

"Not for you skelly!"

Kraeno stabbed the box-headed humanoid below his chin with his bony index and middle finger, then pushed his dying body to a shadowy corner.

Whoever saw, watched with peculiarity but did nothing. In Hell, death is akin to the environment.

Depression overwhelmed Kraeno as he lifted the dead oven helmet off the ugly big eyed fleshy freak and slipped it right onto his own dusty skull. He flipped his hood back on, took his black coat, and checked for cigarettes.

Motherfucker did have cigarettes, Kraeno thought, as he rose and walked out of the saloon, sparked his cig, and watched the streets sway with parading soldiers trying to stabilize themselves for their demon lord's presence.

He noticed his glove was ripped and his middle and index fingers were showing. Without diffidence, he tore a strip off his sash and wrapped it around his fingers. *Should have used my obsidian spear hand…*

After trying to suck in the cigarette smoke, he realized the fag wasn't actually clogged; he just had no lungs to pull in anything.

Damn phantom organs. His spirit instantly dropped back down to nothing.

The energy around him had a rumbling of devilish ambiance, a feeling that darkness was swallowed up by a loathing evil that tore apart every particle of air.

From afar, a dark angel turned the corner, looking like a badass of all badasses. Doomali strutted a few feet behind her, his spiky beard and armor parted his black cloak in abstract ways, creating awesome looking wrinkles and waves.

Kraeno decided he looked rugged enough for a deadly fighter and possible conqueror of his home world. He whistled for Noble. It was loud enough that it turned Doomali's head as well as his guards.

Kraeno's new helmet amplified the whistle into a very hollow blare. He then lazily threw another can close to Noble's peripherals, and Noble tore it apart like the last one. He leapt comfortably onto Noble's back and awaited whatever fate that may cometh.

Guiding his platoon, Doomali pointed his three-pronged armored elbow at Kraeno. Now Kraeno had gathered Queen Lextana's attention too. Her face was pale and smooth. Her hair was in a tight black braid, and her chin had an indentation. She wore a long black coat and tight, clingy leather straps for clothes, reminding Kraeno of someone from the Matrix, only alien looking. Something was vampiric about her.

"Oven-head." Doomali spread his fingers with his palm tilted upward, elevating and descending in a gesture like, What the fuck is this? And how'd you do it?

Noble began to growl and became the wild looking beast that he was, ferocious and ready to fight anything, no matter what the chances of survival.

That's why I'm here bub. Kraeno patted Noble's shoulder.

"He was a tough one. I killed three deserted skellys and then found this one traveling alone and wounded close to Melcruso's castle. He ripped my face off, but ever since, he's fought with me."

Doomali leaned into Kraeno. A stark cling was made when his metal beard collided with the bars on Kraeno's helmet. Those demon eyes inches away from the dark sockets of his skull.

Sniffing came along with Doomali's glazed stare.

"I see you boy! You are the rookie Skel that's been hunting Demon Lords. Well, you won't be alone for long, boy; Mareridt is in the middle of destroying your soft little blue planet as we speak."

One small whimper came from below the demon versus skeleton face-off. Doomali's gauntlet was hovering over Noble's head, cursing the Hound in a wicked paralysis.

The Togmehoian demon lord pushed both Kraeno and Noble away from him with an invisible force.

"He fights with you, and you both fight for your Queen." Doomali looked at his Mother for appraisal while Kraeno frowned under his helmet…

She was busy half organizing her troops and half watching over her son. "Yes, yes Doomali. Your little Skel can join." She said in a beautiful voice, maybe the most beautiful voice he had ever heard. Kraeno shook. *My mother's voice was the most beautiful. My mom, my brothers. Never forget who you are.*

Doomali laughed at him and turned to start ordering his troops for departure. "Planet Earth is ours little Skel, and at this point there is nothing you can do except try and die in our ranks."

Kraeno jumped off Noble, unbuckled the sheath for his short sword, and began tying his satchel and other bags to Noble's saddle, totally ready for a long ride of relaxation. Another bit of luck made him smile behind the bars of his helmet.

He wondered why the demon army would split its forces. One force to fight the warriors of light on the outer rim and another to battle the angels of Earth. And my brothers, Shaki and Favin! Kraeno looked around and fathomed how stupid demons were, arrogant punks that always believed they were the end-all Gods of the universe. He giggled to himself.

Noble, on the other hand, pranced around so his rear was never to the guards. The guards and other soldiers slowly moved past them to the second spaceship. Noble torqued his neck at least six times to get a full and able look at the Lycans.

Kraeno and his companion were the very last to finally peter onto the ship next to Doomali's ship.

"This is your spot newbie." A Lycan Captain told Kraeno as he entered the ship. Kraeno sat down with his back against the wall. He watched the gate slowly creep up and Hell shut away. This was one of the first times he felt comfortable being dead. In a dark closed area, about to ascend into space with Lycan, with a daydream of hope tingling throughout his bones.

Tales of Doom

Kraeno slouched in the ship's corner with his feet propped up on Noble's back. The Lycans were easily in earshot, and the darkness between them and Kraeno was so dense that watching them sit and chat in their red fluorescent-lit enclaves was almost like watching a film.

"The World is called Earth. The planet is blue with an ocean that holds weird water beasts, and it has tons of islands running all different sizes. One of the biggest landmasses is called Africa, our spirit fall location. The lot of us found our wooden bodies there.

"The night of possession, or what Doomali called, 'the Night of Doom', was dark and humid, and the sky was clear enough to see a million starlights in the open atmosphere."

"Ha. Kinda like here." An arrogant older soldier interrupted, with a long white beard tied together by triangular silver plates clasped at every other inch.

"No, on Earth the stars and planets were far, far away, not stacked on top of each other. They all seemed like white glints, snowflakes in the dark sky during a full moon hunt. There, the entire sky has silver little dots."

"Hm, go on then." The white bearded Lycan said intrigued.

The younger Lycan soldier huffed a deep sigh and itched a scar over his eye.

"So, Earth is tucked nicely away from it all, and we came in HOT baby! Terror and awkwardness wreaked their plains as we dominated the natural spirits of that world. I fell into this lanky wooden mother fucker that just couldn't stop moaning. Like a constant exhale, as if its beaten spirit was leaking out of every hollow and crevice. What was weirder was the spirit tried seeping back in to push me out… There were other demons running around like maniacs even-"

"Wait, what? How'd you handle it, or were you just as wacky as everyone else the whole time?" The older Lycan soldier cut in aggressively.

"Listen Sheldon, you have to have faith. I was going to tell you that the other trees were flopping around like their heads were cut off. So I haphazardly went over to one of them and broke one of their limbs off so I could use it to carve an equalization spell into my dense ass skin, or bark, whatever you call it... So don't fucking interrupt me. I know you're an old bloody legend, but this story is greater than you mother fucker." The young Lycan said with a crooked smiling snarl.

"Go on then," Sheldon gestured, preceding with his hand.

"Yeah, alright," The young Lycan rolled his eyes and preceded verbalizing his story toward the other two Lycan warriors sitting across from him, his voice raspy and wolfish.

"I smash into this tree, break a branch off, and start digging in the symbol to summon little mischievous spirit demons from the underworld. One of Six's ideas. So I carve out the symbol, but with my haste came an even greater punishment..." He paused to encapsulate the other demon Lycans and watched for their reactions.

"It was really just an annoyance. It seemed the branch I used broke off with thirteen jagged points, so the symbol had thirteen identical carvings surrounding the first. The little spirit demons devoured the tree spirit and silenced the moans; however, they chattered, giggled, and joked in my head, pretty much until we fell off this damn cliff.

"Damn things were bound to me. Not even an etch or scratch on the original symbol could wipe them out. It was like a thousand horrible voices having a laugh in your head." The Lycan gave a sigh of agony, which turned into a sigh of relief.

"Anyway, even with those little fuckers in my head, at least I had full control over the wooden body, so I watched everyone else's struggle in the forest upon a ridge; demon trees picking flowers, demons babbling to themselves, demons zipping around like mad souls with no sanction. But I watched Doomali in particular. Let me tell you, that mother fucker is a beast with class! He scared the shit out of me with his calm demonic demeanor. He flooded into his wooden body. I mean poured into that mother fucker like it was no one's business. I about soiled myself. My little demon spirits were even quiet for a time. We all watched Doomali stagger to the forest's fringe and slowly, very very slowly tear into his bark, focusing in on the environment and creating his stature of old power within a new being. I mean…"

****

Kraeno watched and listened to the Lycan speak of Doomali and his goons raiding his home. He was comfortably on edge, mad with restlessness and worry, lost in his scarce bond with berserk.
Brothers, I will avenge us, I will…

Words could not creep into his shrouded mind. His anger had turned him into a devilish animal. He listened under his hood, and there were now Two hounds in the corner, ready to tenant evil with a greater evil.

****

The Youngest of the Lycan went on, "This flipping witch, Mareridt, had us in this massive storm circle, marching in the sand, for who knows what. She felt a rebellion and went after it. And hell yeah, there was a fight. Another witch, Mareridt's sister from before, swooped into the eye of the storm with blades rotating around her body.

"She and her blades were actually pushing around our witch pretty good in the sky, chasing her around with another massive blade made out of more blades. Flipping and flying, it was crazy stuff. I mean this sword sizzled the air and started cutting n' drilling right through our army. Anyways as soon as Doomali got involved it was over.

"The witch lay dead in the desert, already half buried by the sand. Swords rotated around her like prowling tiger cubs protecting their fallen mother; however, eventually, their life force simply tinkered out. That was when this brutal earthquake that split the earth and separated us from the witch's human rebels, and also put the witch, I guess Blitzen was her name, on her own little grave island.

"Afterwards, coming back into our forest headquarters, Hantos was waiting with a message. Bloody Hantos!" The Lycan said, with a boast and a smirk.

"He told Doomali, Queen Lextana came back from the assault on a powerful outer-rim planet and demanded his presence for battle! A mother fucking battle against Heaven! A huge honor that no demon could ever pass up.

"Doomali stood there perplexed, tree bark fully covered in spell symbols looking like tribal war art. After a moment, he finally made a confident decision."

The Lycan changed his voice to impersonate Doomali.

"'These earthlings cannot compete with the force of a demon army so great as this! I shall go back to Plaztex, gather our troops, and defeat this angelic snip! Hantos will take my place and turn this world into chaos, bringing fire to the skies and blood to the sea. The blue planet will turn red. Our kingdom come!'"

The Lycan cleared his throat. "After Doomali spoke, the roar from the forest felt like another earthquake and rattled the fresh spring leaves off the dead tree limbs. Later, Doomali had me and twelve others fight him to try and end his body force here so his spirit may escape and retire back to Plaztex. The battle went on for a solid day. The orange sun rose and it was Doomali and I standing there, the only ones left. Then when Mareridt came back she used the dead woods in Doomali's arena to telepathically brush us off the cliff. It was a nice fall into Plaztex. And now we're here, flying into a battle against our greatest rivals."

"Oh ya, you guys fought for twenty-four hours, eh?" Sheldon asked.

"Ya!" The Younger Lycan rebelliously replied.

"Because I heard you and a bunch of others immediately got to the planet and fell in an earthquake hole." The werewolves howled with laughter and amusement of some good ol' fiction.

Kraeno continued to watch them as they laughed.

I must kneel to peace now in order to find glory later... I'll be here. Doomali will be here. And time is on my side. Death is finally, on my side.

Colors of Rawwar

A white owl flew over the early morning chaos in the City Pointe-Noire. It tilted its idle wings and simply glided in the Western breeze. Screams, loud wooden creaks, booming timbers, and crashes tickled a sky illustrated with flickering fire and faraway stars. A hint of gray brushed the horizon with the incoming sun.

Usually during the day, everything and everyone hustled on the docks. When they weren't out on the water or hoisting up nets and carts of fish, they were drinking or sleeping in the city that impressively loomed over its own reflection in the sea. The city prided itself on its fisheries and the size of its bay, naturally capable of having a litany of docks. The buildings were old, industrialized towers that stood tall but looked rickety. Whatever kept these buildings standing seemed to have been doing so for a very long time.

The owl flew out of the city above the docks.

Slash.

It separated in two symmetrical pieces, one slapped against a cargo crate and the other half thudded on the deck of the Saint, roped up at the furthest point of the bay from the city.

One of the ram-horned monks flipped the owl's slashed bloody guts over to the white feathery side with his boot. Pads watched the monk do this and gave him a smile and a 'good luck' nod and then scanned the skies for any other sign of Mareridt.

They knew Mareridt would be in flight looking to punish her sisters, so their plan was to help with the demonic ground troops.

Pads jumped onto the cargo dock where half the Awakened from Crete were preparing for a brawl. Some tied up weaker branches in bundles, others unraveled old Gothic weapons, mostly on the end of chains.

Many grew restless and agitated at the incoming wails from the locals. The whole population was running from the disturbed city and onto the docks.

Most of the Lantos were there already; these warrior trees occupied fifty or more docks and that many boats anchored at their slips. The Macaton, sorcerer trees, were still making their way from the last two ram-horned schooners, slowly moving their roots from ship to dock, carefully, as if not to timber into the water. It already had proven difficult for the wooden ship replicators to ascend from the sea and onto land. So the water-logged Awakened had mostly gathered a little ways downshore and were slowly making their way over to the main battle front.

Pointe-Noire city's population was at 750,000 people. The fishing locals called the city the Black Point because of the mounds of black rocks on shore. Now the local name would be remembered by the darkness eating up its streets.

The huge bay had a boxy, elongated point filled with shipping containers, creating a hook-like landmass in the Atlantic. A broken railway ran in between the bay's marina and the city. It was the line of skirmish between good and evil, Crazed Demons versus the Guardians of Mother Earth.

The regular people running around in horror jumped in boats or simply just jumped straight into the water when they saw there were more trees moving around like warriors preparing for war.

Pads met up with A.D who was helping Lingo and two other tree warriors equip their armor and weapons. Walking up behind, Pads flicked the back of his older brother's ear, and A.D barely budged. He slowly turned and winked at his younger brother, his two long scars under his eye running down his right platform cheek and jaw. He brushed over his bashed nose with his thumb and started rifling through their duffel bag. He pulled out Shaki's crossbow and set it next to another bag full of dynamite.

The sound of helicopters, bombs, and gunfire came from the East, where the city was brutally caught in a hellish fire.

Two of Captain Sharp's deckhands were spraying the Awakened with sticky fire retardant once they became reasonably dry after ascending from the sea. Spear and Arrow, AKA Johnny Twinkle Toes, had a mini anchor resting on his shoulder and a smaller chainsaw hanging at his waist. Johnny walked over to where Favin, Panda, and Afwat waited at the head of the troops and fully loaded with guns.

Pads smiled at the dangerous day ahead, awaiting death joyously if it came to that. A rope crossed his chest, and he had Tracher's spear gun strapped across his back. He crouched to look through the duffel bag after A.D was finished and pulled out Captain Sharp's grappling hook. Pads looked around and really consumed the day.

The warrior trees wore metal circlets around their trunks with dark green drapes hanging from thick branches to signify their guild of Mother Earth. Wizard Macaton trees summoned heavy rain clouds in the streaked, orange-tinted sky. Their idea was to put out fires and wet the soil so root goers could slip through the mud quickly from one spot to another. Most trees carried buckets of water in their highest branches for fire extinguishing reasons.

To walk in the fiery pits of Hell, you must be prepared for the heat.

The troop of Gaia's Hollows stood around in awe, watching the panic of people, and jiggled with excitement.

The smaller, close-combat Landtos trees, Rooter Tooters, and Birchwood Hooters could magically be pushed through the dirt by Mother Earth in order to reach their destination.

The larger Landtos that couldn't dive into the soil or stay back summoning elementals were specialized brawlers. Afwat being one of those, rolled his branches forward, looking like he was rolling his shoulders before a fight. Two miniguns hid in his branches, hanging around like bird's nests.

The time was dawn, and the encroaching darkness of night brought a brisk terrorizing wind in the air…

"Where'd you find the dyno-mite?" Johnny asked in a playful yet fully interested manner. His voice rumbled a little deeper this evening.

A.D knew it was stressed nerves. He felt the fear as well—but to him that just meant they were about to have a truly elevated experience. He wasn't called Adrenaline Devil for nothing.

A.D rubbed his scars on his cheek and patrolled his eyes in search of someone.

"Those ram-horned monks. The girl actually gave me the bag." A.D blushed.

Right then, as if to extinguish the heat in A.D's rugged cheeks, sharp ice shards started spilling from an abruptly forming dark cloud overhead. Pads tossed A.D his lucky, busted-eyed shamrock lighter, then turned to run up behind Afwat, throwing his grappling hook at the fourth branch about thirty feet up. The rope that crossed his chest unraveled itself beautifully as the hook flew upward.

Pads began to climb Afwat's side, hand over hand with two-legged thrusts, to reach the fourth branch. Afwat used Rowan's golden shield to block most of the incoming ice shards, unlike one unlucky Lantos tree behind them, left open to be pin-cushioned by little blue spikes.

Pads looked up into the higher tiers of Afwat's collection of branches, hideouts, and glinting tools of demolition. Furthest away from his trunk, nestled under the shield, was an entangled M60 Gatling gun. Pads realized he should go to Afwat's more protected side if he were going to avoid the fate of the ice-impaled Lantos tree.

He continued to look up while dodging long icicles. Once he made it to the other side, he settled under a heavy branch and sat down to dangle his legs. He took out his knife and dug out the anti-demon symbol in one of Afwat's trunks.

From above he saw Favin, Panda, and A.D climb into Lingo's leafy shelter. Favin hugged the trunk with one arm, machine gun in the other, and whispered into Lingo's hollow. Lingo lurched forward and created an ice elemental on the move. The spiny blob scouted ahead, collecting the additional shards that still fell from the sky.

"Here we go Afwat. May the strength of Gaia be imbued in your wood." Afwat didn't respond to Pads, nor did Pads expect him to. A Forest Within A Tree was concentrating on creative ways of deconstructioning demons. Praises were unnecessary to him.

Afwat begun a slide toward Lingo, and Pads looked back at the flat ocean. In the water he watched the massive reflection of the fire at the city's heart. It blazed up, threatening the sky but leaving the surrounding buildings alone. Then suddenly, the enormous fire embodied itself with a distinct, blood-red face, laughing within the flames.

Before Pads could tell anyone, the flame elemental hid itself again in the inferno environment.

ScorcWushh! It was the first sound that didn't quite make sense. Any burning city was going to have fire noises; however, this was a jet. Then they heard the slapping of icy slush hitting broken cement around the corner.

As Lingo and the crew turned down the first main street, trailing the ice elemental, Pads yelled, "Flame Thrower! Watch out!" The crackling fire and other screams overwhelmed Pad's warning to Lingo, but Afwat had a similar feeling and quickened his roots.

Lingo and the monkeys hanging in his limbs—A.D, Panda, and Favin—approached the middle of the main road and the steaming puddle of their fallen ice elemental. Lingo advanced cautiously, readying his curved metal shield for a flame burst. Finally, after fully rounding the corner, the fire stood like a skyscraper, precise, contained, and waiting.

Then it attacked. Waves and waves of fire shot out of the monstrous tower, pushing the parrying Lingo back toward the building across the street.

The older men were as chill as a slab of steel. They waited for either an opportunity or death, treating them as the same and letting Lingo do the work.

A.D shattered the building's front windows with Panda's assault rifle, then threw it back to him. After tossing the rifle, A.D jumped through the broken window and charged through the small rooms, shoving things aside and breaking through doors and walls to get to the stairwell.

One room had a radio playing *Monsters by Sault* full blast. It reminded him of the old times, charging through backyards to escape local gangs. Those times all seemed so peaceful and easy. Now it was all about urgency, integrity, and blocking out an inevitable fear of monsters.

He reached the roof and shot two flare guns into the sky. Then other flares raced to the upper regions; little fiery bullets from all over the burning city. A.D guessed it was probably a diversion trick from Mareridt's minions.

Not giving a shit, A.D threw the flare guns to the side and slowly walked up to the edge of the building to take it all in. A fire elemental burned on the corner of the first block and the ominous sky overhead was filled by covert witches and manipulated elements.

On the dockside of the block, A.D saw his family pinned down by the jet flames blasting in on them. Lingo and Afwat were there, blocking most of the scorching flames with Rowan's Shield while at least twenty-five trees stood ready for battle behind him, waiting by the water's edge.

A.D followed the flame back to Mareridt's elemental and found what they'd been looking for. Heavy demon trees were coming out of the tower of fire, unharmed by the flames and prancing around in a jolly manner. They poured out like the burning tower was some kind of scorching portal. It must have been some demonic spell from Hell that kept their woods from burning to a crisp ash.

While equipping the crossbow with his first dynamite stick, A.D looked back toward the bay. The rest of the Awakened army was just about to turn the corner to support Lingo and Afwat. Each Lantos had a Macaton water elemental next to them. It was blue squirting out red, and red glistening in the reflections of blue. Water was balancing out the fire, good was rivaling evil, and explosions versed conscious elementals.

A.D lit the fuse and put the crossbow up to his eye.

Mum would smack me if she saw me doing this.

There was a large open space in the middle of the army of fiery woods. The space shimmered with flames a little more than the others. A.D pinched the fire out on the fuse and peered harder at the awkward space. It was almost a reflection of the fire from surrounding flames, a mirror, or camouflage, or…

A.D gritted his teeth so hard a tooth cracked. A wave of fury went through him and it flushed his vision away. He put his hand on his forehead and tried to regain his vision by taking quick breaths and thinking about his happy place. He inhaled slowly, lit the fuse, put the crossbow to his eye, exhaled, and let the dynamite fly at his brother's killer.

The last time he saw this devil, there was a branch covered in his brother's blood, transmuting into the starry night background, looking like the Universe stabbed through Kraeno's neck.

The explosion set the camouflage tree back and tossed a couple others around as well. *Sorry to ruin your masquerade party boys.* He taped another piece of dynamite on a bolt and watched flaming trees walk around the base of an adjacent building from him. The lash of a root shattered windows and more demon trees stepped out of the building.

Holy crap there are a lot of those demonic bastards.

Light. Aim. Fire. And boom. A.D stood there loading and reloading, wondering how he acquired such an awesome spot for redemption.

After four good shots, he lit his wick again, and then a plop of water put it right out. It finally started to rain.

The flames still existed even after the clash between Sentinels and Demons. However, it just created a balance, not an advantage. The flames stopped jumping from one place to another, and they slowly dwindled as the rain poured harder. The fire tower elemental retracted its jet flame and assisted his demons with reigniting their flames while the main sources of fire burned inside the buildings now.

Lightning bolted across the sky and suddenly started blasting down at the demon trees, while thousands of shells riddled and ripped their demon woods apart from the Gatling guns.

The winds began blowing so hard that A.D had to unbuckle his belt and tie himself to a vent so he wouldn't fly off the building.

With Mareridt's fire elemental powers now completely countered, she realized why she couldn't find her sisters. They were too high in the sky for her to detect. She rocketed straight up above the black clouds and into the white puffy ones, away from the tornadoes and wooden clashes in the city arena and right to where Tienilla was hovering 20 sky yards out, feet hidden in a cloud.

A yell echoed over the clouds. "Always waiting Tienilla. Turned from a natural warrior into a spectating slug. How pathetic." Mareridt gave Tienilla a chance to respond, but she did no such thing.

"Once I get the Glasir," Mareridt nodded at what Tienilla was holding in her hand.

"I can open a portal straight to Dyathsake. No more possession, bullshit. Just. Pure. Chaos. And this world will be mine! It looks like this is going to be a lot easier than I thought.

"Giving the Scepter to you! What a laugh! I thought I'd have to go through all of you to get it," Mareridt's beautiful black face turned mad and elongated with evil. She pulled her dagger from her red kimono and flew at muted little Tienilla.

They instantly vortexed around in a literal fight puff. The water particles of cold air were sucked into their cloud scuffle. The cartoon brawl ball gave a golden glint as the Glasir popped out every now and then. The Shield of Mother Earth, now roughed around like the newspaper funnies.

Brick, planks, and dust got into the mix as the circular vortex plummeted down into the building adjacent to A.D's position.

****

Pads saw the tornado go deep into a fifteen-story building. He gulped, knowing that it must have been Mareridt and one of the sisters. He gulped again, wondering how he could get down from twirling, brawling Afwat.

Pads watched Afwat wrap his armored root around the base of a hysterical demon oak and his thick branches around its canopy. The crack of wood crushing all the oak's branches sounding like a synchronized forest fall.

Right as Pads threw his grappling hook onto a tall Sequoia, Afwat stuffed the entire oak tree in the seventh floor of a nearby building.

Pads made the swing over to the protruding roots of the demon Sequoia and carved the anti-demon symbol into its wood. This didn't stop the demon tree but infuriated him, slowly disintegrating its powers while the true Awakened inside rejuvenated theirs.

Pads ran through its branches and looked for his next victim to turn into a timbering bridge. Sadly, the Sequoia was stomping the wrong way, past the Lantos Awakened trees and towards the docks. Lantos were clawing and climbing up the Sequoia to try and pull it down. As this happened, Pads was getting further and further away from helping the Sky Sister caught in a battle with Mareridt. He searched desperately to find a transport tree, and then he saw something he had hoped not to see.

A humongous demon oak, rivaling Afwat and given the gift of fire still burning under its sheltering dead branches, began to tie its extensive roots into bundles of broken-up railroad tracks. It had the strength to not only rip away the tracks but also bend them around its branches. It stared right into a large Cretan Lantos, letting it know that as soon as it was done with the train tracks, it was coming after her.

Still tunnel visioning this poor Cretan Lantos, the beastly tree conductor picked up and smashed an incoming thorn tree into the dirt, then devoured it into his own wood, malevolently stuffing the thorn tree's trunk and wide branches into his own hollows, leaving a smoldering broken apart Lantos sticking half out of its demon core.

While Pads raced his brain for ways to take out an unstoppable beast, his demon-exorcised mount was in the early stages of falling into the water. The end of the dock creaked loudly as the Sequoia finally tumbled in to cool down the fiery pain coming from the anti-demon symbol. Pads ran down the trunk mid-timber and jumped to make it onto the dock platform, his shoulder slamming against the planks in a tough roll.

He looked up, coughing from the pain in his ribs, and saw a ram-horned exorcist A.D had picked up from Crete. The girl with orange hair and half her head shaved.

In Pad's eyes, everything happened in slow motion. The more epic the scene, the more the scene slowed down, or was it the girl that did that to him?

The ram-horned girl ran up to Pads and picked him up. As he rose, he saw two other ram-horned monks throwing down glitter pops like ninjas evading with puffs of smoke. They hopped around, close to the demon hollows, ice-picking areas of bark away so they could carve anti-demon symbols close to the tree's core and whisper sweet words of exorcism in their voided rifts.

They were extremely fast and aggressive, and Pads couldn't help but wonder how they trained for this kind of action.

Pads looked over to where the beastly oak with railroad tracks was ramming trees into the air, demon and Awakened alike. The ruined top of one of the buildings that flanked the bashing and smashing was where Mareridt and one of the Sky Sisters were.

"I need to get into that building!" Pads yelled.

He was in the middle of the back-line tree warriors. Protected for now, but not for long against the incoming tree conductor slowly pressing its way to the docks where thousands of civilians flocked.

Pads could see the building he needed to be in, however, there was a wall of raw warring trees between them.

Once he got past that wall, he knew that layers and layers of other tree walls would exist. He squinted his eyes at the idea that his world could come to ruin because of these babbling-crazed demon spawn.

The ram-horned girl watched the top of the building as he did, peering over the railroad branched tree.

Suddenly, the tree turned to loom over them both. A movement so fast, even when Pads thought time moved slow in these epic situations.

Its slitted red eyes gleamed with a mad thrill.

Pads nudged the girl to say something - *come on just one whisper* - As an explosion of dynamite appeared over the beast oak's spine. The ram-horned girl backed up, slapping her arm over Pad's chest like a mother protecting her kid from an abrupt traffic stop, as the beastly oak raised its train track roots for the final dunk on the two humans.

For a second, Pads thought he could take the hit, just like before in school fights or rugby matches, but then it clicked: the orange haired girl can't take the hit. A whisper can't stop the slam of a train track either! The red slit face revealed itself in the dense wood, and Pads was all out of ideas.

****

A.D sat at the top of the building pulling dynamite after dynamite from his duffel bag. His focus was on his little brother, Padrick, and the hulk of a tree looming over him. Pads was too close for A.D to shoot the dynamite without hitting them both. So he watched and hoped for something to change the tides of war.

A possessed witch elm climbed the building in search of the recon boomer, A.D. Afwat took a second from blasting the fiery trees and turned around to gun the witch elm down. Bullets from the m60 tata-tat-tatted the building where A.D was, but he cared very little about his own safety, and he saw that Afwat had similar feelings while being poked by demonic wooden worms while his attention was elsewhere.

A.D looked into his duffel bag and found only five dynamite sticks left, out of the thirty-five he had before. He locked another into the crossbow and aimed. The tree was just about to slam down on Pads and the orange-haired girl when Sky Sister Kendra suddenly flew in to intercept the train track roots. It almost seemed like her dual-sided black blade was twenty feet longer.

She beat the roots back and slashed at them with her sword, left, right, left, left, right. The strength of the tree conductor slowly failing under Kendra's assault.

A.D saw Pads make his way around the hulkish oak and towards the first building on the block.

There you are little brother.

The tree line was dense, and seemingly impossible for his brother to pass through to get to Mareridt and Tienilla. Quickly, through rash calculations of engineering expertise that he did not possess, A.D shot the dynamite at the base of a leaning building in front of Pads.

Were we the only ones that saw them crash into that building? A.D thought as the building slowly crumbled into ruin, safely away from Pads.

****

A litany of pebbles and heat blew into Pad's face. He peered up where A.D was posted and gave him a wink. The building next to him swayed, and Pads thought it must have been the battle fever, a concussion, or even an abstract transcendence into the afterlife. Pads snapped into believing this dreamlike day was nothing but reality because regardless of lucidity, Sky Sisters needed to be saved; the world needed to be saved. The first building from the docks crumbled on top of the Awakened and demons alike, creating a path of rubble and dust.

Pads wobbled through the uphill climb of wreckage and debris, feet slanting and slipping down the slopes of the ruined cement blocks. He enjoyed the space given in the destruction. An all around focus on the warring around him was all he could concentrate on before. Now fumbling and tumbling through the ruins, blind in the dust of the recent collapse, he simply focused on moving forward and moving forward only. The second building was close.

The feeling that something was wrong was already there. An army of bloody demons fully encapsulated in wooden armor wasn't a trip to Disneyland, but now there was something even worse; Pads felt like the balance of the universe was shifting under his feet. As his foot slipped, his thigh hit an extended piece of rebar and his following step accompanied no landing. At the last moment Pads grabbed hold of the rebar with his right hand and waited, suspended in the air. The rubble dust was clearing overhead, and soon, the terrain would be somewhat revealed below.

****

The ancient Glasir protected Tienilla from Mareridt's dark magic. Mareridt herself had some magic protection as well and became invulnerable to what little water summoning Tienilla could produce in such tight quarters. The fight became more physical and sometimes even upside-down.

The Pointe-Noire people still in the building watched a petite white girl holding a golden scepter fighting against a black woman with a knife. To them, Tienilla was the obvious enemy. They threw chairs and other pieces of furniture at her as the sisters blocked and attacked each other with their Kung Fu art.

The Glasir Scepter guarded Tienilla, but not for much longer. Mareridt had Tienilla retreating and narrowly dodging her attacks.

Heavy tornadoes twisted vigorously over the hole in the roof of the building. Through the levels of burrowed wreckage, Tienilla gave a sigh of relief; her sisters had arrived. She looked back, straight ahead, only to stare into the fiery eyes of her other, very twisted sister.

Mareridt used the angelic moment as a chance to capture, grapple, and force Tienilla to submit. After a smooth re-position of bodies, they both ended up on their knees, Mareridt breathing heavily behind Tienilla, her knife pressed to Tienilla's throat, waiting for the family reunion.

With haste, Freya and Shay flew into the building's crater and immediately halted at the hostage situation...

Breathing hard from his sprint up the stairs, Pads watched in the shadow of an extremely dark office down the corridor. He sat on the table looking out, blood spilling down his calf, knife leisurely dangling in his hand. He was bare: ragged clothes, no rope, no grappling hook, just him and his blade. He listened closely to Mareridt's tone, waiting.

"Hello Freya, Shay. I haven't seen you for so long…" Mareridt moaned as if in sarcastic agony.

"I'm going to tear you a new one Mareridt! You're dead!" Freya growled. She grabbed the zipper lining of her leather jacket and puffed it forward, tightening the jacket around her shoulders. Her strawberry blonde hair tied in a ponytail, tight enough that being in the heart of a twister couldn't even unravel it.

"I'm already dead. You killed me, remember! Remember that!" Suddenly furious, Mareridt looked around at Tienilla's face. "Remember Tie…" With a flash, Pad's throat was slashed.

Triumphantly, Pads turned around to peer into Mareridt's eyes and winked.

Mareridt pushed him away in utter shock and surprise. She looked down the corridor at the far office, and there stepped out Tienilla. Her bright blue eyes and red tick of blood on her neck were the only things visible amongst her shadow.

Shay, black, bald, and beautiful, formed a surface of air decorated with four golden rings, mimicking her own hand, and lined up as a replica of pain. Freya flicked fire from her thumb, igniting the hand as it slapped Mareridt across the dark room. Freya and Shay approached the thud where Mareridt hit the wall.

Pads calmly held his throat closed to try and breathe while his eyes followed the two silhouettes stepping into the gray, wispy smoke rising from Mareridt's smoldering body. Freya flicked up some more fire, just enough to light up half of Mareridt's face.

A moment went by, and all that was heard was the singe of Mareridt's shirt and the woodland booms and squabbles outside.

"This isn't the end, Sisters," Mareridt said as if it were a bad word. Her black hair wept strands in front of her black face with rosy cheeks.

"I have something special for you, older sister." She smiled under her veil of hair. "I will stay with you…" She cackled and slid out another dagger. "From the depths of where I end up…" She moved her hair back and raised the dagger to her forehead. "I will haunt you for eternity!"

Mareridt ran the poison blade down her face. Her eyes were now seen as little spheres of hate, her nose flattened to the bone, and blood squirted and spilled from her cheeks onto her bare and revealed teeth. She would get along nicely with the Skeleton Crew.

Green poison oozed down from her forehead, accompanying the blood - somehow her dagger always rendered poison. Mareridt continued her cackle, but out of that cackle, there was something else, a wail perhaps from Beth, the lucky lady behind the scenes watching the horror unfold. Mareridt, pleased with at least terrifying someone, flew up out of the building and off into the rising sun.

"I'll go get her. Alone." Freya said and then took off.

Shay crashed down on top of a demon tree, crushing the tree's entire flank like a lightning bolt would do.

After their landing, Tienilla kissed Pads' forehead and passed him over to Shay.

Kissed by an angel while I die, I don't think it gets better than this…

Her forklift-angled arms carried Pads as if he were a leaf. Her eight-ringed fingers folded around his ribs and stomach with the Glasir Scepter resting in his lap.

The crew began to clean up what was left of the demon army, finally honing their skills and abilities after the long fight. The beginning of the battle was basically a struggle to survive while witnessing an elemental carnival go apeshit on a bad piece of acid.

Johnny was deep in the city streets with two deckhands. It's a world wonder how all three of them got there, but Johnny made the best of it by swinging the anchor around to clip trees and break branches, while the other two crouched and kept steady fire with their assault rifles and rocket launcher. They were so far in the war crowd that when the first building fell, it smashed a row of babbling demon trees encroaching on Johnny's rear.

When Lingo saw the sisters come out of the building, he began juggling up pockets of air. He wasn't thinking about pushing the enemy back with a wave of wind. Lingo wanted to juggle out volatile elements like Freya did. His branches rotated hypnotically while he cleared a path for Shay and Tienilla, squinting his hollows, encapsulated in wooden fury.

Kendra zoomed around the two giants, Afwat and the hulk oak tree conductor as they duked it out. Afwat's branches were mostly bent and mangled, but the thud and checks of his thick trunks still proved to be effective while Kendra got her licks in with her black dual-sided blade crackling with lightning.

The tattooed ram-horned exorcists and Tasmanian Birchwoods rushed around the streets. Different variations of the anti-demon symbol were scribbled all over the Demon woods within moments of them passing by.

The Awakened didn't have a large army to begin with, and that whole morning the battle was being won in some areas but lost in most, just from the sheer diabolical numbers of the Congo Forest; however, now, as far as A.D could see, the tides of war were changing.

****

When the sun cast the shadow out of the inner city, Shay rose to eclipse the burning sphere and absorb the light with one jeweled hand, raining an angelic sun ray amongst the inner and outer tiers of war with her other. The light did no direct damage; however, it distracted the enemy with a warning signal of triumphant luminosity for the Sentinels. They pressed the streets and trampled the rest of the out-world invaders into the asphalt. It was an all-day battle of raw war.

****

A.D ran up to the docks with Shaki's crossbow in hand.

"The golden Glasir will protect him from Charon, the dark Ferryman of the Dyathsake Galaxy. He will be led straight to the Outer Rim of sublime light." Shay told A.D. Her voice and demeanor, as always, calm and collected.

"How?" A.D asked as if he dedicated his entire life to keeping Pads alive.

"He died for me…" Tienilla whispered in his ear, gesturing Shay to move on past the litany of wood chips and to the Saint. Tienilla's bare chest was smeared with blood, dirt, and ash.

****

Mareridt slumped in her landing at the entrance of a cave found in a Scandinavian Forest. She tore her kimono off and walked into the darkness at a steady and unhesitant pace.

She stood there in the dark.

The heavy rainfall during her thousand-mile flight made her face drip liquids that ran down her faceless skull and through canals of meat and bone. The blood slipped and gooed, spilling in sporadic droplets onto the previous body owner's neckline. She sat down after a moment and rolled her eyes to the back of her head.

Mareridt revealed her spirit in the X vapor of the Citadel Catacombs in Plaztex. Six was already standing in the open room, pouring potions into potions and meekly stirring pots.

"Six, call for Doomali and another army to fly into Sweden's Boreal Forest. The trees there are ancient and powerful!"

Six turned around, somewhat taken aback to see Mareridt in distress.

"Ahh, Mareridt, I already sent our prisoners and everyone we could spare. Beauty and the Beast was the last of them. I'm sure he caused a ruckus! Enjoy conquering their world. We have our own battle to attend here. A Skeleton army is on the fringe of our city gates. We may need your hel-"

Mareridt returned to her cave, only this time the walls were lit on fire all the way up to a fork in the path.

Even in Mareridt's madness, she knew this expedition was a loss, and she needed to return to Plaztex to help smash some skellys to relieve her stress. She turned towards the cave entrance. Her eyes were glazed with joy toward the future destruction of the dead. Then through the blur of her glaze was Freya, her hands flared out to maintain the heat on the walls.

"Ah if it isn't Freya, the little fire b-"

"This is Mother's fire. She wants to see you, Ruza." Freya breathed maliciously.

"That name has nothing to do with me now. I am Mareridt, caller of storms and bringer of NIGHTMARES!" Mareridt's voice proceedingly became louder while cackling throughout.

"Your nefarious ways are FINISHED!" Freya flew out of the cave and turned it into a furnace.

Mareridt raced out, completely engulfed in flames. Freya, already turned around and waiting, welcomed her escape with an abruptly thrown spear, driving Mareridt back into the cave.

Freya pulled the flames back to dance amongst the walls as she flew back in.

"Holy light let me guide thee into a passage of eternal sin, so thou can smite thee whom is bound to Hell."

Freya walked up to impaled Mareridt, pulled the spear out of her stomach, and sunk it back into her skull. She pulled it out again and spat into the spear hole in Mareridt's head, flipped off her invisible spirit leaving Earth, and turned around to leave, having the flames die out like winter candlelight.

Flood

With weeks of work, the fresh recruits were acclimating well to their new skeleton bones. They walked like high school all-stars who slept in tattoo parlors filled with hot babes.

As their skeletal feet balanced on the tightly knit bone structure of the ship's deck they occasionally would cross paths and clank bone to bone in amity. The white-striped army was feeling the comradery of their new crew. '*No sleep for the wicked,*' they'd whisper during the darkest hours of the night as they approached Plaztex.

The Dyathsake Galaxy was funny in the ways of light and dark, day and night. Planets closer to the Halo that wrapped around the Galaxy always resided in daylight, with neighboring suns of youth and glory. They rejoiced when moons crossed between them and the Halo, casting a nice shadow for a time.

The planets closer to the Dark Bulge were always in darkness, unless certain moons rotated above and reflected a dim or half-obliterated old sun's light in the planetary revolution. Densely loaded ghost moons would also flash with a luminous, spectral blue light more than others. More double-dead, more ghosts on a moon, the more light. Almost making it a contest within each dark bulge planet to see how bright they could get their moons.

This particular night, there were three bright ghost moons overhead, accompanying an intensely glowing lava river on the brink of flooding into the city gates. With the blue moons and red river, the sky held an eerie purple tint.

Max peered down the crossboned bow, watching the haul of bones surge against the boiling lava. His hollows filled with fire and retribution. The flood was here.

The bone ship was centered in the river, completely surrounded by forty yards of lava on either side. Archers confidently stood around the ship, glaring at the incoming raiders. Stonolf and the boys began their early morning drum and bass battle beats to steady other bow hands before the final approach. Their ship was fortified and ready for the siege.

Further ahead of the ship, shield maidens bashed the incoming raiders who were trying to stop Max's diggers and drills. The sound of bones clacking against steel was dull and stifled against the drone of three massive drills curling into the dead desert dirt.

The fire burned hotter and brighter as they approached the gates of Plaztex. Twenty-foot flames roared up every time a raider's body took a spill in the lava. Max could barely see his third and fourth tier of shield maidens at the fringe of the lava scar.

He could see Plaztex though, large on the horizon, wavering in the mirage of heat. Slanted buildings seemed to shoot up in the air, with crooked roofs and loony characteristics, under the towering Citadel leaning over them all. Saul's Citadel was able to see into every alley and dark patch of the city. It was a gothic white tower with so much darkness inside. Constructed of bright white stone and caressed with yellow and blue slashed tapestries and flags hailing their Togmehoian clan.

Max pressed on his hilt with the blade still sheathed. He chewed on weeds while overlooking the city's layout as a canvas, a piece of art that he and his team of scallywag skeletons could drill into, creating their own design and their own home in the soon-to-be fallen city. Max did not smile, he only chewed, a sober and jolly chew.

The music was now heard above the drone. The beats switched the skeletal shield maidens into a bashing flurry. If they fell, there were others to take their place, giving time for the fallen to rise again. As long as too many limbs weren't taken from them, they could reconstruct themselves in short order. It seemed like the Skeleton Crew liked this new way of living. The new recruits were unskilled, but they made up for it in numbers. Max's plan was simple. Prevent the demons and their dead soldiers from breaking through to the diggers and stopping their crease in the earth.

The river of lava was now so close to the walls that the bordered banner on the left side of the city gate caught fire.

Saul's raiders stood five hundred strong with their backs against the wall, frowning at the imminent, burning flood. Nothing to do now but watch the river flow through.

The gates creaked and suddenly opened.

Saul, the King of Plaztex, father of Doomali, flew out with his armored dragon cavalry to make time for his raiders to regroup inside. The dragon cavalry trampled and crushed any skeletons on the outside of the river of lava. The shield maidens retreated slowly back into their natural habitat, and the winged guard flew back to perch on the city walls.

The first tier of maidens that retreated into the lava had their shields melt onto their forearms, creating a metallic bone. Their instant response was one of frustration with their forgetfulness, but only an instant later, they rejoiced with laughter, pumped that they could soon live a Terminator'esk lifestyle in Hell.

Max thought a lot about his new Skeleton Crew during their flood. He surmised that these folk must have been a little crazy in the first place. To die from any demon on a planet outside the Dyathsake Galaxy seemed a little strange to Max. These people must have been fighting the dark forces or perhaps looking to join with them in order to die by them. Of course, they could have been in the wrong place at the wrong time as well. Regardless, this new lot was taking Hell way better than most.

Saul watched the skeleton maidens through the elevated flames. They crouched in the lava, holding their metal shields over their heads, which caused the metal to drip and layer their bones with steel. Some even donated their shields to top-dog maidens, making them full-metal sons of bitches.

The drills were extracted and moved to widen the river while the diggers were now at the city edge. The Skeleton Crew devoted most of their efforts to digging in the lava with bone shovels. One skel even had a wide-mouth skull as the shovel point and an attached spine as the handle.

An arrow flew from the bone ship and thudded a couple of feet away from where Saul sat mounted on his dragon. Saul growled at the white, spiky-boned ship gliding on the lava's surface. He saw the troops occupying the deck. He saw the spook who released the bowstring.

Saul shot out a treachery spell that only he could see the making of. He focused and watched the spell trail until the invisible force reached the archer. The skeleton dropped her bow and lifted into the air. Then her head came off, spinning into the air and returning down onto her body with a vengeance while the body twisted and broke apart itself, putting a leg into the ribs and shoulders intersecting the hips. After a moment of jumbling the skeleton into a ball of bones, the remnants dashed into the drum stand, splintering bones all over the band's stage.

Saul's long, prominent, proud jaw "hmph'd," in his success.

The diggers took steps back as the lava softened the dirt under the castle stone, slowly disintegrating its foundation.

"Call," Saul ordered his dragon. A roar followed by two screeches commanding more dragons from the city to reinforce their leader. Saul's mount beat its wings into a fluttering hover way over the Plaztex walls.

He saw the long, fiery river of lava make an indent through the desert in a meandering line as far as he could see. Every settlement along the way had been burnt and plundered. He returned his gaze to the beautifully crafted bone ship, a well-executed plan indeed; however, the bone ship tilted heavily to one side, either due to undistributed weight or a sloppy construction job.

"Flank starboard side of the ship with your kin and rock it until it flips," Saul growled, lifting his great hammer, usually strapped onto the dragon's neck as a riding brace. He popped up and stood on the fluttering dragon to intimidate the new recruits on the ship.

Two legendary dragon riders posted on top of the wall towers like gargoyles, flaring out their wings as soon as they caught the signal to fly with Saul. Considering it has been 150 years since the last flight with their leader, this was a very special moment.

Dozens of dragons flew out of the city. They moved competitively amongst one another in their race to reach Saul, who had already taken off towards the bone ship, standing on his mount and surfing his dragon, streamlining towards the bone parade. His hammer grasped in both hands as he surfed, and puny arrows whistled by his head. His dragon aimed itself at the bow of the ship taking the chance of crushing their skeleton leader Max. All dragons intuitively knowing that the skel officers wore clothes.

During Saul's mounted dive, he jumped off, driving his hammer into a disoriented archer, probably thinking this was one hell of an amazing nightmare. The hammer crushed the skelly, leaving its head between its feet. Saul looked back and his dragon already had two other skeletons in its mouth.

The ship smashed into the city wall, catching Saul in a brief stumble. After his recovery he begun slamming his great hammer through bones to reach the deep hull of the ship with a smile, his muscles rounded and defined.

As the other dragons and dragon riders hit the flank, ripping the deck to shreds, Max was rolling in between masts and obstacles like the swordsman Inigo Montoya, occasionally beating back a dragon rider and Saul's dragon with his scimitar. The dragon rider reared his dragon up on two legs to flap its ridged wings, blowing Max right off the ship.

After his slow, welcoming fall, Max rose out of the lava, skull and hollows peeking out of the red goo. He watched the Togmehoian leader destroy his ship from the inside, swinging around his hammer in broad and precise strokes. He listened to the dragons screech and clatter bones between their teeth. The ship wouldn't last long, but the river would.

He turned around calmly, like a navy seal along the banks of hostile waters. He breast-stroked toward the Plaztex wall as it crumbled, toppling over on either side.

Gathering on the rubble, he saw the five hundred demons that had been trying to stop the diggers before; however, now they were in a much better position without the shield maidens on the defensive.

As the roar of the five hundred stampeded over the rubble, the shield maidens advanced, rising out of the lava to meet the demon's heavy blows with bone and steel, agility and invulnerability. There were a dozen maidens with the shield's melted metal guarding their upper bodies. The rest of the skellys behind them were roused and fumbling over the fallen stone when they got to it.

They gained a momentous thrill for battle at the banks of the lava river, and as the bow of their ship crumbled, they passionately pushed the demon wall defense away from the diggers.

"Diggers! Maidens and Men! Raise your hip bone shovels and overwhelm the town with chaos and collision. If you haven't pulled out the maniac inside of you yet, then they will surely smash you with the maniac inside of them."

As Max was yelling his battlements, an undead-looking warrior with two morning stars stood opposite, perched on a pile of bones, crushing incoming skulls. One digger thrust a sharpened shovel at his midsection; the deteriorating warrior retaliated with a double morning star swing, one crushing the skelly's head and the other obliterating its ribcage.

Max, now unclothed, stepped to the challenge. He took a bone shovel from each digger to the side of him and spread his arms out, taunting the undead. The warrior swung predictably, as he had done before, and the morning star chains wrapped around both shovel shafts. Now connected, Max moved forward, chest to chest with this undead, and leaned back, causing them both to fall back into the lava. Max came out and quickly jogged up to the rapidly liquefying stone wall.

"Use lava as your weapon. Fling it their eyes, pull their asses in. Dig and fight! Let's hustle, Argh!!"

The men joined maidens in the press against the city's defenders. It was dirty fighting, carrying lava in skulls and splashing it over demons and undead warriors, but this was Hell, and in Hell anything goes.

A crooked building collapsed behind the demon army, making their end an imminent reality. There was no stopping the Skeleton Crew now.

****

As the ship toppled in on itself, the lava river had already made it inside the city walls, burning the city's buildings in its path to the Citadel. The flood wallowed forth effortlessly, based merely on its width and surging elemental power. Max grabbed a team of his best fighters to attack the Citadel head-on, leaving the river to flow.

His team was comprised of three full-metal maidens and eight skeleton warriors armed with the enemy's swords and spears. They half stalked, and half charged the Citadel's guards, feeling a little awkward running on land instead of wading through lava.

The first metal maidens made it through the guards easily while the others cleaned up the scraps. However, when the first metal maiden made it into the doorway, they were immediately shot out with balefire.

Six, the demon sorcerer walked out after her, rubbing his shadowy face, then put his hands out like, 'Oh, what happened?'

His dark blue robe encapsulated tormented souls, continually taking turns to peek out of the creased opening. Six sanguine guards stepped out from behind him.

"Now what will you do Max? You made it this far." Six asked in his deeply amused yet evil voice.

Max turned his skull to speak to his crew in low, hard-to-hear tones.

"Maidens guard my rear tight." Max turned to Six and growled out.

"Hit!"

He then met Six's six guards. The sanguine were beaten in seconds, and Max used his opportunity. He pressed through, reaching the last of them, and then repeatedly stabbed the Citadel guard through the stomach up to his neck.

Losing the sword in the guard's body, Max pushed the guard at Six. Six waved his hand and disintegrated the guard while winding up for another balefire. Max crouched into a bone ball and slipped back between the maidens' bony thighs, pushing them forward into Six's blast. This sent the two metal maidens and Max sailing, thudding into the desert street.

Six, however, was now dealing with the balefire ricochet, spilling imprisoned souls out onto the Citadel's welcome mat. He retreated back into the Citadel, holding his robe closed like a streaker that just shat himself.

Max lay there, wounded, tired, and grateful that he was able to humiliate Six in such a way. He got up and started looking over his skeleton team. They were all gone, souls already drifting towards the eerie blue moons.

The souls all blew away in one fluent direction with a heavy gust of wind. The heavy gust came from Saul and his dragon as they made an aggressive landing, stepping at Max with their momentum. Behind Saul, the drakes and dragons annoyed and interrupted the diggers and the rest of the Skeleton Crew, still dedicated to their mission.

Good job lads, just a little closer, and we'll burn this baby down.

Saul hopped off his mount like he wanted to say something to Max, but all that came out was pissed-off grumbling. He advanced on Max with no hesitation and raised his war hammer behind his shoulder. Max, acting like he'd given up, jolted forward and stuck Saul through his center.

Saul grinned, dropped his hammer behind him, grabbed Max's cervical vertebrae, and raised his fist to crumple Max like Max had crumpled his city.

Aussie Max looked into Max's hollows over Saul's shoulder and waited for the kill. Max looked back like an already empty skull, hollows cradling the last of their life on the eve of being forgotten.

Bones crackled all the way down his spine by a crazy Togmehoian power slam.

Other Max, Aussie Max, backed up and did a 'bird whistle' like a wolf on Haley Street. Saul turned around to see his call boy and then noticed the burning fuse at his feet. Aussie Max had put a ticking bomb under Saul while he was playing with Captain Max.

KaBoom!!!

****

Max walked away from the dead. Away from Max, the exploded Togmehoian, and finally, Saul's slain dragon, previously impaled by his twenty-foot spring-out blade, install-killing the beast.

"Ahhh, the Skeleton Crew is mine. Ha. And the city, look at that." Most of the buildings burned, and the lava flowed around corners. The place was in ruins, and Max was happy.

I'll change my name to Lavos, The Scape Conqueror. The Terror Between Worlds. The Ghost of the Weapons Closet.

The Halo

We lay on our multicolored bedspread with a patchwork of colorful abstract designs. The oil of jasmine and cherry blossoms roasted under a candle wick, filling my head with my lover's routine scent. My veins ran hot and steady. Her face rested on my chest with her open palm on my lower stomach.

The world was mine, and if that were not completely true, I felt as if I were a king mad with happiness, perched just right in the kingdom.

We lay relaxed and in a dreamy state of awakenings as her lustful eyes stared up at my chin.

Just like the slow progression of a teapot beginning to whistle, the room filled with noise, a rumble, a terror advancing on the room's savory energy. A beautiful woman's voice from, *The Skints,* sang in cute tones, though it was submerged under a fat sound bubble like the music was pushed out of the room, as if the music came from the other side of the wall.

The candlelight grew dim, soaking up the hidden shadows in this cube where we lay to rest. Suddenly, the candlelight fluttered like it was about to extinguish, and a trailing yelp of air blew in with a maddened force and suddenly halted. It didn't disperse into the room or go back out the crack of the window. It stopped at the foot of our bed.

Now, as we lay with our adrenaline spirits jacked with fright, a change of energy twisted over the room. All the colors in the room turned to black and gray. The gray smoke rose from the extinguished candle, and the smoke was being eaten away by shadows of petrifying darkness. I slowly sat up on my knuckles as if I was posing as a beast in his cave, and then a growl came from the mouth I knew as mine.

The shadow peered at us, dark with no face; however, its stature showed that it was looking directly at us. Again, with a shocking thrill of supernatural surprise, the shadowed figure fell lickety-split down into me.

All the voids and rifts of my body and soul were filled with aliments of destruction and chaos.

Now, I no longer feared darkness, because I was darkness.

****

Kraeno woke up. His hood blocked out most of the interior starship, but he could see Noble, who watched him while lying on his paw. He watched Kraeno with eyes careless of his troubles, careless of his nightmares, only consciously caring if he had enough strength in him to kill things. To be a companion of ambition and bloodshed.

Time for Guts to play with the big boys eh Noble? Guts was Kraeno's new nickname for himself. He thought it fitting being a skelly and all.

Kraeno peered under his hood, deep within his grilled helmet. The starship resting bay was in full view now. Some of the Lycans were dozing, and the others were staring into space, except for one, looking straight at Kraeno.

Ah, I've found my first kill.

Lycans hunt at night so they could easily see Kraeno through the barrier of darkness. Kraeno relaxed his bones and didn't move a muscle; he only stared back. Noble would spark up and be ready to fight as soon as Kraeno flinched or twitched, but this wasn't the time to fight, it was the time to wait.

The enclave seats where the Lycans were sitting had dim fluorescent lights on the trim. The starship rumbled and rocked with turbulence every now and then, which made Kraeno more comfortable, like rocking a baby to sleep.

When Kraeno was still alive, he always felt comfortable watching movies with starships. It was something about being shuttled up in the middle of eternity, life's original beginning. Like his father always told him, find your happy space; and now, when Kraeno finally found it, he was dead and headed straight into a conflict between demons and angels.

Kraeno felt a rumble, but this time it wasn't just turbulence, it was an explosion from outside.

The Lycans all started to perk up, grinning for battle, but there was still one of the quiet ones looking directly at him. Kraeno thought about how he looked.

What the hell was he staring at?

Under his hood and oven-looking helmet, his eyes were hollowed out. The drape of the clothes he wore were ragged and dark, and Kraeno expected he looked like a pretty threatening mercenary, especially with a Hellhound. He remembered what was under it all: his bones, his hollows, his skeleton, something that was definitely going to take some time getting used to.

The Lycan stood up, looking like a wolf on its hind legs, and began to approach. Noble got up and was as tall as the Lycan's chest, even on four legs. The fight wouldn't go very well if they chose to dance in such small quarters, so the Lycan halted in the darkness.

The other Lycans looked away, uninterested. Behind them, the windows showed an extensive amount of white light, reminding Kraeno of back home during a hot summer day when the rays were blasting down through the light fluffy clouds. The Lycans didn't much like it, peeling away from the light as it shone through.

There was an even closer explosion that rocked the ship to a full tilt. Noble became a little unstable, but everyone else stood in their places unmoved. Once again gaining his balance he barked out a blood-curdling growl at the hovering Lycan.

The spaceship's intercom clicked on, and the pilot said, "Entering Elvmerick's Plains! We are coming in for a landing. Get ready. There is a full-throttle shin-dig going on out there. Hold on!" The pilot's voice was buttery, and then he put on *Flowers in my Hair, Demons in my Head by The Mystery Lights*. Then, the rear drop gate started to open.

An imp came flying up to the opening gate, crazed with excitement and skittering to get in. Noble jumped and clawed at the little imp, but with the imp's excitement plus its extraordinary dexterity, Noble missed every swat. The further it opened, the closer Noble came to the edge of the increasingly declining gate.

Still biting at the Imp, Noble slid down the gate, giving a yelp when he found out he had gone too far. Kraeno grabbed his furry tail and whipped him back into the ship. They both sat there in awe as the imp fluttered off with its little red wings, joining the other airborne creatures of the afterlife.

There must have been hundreds of thousands of demons in the sky, along with starships carrying other soldiers. The demons brought a tint of red with them, an aura of darkness, creating a definite contrast against the light blue sky and godly golden Halo in outer space.

Swords had dark smoke streaming off of them. Chains scrunched up in wiggly lines and whipped out in the cool breeze. Scythes looked as wicked as Death's own. Black and red brutes with fists and forearms the size of small boats, blobs of monstrous masses, smiling faces of dangerous insanity, straight faces of pain and brutality, sad faces of psychological distortion.

The armies of the Bulge marched like they were waiting to get into the Super Bowl Stadium. Thousands of spiked pikes - sometimes triple or quadruple spiked - all tilted in the air, accompanying hundreds of flags with different colors and signets for each block of troops.

Zip!

A ballistic bolt clipped the underbody of their starship and proceeded directly into a monstrous mass of long, razor-sharp teeth, which in reality was the army of thousands of spiked pikes.

During the starship's tilted descent, Kraeno became more aware of the upper tiers of the sky. In the outer region of Dyathsake, there was a light ring that was so large it wrapped around the entire galaxy, holy and bright. It had Earth's sun color and brightness, however, it was completely majestic in its form, like a golden star of glory nourishing all the planets in the outer rim of Dyathsake, the Galaxy of the Dead. A silhouetted moon zealot twirled in the Halo's radiance, enthusiastic about the major clash of galactic rivals.

The starship evened out and flew low, trying not to crash into the demon army. Flags blew away from the ship's thrusters and snapped some taller shafts as they made it closer to the ground. It was as if they marched for years, flooding in endless amounts of waves, never ceasing to test Elvmerick's defenses.

A bright light with white and blue wings flew by and sliced a ghoul in its midsection, so it dropped and impaled itself on a flag shaft. The blue and white specter flew around the sky, cutting down enemy demons twice as buff as the largest bodybuilder on Earth, until a humongous whistling swing of a halberd hit the blocking specter and bounced him far, far away, sending him crashing into the warriors on the ground.

The halberd welder was Doomali's Mother, leading five starships that hovered as low as Kraeno's ship. She previously slipped out and rode on top of her starship, obviously feeling high and mighty.

Doomali… Kraeno thought.

Catapults hucked boulders and the ballistas shot bolts that were taking out ships much higher than the one they were on. Kraeno let out a relieved sigh that crackled through the hellish oven helmet. They were below the cannon fodder.

The ship jolted down, occasionally hitting what felt like bodies in suits of armor or heavy weapons they had lifted above their heads. And even while the dead died again and Lycans breathed down Kraeno's neck at the edge of this plummet into insanity, he still had his full attention on Doomali's Mother. If he followed her, he would find Doomali.

Anti-aircraft grapple guns shot up behind Queen Lextana and pierced through two following starships, pulling them down without a problem. One after the other they fell… and then Kraeno's starship was caught as well.

Not far, not far at all... Doomali is near. The thought repeated itself as the inhabitants of the ship were bashed around the metal interior during the crash.

Kraeno got up as quickly as a skeleton could and raced out of the starship, leaving only a moment to scan the perimeter of the crash zone. Their wreck had killed many that it landed on. Blood and limbs splattered around the outside of the cockpit. In the case of this crash, the zone seemed to be on the main battlefront line.

Behind Kraeno, there were the good ol' boys from Hell, and in front of him were huge giants in white cloaked armor. Tall, absolutely massive soldiers bordered the space either in front or behind him. Kraeno did not fit the size for this squabble, but his drive to kill only one gave him the advantage.

"You first dick."

The hovering, staring Lycan put his hand on Kraeno's shoulder and pushed him toward ten white-cloaked giants, twisting their hammers of light back into a solid two-handed grip. Kraeno stuttered, knowing that this could be the end of him. Being crushed by a holy hammer would totally be the ideal way of killing off a skeleton from the lava pits of Hell.

The Lycans prepped themselves behind him, pulling their blades out and solidifying the right stance. Kraeno stuttered again.

"You're a boney little fuck aren't you!" The Lycan with the earrings told him.

"Let's make Doomali proud, boys," said the Lycan that had gone on the possession tour with Doomali.

These bastard werewolves reminded Kraeno that he'd rather fight than be obliterated into the ground and have a war parade trot all over his powdery bones.

He spun around, twisting his coat in the grasp of the jeweled Lycan. Kraeno was always shocked by what he could get away with, and took off his helmet and shoved it into the closest snout behind him. Afterward, the other six Lycans were static from the revealed skull and deceiving hollows of Kraeno Kalmc, the slyest bone pirate around.

Noble sensed their displeasure and decided to react to Kraeno's actions, toppling both the white-bearded elder Lycan and Krae's hovering, staring nemesis to the ground. All claws were out, but the Hellhound's teeth were what went deeper into the skin. Kraeno pulled out his sword and stuck a jester-looking demon in the stomach.

Kapow Biatch. Freaking hate dolled up evildoers.

Other jester buddies pushed up fast, waving their blades at him like the crippled humor ghouls they were.

One second, a bundle of blades, and the next, one gigantic hammer. It slammed down next to Kraeno, saving him and Noble for the time being.

He didn't have time to see if the giants were protecting him or had just missed him. They did seem like giants of ultimate judgment, so maybe. Kraeno hopped on Noble and pounced into the ugly crowd of demon spawn toward where Queen Lextana's ships had crash-landed.

They pushed through howling faces and frantic banner men.

Was there not one stoic demon in Dyathsake? Had they all gone hysterical? Even quiet, controlled horn jobs could fake the look of a battlefront hero, but none of these darklings had a stoic ease.

When a mace hit Kraeno in the chin, almost knocking his skull clean off, he took the opportunity to see. His hollows tilted toward the sky, where there were birds and radiant shields with wings soaring through the red spray of demon blood.

As his gaze fell back to the crowd they were charging through, he saw bodies being tossed up into the sky that—unless snatched up by a nearby angel—fell back down with a vengeance, clenching onto every moment of vitality, fully flexed, blades out and pointed toward their enemies in their decent.

It all happened up ahead near Doomali's crash site. Only a dozen more layers of dead to go and they were there. But something happened; the crowd became so thick that plowing over soldiers wasn't enough.

Kraeno whispered to Noble, *kill*, and the Hellhound proceeded with a slow but steady slaughter forth… He would tear out the legs from under the demons and then stomp on their faces. Kraeno knew Noble was getting worn away with all the slashing and bashing against the grain, but in the end things just got rough.

Kraeno became tangled up, wrestling a snarling demon with bloody horns and guts splattered around its ivory club. Noble toppled the monster under them and Kraeno slid his obsidian point spear through the demon's neck.

The falling warriors from Noble's claws and Kraeno's machete spear started to create a little more space so they could curve in and out of them, like they were headed to the front row of a *Black Flag* concert. The harder the bashing, the further they went.

Noble pounced the last couple of yards into Doomali's crash site like a dog pouncing on bees in poppy fields. *My happy space. Oh boi!*

"Move aside." Amazed at Kraeno, the guards moved easily at Doomali's orders. Now, the only thing in between Doomali and Kraeno was one ray of light.

Doomali grabbed a holy hoplite from one side and a demon from the other and threw them both at Kraeno, knocking him and Noble over. Doomali approached slowly. Queen Lextana and her guards defending him as he walked.

He reached Kraeno, pulled him up off the ground by his vertebrae, did a low squat, arm fully extended back, and chucked him straight up with all his might.

Kraeno was in the air, watching all that was around him. He soaked in the glimpse of the City Elvmerick and the towering white gate fortifying Elvmerick's castle, beautiful and gothic, just like he had imagined it. *Smashing Pumpkins, Today,* played in his head.

Is that where my brothers will go?

He thought back to when he had the dream of being surrounded by whales, sharks, and sea critters, always ending somehow with the twirling bark in the universe. Everything just is. Everything had its equilibrium.

He floated, reaching his peak, and fell back in peace, looking up at the Golden Halo that ringed around the galaxy, watching the Moon Zealots rotate in their luminosity, like hammerhead sharks swimming above a diver.

He landed, crumpling right at Doomali's feet. Noble nowhere to be seen. Doomali lifted his heavy war boot, though behind him came a crashing, cometing Moon Zealot to wipe them all out.

Doomali tilted his head up, his beard tinkling in Halo light, "This isn't the end Skel. This is just the beginning." His voice chill as ice.

The Moon Zealot's shadow darkened the battleground.

"That Zealot chose us for the holy conversion. Where demons go to Heaven and angels go to Hell. The ultimate balance of the dead." Doomali coolly said while pulling out some kind of orb from his coat. Kraeno looked around and saw demons praising the Moon Zealot's fall while an Elvmerick Hoplite sat on his heels, peering up with hopeless eyes of sorrow.

We switch? No… Pads?!

Kraeno let out one last giggle while watching Pads hang onto a long front tooth snarling out of the Moon Zealot's city-wide mouth.

A crater quaked into the Elvmerick's Plains and rippled, sending demons and angels flying. The magical impact slowed down time and made the battlegrounds the Moon Zealot's bitch. The beings of good and evil were now wonderous spirits inhaled by the galactic dragon, later to be spat out to either the shining gates of Heaven or into the fires of Hell.

Galaxy of the Dead

A large upheaval for the balance of the universe. Heaven focused on crippling Hell, while Hell fixated on dominating Heaven, and in between the stars and moons rested the true keepers of balance, for they all are one. They all are, the dead.

Epilogue

The last thing Padrick Kalmc remembered thinking was how good his balls felt resting on the front tooth of a galactic dragon diving straight into an Angel and Demon filled battleground.

Now, heat boiled around his comatose body, sprawled out on the broken boards of a demolished building. The sky swirled with the purple mists that made the outer reaches of space twinkle in a midnight haze. A white-striped figure waded through a creek of lava between two collapsed wooden buildings. The figure and its friends were barking with laughter at the ruin and what had come along with it.

"New Recruits!" The last of the boney figures giggled. "They missed all the fun!"

Pads shifted and began to wake up with the increased temperature and clatter of laughter. He pulled his right arm out from under his body with his other hand. The arm was broken, yet numb from laying on top of it. He was simply face-down amongst slowly burning slats of wood, yet there was little reason to rush around in an eternal afterlife.

The first skeleton, apparently the funniest of the bunch, spoke to his mates nonchalantly as they trailed away through the lava alley.

"Leave 'im be. He'll figure it out sooner or later."

However, there were other sounds. Sounds that forced Pads to cough his way to his feet to see what lay in the chaos of that asteronomous dragon fall. As Pads stood and became more awake, many questions and curiosities ran through his head.

About five city blocks away swayed a lone church tower, epic in height and grandeur, with none to match as far as he could see. Rivers of lava curled around every street, alley, and crevice in the lower city. Most buildings still stood even though their walls were freshly burning. The stone was mostly intact, except for the Western battlements that had collapsed from the lava river.

Pads stepped back as a piece of wood caught on fire right under his foot. He was surprised he felt it. Every inch of him was so hot and numb that he could barely keep his eyes open from the sweat beading down.

The burning wood read, '-ning Christ', almost like a storefront sign or bar name.

This is Hell, but when I fell... It was so bright, so heavenly. There was a battle at Heaven's gates.

Pads squeezed his eyes shut in the despair he felt losing his place in Heaven. The cool wind, the angels, the righteousness, it had all been right there in front of him. But now...

The far-off Church now seemed more an Evil Citadel. It began to crumble from the bottom up, leaning hard in its stone timber. Blocks fell, slapping into the surrounding lava pits.

Okay, so buildings and things don't just eternally burn in Hell. There must have been a volcanic eruption or...

He looked around for a nearby mountain with a spewing red tip but instead found himself surrounded by a weird battle zone. He held his broken arm and leapt over to a two-story building, with only its front wall disintegrated by the lava flames. He ran up the interior steps to gather a better look at the city's disorder.

Suddenly a blue mist spirit wisped under his chin, making a pleasurable exhaling sound, "Ahhh." His confusion found no end on this night. Pads watched the spirit curl her hand to beckon him closer, but he shivered the moment away and walked up to the roof.

Skeletons were wading through the lava creeks and regular-looking Hell residents were being captured or slain on any other solid mass, some being pulled into the lava river just for fun.

Up above, on the Southern battlements were twelve skeletons that had twice their number in prisoners. They had forced them to kneel with their hands tied behind their backs.

Pads had a flashback of a skeleton as he rode naked on the tooth of the galactic dragon while plummeting towards Heaven's Gate. *Was this the same place? It seemed so different.*

Pads looked to the stars. The wind ran purple and dark, like a goo, like there was a sticky film all over the world. As he fell before, while hanging on the dragon tooth, he rode in on a clear blue sky with a golden ring fortified in outer space. This definitely wasn't the same place. There were no meteor remnants and no massive crater of destruction. However, he did remember a funny looking skel looking up at him as he fell. There had been something personal about that moment.

Fingers itched at his skin as he rotated around. He became terrified in his thoughts. Pads liked this place for some reason. It felt like home to him, but at the same time, he wanted to escape… the heat... no. It was something else. The itch. *You're itching because of the heat you dumb dumb.* He was so confused he turned and sat on the top step that led up to the roof.

There was a horrifying scream that came from the final collapse of the Citadel. A maddened yell that seemed muffled, like they were trapped and super pissed off. The scream went on, never ceasing, belting out its poisonous screech.

"Jump in…" a wispy voice whispered. The spirit from before appeared close to Pads' broken arm. It nodded outside. Pads just sat, letting be, be.

"Jump in laddy. Come on."

"Dude!" Pads got up and went back up the stairs. From here, planks crossed multiple roofs, eventually leading to the back Eastern Gate. The mass of demon looking monsters and skeletons encroaching on them was a little daunting, but Pads decided that was his only way out of the forbidding lava city. He also desperately wanted to get away from that scream.

He went to the edge of the roof and inched off, hanging on the ledge sideways with his left hand. He pushed off the wall and just made it over the lava to the top of another building.

He ran across some planks and made one final leap. As his feet hit the edge, he leaned too far back with his upper body, and he had to wave his arms to keep from falling. Even then a large spirit gust pushed him back. Pads quickly knelt in his fall and grabbed hold of a piece of metal acting as structural reinforcement. The rebar sticking out of the roof was sharp all around, every bit of it. Everything was freaking sharp around here.

All things in Hell were dangerous. He reminded himself. He stabilized himself on the roof and analyzed the torn flesh on his left hand. *And this is Hell.*

Pads crouched to the other side of the roof and peered over, watching the skeletons rotate around their rivals. It looked like a stalemate for the time being, and everyone was very distracted by all the high pitched screaming. The skeletons didn't advance because it would pull them too far away from their lava, and the demons were just trapped in the corner; lava being too close to the Eastern Gate to escape.

A dirt alley wove in between a couple unharmed buildings that reached the stairs to the wall. If he could make it to the stairs then over to the gate... He had to risk it. The screaming was painful now.

Pads jumped down and moved through the alley in the shadows. He made it to a wide opening before the battlement stairs. Two skeleton shield maidens stood watch, but were focused on the demon horde in the corner. Pads tiptoe dashed across, but on his second step, the screaming ceased and one of the maidens turned around and stuck Pads in the gut with her metal spear.

"Aye, what's this you sneaky beat?" She held the spear point through his stomach, waiting for his response. The other maiden turned around as well and rested her shield hand on her hip bone.

Her skull curled in a smile and she huffed out a laugh, "Ah, let him go, Mego. I can smell his rotting flesh from here."

Pads stood there surprised and bewildered once again. *This spear through my guts doesn't bother me at all, and what does she mean by letting me go. And why is she somewhat covered in molten metal? Hell is so weird.*

"Aye Blitz, them scallywags be moving," the Maiden indicated while pulling the spear out of Pad's stomach. Blood spilled out, but it felt good. He felt like he could run. Pads made it to the top of the stairs and halted, holding his head. His mind flooded with thoughts.

Blitzen…

****

Kraeno came back into consciousness. His hollows focused in on one strand of grass, the other million were just a blur.

Grass? Pads? Wait!

He sat up and looked around, his skull barely popping over the field's tall greenish blue grass. The golden Halo magnificently arched over,

not just the field, or the planet he was on, but the entire galaxy.
It still baffled him. What was that Halo all about? He needed to find out, but what really had him twisted was why he was still a skelly, not a double-dead ghost. And where the fuck was his brother Padrick!?
It was time for some answers.

Epilogue

Epilogue

www.ingramcontent.com/pod-product-compliance
Lightning Source LLC
Chambersburg PA
CBHW010745310726
48980CB00004B/373

* 9 7 9 8 9 9 2 3 0 8 8 6 0 *